ZEALOT

C. VONZALE LEWIS

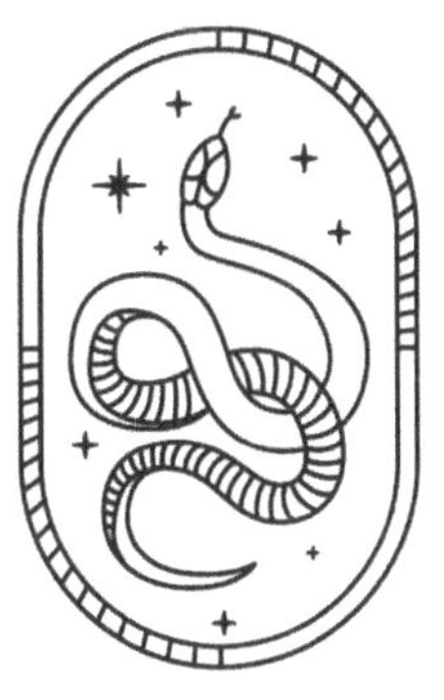

BOOK TWO
BLOOD & SACRIFICE CHRONICLES

Midnight Tide
PUBLISHING

Also By C. Vonzale Lewis

Blood & Sacrifice Chronicles
Lineage
Zealot
Tribe

Novellas:
Descendants of the Big House

Short Fiction:
The Recipe for Cornbread (Link by Link)
The Soulless Ones (Beyond the Cogs)
An Ax for the Storm (Emporium of Superstition)
Harbinger (This Fresh Hell)
When You Hear Them Scream (The Darkest Lullaby)

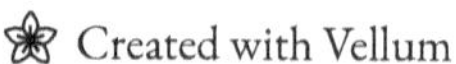 Created with Vellum

For my husband, Bobby,
thank you for the support you give.

For my loving mother, Gynda,
your strength has inspired me.

And for my Aunt Louise,
who is resting in Heaven.

*...Footfalls echo in the memory
Down the passage which we did not take
Towards the door we never opened
Into the rose-garden...
T. S. Eliot*

The first package from Doc arrived two weeks after we killed his sister and brother; a battle that took place on his family's land, hidden in the small marshland between Sandpoint and Alice. Doc, after murdering his nurse Emilia, had left a note for me, along with directions to the barn-like structure. There, his family was holding close to fifty people, including Marta, for their Harvest ritual. We'd won that fight. And I'd barely escaped with my life.

Like his first letter to me, he'd written in graphic detail about the torture he'd inflicted on Felicity Markum. Ronald had carved her up and eaten pieces of her. He'd even included photographs of his work. Unfortunately, he never signed the letter. It would have been proof of what he was doing—a confession written in his own hand. But he was too smart for that.

Mixed in with the gruesome photographs was a picture of him in Thailand, arms around a group of kids, while wearing a doctor's uniform. And while blending in with other physicians and treating the locals, he killed without the constraints his family had put on him. We'd scoured online news outlets in the locations he'd sent me boxes from: Thailand, Philippines, and Malaysia, and found articles on his victims. Local women who bore a passing resemblance to me. I still get nauseous thinking about those photographs and the fact that he, in his mind, was obviously killing me over and over again.

It was only when he left the area that he'd send me mementos with a bottle of Asbach Uralt—his favorite brandy—and photographs of his latest victim. Devlin sent copies of the first letter and set of pictures to the embassy in Thailand. Sadly, we never got a response.

After some debate, we'd sent the pictures and the note to the Markum family. I wanted to shield them from the horror, but Devlin argued since they'd hired him to find out about their daughter, he was obligated to share the information with them, no matter how much we wanted to protect them from the reminder of their daughter's death the pictures would surely invoke. And in the end, I understood why they needed to know, and it wasn't my decision to make.

A few days later, Devlin had received a letter—a check with an obscene amount of money along with a signed contract from the Markums. Regardless of their daughter not dying from the ritual, they hired him to investigate the other blood magick users on Tulare Island. The letter contained carefully worded instructions on what to do when we found them. While not direct, we all understood they wanted us to kill them all.

Despite their wishes, we simply couldn't do that. At least that's what Devlin said. I was firmly in the Markums' camp. We could, he said, investigate the five remaining families to determine if they were practicing blood magick. And if they were, we'd stop them. It seemed simple enough. Yet, I had a feeling it wouldn't be.

I stood up. My hand shook as I tried to ram my key into the lock—scratching at the polished brass. Pulling in a deep breath, I closed my eyes and pushed down the pain. Pushed down the images that were inside that dirty package. Pushed down the guilt and finally, hand steady, unlocked my door. Picking up my bag from the floor, I rushed inside and came to an abrupt stop in the middle of my living room.

A sudden kaleidoscope of memories cascaded through me, keeping me rooted in place. My bag thumped to the floor as I let the onslaught of them overtake me. The numerous instances clues had presented themselves—practically smacking me in the face. My chest heaved and blood rushed through my veins while black spots blocked my vision. I gripped my shirt, burying my knuckles between my breasts.

It all started with me walking into Tribec Insurance and smelling blood. Instead of running out of the building, I stayed.

When I spotted the magick wards and symbols peppered throughout, sure, I questioned it, but still, I didn't leave.

Then, when I was presented with the option to leave, I'd stayed.

And with Doc, I'd let hormones and anger at my having to

take a job I would hate fuel my decision making. Turning a blind eye when I sensed, deep down, something was off about him.

I couldn't change the past, no matter how much I wished I could. But accepting what had happened felt wrong too. Like giving up, somehow. Each time I was faced with it, my body, mind, and soul wanted to shut down. To block out the world and just forget. That was how I usually handled things. But lately, it hadn't been working. Alek advised me to use cleansing breaths and mantras to help.

Fuck mantras. I wanted blood.

But sadly, until we stopped Doc and all the other blood magick users on this damn island, I would probably keep having these episodes.

I could do one thing to help myself, though: I could stop referring to that sadistic monster by the pet name I'd given him.

I threw my keys on my brand-new coffee table. They skidded across the glass, most likely leaving little dips and grooves—permanently damaging the surface—and came to rest near the stack of self-help magazines I'd started accumulating. I had hoped the articles would help me deal with the panic attacks. But sadly, they, along with the book on surviving abuse I'd purchased, weren't working.

Figuring if I couldn't get my mind right, I could at least give my apartment a makeover. I'd bought a few items of furniture with the money Devlin gave me. Along with the coffee table, I found a small dinette set in pretty good condition at a yard sale. Eventually, I'd get some towels and a few pictures for the walls.

The only drawback of me making my apartment into a home was that I still pictured my previous neighbor, Wade, dead on the floor in the corner of my living room. And sadly, no amount of gussying up would ever wipe that gruesome apparition from my mind.

Kara walked up behind me. I could feel her eyes boring into my back and feel the weight of her concern hanging in the air.

"Why did you pick it up?" I asked, not turning around.

"You know why," she answered, her tone cautious.

I dug my fingernails into the palms of my hands.

"Devlin said we need to keep tracking him," she continued, her voice softening. "And if he's crazy enough to send us information on where he is, we shouldn't just throw it away."

I whipped around and snatched the package from her. "He sends these sick little mementos *after* he's left the area. How can that information help?" I was arguing with the wrong person. But my anger had to go somewhere. And sadly, Kara was the only person in the room. I threw the package on the ground; the *thump* was like nails on a chalkboard.

My damn fault. All of it.

She didn't move. Just stood there with love and patience in her eyes. She, like everyone else, had become used to my sudden outbursts. I hated that. I'd promised myself I would stop, but today, it really couldn't be helped.

I didn't understand why Devlin wanted to start with the church. It made more sense for us to focus on the Sinclair family since they were the ones who had hurt Marta's kids. But he pointed out the protection around them right now would pose a risk to us, so we'd begin with the Young family.

When I continued to argue with him, he must have picked up on my hesitancy and figured out there was more to my not wanting to deal with the Young family than what I was saying. He stopped insisting and had given me the opportunity to explain my reluctance. But true to form, I had declined to go into detail, leaving me with no way out of the situation.

Kara continued to stare at me as I cycled through my anger.

Pull it together, Nicole.

It was the love in her eyes that chipped away at my resolve.

Besides, our friendship was the one thing that kept me sane. I couldn't afford to lose her. Not now. Not ever. And more importantly, she didn't deserve my rage.

"Sorry," I said, reaching for her.

She smiled and wrapped her arm around me, pulling me close. "You know I will always have your back, Nicole."

"I know," I mumbled. "I just..."

She stepped back and looked at me. "We all, just... The key is to keep it together. Let the fury build." Her mouth stretched into a wicked grin. "And when the time is right, we strike. Letting all that rage feed our magick."

"And bathe in the blood of our enemies?" The last of my anger slowly seeped out of my pores. I could do this.

She laughed, her body also relaxing as she studied me. "That's right. We will bathe in their blood and let their screams be our soundtrack."

"Have I told you lately that I'm a little frightened of you?"

Her face took on a pensive look while she tapped her finger on the side of her cheek. "No. But I'm thinking I should get that printed on a t-shirt." She gestured across the spans of her chest. "Fear me."

I shook my head. "I've corrupted you."

She picked up the package off the ground. "Well, maybe I needed a little corrupting." She pointed toward my bedroom. "Now, why don't you go find something proper and decent to wear to church."

"Shit," I said and rushed out of the room. Despite not wanting to go, I still loathed the idea of being late. Hated having to rush in at the last minute. It made me feel as if I were missing something. Like in my haste to beat the clock, I'd left out a crucial task or step when getting ready. That's why I always left early. It gave me time to not only think, but also circle back if I had, in fact, forgotten something.

I opened my closet door and stared at the mounds of clothing crammed into the small space. I didn't have church clothes, at least not according to society's standards. But then again, I never much cared for the boxes the illusive "they" put people in in the first place. So, fuck them.

And it was that very attitude that had me staring at the many clothes in my closet, contemplating wearing a short red dress to church.

"He's in Cambodia," Kara said as she walked into the room. "And yes, there are pictures."

Why the hell had she opened the package?

"That's inconvenient," I said as I stared at a skintight green dress. I doubted I could blend in showing off my cleavage, and if I had to bend over for any reason, I was sure to cause an uproar. Might even get a few people offering to pray for me. I groaned and shoved it back in the closet. It landed on the floor with the rest of my clean clothes. I really needed to do something about my closet.

"The pictures?"

I glanced over at her. "No, Kara, the fact that he's in Cambodia. How the hell am I supposed to kill the sick bastard if he's not here?"

She set the pictures on my bed and joined me at the closet door. "Remember what Devlin said," she slanted her eyes toward me, "he'll return eventually."

Devlin believed Doc was obsessed with me. Even after he'd gotten away, he continued contacting me. Taunting me. And that level of fixation would not only make him careless but also force him to return to Tulare. So, he wanted us to keep the sick mementos Doc sent. That way we could keep an eye on his progression into madness. It would be the only signal we had when he inevitably returned to Tulare Island.

When I objected, he pointed out that I got away from him once and would do so again. This time, with the team backing me. Yes, it's true I did survive. Even if I hadn't known my life was in danger. But it didn't mean I liked the idea of waiting around patiently for him to come and finally finish the job.

The bastard had told me in one of his letters he wanted to kill me—that his desire to do so was so overpowering that he had to fight hard against it. So, instead of raping and killing me, he had turned me into a useful pawn in his scheme to get away from his family and free himself from the shackles they'd imposed. He'd wanted free rein to continue with his sick proclivities, and I was the useful idiot who helped him get away.

I shook my head. "Eventually? How many women will he kill between now and then?" My stomach flipped and bile rose, burning my throat. A wave of dizziness came over me. I stumbled toward the bed, shoved the pictures out of the way, and sat down. "I can't do this."

Kara turned and extended the dress to me. "This will work."

"Did you hear me?" I took the pale-yellow summer dress from her. "I can't do this."

"I heard you. And"—she smiled sarcastically—"I'm ignoring you."

"Fine. If I fuck up, I will blame you."

"That's the spirit," she said, and went over to my jewelry box. "Do you have earrings to match?"

Honestly, I couldn't recall when I'd bought the dress. So, there was no way I'd remember having earrings to match. While Kara rummaged inside my jewelry box, I slipped out of my clothes, pulled on the dress, and groaned. The damn thing was too tight.

Kara handed me a pair of gold hoops. I put them on and surveyed myself in the mirror. My hair stuck out all over the place, looking as if I'd stuck my finger in a light socket. Red splotches covered my cheeks, forehead, and chin. And the bags under my eyes made me look as if I'd been awake for the past thirty days. I could cover it all with make-up, but I refused to put any on in this heat. And doing my hair would take too much time. So, tight yellow dress and wild-woman-do, it was.

Kara took the box back into the living room and put it on the coffee table while I grabbed my purse. Before we left out, I debated briefly on whether or not we should take the damn thing with us. I didn't want it in my house. But I also didn't want to touch it again, either.

So, I left it where it was.

Wade's apartment sat next to mine near the entrance. As we

made our way to the front door, Kara stopped and stared at the for-rent sign affixed to the frame.

Mr. Wan still hadn't been able to find a renter, especially since he was required to disclose Wade had been found dead inside the apartment. We had moved him to his own place after our confrontation with the men sent to kill me by Andrew Snow, a former trainer at Tribec Insurance.

The other tenants had speculated about Wade's death for weeks. At first, they believed his murder had something to do with the previous tenant who used to live in my apartment. After-all, the man had started growing marijuana in the garden outside. Eventually, they started giving me accusing glances as if I was somehow responsible. It was my fault. I should have shut Wade down long before that night. I'd told him I wasn't interested, but obviously not in a way he understood. If I had, it would have stopped him from coming over every time he believed I was home.

"How much is the rent here?" Kara asked.

"Don't tell me you're giving up your house? I thought you said your grandmother left."

"No." She continued walking. "Paul is looking for a new place."

I stood there for a minute, watching her. She better not suggest Paul move next door to me.

"Kara?"

She turned. "Come on, Nicole. We need to get going."

I caught up to her. "If this is some weird attempt on your part to have Paul keep an eye on me, I will be pissed."

"You have got to stop being so paranoid." She pushed open the front door. "Now, come on. Let's go join a cult."

"You actually managed to put those two things together," I said, following behind her. "Paranoid and a cult." I turned away before she could see the fear in my eyes.

She unlocked the doors, and we climbed inside the stifling car. We rolled down all the windows, and Kara turned on the air-conditioning full blast. Humidity made it easier to cool off the car. But nowadays, despite the moisture in the air, it seemed to be taking longer for the air-conditioning to work. The lack of rain puzzled a lot of people on Tulare Island—especially the weatherman, who had grown increasingly agitated every time his prediction for rain wasn't fulfilled.

Once the car had cooled down, Kara faced me. "You don't have a problem with Paul moving in, do you?" she asked, looking as if she were bracing for the worst.

I shrugged. I'd gotten over my petty jealousy of Paul a few weeks ago. It was misplaced and stupid. Paul was a decent guy. Strange? Illusive? Yes. But also nice, and fun to go drinking with. The man could not hold his liquor.

"I hope you told him about what happened," I said. "I'd hate to have it slip out when he comes over for a night of drinking."

Kara smiled then reversed out of the parking spot. "See, you've already found the bright side." She slanted her eyes toward me. "I thought you gave up drinking."

"I'll probably be drinking again real soon. And it'll be nice to have someone to drink with."

Kara frowned and pulled out onto the street. She wouldn't say anything about me going back on my word. It was a song and dance we were used to, only speaking up when things got too bad. She gave me the space to decide if I wanted to talk to her when something was bothering me. My usual way of dealing with these uncomfortable situations was to make some sarcastic remark. Opening up and expressing my feelings just wasn't me.

My apartment was a few blocks south from our old stomping ground, Jordin Cisco's. I should have told her to take the long way around to avoid the place, but it was too late now.

Kara slowed as we came to the gray brick building with blacked-over windows and a single reddish steel door. The neon sign wasn't lit. The bushes were still thriving. Which meant someone was still pissing and pouring beer on them. In the daylight, the once-familiar spot had taken on a more sinister caste.

As if the light, finally showed me what had remained hidden for so long.

I'd learned weeks ago that Jordin Cisco was an Old One—a god created by blood magick a few thousand years ago. And I had taken to him like a moth to flame. He had been my lover. The one constant in my life that I could depend on never changing. Sure, he slept with many other women, but I never had an issue with it. I enjoyed his company when I could.

"I still think you should confront him," Kara said, stopping at the intersection.

Ezra, another Old One, had warned me about the pact he and his siblings had made regarding people with my strange type of magick, a power that allowed me to keep a dead person's soul tethered to their body. I'd learned about this rare ability during a battle with the employees at the Sinclairs' at-risk youth facility. During the attack, a man had died. And my hand on his body had kept him somewhat alive—his soul resting inside his long-dead flesh.

He'd told me they would either kill or protect me.

Ezra had chosen to protect me, marking me with an elaborately drawn brand that I was still trying to decipher. Unlike the shen ring on my wrist, his brand was engraved into my bottom lip and only showed when I was in danger. Yet, Jordin had only slept with me. He had to have known about my magick, which made me wonder why he decided not to brand me for protection as well? And since he hadn't, that left him with only one option.

To kill me.

Jordin was the true embodiment of Dionysus. The original basis for the mythical god of wine and madness. Often driving women insane. Turning them into Maenads. The raving ones. Women who were given to divine possession and frenzied, ravenous like behavior.

When I learned this, I thought of the women who had become fixtures at the bar, sitting on bar stools staring raptly at him, hoping to gain his attention.

I must have sensed the danger inside of him like a coiled snake ready to strike. His attentiveness was intoxicating and always left me in a drunken state. Could that have been the reason I'd been so drawn to him? Yes, I loved sex. And yes, Jordin was extremely good at it. I'd slept with many men but with Jordin, it had been different. My nights with him had always left me high, feeling as if my skin were on fire.

I never questioned it, though. Like I said, I enjoyed the ride.

But now, I worry what my time with him could have done to me, if seeing him again would have the same effect. Would I be able to refuse him? Or would I let him pull me back into his powerful embrace?

I turned away from the bar and Kara continued driving. I pushed the thoughts of him down deep, burying them in the vast basement of my painful past. I couldn't dwell on the *many* opportunities Jordin had to slaughter me while I'd lain naked and vulnerable in his bed. The many ways in which he could have killed me was too much to think about. And I already had the images of Ronald's victims in my head. I didn't need anything else to keep me up at night.

We drove in silence—cutting across the island using the back roads instead of the main highway. I appreciated the detour; it gave me time to get my thoughts in order and review the plan the team had gone over this week.

A few years ago, most people on Tulare started referring to The Better Day Church as a cult. Including myself. Of course, this certainty was never anything anyone could prove. It was just rumors and conjecture based on the odd beliefs of its parishioners.

The lack of concrete details was why Devlin outlined that our objective today would be to determine if the church was in fact a cult, and if so, secure an invitation to join. If not, we would have to keep digging and find another way to verify if the Young family was using blood magick. We all doubted their true purpose would be revealed to those who attend church services occasionally—so we'd also have to show an interest in all their activities.

I was not looking forward to purchasing more useless clothes like I did when I got the job at Tribec Insurance. And I drew the line at elaborate hats and white gloves. There was no way in hell I would ever wear some extravagant hat. Especially in this heat.

I turned to Kara. "I can understand why Jonah is part of this recon mission. He is a faith mage." I paused. Maybe asking why she chose to come today would sound unappreciative. Fuck it. She knew me. "Why did you decide to join us today?" I sounded like a damn self-help guru. *Why did you decide to join us today? Seriously?*

She laughed. "Did you just say, 'recon mission'?"

"Devlin's words. Not mine," I said, smiling. "I think he's wearing off on me." *Was she stalling?*

Kara blew out a noisy breath and shrugged. "You..." She trailed off, then glanced at me. "I knew you were struggling. I saw it in the way you kept staring off into space, wringing your hands like you needed something to take the edge off. I'm surprised you didn't buy any cigars." I let out a bitter laugh. I had been entertaining the idea of buying a pack for a while. "And," Kara continued, "I wanted to be there in case you needed me."

I rubbed my temple and looked out the window. "Yeah, this is going to be hard." I stopped short of telling her why. No one knew about my past dealings with a religious cult and now was not the time to go into it. I needed to stay focused on the job at hand or I'd breakdown into a useless puddle of emotions. "Thanks. I appreciate it."

"And Nicole," she said, drawing my attention to her. "Try not to be cynical." She smiled. "Make it a mantra: *I will not by cynical.*"

"What about questions? Can I ask those?"

She laughed. "Of course. It would show interest. Just"—she gave me a look, her eyes dancing with humor—"try not to add any cynicism to them."

Her suggestion was eerily like the advice she had given me when I was applying for a job at Tribec Insurance. Kara knew I had a hard time not peppering people with questions. Truthfully, I'd been this way since I was a child. It used to drive my mother crazy. But the cynicism came later, when life had dealt me a shitty hand, and the only way I could cope with it was by using an unhealthy amount of sarcasm at the wrong time. I was working on it. Well, at least trying to work on it. But until I did manage to deal with the lemons I refused to make into lemonade, I had Kara to keep me grounded.

Kara crossed the border from Pleasanton into Alice, and I shifted my focus.

My limited abilities with magick disturbed me. It was a constant reminder of my parents and Luisah's betrayal of not teaching me the things I needed to know about my own abilities. Ones that had been locked away behind a black mass of energy that had been destroyed weeks ago. Now, my body had this thrum of power running through it—waiting to be used. Only, I had no idea how to use it. Sure, I understood all the rituals and even knew about the roots and herbs used in earth magick, but I didn't know how to wield my power to make a spell work.

When the team started teaching me, *the right way*, about magick, they gave me a strange analogy. They said to look at my magick like I had a green thumb. While two people could use the exact same methods to care for plants, it was always the person with a green thumb who managed to keep the plants alive and thriving—able to connect on a cellular level and assess the plant's needs. While the other person, time and time again, ended up with dead vegetation.

Magick was in the blood. In our very DNA. And surprisingly, everyone had it to some degree. However, like the green thumb analogy, only a few could access and wield its power.

Devlin considered those who couldn't use magick as having none. During his entire career in law enforcement, he had refused to use his own magick against those who didn't have any active magick of their own.

I had a strong suspicion this rigid belief would change eventually.

Given this, I decided to start off small by working on viewing the human aura or soul as some referred to it. It was where a person's magick resided. My first encounter with this was when we fought the people at the Sinclair at-risk youth facility. Alek had been bathed in a rich orange that looked like the sunset, Rachel a dark green, and Devlin a vibrant, lush blue. Using Jonah as a test subject, I was able to see his aura consisted of a white-goldish color tinged in black. My own had a green hue, representing earth, but it also had striations of red running through it. Which could possibly explain the anomaly in my magick. Kara, being an earth practitioner, had a dark green aura. But she also had blue ridges cutting into the green. The more vibrant the color, the stronger the magick. Only earth and mind practitioners had the ability to see the magick in others.

But unlike other earth practitioners, I had an additional power that they had never seen or heard of before.

I could keep a dead person's soul tethered to their body. Recently, I've practiced both seeing and feeling the small ball of energy pulsing in the center of an individual's aura. Alek had graciously volunteered for this experiment. When I touched his soul, it felt like a cold orb of energy, crackling in my palm. Alek said the sensation made his fight or flight response kick in, giving him a level of fear, he never thought he would feel.

It was going to take more practice, and understanding, before I could use my strange ability in battle. And while I would have loved to continue working on it, learning about the other principles was also important. Especially given what we were setting out to do. So last week, I switched gears.

According to Jonah, faith magick had never really been about religion. Its power was meant to create. But some thousands of years ago, after creating the first god using faith magick, the practitioners also formed religion. Using mankind's spirituality against them to garner control over the people. Today, it was the most common principle used across the world, which was why it was too easy for people to become fanatical in their beliefs and try and impose them on others—creating Zealots.

And in the wrong hands, faith magick could be the deadliest.

Given my own experience with religion, I had to agree.

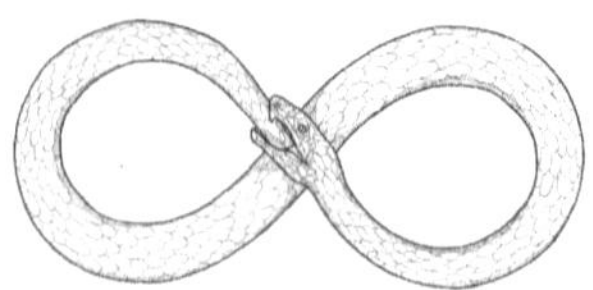

TWENTY MINUTES LATER, a little after eleven, we pulled into the packed parking lot of The Better Day Church, located in Alice, two miles North of Tribec Insurance. The service started at eleven thirty, so we had made it on time.

Kara circled the lot as I took in the garish structure: a towering white and gold cathedral with Roman columns and white marble statues of lions on either side of the walkway leading to the building.

One Sunday, when I was younger, my mother and I had ridden by the place on our way to Sandpoint. It was a year before David and Karen Young had been killed. A massive white tent had been erected in the parking lot. Scores of people roamed about, holding plates of food. My mother had called it a revival and said most churches held them. I had been curious and asked if we could go. She gave me a look I will never forget; one so laced with fear that I'd turned away and just stared at that tent as we continued to drive by.

Looking at the giant cathedral now, I wondered about that look. Did she know something about the family? Or was it just the aversion she and my father had to organized religion?

The original church had been modest—a small white and black building with a large lot. Once Gavina and Boyd took over the church after her parents' death, they'd turned it into a spectacle.

Kara pulled into a spot in the last aisle close to the exit and shut off the engine and, sadly, the air too. I sat there, staring, trying to build up the nerve to get out of the car.

"Are you ready?" Kara asked.

"Yeah, I just need a minute," I said, not looking at her.

She didn't push. I appreciated that. Instead, she turned the car back on and the air on full blast as I continued to gaze out at all the people making their way toward the large building.

The last time I'd been in church was four months after my best friend Steve's death. Two weeks after my boyfriend Frank had been killed. After pumping ten bullets into Frank's chest, his uncle had turned the gun on me while I lay there in a drugged-out state, unable to muster up enough willpower or concern to save myself. If not for him using all the bullets on Frank, I would have died that day.

I spent the next few weeks in so much pain, it felt as if my very soul was clawing away at me—hollowing me out until there was nothing left. My skin burned. My heart ached. And I just wanted everything and everyone to go the fuck away.

My parents tried. Especially my mother. But in the end, I climbed out of my window and ran away to stay in New Orleans with a woman who I had believed was my Aunt Delilah.

Her way of helping involved her church, a congregation whose roots came from twisted rituals and lust and power and subjugation. Pastor Jeremiah ran this small cult-like church with a zeal born from madness. Every once in a while, I still saw his dark, evil eyes staring down at me—willing me to believe in him.

Their place of worship was hidden in a deep, shadowy part of the bayou. Away from prying eyes and those who would question their beliefs. They had tried to convince me I only needed to have my soul cleansed to free myself of my pain.

Even now, all these years later, I can feel the rough, pitted texture of the concrete slab they had laid me on. Still feel the cold biting into my naked skin as the pastor stood over me praying while my aunt stood by watching. When the rest of the men surged forward and the pastor's wife handed him a knife, I yanked free of my loosely tied bindings, jumped off that slab, and ran.

When I'd returned home the next day, I didn't tell my father what happened. But somehow, he must have known. He told me Delilah was not really my aunt, but a family friend, one who they had long stopped talking to when they learned the depths of her beliefs. Only, no one ever told me this before. But then, why would they? We had left New Orleans and settled on Tulare Island when I was young. And while my father's brothers kept in contact, we never stepped foot in our old neighborhood again.

After all, my mother had buried the man who raped me when

I was six behind our house. To them, the land would forever be poisoned.

On a sigh, I pushed open the car door and stepped out into the sweltering heat.

Kara turned off the engine and got out of the car to join me. "Well, I hope we'll be able to find seats," she said as we started toward the church—mixing in with the other people making their way across the lot.

"The size of the building says we will. Besides—" The humidity made me gasp. *Please let them have air-conditioning.* "Jonah's probably already here. And he would have saved us one."

Kara made a non-committal noise that sounded suspiciously like a moan and continued walking.

The closer we got, the more my stomach turned. I had sworn to never set foot in another church again. But here I was, swarming to Enlightenment like the rest of these people.

Halfway to the building, my steps faltered. A man, leaning against a white Cadillac with dark tinted windows, caught my attention. Bald head, tanned skin that suggested he might be mixed with something, with a long, jagged scar tracing from his ear to the middle of his neck. He wore a pair of dark jeans and a tight gray shirt, molded to his massive physique. Even though his shaded gaze remained fixed on the church, I got the impression he was watching us. A chill ran down my spine and I reached out and stopped Kara.

She turned and gave me a questioning look. I pointed to the man. "Does he look..." I paused, unsure of what I wanted to say. All I knew was that his presence felt wrong.

"What?" she asked, glancing between me and him. "Do you know him?"

I shook my head and turned to her. "He just seems out of place," I said finally.

She studied him for a moment, her face going pensive. "Probably just some rich guy's driver," she said after a while. "We should keep walking. I feel like my skin is on fire in this heat."

I nodded. She was probably right. I was on-edge and most likely looking for danger when there wasn't any.

By the time we reached the front entrance, my entire back was covered in sweat. My hair was plastered to my head; strands lay across my face as if they had grown directly out of my pores. My sandaled feet slid forward on the verge of slipping completely out of my shoes. And my throat screamed for water.

"Fucking heat," I croaked. I should have brought a bottle of water with me.

"It's like the sun was trying to cook us as we walked." Kara wheezed, her breathing shallow.

"Please tell me you have a tissue or a bath towel in your purse."

"A bath towel?" Kara ran her hand over her forehead. "I might just go dive in that enormously large fountain they have over there."

I glanced over in the direction she was looking and found a marble statue of a woman wearing a toga in the center, holding an upturned jug in her hand. Mist smoked out as water cascaded down into the pooling water below. "You make the first move, and I promise I will follow."

She laughed. "No, I think that's more your speed."

"Don't tempt me." I ran my sticky arm across my forehead as if that would help. All it did was add to the already gritty, clammy sheen of sweat covering my face.

I spotted Jonah standing outside the large gold and white cathedral doors waiting. An immobile force of a man wearing a short-sleeved white button-down shirt and dark green pants. Parishioners gave him a wide berth. I didn't blame them. He was giving off this 'get the fuck away from me' vibe that was hard to ignore. I loved it.

He watched us as we made our way toward him. Correction, those brown eyes were *glued* to Kara as if she were just the spiritual healing he needed. I chuckled.

"What?" Kara asked, her eyes on Jonah as she straightened her cream-colored short dress.

I glanced at her. She had worn her long red hair down and had even curled the ends. Something she almost never did. I didn't have the heart to tell her what it looked like now.

"Oh, nothing," I said, smiling.

In the past few weeks, she and Jonah had been giving each other some extremely heated looks when they thought no one was watching. It was cute. And I really wished they would just go ahead and get down with it. Kara needed to have someone put a smile on her face.

"D, that man is sexy as hell," Kara said.

I turned to her. "Wow, you managed to curse. Well, your version of cursing, at least, and you said hell before we even got inside." I shook my head and linked my arm with hers. "You're such a heathen, Kara."

"Shut up, Nicole. And I'm serious. Give me some pointers."

"Outside of church?" I asked in mock outrage.

"Forget it." She turned to me. "Do you remember your mantra?"

"Yes, I will not be cynical."

She nodded. "Good."

"Welcome. Are you new?" a woman asked.

Kara and I whipped around and came face to face with three young girls. They stood behind us, wearing white lacy dresses that came to their ankles. Smiles stretched across their faces as they took us in. I was surprised they weren't covered in sweat. I mean seriously, how the hell did they manage to be covered from head to toe and not be affected by this heat?

The blonde-haired girl looked like she was the oldest: maybe early twenties. She kept her gaze steady as she continued to smile, waiting for our response. She gave off an air of authority, as though she commanded the space around her and everyone else were mere obstacles in her way. *Okay, yes, I was telegraphing.* Honestly, while she did give off this sort of, 'I'm in charge' vibe, she also had an openness about her. Like she wanted to invite you in.

The dark-haired girl looked no older than eighteen. Her dark green eyes held a well of inquisitiveness that gave me the impression she was trying to figure something out about us. Her slight build looked unassuming. But then again, the dress she wore was probably meant to give that impression. The younger girl, maybe no older than seventeen with similar features, stood by her side. Her dark brown hair was pulled up into a tight bun—stretching her face into a porcelain mask. She kept her green eyes averted, only stealing a few fleeting glances at us as she pressed into the other girl. Sisters?

I felt movement behind me but didn't look away from the girls. Jonah's familiar cool woodsy scent washed over me. The girls' eyes tracked up, taking him in.

Kara smiled and I worked my mouth into a facsimile of the gesture.

"Yes," Kara said to the girls. "We are most eager to hear the wisdom of Boyd."

Most eager to hear the wisdom of Boyd? When the hell did Kara start talking like that? I glanced at her. She was serious!

Don't laugh, Nicole. Please, don't laugh. I will not be cynical. I will not be cynical.

Kara turned to me. "Isn't that right, Nicole?"

"Yes," I said, and immediately went into a coughing fit. Me being here was a bad idea. I'd be surprised if I managed to hold it together for the entire service.

"I'm Sara," the blonde one said. "And this is Juliette and Bridgette. It's very nice to meet you. All are welcome to enjoy the word of Boyd. And we'd love for you to sit with us."

Jonah placed a hand on both our shoulders. "They're with me."

I smiled. Jonah sounded like our pimp.

"You're welcome as well," Juliette said, her voice small, as if speaking up wasn't what she was used to doing. Interesting. Especially since she had no problem making eye contact with us.

Sara turned to me, locking eyes. "Are you sure you won't sit with us?"

"Umm..."

Something in her eyes frightened me. It was a predatory look I'd seen before in a similar situation—the sinister hunger I received at my aunt's church from all the parishioners as they watched me walk toward the altar.

A breeze pushed at my back and suddenly I was back at the outdoor church hidden in the thickness of the bayou. The cloying smell of dead things filled my nose. Water lapped nearby, but I couldn't see it. All the men and women that surrounded me wore false smiles. "Welcome," they'd uttered. "We will heal you," they'd said as they led me to the middle of the clearing.

But I didn't look at them. I had become transfixed on the concrete altar in the middle of the clearing. The ground appeared to have given birth to it. All the vegetation caressed its sides, keeping it cocooned. Safe. The surface gleamed in the moonlight. And the leather straps nailed into the stone had been polished, laying wide. Waiting.

I'd gone so far beyond fear and hope that I never registered the tears streaming down my face until the scene became hazy. Or the fact that they had to carry me the last few steps until my feet no longer felt the ground beneath me.

"No thank you," Jonah said, the timbre of his voice pulling me out of the memory.

I shook myself and both Jonah and Kara looked at me. I turned away from them and swallowed the lump in my throat. "Yes, no thank you," I whispered.

I really didn't need to say it again. I was sure the women had gotten the message. But I needed to say something. They were all staring at me; their scrutiny made my skin itch. It was almost as if they were scratching away at the surface, digging into me. At any moment, they would see the fear building inside and the raw anguish that was taking all my strength to bury once again.

I will never let anyone tie me to an altar again.

"Yes, of course," Sara said finally and extended her arm toward the church. "The service will be starting soon."

Jonah's hand went to my back, urging me forward, and I took a step. Sweat had accumulated at the base of my neck. I pulled my hair up and a warm breeze blew across my nape. I glanced up at the sky. White clouds rolled overhead. Our frequent showers were no more. It was almost as if something was holding the water back with an invisible dam. The pressure could be felt in the air, and at any moment, it would become too much. The dam would break, releasing all that water. And with it, an enormous amount of power.

L ike the outside, the inside of the church reminded me of a gilded homage to the gods. Tall white columns lay flush against the walls with ivy vines intertwined around the posts. The floor was covered in white and gray marble. A display case filled with religious items sat just inside the door. Sitting beside it was a rack filled with brochures for church activities.

A woman stopped us before we could enter the chapel. "We like to have all the new people sign the guestbook." She beamed at us as she held out a gold pen.

Jonah took it and scribbled down his name and address, then handed it to me before I could formulate a protest. I stared at the long list of names and addresses and froze. I didn't want to give these people my information. Jonah nudged me, dipping his head toward the book. I glanced at Kara, and she too gave me a look that said, 'do it.'

I swallowed the cynical reply on my tongue and wrote down my name and address, omitting my apartment number. Let them figure it out. It wasn't until I started to turn away that I noticed Jonah had written a bogus address.

I narrowed my eyes, trying to keep my ire contained, and Jonah shook his head and mouthed, *later*. Damn right we would talk about this later.

Once Kara had signed the book, we continued inside.

Light wooden pews with red cushioning curved in toward the altar—or pulpit—as if they were being moved by some unforeseen force. A strange earthy scent hung heavily in the air. I held back a sneeze as we moved to the center of the room and found the last of the available seats.

Only to have my nose assaulted again. The man next to me—late forties, greasy dark hair streaked with gray, wearing a wrinkled dark blue suit—smelled like he'd bathed in motor oil. When he shifted, I got the faint whiff of peppermint and a tangerine scented aftershave that was trying to compete with the oily smell.

I will not be cynical. I will not be...fuck!

I turned to Kara. "Can we change places?"

She looked around me, wrinkled her nose, and shook her head. *Dammit.* There was no way I could keep my mantra in my head and block the man's scent at the same time. Especially not with old memories pushing their way to the surface too.

Jonah leaned over and whispered, "There are only a handful of people dressed like those girls."

I turned and surveyed the crowd. Hushed voices overflowed the large space, echoing off the walls. He was right. Most of the people were dressed in either suits or dresses. Only a few individuals wore the white lacy number that Sara, Juliette, and Bridgette wore. And it was only the women. I didn't see any men wearing white. Come to think of it, I didn't see many men at all.

Jonah told us most cults had more women than men. Because underneath the ramblings of a professed Prophet was really a deviant mind that used his charm to cajole women and young girls into sleeping with him. Seeing all the women in white all but confirmed this.

I spotted the Young family sitting in the front pew.

Andrew Snow had compiled information on seven families on Tulare Island he believed practiced blood magick. The Young family was among them. While he was able to determine their magick, he had little personal information on them. We had to fill in the gaps in his research.

Salome, the oldest at twenty and an earth mage like her sister Oralee, stood, arms crossed, watching the crowd. Rachel had managed to find her class schedule at Red Oak University when she hacked into the database, and it seemed Salome wanted to be a teacher. Unlike the rest of the girls in the crowd, she wore a simple blue dress. It complemented her blue eyes.

Her sister Oralee stood next to her. Instead of wearing the white frock, she wore a tight white dress that stopped just above her knee. Large gold hoops adorned her ears. She wore her dark brown hair pulled up in a tight ponytail. She looked bored and a little irritated. While she had graduated from high school, she had yet to apply for college.

Vidette, a faith mage like her mother and sister Hedia, sat with her back to everyone. She was supposed to graduate this past year but dropped out before she could complete school. The youngest, Hedia, sat next to Vidette, resting her head on her sister's shoulder. At fourteen, she spent more time in the principal's office than she did in class.

Their only son, Xavier, stood near the stage with a smirk on his face, his eyes wandering over everyone. He was the only one of their children who didn't have magick. If I had to guess, being the only male child, he might resent that. At least that was what I was getting from his body language. Like he was above everyone and everything. Men often went through that phase in life. Some settled into it like it was their calling in life. I've encountered quite a few of them in my vast-experienced dating life.

When I asked Rachel about the family's array of magick, she said it was possible. Especially if Gavina's ancestors had mixed with other magick families. The same way a child could be born with blue eyes when both parents had brown eyes. Somewhere in their family history someone had earth magick and that trait, through DNA, would have been given to the child.

From their indifference, I had to wonder if the Young children even took part in their parents' activities. None of them seemed interested in being here. That had to be important. I filed the observation away for later examination.

Sara, carrying three books, made her way toward us. She smiled at a few people along the way. Juliette stood in the front with a group of other women, her gaze transfixed in our direction. Her sister stood next to her. I followed her line of sight to Jonah. He rubbed his chest as he watched her. It was almost as if he, too, was transfixed.

"Jonah," I said. "What's going on?"

He shook himself and turned to me. I raised a brow in question.

"Nothing," he said. "Just..." He turned back toward her, but Sara stood in his way.

"I noticed you didn't have our Holy Book." Sara handed the books to Jonah. "You can use these for the sermon and pay for them before you leave."

"Pay for them?" I asked, as I took a copy from Kara. *The Wisdom of Boyd: A guide to Spiritual Enlightenment and Worship.* Seriously?

"Yes, of course," Sara said as if it was a given.

"Why the—" I started. Kara placed her hand on my arm.

I will not be cynical. I will not be cynical.

"That will be fine," Kara said.

No, the hell it wouldn't. I wasn't paying for this shit.

"Enjoy the sermon," Sara said, cut her eyes at me, and walked away.

Bitch.

"I'm not paying for this book, Kara," I said through clenched teeth.

"I'll take care of it," Jonah said. He glanced at me. "We need to secure an invite, remember?"

My mouth moved, but no words came out. I wanted to argue. My fists clenched on my lap, the short nails biting into my skin— most likely breaking the surface. While my head pounded, a lump formed in my throat. I swallowed it down. He was right. I tried to fill my head with my mantra again, but it wasn't working.

Why the hell was I getting so emotional?

Oh, I knew why. Because long-buried memories were surfacing, and I couldn't do anything to stop them. I toyed with my charm bracelet, trying to find comfort. The bracelet had been a gift from my father when I was nine. The charms on it—an ankh and a fleur-de-lis—represented my parents.

Jonah studied me, waiting for a response. Finally, I nodded and turned away before he could see the tears filling my eyes. I sucked in a deep breath and willed the pain away.

Rubbing my suddenly chilled arms, I faced forward and let my mantra fill my head. He was right; I needed to pull myself together.

Come on, Nicole. You got this.

I didn't have this. Dammit, I should have told Devlin I changed my mind and wouldn't go. But then he would have asked why, and I would have stumbled around for a plausible reason that didn't require me to relive the past. Alek would have pulled me aside and stared at me, willing me to tell him. I wasn't ready to share my past pain with anyone.

She'd told me once that Jonah didn't do undercover work. Yet, he had volunteered to do this assignment. Come to think of it, he had suggested I help.

I glanced over at him.

Curiosity wormed its way inside of me, a welcome distraction from the emotional turmoil that had started gnawing at my insides and unlocking the long-buried trauma I needed to ignore.

Why did he want to go undercover at church? True, he was a faith mage, but he could have stayed on the sidelines and offered support like he'd done when Devlin, Rachel, and I were at Tribec. Was there something in his past that he needed to atone for? Devlin had alluded to Jonah having a troubled past when he'd first talked to me about what his team did.

Before I could ponder it further, a rush of excitement ran through the crowd. We turned and watched Boyd and Gavina Young make their way up the aisle toward the dais with smiles plastered across their faces.

Confidence oozed off the short round man as he strode forward wearing his white robe with gold embroidery running down the front. I was somewhat surprised to learn he didn't have any magick. I would have thought it was a requirement for running a cult. But what he lacked in magick he made up for with his gift of gab. Boyd had spent his youth in and out of juvenile detention. And his adult life running cons. Despite his shady past, he was never the one in the spotlight when the church came under scrutiny. It was always Gavina.

Gavina walked next to him—arms linked—looking regal and refined, a slender woman with long raven hair that hung around her body like a veil. The front had been pushed up in a tall bump making it look like a crown.

Boyd took his place behind the lectern while Gavina sat behind him on a marble chair with red cushioning.

Boyd looked out over the congregation with his large hands gripping the sides of the polished wood.

"It's great to see so many new faces here today," he said, his voice filled with false joy. "So many people ready to receive wisdom." He paused, morphing his face into a mask of skepticism and concern. "But how many of you will deny that wisdom?" He paused again. Staring. Waiting. I had to hand it to him; he even had me a little curious. "Would the new members please stand? Show the congregation—your fellow brothers and sisters—who you are."

People rose slowly from their seats. I glanced around and counted close to forty. Finally, Jonah and Kara stood. I remained seated. Besides, I wasn't ready to receive any of Boyd's bullshit wisdom.

Jonah and Kara looked at me with concern in their eyes. *Dammit.* I stood.

Boyd continued, "Tell me. Are you all ready to receive my wisdom?"

Murmurs filled the space. I mentally flipped him the bird.

Boyd gestured for everyone to sit.

Again, he paused for effect. I wondered if he practiced this song and dance in front of a mirror. "We grew up poor." He shook his head, gripping the side of his lectern. "No money for even our basic needs. We relied on charity and the good will of our neighbors." A tear slid down his face. He pulled a white handkerchief from his pocket and dabbed at his eyes.

I wanted to call bullshit, yell at him that it was too early in his act to turn on the water works. How the hell could people be so caught up in this crap? Kara squeezed my hand. It was like she was reading my damn mind.

She leaned over. "Remember your mantra," she whispered.

I will not be cynical. I will not be cynical.

"One day, while walking home from school, a voice whispered to me." His mouth turned up into a knowing smile. "It told me that I had been chosen to spread its word and I had to convince my parents to move out of our town and into the next one." He stopped and drummed his meaty fingers on the podium, staring at each person in turn. "I asked this voice how we were going to do that with no money. It replied, 'I will provide the way.' So, I ran home and told my parents exactly what it said." He smiled, again looking around the room. "You can guess what my father said. And my backside was good and worn by the time he finished saying it." Everyone laughed as if on cue. "But I didn't give up. I kept at it. Until finally, he agreed maybe we should move."

Boyd moved from behind his lectern. "And I promise you," he said, raising his voice as if he were shouting to the heavens. Some of the congregants stood, lifting their hands up to join in his rapture. "The very day we settled in our new home was the day our lives began. No more struggle. No more worry. And from that day on, I have been blessed with more wisdom. More knowledge than I could ever hope to use in one lifetime." He lifted his book again. "And it's all right here."

The congregation applauded. And I crossed my arms over my chest. His story sounded so much like every other con artist's bullshit and lacked any substantive detail. He should have come up with a better story; at least given us the reason his father changed his mind. And who suddenly has no more problems? If I spotted a suggestion box on my way out, I was so going to give him some critique notes.

As Boyd waxed on, Gavina's gaze roamed over the congregation, hungry, like she was scenting out fresh meat until finally settling on me.

Our gazed locked, and the room seemed to shift. My heartbeat slowed, keeping rhythm with the second hand on a clock. I tried to turn away, but her dark eyes held me there. Heat pooled in my stomach and warmth spread all over my body. I remembered this feeling. Sexual. Tender. But I've never been attracted to women. Yet, Gavina kept me rooted in place, snared in her seductive web. Boyd's voice grew smaller and smaller as if I were sinking into a pit. Getting further away from him until all I heard was the roaring of my own blood in my ears.

"I can heal you," a feathery voice whispered, waking the mark inside my head. *"I will heal you. Just let me inside."*

An invisible finger ran down the side of my face and the phoenix's wings opened.

When I was a child, my mother had bargained with an Old One to block the part of my brain that would allow me to access my magick. They had placed a mass of darkness, a sort of magickal seal, around it. To keep it in place, they put an elaborate mark in front of it—a golden glyph of a phoenix outlined in red with a fleur-de-lis rising behind the mystical bird. The entire mark was enclosed in a shen ring. Outside the ring were hands, held up as if in prayer. Many different types of wards had been used but given what Alek told me of magick wanting to be used, I understood the need for the intricate design.

It also explained the tidal wave of power that was now constantly rushing through me—waiting for me to wield its power.

Alek was the first to try and use magick on me and paid the price with pain. He wanted to stop the onslaught of memories flooding me when a fissure split down the black mass, creating an opening that gave me access to my power. And now, as Gavina cried out, it seemed she would pay the price as well. She sucked in a breath, the sound so loud it echoed off the walls. As she struggled for breath, she kept her eyes trained on me. Her kids followed her line of sight as if searching for the reason their mother was in pain. Boyd whipped around and looked at his wife. Hushed, worried voices filled the church, sounding like an infestation of bees.

Her children rose from the front rows and converged onto the dais.

Xavier turned his head slowly until his gaze landed on me. I expected to see anger, but he only smiled. Not handsome. But intriguing. And obviously he was not too concerned about his mother. His sister, Vidette, said something to him, and he turned back to his mother and slowly got up, taking his time as he joined his siblings on the dais.

Gavina continued to wheeze as if someone had their hands around her neck—squeezing. Boyd went down on his knees in front of her and their flock of girls in white moved toward the dais as if summoned. All the while, her eyes remained fixed on me. Accusing. Finally, her head shifted slowly away as she murmured —her mouth moving sluggishly. Was she working a spell?

I leaned toward Kara and whispered, "She tried to attack me."

"Yes," Kara said, glaring at Gavina. "Are you all right?"

I rubbed my head, trying to dislodge the residual pain. "Fine," I said, my voice trembling. Raw emotion clogged up my throat. I bit back the tears that were forming and latched onto anger, letting it infuse me with strength. "I hope that bitch suffered," I gritted out.

Kara squeezed my hand. But I didn't look at her. Instead, I kept my eyes focused on Gavina—letting my gaze go distant as I studied her aura. I'd expected to see a gold sheen covering her body but instead found steel gray. I nudged Kara. "Something is off with her magick," I whispered.

Kara stared at Gavina as one of the girls in white gave her some water. After taking a long sip, she pushed them away and leaned in to talk with her husband. He nodded a few times and then returned to the lectern.

Kara looked at me, confusion in her eyes. "Maybe she's not a faith mage," she said and turned to study Gavina again.

I didn't know. And there was no way we could question it now. I scanned the rest of the family—noted their auras as well. When I came to Xavier's, I almost gasped. He didn't have one. In its place was a void. I looked deeper and saw his soul pulsing inside of him.

I checked Boyd, wondering if a person without the ability to use magick in fact did have no color to their aura, and found a pale gold light surrounding him. I had to squint to really see it, but it was there. So why didn't Xavier have any color inside his aura?

"To heal oneself and accept the wisdom," Boyd continued, pulling me out of my thoughts. *Oh, okay.* They were going to *pretend* like nothing happened. "You must give in. Let the desire to be whole fill you." He paused, looking around at his audience. They had returned to their rapt state, watching him as if he truly were some sort of god. I chanced a look at Gavina and found her staring out at the crowd, her mouth moving again in what I was coming to believe *was* a sort of spell. Which made me even more curious as to what kind of magick she had.

"We need a path in these dark times to find light and satisfaction and prosperity."

I'd heard those exact words before.

The more he talked, the more the room spun. Until finally, his voice grew deep...morphing into Pastor Jeremiah's.

I blinked and was no longer in a gilded cathedral sitting next to Kara. Now, I lay in my underwear on a cold slab of concrete, shivering. But not from the cold—from fear.

My aunt stood next to me, speaking in an urgent whisper. And I watched her through a haze of tears.

"We need a path in these dark times to find light," Pastor Jeremiah said, gazing down at my body with a hungry look in his eyes.

Someone grabbed my arm, jarring me from the memory. Before I could cry out, Kara slapped a hand over my mouth. I closed my eyes, pushing the rest of the flashback down. *Fuck*, I mouthed behind her hand. She smiled, but I still saw the concern in her eyes.

"Old memories," I whispered when she took her hand away.

Jonah lifted his eyebrow in question, and I shook my head.

"It is for that reason we have gathered." Boyd's voice pushed the last of my memories away.

Everything in me wanted to run out. Scream. Something. Being in here was tearing me apart. I couldn't keep the memories away. Why had they started surfacing? Was it because they had been on my mind? Was I responsible somehow? Like when someone says, 'Don't think about elephants,' and then that's all anyone can think about. Only, no one told me not to think about the past.

I shifted around in my seat, anxious, and took in the rest of the congregation.

Spellbound in the melodious words coming out of Boyd's mouth, hardly anyone moved. Small smiles played across their faces as Boyd promised them a path forward. The only ones not caught in his web were the women in white. They were too busy studying the faces of everyone in the room—like ravenous wolves scenting blood.

The parishioners reminded me of the employees at Tribec Insurance on the day I arrived for my interview. And the constant drone of their voices as they repeated the well-rehearsed script the company had provided them. They too had this sort of deadness about them. Like they were ensnared in a spell that drained them of all their free will. Which I later learned was actually true. Tribec Insurance had set up a ritual to drain the life out of their employees. The spell was called Athanasia and created by a Druid Priestess to help revitalize one's life. Was the Young family using the same ritual?

Either way, Gavina had to be working some sort of spell on the congregation. Boyd's ramblings just weren't filled with much more than repeated promises of salvation. One could find those hollow words anywhere.

I glanced at Kara and Jonah. They, at least, were able to keep up the façade of attentiveness. After what just happened, I refused to keep up the pretense. Of course, that might mean we wouldn't get that invitation we needed to join their cult. But at that moment I was finding it extremely difficult to care. Devlin could yell at me later. Correction: Devlin *would* yell at me later.

I turned away from the spectacle, and my blood froze in my veins.

A few pews behind us.

Ronald Stewart.

I reached inside my purse, wrapping my hand around the gun Devlin had given me.

They told me I should leave it at home. I was happy I didn't.

And from one blink to the next, I realized it wasn't him. He might have had the same slim build as Ronald, but the wrinkles around his brown eyes gave him away. Ronald, of course, didn't have wrinkles, and his eyes were blue.

Gerald Stewart, Ronald's father, sat in the church, staring daggers at me.

He tipped his head in my direction. My heart rammed in my chest so hard, I worried that everyone could hear its frantic pounding.

There was no way his presence here was mere coincidence.

Someone jabbed my arm, and I glanced at the smelly man sitting next to me. He handed me a basket full of money. It took me a few seconds to understand why. I let go of my gun and fumbled for my wallet. Hand shaking, I pulled out a dollar. After setting it on top of the other bills, I gave the basket to Kara.

"Surely you have more to give?" the man asked.

"I need to eat, so no," I said before I could stop myself.

"Nicole," Kara whispered.

Fuck me.

I pulled a five out of my wallet and set it in the basket. "I am thankful," I said through clenched teeth.

He patted my arm and smiled. "You are most welcome."

That word again. In any other circumstance, I wouldn't mind it. But here, at The Better Day Church, the word felt like a dagger. Underneath that cheerful uttering was menace.

"We can heal you."

Please, not again.

The room spun and the walls started to close in, the ground seeming to shift beneath my feet. The cloying smell of the swamp pushed its way inside of me. I should have stayed away from this church. A single tear slipped down my cheek as my heart rammed in my chest. I should have banished these demons. But I didn't have the strength. And all these years later, I still didn't. I probably never will.

I stood up. The book Sara gave me clattered to the floor. Its *thump* filled the cathedral. Boyd's voice cut off abruptly. Some-one's magick brushed up against my skin. I scanned the room. All eyes were focused on me, filled with scorn and hate—obviously pissed I'd interrupted the sermon. I wanted to yell it was all bull-shit, but instead, I turned away from them and moved past Kara so I could make my way outside.

"Nicole?" Kara whispered.

"I need to get out of here," I said, my voice thick with sadness and frustration. I pushed my way out of the row.

"Nicole," Kara called again in a pleading tone.

I ignored her and rushed down the aisle. Sucking in a calming breath, I shoved open the door and emerged into the damp heat.

If I could have ripped off my stupid ill-fitting dress, I would have. I didn't care what Devlin said, I was not going to be able to do this.

An image of me on the altar in my aunt's church flashed through my mind again and bile rose in my throat. I bent over, ready to throw up.

"Not very religious, Ms. Fontane?" His voice crawled over me.

I eased up and turned to look at Gerald Stewart. He stood, leaning on a cane, just outside the double doors, his face blank while his eyes blazed with hatred.

"Well?" he asked.

"No. I'm not," I said, finally able to dislodge my tongue from the roof of my mouth.

Beads of sweat gathered at the base of my neck, despite the chill that had settled there. I flexed my hand, trying to work some blood circulation back into it. I didn't want to show the fear brewing inside of me.

"A murderer wouldn't, I suppose," he said in a pretentious tone.

His snide comment was like a slap across the face. And it was all the fuel I needed to push the irrational fear I had of him out of me. True, Devlin and the team—myself included—had killed his adult children. They deserved it. And no matter how many times I told myself that, it still troubled me. Not enough to regret it, just enough to concern me.

"Tell me, Gerald, does sacrificing dozens of innocent people count as murder?"

He walked around me, purposely invading my space. I guess he expected me to flinch or move out of his way. Fuck him.

The bald man I spotted in the parking lot earlier walked up and stood next to Gerald. His dark gray eyes seemed to bore into my soul. I should have trusted my instincts when I first saw him. Because he, despite Gerald's posturing, was the real threat.

Gerald spared the man a quick glance. "You will refer to me as Mr. Stewart."

"Not on your fucking life, *Gerald*. Say what you came to say and leave," I bit out.

He smiled. "Brash and stupid, just like Thomas said." He shook his head. "I should have pushed him to get rid of you. Instead, I indulged Ronald once again."

Which meant he knew what his sick son was up to and did nothing about it—only hired a nurse to watch him. A nurse who, in the end, became one of Ronald's victims.

Gerald took a step forward, and I stuck my hand in my purse and wrapped it around my gun.

The man's eyes narrowed, watching my movements like a hawk. He took a step forward, hands held loose at his sides as if he was getting ready to pounce. Gerald put a hand on his arm. "Don't, Logan. Ms. Fontane isn't a threat."

Logan? I'd heard that name before.

The door opened behind me, but I didn't take my eyes off Gerald or Logan. Instead, I pulled the gun from my purse and held it casually at my side. If either one of them moved forward, I was going to shoot them.

"Don't, Nicole," Jonah said, placing a hand on my shoulder.

Gerald and Logan looked at him, dismissing me as if I wasn't even there. Unbelievable. I was the one with the gun! I still didn't know how to use it properly, but this close, I could hopefully do some damage.

Kara moved up beside me and crossed her arms.

Logan turned to her, and a worried look crossed his face. He covered it quickly. His gaze never left her face.

I glanced over at her and fought hard not to flinch as well. Coldness crept into her green eyes making them appear black. She took the gun from my hand and put it back in my purse, her movements mechanical. All the while, she kept her cold, dark gaze glued on Logan and Gerald as if daring them to attack. Remembering her during the battle with Thomas and Lisa, how she was able to pull the soil up from the ground and wield it, and the look of pure glee on her face, I got the distinct impression she was hoping they would.

"You don't need it," she said, and smiled.

What she probably meant was I couldn't use it, so why show it off. And of course, she was right. No matter how many times Devlin tried to help me with my aim, I just couldn't get the hang of it. Everything I shot at, I missed. By miles.

Gerald cleared his throat. "Now that all of you are here, I can warn you together. When you maliciously killed my children, you took something that belonged to me. My wife mourns them. But I just want the Ark back. We worked too hard to secure that relic, and I want it returned immediately."

I laughed. The Ark was used in a ritual to create the Old Ones —gods born out of blood and sacrifice. When we'd defeated his children in battle, the Ark had been lost. And we confirmed the police hadn't taken it, either. So why did he assume we had it?

"We don't have it," Jonah said. "And even if we did"—he smiled and leaned in as if Gerald were two feet tall—"we wouldn't be returning it to you."

"Is that so?" Logan said, once again stepping forward.

Gerald stuck his cane in Logan's path and stared up at Jonah. "We'll give them some time to think about it." He glanced at me. "I believe my son, Ronald, is quite taken with you, Ms. Fontane. You better pray he never returns to Tulare."

"No, Gerald, you better pray he doesn't. You have already lost two kids. It'd be a shame to lose the last one."

He shook his head and walked away, dismissing me once again. I really needed to work on projecting menace. I was getting a little tired of being underestimated.

As Logan spared me one last glance, it finally dawned on me where I'd heard that name before. It was during the conversation Ronald had engineered for me to overhear. Lisa had threatened to send Logan after me when they feared I was becoming too attached to Ronald and could possibly learn about their Harvest ritual. Ronald had managed to deter her.

At first, I believed it was in an effort to protect me. I learned later, he had plans of his own. He wanted us to expose his family's blood magick practices so he could break the weak ties that kept his sick appetites at bay.

So, if Ronald, a serial killer, was worried about Lisa sending Logan after me, then the intense bald man had to be a serious threat.

One who seemed to know Kara.

Since Devlin wanted Jonah and I to report in after our day at the church, I opted to ride with Jonah. We stopped at a local burger joint around the corner from Devlin's and I ordered two fully loaded burgers and a large fry.

Jonah gave me a pointed look. "You think you ordered enough?"

"Don't judge me." I refused to look at him.

He pulled forward after placing an order for himself and the rest of the team. "No judgement. Just wondering if you'd rather talk."

I sighed and let my head rest against the seat back. "No. Right now, I'd rather eat my weight in food."

"Whenever you're ready," he said and let it drop.

I appreciated his concern. More than he would ever realize. I also appreciated that he didn't push and instead gave me the space I needed.

A short while later, we pulled up to Devlin's rental house in a family-friendly neighborhood located on the border of Pleasanton and Alice. Before we got out of the car, I turned to Jonah and asked, "What address did you write in the guestbook at the church?"

He shut the car off—it immediately filled with the stifling heat—and grabbed their food bags. I always got a separate bag. I didn't like getting stiffed on my portion of fries. Not that I needed them. But still, they were mine. "The hotel Devlin stayed at," he said finally.

When they first arrived on Tulare to investigate Felicity Markum's disappearance, Devlin and Rachel had stayed at separate hotels closer to Tribec Insurance while they were undercover. Alek and Jonah had stayed at the rental house. Now, all four of them were living there. Including me on a part-time basis—still sharing a room with Alek, even sleeping in the same bed. And not having sex. More reason to eat my weight in food.

"I should have copied the address you wrote," I said.

Jonah gave me a questioning glance. "Why didn't you?"

"I wasn't thinking." I shook my head and followed him up the walkway to the front door. "You know, I'm surprised Gerald Stewart hasn't found the house."

"What makes you think he hasn't?" he asked, pushing open the door—letting out a blast of cool air.

"He and Logan would have come here to threaten us instead of showing up at the church."

"Not necessarily. It could just be a show of power." He continued down the hall toward the back of the house where Devlin and Rachel were. They both sat at the large worktable Devlin had exchanged for the foldout table that was in there originally. He'd added a few other pieces of furniture to the house as well: a sleeper couch in the front room for him and a bedroom set in the room Rachel was sleeping in. He left the fourth bedroom empty.

I'd been referring to it as a safehouse, but really, it was more of an operation center.

Devlin looked up from the computer when Jonah set the bag of food on the table. Jonah unbuttoned his shirt and sat down at the table. "Coming here," he continued while he pulled a burger from the bag, "would have been obvious. But showing up at the church makes a bigger statement."

I sat across from Rachel and tore open my bag, spreading my

food out on the greasy, brown paper. Rachel smiled at me, and I smiled back. "What statement is that?" I asked.

"I can find you anywhere," he said, then took a large bite of his burger.

He was right. They had to be keeping tabs on us. Probably had someone watching the house. How else would they have known where we would be? But that wasn't right, either. Logan had been in the parking lot when Kara and I arrived.

"Do you think they followed you from here?" I asked Jonah.

He nodded as he chewed.

Well, that wasn't scary at all.

While we ate, Jonah filled both Rachel and Devlin in on what happened at church. Since I was still getting used to the old 'report to Devlin' portion of my job, I'd let Jonah do all the talking while I stuffed my face and reflected. Or rather, while I prepared myself for one of Devlin's "training" sessions. Or as I liked to call them, 'shine a light on the many ways Nicole keeps fucking up,' sessions. Everything he did with me was used as a teaching moment. And I hated it.

I looked over at the three white boards Devlin had tacked up to the wall. A condensed version of Andrew's information was spread out all over the surface. Each family had their own little section that contained notes, pictures, and their type of magick.

Refusing to part with the original, I'd given them a copy of *The Land Guarded by People of Colour* written by Louis Badet. It sat off to the side with the names of the four Old Ones we had identified thus far written alongside their images. Luisah had already shown me a depiction of one of the Old Ones in a book on the Naqada culture. He had been drawn with different color whorls covering his skin. She told me the designs represented his name in a language that sounded like musical notes.

Louis Badet had referred to the Old Ones by the names they'd been given much later in Egypt.

Ezra was often referred to as Anhur—god of war and hunting. When I'd gone to his dojo after learning about the Old Ones, he had invited me in to talk. I recalled the stray thought I'd had of him hunting me as we made our way to the small apartment he had in the back of the dojo. He didn't have many personal items in that small space. Only war memorabilia lining his walls. Now I understood why.

The woman who had helped Ezra save me when I was almost killed by their brother was called Hathor—goddess of the sky, the sun, sexuality, and motherhood. She was also responsible for blocking my memories and magick when I was six years old.

Jordin Cisco was called Shezmu—god of wine and sex. In the Greek pantheon, he was called Dionysus, and the Roman— Bacchus. He fit his godhood perfectly.

And their brother, the Old One who attacked me, was known as Set—god of violence, chaos, and strength. Oftentimes, Set was referred to as a trickster god as well.

It made me wonder if they had molded themselves into what the people expected. After all, human beings created the myths, not the gods. And the Old Ones were considered gods.

"Nicole," Devlin prompted. His tone was like nails on a chalkboard. He leaned back in his chair, shifting his body so that he was facing me.

I pushed my empty bag away, got up, and stretched. "I saw Logan in the parking lot when we arrived." Might as well get the embarrassment over with.

"What was your first thought when you saw him?" he asked, standing.

"What do you mean?" I knew what he meant, but I needed to stall; find a way to organize my thoughts and put them into words he would understand. Who was I kidding? Devlin understood only two things when it came to a job: success or failure. Despite him treating missions this way, he operated in the gray—seeing some of their illegal actions as neither right nor wrong. Only justified and necessary. I was still struggling with that. But not as much as when I first witnessed Rachel giving a guard from Tribec Insurance a concoction she knew would eventually kill him.

Devlin sighed. He had been doing that a lot lately when having conversations with me. The first time, I told him he might want to tattoo 'Patience' on his forehead like Jonah had tattooed on his arm. He didn't like the suggestion and gave me some crude advice I didn't think was humanly possible. It was not one of our better sessions. We might have devolved into childish name calling had Rachel not step in. She did, however, take her time doing so. Now, I chose to ignore him. After all, I was still in my damn church clothes.

"You have instincts, Nicole." He continued after a pause. "Yet you keep dismissing them. You need to work on listening, assessing, and making split-second decisions." He moved closer to me, crowding into my space. The smell of coffee and his spicy aftershave filled the miniscule room between us. I'd never admit to him how much I liked the smell. Might give him the wrong impression.

Placing my hands on my hips, I stared up at him, trying to keep the defiance off my face. His nostrils flared as he glared at me. Maybe I shouldn't have put my hands on my hips. "Now, think back to when you first saw him. What was your first thought?" he asked, his jaw clenched. I couldn't have gotten to him that much. Why was he so angry?

"I was suspicious."

"Why?"

I paused. Why *was* I suspicious?

"Don't think about it! First feeling."

"Dev." Rachel got up from the floor, walked over and placed her hand on his chest. "She's trying." She kept her gaze steady on his. A quick burst of green light pulsed from her hand and Devlin sighed, eyes closing. I rubbed my eyes wondering if maybe I were seeing things. I looked at Jonah. He hadn't reacted so maybe I had imagined it.

Devlin cleared his throat. "Sorry, Nicole. Go on."

"He didn't belong," I blurted out, my mind still whirring. I pulled in a deep breath and tried to focus. Whatever Rachel did, I doubted it would last too long.

"How so?" Devlin asked.

I yanked my hair, frustrated. No, not belong. He did not fit. That still wasn't right. None of us really fit in at The Better Day Church.

Dammit. I could do this.

"I pushed that feeling down," I started, blowing out a frustrated breath. "Fuck. Neither one of us belonged there. But…" I held up my hand to stop him from pressing me. If he kept pushing, I would shut down. "No." I shook my head. "No, it was more than that. His presence felt…wrong. Like he didn't come for the same reasons as everyone else. Including us. And when I looked at him, a chill went down my spine. I was worried."

"Why didn't you say something?"

"I didn't want to be wrong."

"Don't hold back again."

I saluted him. "Yes, Boss!" Damn bossy bastard.

"What happened to you in there?" Jonah asked.

I'd put off telling him about my encounter with Gavina knowing I would have to tell Devlin as well. Saying it more than once would have been too hard. I paced the floor, not because I was nervous, but because I didn't want to look at them. "Gavina attacked me, and my protective mark repelled her."

I recounted everything. Even described the way her probing had made me feel. I rubbed my arms and cringed as I described the sexual feeling she elicited in me. I left off the description of the warmth that had spread throughout my body and just how much I wanted to feel that again. Craved to feel it, really.

Devlin turned to Jonah. "What do you think?"

"Sex has always been used in cults." He balled up the takeout bag and threw it in the trash. "It's the best way to control someone's mind, body, and soul. They target them when they're young and still trying to find their way both sexually and spiritually." He paused and rubbed the back of his head. "It doesn't make sense, though. The people who attended today were there for a sermon. Not to be indoctrinated into a cult. So, it has to be something they're doing with just the women. And Gavina being able to invade Nicole's mind doesn't make sense, either. It's not something a faith mage can do." He glanced over at the board. "Andrew underlined her magick and put a question mark by it." He rubbed his head, thinking.

"I watched her working a spell while Boyd waxed on poetically about nothing. And her magick was...different."

Jonah turned to me. "Faith magick only works if the people involved have faith to begin with. She couldn't spell them into believing. Different how?"

"Her aura was a steel color." I thought about Xavier's lack of aura. "And her son didn't have an aura at all."

"A faith mage would have a gold tinge to their aura. It must be some sort of taint." Jonah sat down and rested his forearms on his thighs. "I would say it could be a demon, but they have more of a burnt gold and red color to them. And I don't know what would cause someone to not have an aura." He paused. "We're missing something."

He was right. Given what Gavina had managed to do, I was having a hard time believing she was a faith mage. Maybe that's why Andrew put a question mark by her magick. He wasn't sure, either. We needed more details. Especially if a demon could be involved—something Jonah had refused to talk about before.

"Can you dig into it?" Devlin asked Jonah.

Jonah checked his watch. "I'll call my Uncle Troy later. He's probably still at his church. He might know something about it." He sighed heavily. "This situation is dangerous, Dev. We need more facts."

"I agree. And Nicole shouldn't go back there," Rachel said. "Not after that bitch hurt her."

"We can't hide from danger," Devlin said. What he meant was *I* couldn't hide from danger. They ran at it like it was a ride at Disneyworld. And how nice of him to put me in the line of fire.

"I believe it's my decision," I said through clenched teeth.

He watched me. Obviously waiting for me to retract my statement. Not going to happen.

"Did you want to sit this one out?" he asked finally.

I glared at him, knowing he was really asking: Did I want to give up? Also not going to happen.

A brief thought pushed its way inside my head. Earlier, I'd been thinking of the ways in which I could have avoided being caught up in the horrific events at Tribec Insurance if I had only listened to the alarm bells going off in my head and left. And now, I was being given an opportunity to step back from a situation that had dredged up painful memories and I refused to take it. I had to wonder if it was pure stubbornness or idiocy that stopped me from taking the offered out. Could be a little of both.

"No, but I still have the choice," I said finally.

If I did step back now, I would be giving up. Besides, like Rachel said, Gavina had hurt me. If anything, I wasn't going to let that bitch get away with it. If that meant putting myself in danger, so be it. I was used to it anyway.

He dipped his head in agreement. "Gerald believes we have the Ark. That's a problem." He moved away from me and went over to the coffee pot and poured himself a cup. "Rachel, did you ever hear back from Alek's source about the Ark's purpose?"

"Alek said he would try talking to Petronela again after the funeral," she paused. "I'm worried about him, Dev."

Vincent—a former employee of Tribec Insurance and Alek's distant cousin—was burying his mother today. I had offered to go with Alek to the funeral, but he said he had to take care of something after and would see me later. It was a good thing. Petronela hated me.

"He'll handle it," Devlin said sounding unsure. "We need to give him time."

"Time for what?" I asked.

"It's not important."

He was lying, but I couldn't figure out why. I looked at

Rachel and she looked away. Why were they keeping secrets from me?

"I need a ride back to my apartment," I said finally, not wanting to start in on it now. Because if we did, I would end up being late for dinner at Marta's, and I couldn't disappoint them. Not after what they'd been through.

Devlin studied me for a moment. "We have a lot of work to do."

"And I told you yesterday I was going to see Marta and the kids this afternoon. I'll be back first thing Monday morning."

His face softened. Devlin had taken on the responsibility to care for Marta and the kids financially. He'd been sending her money for the past few weeks. Marta hated it. Not the kind gesture, but the fact that she needed handouts. She had way too much pride to accept it. I'd like to say I didn't suffer under that way of thinking, but honestly, I too would have had a problem with just taking money without earning it.

He nodded and looked at Jonah. Without a word, Jonah pulled his keys out of his pocket and started toward the door. I guessed that was my cue to follow. I said bye to Rachel and followed Jonah out.

I stepped out of the coolness of Devlin's house and into the swampy heat. It settled over my skin like a wet, warm blanket, digging into my pores. I pushed past its weight, shielding my eyes from the glare of the sun as I descended the stairs and started down the walkway.

Jonah's gray Chevy truck idled at the curb, and I sent out a silent prayer that he had turned on the air-conditioning.

An ice cream truck turned down the street. Its happy melody filled the neighborhood, luring children toward it. My mouth watered at the thought of an ice-cold big stick—a childhood favorite. Its cool, sticky ice would be a welcomed treat right now, even with my aversion to sugar. Too bad I didn't have any room left in my stomach. Otherwise, I would have joined all the anxious kids now bouncing up and down in front of the truck's open window.

Adults stood outside, still wearing their church clothes—although the women had removed their hats and the men were down to just their dress shirts and slacks, talking and laughing. The area had come to life since we'd been inside. I paused midway, staring at the picturesque family neighborhood. It was the first time I had thought about just where Devlin's operation center resided.

Right in the center of a family-friendly neighborhood.

I was surprised Devlin hadn't rented a house or apartment in

Brunswood. The people in my neck of the island stayed up all night partying—oblivious to the illegal activity going on around them. Making it easy for the team to blend in and hide what has and will transpire while we investigate the blood magick users on the island.

As I stared at the people in the streets and in their yards, I wondered how safe they would feel if they knew about their new neighbors. How a team of vigilantes had set up shop and were staying until they had killed every last blood magick user on the island. Hell, they probably didn't even know blood magick was being practiced on Tulare in the first place. Everyone was familiar with the other four principles. Not many knew about the fifth.

I opened the truck door, and a blast of cool air rushed out, drying the sweat that had accumulated on my skin. After hoisting myself up into the cab, I slid in and relaxed against the cloth seats, thankful he didn't have leather ones like in Devlin's SUV.

I turned to Jonah in hopes of asking him a question, but the look on his face screamed loudly that it wasn't the right time. Deep in concentration, he kept his eyes glued to the windshield as he pulled away from the curb and navigated around the children, still standing in the street, holding their sugary goodness, after the ice cream truck had driven off.

The quickest route to my apartment cut through the center of Perry and what the locals called "The War Zone," a twelve-block radius with Greenwood Apartments at its epicenter. The very place I had witnessed Frank get killed by his uncle while I lay next to him, high and helpless, awaiting my fate.

The team knew about my fear of the neighborhood. They learned about it after Alek and I drove through there over a month ago and, if not for Alek using his mind magick to shut the crowd down, we would have been attacked. So, instead of heading west toward Brunswood, Jonah headed north, taking the border line between Dulean and Pleasanton, a good twenty minutes out of the way.

He drove the streets on autopilot, as if he had driven the same path a thousand times and didn't need to see the road to know where he was going. I'd done the same a few times in my life. It always freaked me out when I'd left Kara's house and ended up at my parents without remembering the trip.

I studied his handsome face for a moment. Kara's crush, or lustful intentions, were understandable. He was a gorgeous man. Chocolate skin so smooth it would make anyone want to run their fingers over it. Or lick it, for those more adventurous and not afraid to put themselves out there. But underneath his handsomeness was a quiet and reserved man. He often took to communicating with meaningful gazes and facial gestures and, on rare occasions, he could go into long soliloquies that kept the listener glued to every word. This might have something to do with the soothing timbre of his voice as well as the knowledge he imparted. It was funny how I'd gotten so used to spotting the subtle twitches and changes in his demeanor that signaled a change in mood. But then again, he broadcast them loudly. They all did.

"What's on your mind, Nicole?" he asked, patience lining his voice.

"Just wondering."

Despite having worked with them now for over four weeks, they were still strangers to me. Yes, I had gotten to know them a little, but there were things I knew they kept from me. Especially Alek. I'd like to say Rachel was an open book with her need for friendship and her unwavering willingness to defend me when Devlin was in one of his moods, but even she had secrets. And with Devlin, there had to be something buried under that rigid posture. He'd told me his mother had named him Devlin Grey after the famed Dorian Grey because she wanted him to live forever. I still hadn't asked him for the full story. Maybe I would soon. It might help pull him out of the funk he was currently in.

Of course, I'd have to tell them about my past as well. And I wasn't ready to do that. So, for now, I would have to remain comfortable with our secrets.

Jonah spared me a brief glance before turning back to the

road. I, too, looked out at the houses as we drove at a steady pace. We were close to my parents' house. A slew of emotions swirled inside of me. I blinked back the tears, swallowed the pain, and turned away from the familiar streets.

I wished things were better between my parents and I. My mother called every day. I'd talked to her only once after I'd healed completely from the attack. Now, I never answered the phone when she called. I couldn't face the turmoil right now. So many things we needed to say to one another. I'd written them all down in my journal. Anger. Frustration. Shame. And then anger again. They had kept a life-shattering secret from me, and I didn't think I'd ever get past the betrayal.

When we crossed over into the northern part of Perry, I said, "I'd swear you've lived here all your life, the way you drive without really seeing where you're going."

He nodded. "One of the first things I do when we arrive at a new place is get to know the area. I don't like relying on road maps or technology to tell me where I am. Just one of the many lessons the military drilled into me. Always know where the exits are." He tapped his head. "Tulare is imprinted in my head."

I've lived on Tulare Island for twenty-two years, only leaving the island briefly twice in my life. Once, when I went to stay with the woman I believed was my aunt, and the second time when I'd married an out of work saxophone player I met in New Orleans. We were married for only a month before I found him in bed with another woman. After destroying what little possessions he had, I got our marriage annulled. I still try to pretend it never happened.

There were still areas on the island I needed to look up directions to find. Yet, Jonah had managed to memorize the entire island in a few short weeks. Amazing.

He chuckled. "The only thing that continues to puzzle me is the way the locals keep referring to the different areas as settlements."

I nodded "According to the map, we're supposed to be a city in Georgia since a road connects the land bridge Coeur d' Alene to the state. But the locals have maintained the land designations, named after the first six families who settled here. They called the areas settlements back then. And the descriptions stuck." I laughed. "When I was younger, I didn't believe it was much of an answer, honestly. I mean, settlement? That didn't even sound right. I peppered my teacher for most of the class. Until finally, I let it go."

He laughed. "You let something go?"

I turned back to him. "What's that supposed to mean?"

He gave me a half smile. "You're like a dog with a bone. Relentless questions all the time." He turned and winked at me. "It's a good trait to have."

"Yeah, well, I lost interest." I pondered what he said for a short while, thinking of my interactions with Devlin.

"Boss Man doesn't think it's a good trait." I sounded petulant. Like a child who needed constant approval and when they didn't get it, acted out until they were noticed. Was that how I was behaving?

His mood sobered and he shifted in his seat. "Devlin is having a hard time right now. We all are. But him especially."

"Why?" I asked.

"This is not the type of job we normally take. But after seeing what the Stewarts had done, he couldn't just walk away." He turned down the road leading to my apartment. "Now, he has to change tactics. Look for a reason to kill." He shook his head, his face clouded with sadness. "That's not an easy thing to do. But blood magick has only one purpose. And if anyone is using it, that means they are killing innocent people. Devlin won't walk away."

Jonah pulled into my complex and parked. I thought he was going to just drop me off, but he got out of the truck. After a brief pause, I climbed out as well. He leaned against the passenger side back door and stared up at my building. "Rachel did some research on this place."

I joined him, leaning against the hot metal surface. The heat was uncomfortable on my back, but I didn't move. "Yeah. Before Mr. Wan bought it, it was home to a cult."

"Wasn't there a mental hospital here before that?"

"Yeah." I dug in my purse, searching for a cigar I knew wasn't there. Dammit. "Back then, it was called an asylum, and it was closed down in 1978. The cult started two years later. And five years after that, they stormed the place and found everyone dead except for the leader—Lemuel Oren, who had escaped."

"Not everyone was dead."

I jerked my head up and looked over at him. "What? Who told you that?"

He glanced at me. "Rachel. Five women survived. Gavina was one of them."

My mouth dropped open as I absorbed what he just said. Gavina was part of that cult too? Could that be why she started one with her husband? "Why didn't anyone tell me this?"

"Rachel found out this morning. Figured I'd tell you now. She didn't find much. Just a picture in the paper and a reference to the cult. She wants to dig into it some more. Hunt down the leader, Lemuel Oren, to see if he has a connection to The Oren Group, before we can decide if it's important."

Gavina had a connection to my apartment. It didn't matter if Rachel wanted to dig into it more or not, I just knew it was important. And I should have made the connection with the name Oren the first time Kara told us about The Oren Group. Damn, I was slipping. I pushed off the truck. "If you don't mind, I seriously need to get out of these clothes. Yes, that sounded wrong." Jonah laughed. "Come inside so we can talk."

"Is there something on your mind?" he asked, his tone softening.

"Several somethings. But this heat is too much."

I wanted to know why Jonah had decided to go undercover at the church. And why he wanted me to work with him in the first place, since I knew this might involve his past, which was a subject he might not feel like going into, it was better if we went inside and got out of this heat. Like he said, I was like a dog with a bone and I couldn't pepper him with questions while sweat ran into my eyes.

We made our way to the front door. While we walked the short distance, I thought about the heat again. Like the bizarre rain showers a month ago when we were investigating the Stewart family, the lack of rain and sky-rocketing heat was different. True, we lived on an island, so the humidity was normal. Even the rain showers were a part of island life. But the subtle changes in the air had become noticeable enough that more and more people began remarking on it. The constant humidity was beginning to take on a more desert like feel.

Outside the church, I thought maybe it was an accumulation of power. Like it was building to something. But now, I wondered if someone—or something—was playing with a dial that controlled the weather, trying to get it to just the right temperature. Devlin said elemental practitioners couldn't create the elements but only used them when using their magick. Able to bend the four main sources of power to their wills. But what if he was wrong and someone could control the weather?

And what happened when they got it exactly right?

Mr. Wan stood outside his door, wearing his usual attire of a white t-shirt and khaki pants. A strained smile stretched across his face as he watched us walk in. I had been a little worried about him lately. Ever since he'd stumbled upon the aftermath of the attack on Alek and me, he's had this haunted look in his eyes. He'd even hinted at selling the place. Thankfully, I was able to talk him out of it. If a new owner came in, chances were, they would raise the rent.

Despite Alek using mind magick on him to explain away the carnage he'd seen, he would still have stray recollections of it. Because, as Alek said, the only way to alter another person's memory is to work with what they had already experienced. The mind mage had to use those memories to craft a new scenario. So, while he suggested to Mr. Wan that he had found Wade in his apartment, he would still get the vague impression I had been there too and possibly been involved in what happened.

"Hi, Mr. Wan," I said, stopping in front of him. "Nice to see you smiling again."

He bobbed his head up and down and glanced behind me at Jonah. "New friend?"

"Sorry, this is Jonah." I forgot he'd never met Jonah.

Jonah extended his hand. "Nice to meet you, sir."

Mr. Wan shook his hand and jerked his head toward the

empty apartment. "Nicole tell you we have an apartment for rent?" His eyes lit with joy.

Jonah smiled. "No, she didn't."

Mr. Wan nodded and scratched at the gray stubble on his face. "If you're interested, I can show you before the other person who called about it shows up."

"Someone called about the apartment today?" I asked, cutting off Jonah's reply. Alarm raced through me as I thought about my giving the Young family my address. Dammit, I should have given them a fake one.

Concern crept back into his eyes. "Yes, that's good, right?"

Even I could detect the skepticism in my voice. *Dammit, Nicole!*

"Yes, of course it is. Sunday is just…" I trailed off unsure what I was supposed to say. I had every right to be concerned. Not only did the Young family have my address, but Gerald Stewart also knew where I lived. And I didn't put it past him to have someone rent the apartment next door just to spy on me.

When did I get so paranoid? Oh, yeah, I remember—when someone tried to kill me…twice.

"They know about what happened and they still want to rent it!" he said defensively.

"Sight unseen?" *Shut up, Nicole!*

He smiled and stepped back into his apartment. "Don't worry. I will screen them good." He stopped inside the door, his smile slipping, giving way to a deep frown. "I still don't understand why those people killed Wade. He was a decent man."

Wade was a pervert. Didn't mean he deserved to die.

I reached out and placed my hand on his arm. "Yes, he was okay."

He glanced at me. "They still haven't caught the person who did it."

"I'm sure they will eventually," I lied.

"Yeah, you are probably right." He turned. "Don't forget to

check your mail. The mailman complained about your box being too full."

"I will," I said, and Mr. Wan shut the door.

I didn't want to check my mail in front of Jonah; I'd have to do it later. So, I continued down the hall toward my apartment, hoping he wouldn't say anything. I was keeping a big secret from the team, and right now wasn't the time to go into it.

I opened my front door, and my gaze landed on the package Doc had sent. The dirty brown box filled with evil seemed to contaminate the air inside my apartment.

Jonah went around me and picked it up. "We should take this to Devlin."

"Yeah." I tossed my purse on the couch. "That's what Kara said." I hurried out of the living room to avoid having to talk about it further. After a brief stop in the bathroom to splash my face, I went into my bedroom to find some cooler clothes. I needed a shower, but it would have to wait until after Jonah and I finished talking.

I pulled on some shorts and a tank top. I was down to my last set of clothes and really needed to do laundry. If there was a way I could avoid talking to my parents, I would go to their house and do it. I could use the machines in the basement, but that place was way too creepy for me. Maybe Devlin would let me use his machines.

Before I left the room, I hesitated at the sight of the Shen ring that had been carved into my dresser. While I'd bought some new furniture, I'd kept that piece.

According to Luisah, it was a mark of protection. Set had etched the symbol into the wood and also branded it on my wrist while I was sleeping. He was one of the reasons I had been staying at Devlin's. His ability to manifest in my apartment and actually inflict harm on me was beyond disturbing. Yet, he'd also branded me and my furniture with protection. Strange, since he *literally* tried to dig my magick out of me, and if not for my father and Hathor healing me, I would have died.

Despite this, I could not bring myself to get rid of something that was supposed to protect me. I figured I needed all the protection I could get. Illusion or not.

Jonah was sipping some water when I stepped back into the living room. The contents of the package were on the coffee table —the pictures fanned out and the bottle of Asbach Uralt set off to the side. The detailed note of what he'd done was on top of the pictures. I stopped midway between the items and the hallway that led back to my bedroom.

A wave of helplessness overcame me.

The walls closed in around me as I stared at the letter, written in long hand like a damn love letter. An ode to the horrific things he was able to do without anyone stopping him. Including me. I was surprised he hadn't said thank you in the first one he sent. I dropped to the floor and cast my eyes down.

"He's gotten inside your head," Jonah said as he studied me. "This"—he waved his hand over the items—"is meant to break you." He finished his glass of water. "Are you going to let him?"

"It's not easy looking at what he's doing," I said, my voice small.

"It's not easy for any of us." He picked up the letter and extended it to me. "But understanding your enemy is the best way to defeat them."

"More army training?" I asked, not moving. I wasn't going to read that damn letter.

"No." He folded the letter and put it and the pictures back in the box. "*The Art of War*. Now, what's on your mind?" he asked again.

"Why haven't you asked Kara out yet?" It was not what I wanted to ask and the look on his face told me he knew it wasn't. But seeing those horrific contents spread out had forced me back into a shell.

He leaned back on the couch, stretching his arm along the back cushion. "That's not what you wanted to know. Ask, Nicole."

I swallowed the lump in my throat and pushed the images of Ronald's victims out of my head. "Did Rachel use magick on Devlin?"

He studied me for a minute. "Yeah. It's a type of healing." He stopped; gaze still steady on me. "You could have asked me that on the way over here. Something else is bothering you. Now spill."

He was right. I could have asked earlier. I was acting like a chicken shit, and I really needed to stop doing that. "Rachel told me you didn't do undercover work. So, why did you decide to go undercover?" I asked in a rush.

"I need to atone."

"For what?"

He got up and took his glass to the kitchen. It seemed like I wasn't the only one uncomfortable with personal questions.

He stood by the sink, filling his glass with tap water. I had bottled water and wanted to tell him so, but I didn't want to break his concentration. Finally, he said, "My third year in the military, I, along with ten other men, were sent to a small town in Georgia to help end a standoff with law enforcement and the New Enlightenment cult. A social worker and two cops had gone there to check on the welfare of twelve children living there with their parents. They went in on a Monday."

He walked back over to the couch and sat down heavily. Bending forward, he rested his elbows on his knees—eyes focused on the kitchen. But I didn't think he was admiring the paint. He sucked his top lip into his mouth, biting on the tender flesh as he shook his head. After taking a long drink of water, he continued. "That night, a box containing six severed arms was left outside the police chief's home. And each subsequent day, additional boxes were left, all with dismembered body parts."

"The social worker and the cops," I said, trying not to picture the gruesomeness of what he was telling me.

He nodded. "All ten of us practiced magick." He stood again, rubbing his hand over his head in agitated jerks.

"Do you need something stronger than water?" I asked.

He walked into the kitchen without responding and grabbed the Dr. Pepper then filled a glass with ice. "I was the only mage-level faith practitioner in the group," he said. "Four were earth mages and four were mind mages. My best friend from high school, Jacob Summers, was an elemental mage." He opened the bottle of Asbach Uralt brandy and poured some in the glass, topping it off with Dr. Pepper.

"You are not going to drink that!" I screamed in horror.

He harrumphed. "I've been drinking it."

"Getting to know your enemy?" I asked, my teeth grinding.

He took a sip and leaned back. "Something like that." Staring at the glass, he continued. "By the time we arrived, they had already sent the heads of the two cops and Laura." He looked over at me. "That was the social worker. Thirty-seven years old with four kids. Two of her own and two foster children. Kids were her life."

I swallowed the lump in my throat and went and got a glass from the kitchen. While I could use a drink myself, I settled on sharing the Dr. Pepper.

When I sat next to him, Jonah tipped the bottle of Asbach Uralt in my direction, and I shook my head.

"We arrived at the barricade that night. I was in charge. I hated that. I never liked leading a team." He leaned back; a pained smile played across his mouth. "I was good at it. But the responsibility of another person's life..."

He polished off his drink and set the glass on the coffee table. A stray memory of Doc entered my mind. His drinking on the job was another thing I should have seen as a sign but didn't. I pushed the memory away and refocused on Jonah.

"Our first goal was to get the kids out safely. Only, we were dealing with mage-level faith practitioners and had no idea what was waiting for us."

"What do you mean?"

"They could have created a god."

"What?" I shifted around and faced him. "How?"

"Remember the circle configuration we saw on the floor at Tribec Insurance?"

I nodded.

"That was a ritual to bring a god into existence. Mind you, they are temporary beings that are held together by using the combined magick of mages, latents, and believers. I found one of the circles when we went into the forest to get closer to the compound. In this one, unlike at Tribec, the red power circle wasn't touching the others."

"I remember." An image of the three green, three gold, and three black circles carved into the floor at Tribec, coalesced in my mind and I suppressed a chill.

He bit his lip again. Resting my hand on his arm, I said, "If this is too painful, you don't have to tell me." He stared at me, as if he was trying to find a lie in what I'd said. "I'm serious, Jonah."

He smiled. "No, it's been five years. I need to get past it." He placed his hand on his right arm. Over the spot where he had 'patience' tattooed in Chinese lettering. "Given the gruesome way the social worker and the cops were killed and the concern for the children, I made a hasty decision that cost lives. I knew I shouldn't use their circle, but if they had a god doing battle for them, then we needed one of our own. So, instead of confirming my suspicion, I showed my men what to do, and I pulled a being into existence." He paused, his eyes filling with an emotion I couldn't decipher. Finally, he continued, "Like all magick, there are rules. I broke all of them in that moment. Only faith practitioners can successfully create gods. What I created slaughtered my men and half the people in the cult. It devoured them. And because I didn't have anyone to help me contain it, I had to absorb it."

My heart melted at the sheer pain and anguish I glimpsed in Jonah. No wonder he was always so stoic and, if I had to give it a word, standoffish—although the word really didn't work, the behavior was there. He kept himself apart and only contributed when it was absolutely necessary. Maybe because he was constantly second-guessing himself. Making sure he never repeated his past mistakes.

I wanted to wrap my arms around him. Comfort him if I could. But I knew that was not what he wanted in this moment. Now, he wanted to tell me his story. And if I had to guess, I'd say it was to put me at ease as well. Maybe even encourage me to open up about my past. Too bad I wasn't ready. Otherwise, it would have been a really great moment.

He got up and paced the room. "Patience." He rubbed his arm where the tattoo was etched into his skin. "I shouldn't have..." He shook his head and swallowed—his throat working as if he were absorbing his pain. "I left the military after that. I didn't even go to my men's funerals. Instead, I resigned myself to a life of solitude. Wrestling with the demon inside of me as it continues to fight for a way out."

I wanted to know more, but the tear running down his cheek stopped me from pressing. "You did what you thought was best," I offered, infusing my voice with understanding.

He laughed—the anguished sound that came out of his mouth was laced with anger and frustration. "I did a stupid thing. Turns out, the god they created was only there to protect them. However, they couldn't hold on to its essence. The demon I made found the congregation hiding in a building and devoured them in a matter of minutes. In the end, I was able to save five children and two adults. The leader, Ryan, had also escaped."

"Shit," I said, expelling a ragged breath from my lungs. I glanced at the bottle of Asbach Uralt as I tried to process what he'd just said. Could I blame him? I wanted to. But I just couldn't bring myself to do it. He'd made a mistake. Hell, I probably would have made the same one in his position.

"Why did you stop drinking?" Jonah asked. I'd forgotten about my announcement to everyone that I intended to stop drinking. Of course, I had been drunk at the time, and I assumed they'd brushed off my intoxicated proclamations as just that. Intoxicated proclamations.

"Because Madeline Foster said I should," I answered finally.

"Who is Madeline Foster?"

"The bitch who wrote the self-help article that has been guiding my recovery."

He sat next to me. "Were you an alcoholic?"

I shook my head. "Not really. But I do have an addictive personality, and..."

"And what?"

I looked over at him, meeting his eyes. "We all have our demons, Jonah. You just happen to have a physical one. True, you acted in haste. Most people would have done the same thing in your position. Hell, I've turned acting in haste into an artform. Right now, given what we must do, I figured I needed a cool head. So, I need to get rid of the things that affect me. Alcohol is one of them. Along with cigars and sex. Well, at least according to Madeline." I didn't mention my past drug use or the anxiety I'd started feeling when the memories of my molestation had surfaced. I wanted to keep the focus on Jonah since I was sure it took a lot of courage for him to tell me about his past. We could visit mine later. Or never.

"You need to throw that article away."

"That might be true." I picked up the Asbach Uralt and went into the kitchen. "But no one should be drinking this crap." I emptied the contents in the sink. "It could be laced with poison."

"Rachel tested the first bottle he sent. It was fine. No need to waste a good bottle of liquor."

I threw the empty bottle into the trash and turned to him. "What happened to Ryan?"

"I hunted him down."

"Did you kill him?"

He shook his head. "Turns out, Ryan was innocent. The whole op was a setup. The sheriff's wife was losing members of her church to Ryan when her demands for servitude crossed the line. She didn't like that. So, her husband called in a few favors.

Killed his own officers and the social worker to ensure we would get involved."

He continued to stare at me as if he was waiting for my judgement. He'd been used. And in the process, a lot of people had ended up dead.

"When did you meet Devlin?"

"A year later."

I stared at him for a while. His answers had become short. He was shutting down. Like he'd reached the point where he no longer felt like opening up. Maybe what he'd told me was all he could manage to divulge at this time. I could understand that. Finally, I said, "I won't press."

He sighed. "Thank you."

"Except, I do need an answer about Kara," I said, grinning at him, trying to lighten the mood.

He laughed and walked over to the door. "I'll see you later." He turned around. "You coming back to the house tonight?" A smile played across his face. He already heard me tell Devlin I'd be back Monday. So, that secret little smile had to be because of Alek. And my not-so-subtle attraction to him.

I matched his smile. "Maybe. I still haven't decided." He cocked his head to the side, giving me an inquisitive look. We both knew I wasn't just talking about going to Devlin's.

I looked away, suddenly unable to meet his eyes, and almost missed him rubbing his chest. I followed the movement, staring at it as if I could see the demon inside of him. "How do you keep it contained?"

He opened the door. "With faith," he said and walked out.

J onah's confession left me in a raw state. The sheer weight of what he had to carry around with him overwhelmed even me. Yet, he managed to whittle down all that horror into a single word to constantly remind him of what he'd done and what he should never do again.

Patience.

I couldn't imagine what he went through after learning the mission he had been sent on was a lie. A carefully laid plan by a corrupt Sherriff—all because his wife did not want the members of her church to keep leaving. For that, they were willing to kill.

I wondered if my sordid past could be shoved into a simple phrase. I mean what would it be? "Never again," came to mind. "Don't do it," also made sense. But I knew dealing with my demons would take much more than a single word etched into my skin.

Besides, if I did manage to find one, I'd most likely have to carve it into my forehead to remember.

I spent a great deal of time in the shower scrubbing my skin raw. Thoughts of Gavina's mental attack had resurfaced, and I couldn't shake the feeling of my body being covered with her evil influence; how the unspoken pleasure of her intrusion left me feeling vulnerable and confused. Unsure as to why I had responded to her in such a way.

My protective mark had done its job, but it didn't stop the

licentious sensations she'd elicited. It did not stop the deep-down yearning I felt when she'd touched my soul. Because that is what she did—pushed her way inside and violated the place in me no one should have access to unless I gave them permission.

I didn't want to classify it. Did not want to say it out loud. Then I'd have to deal with it. And I was not ready for that.

So, instead, I focused on the many ways I could hurt her. Focused on images of me ripping her soul from her body. Holding it in my hands. And watching her take her last breath. I hated the dark place I had gone to. But I hated the violation even more.

I would make her pay.

While I got dressed, I thought about Lemuel Oren. It wasn't a common name. So, the connection should have been obvious. Hell, it practically had a neon sign over it. So why hadn't I thought of it? Probably because my apartment's nefarious history wouldn't have been of any interest to anyone but those who liked to study the creepy pasts of old buildings. But then again, maybe it did take looking into Gavina's past to bring the link into clarity.

Could it be the same man who was running The Oren Group? I did a quick calculation in my head. The hospital shut down in the early seventies. Lemuel Oren had been a former patient. Best guess, he would have been in his early to late twenties at the time he started the cult. Any younger, and I doubted he would have been able to ensnare a bunch of gullible, confused women into following him. So, if he was still alive, he would have to be in his late seventies by now.

I made a mental note to ask Rachel if she found anything, grabbed my purse and keys, and headed out the door.

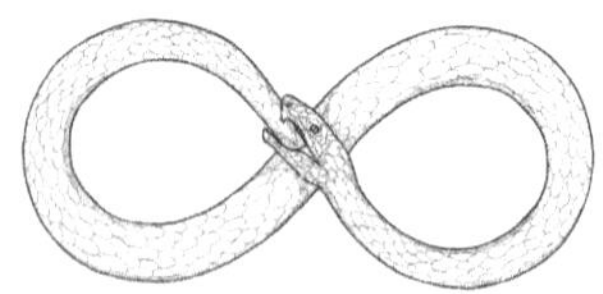

I PULLED into the parking lot of the convenience store around the corner from my house and almost screamed aloud. Every spot close to the building had a car crammed into it.

Marta's kids wanted cookies for dinner. After a heated debate, she'd agreed to let them have some and I said I'd bring them. I should have gotten them earlier...before the stores had become too crowded.

After finding a spot at the edge of the lot, I climbed out of the car and headed toward the store. By the time I reached the front door, my body was covered in sweat—making the shower I took earlier useless. Today was truly not my day.

The bell jingled as I pushed my way inside the cool space. The smell of bread smacked me in the face while I made my way around a crowd of people. Their conversations sounded like white noise. Just constant murmurs filling up the room. My eye twitched when I said, "Excuse me," for a fifth time. If these people didn't move out of my way, I was bound to have a meltdown before I even reached the sweets section. Another customer stepped in my way, I turned and ran smack into a short woman with long, dark hair, wearing a tight white sundress and flip-flops. She stood in the middle of the aisle, telling a tall, brown-skinned man about the benefits of avocados on salad.

He stared down at her out of eyes filled with tolerance while holding a bag of chips in his hands. As I tried to move past them, they both turned and looked at me. She smiled and he dipped his head in greeting. I furrowed my brow when an overwhelming sense of déjà vu overcame me. I studied the man for a minute. Medium brown skin, long hair queued in the back, and a slender build. He seemed familiar, but not as familiar as the woman. She beamed at me and stepped forward as if she were going to hug me.

I stepped back quickly, confused. Before she could touch me, I mumbled, "Excuse me," and weaved my way around them and continued toward the cookie section.

Before I reached it, I glanced back and found them staring at me. I would have said something, most likely filled with expletives, but the look on their faces rendered me speechless. They gazed at me as if they knew me. I stopped for a second. The woman moved forward again like she wanted to meet me halfway.

A jolt inside my head startled me. The woman started toward me. I stepped back, alarmed. What the hell? The man took the woman's arm, and she turned to him, giving me the chance to make my escape.

That was beyond odd.

I stopped at the row of cookies and scanned the many over-priced packages while I tried to figure out why the two strangers seemed so familiar to me. Unfortunately, I kept coming up blank. And the longer I stood there, the more frustrated I became. So, I snatched up a bag of seven-dollar chocolate chip cookies and walked quickly toward the front—only to run into the same woman again.

She turned when I walked up and looked at my cookies. If she opened her mouth to tell me about avocados on salad, I was going to scream. She shifted toward me, her bright green eyes dancing with joy. The familiar scent of jasmine wafted off her.

I turned and grabbed the first magazine I saw off the magazine rack. *Great.* Another self-help one.

"You know, those have the best quizzes in them!" she exclaimed in a thick accent.

Shit.

"I got that issue yesterday. "How to Rate your Personality" is in the back. You should take it. It might make you smile."

I had walked into my worst nightmare. I hated dealing with crowds of any kind. I always managed to attract people who wanted to talk or get my opinion or invade my space. Familiar or not, I really wasn't in the mood to deal with anyone right now.

"You see," she said, oblivious to my unease, "it said I was a giver." The line inched forward, and she moved with it. "I love sharing knowledge with people." She sighed. "People are so lost and it's my job"—she smiled and gave me a wink—"according to the quiz, to give people what they need."

Please shut up.

I turned, hoping the gesture would clue her in to the fact that I was not listening and did not want to engage in a conversation. The guy she was talking to earlier stood at the back of the line watching us. He smiled and I turned away. I didn't need him joining the already awkward confrontation.

"Now, about your smile."

"What about it?" I asked through clenched teeth.

"Don't you hate that? When people tell you to smile?" Her voice grew somber giving way to a sense of familiarity.

I narrowed my eyes and stared at her. *How do I know her?*

"Oh, most definitely," I said eventually. The line moved up again. "So, why are you insisting that I do?"

She winked. "I had to get your attention somehow. Right?"

What the hell was wrong with this woman? "Well, now you have it."

She looked off, her mouth turning down into a frown. "I'm not good at this stuff. My brother is better. Brooding as he is. He can get to the point. Not me." She shook her head, driving her point home. "Nope."

"Next!" the cashier yelled out.

"Oh, that's me." She rushed forward and slammed her bottle of water on the counter. "It's not as hot as the desert, but it is hot." She yanked at her dress as if she were going to snatch it off. "It would be easier if I didn't have to wear these clothes."

"Yes, ma'am," the cashier said, his eyes going wide, holding her bottle in his hand. Finally, when he must have realized she was *not* going to strip down in the store, he asked, "Will that be all?"

Her mouth stretched into a painful-looking grin. "Yes!"

She set ten dollars on the counter, grabbed her bottle, and ran out of the store. *Maybe I should be concerned*, I thought. Or I could just mind my own business and be thankful I did not have to talk with her anymore.

After paying a small ransom for twelve cookies and, yes, the magazine, I stepped outside into the heat, only to stop dead in my tracks as I was pulling down my shades. "Oh, this really is not my…"

"Hi again!"

"Look, ma'am, I don't mean to be rude, but I have somewhere I have to be. Thank you for the advice." I started to step around her but hesitated. I was being rude and this stranger, one who I might know and needed some help, didn't deserve it. I turned and looked at her. "Are you all right?" I asked, softening my tone. "Do you need me to call someone?"

"You don't remember me?" Her tone had changed again. Like she was settling into another persona. Or, the real one. Her mouth curved up into a genuine smile that reached her eyes. A breeze ruffled her hair, carrying that jasmine scent again. She turned into it, inhaling as if she could smell the wind. "I miss the desert."

"I'm sorry, I don't remember you," I said, although it wasn't entirely true. Something about her was familiar. But what?

She reached out and put her soft, warm hand on my arm. "Even if you don't take the quiz, you have to find your purpose. Promise me you will."

"What?"

She backed up. "Have to go. Much more exploring to do." She held up her bottle, her face turning down into a frown. "Maybe I should have bought more water. It takes a great deal of energy and heat to restore power." She turned, and I don't want to say danced away, although it did look like that, but she did move with a sort of rhythmic sway. How she managed that with flip-flops was nothing short of a miracle.

The man she was talking with earlier exited the store and gave her brief glance before making his way down the street.

I made a mental note to avoid the convenience store in the future and climbed into my car. Once the air had kicked in, I merged into traffic and headed east toward Marta's house—my encounter with the woman playing on repeat in my head.

The woman thought we knew each other. I combed through

my memories, trying to place her face or voice, but came up empty. She had a bit of an accent. I was able to detect it when she was not inflicting cheer into her words. Her dark features told me she might be from the Middle East. Why was I wasting time thinking about it? My mind was full enough. I didn't need to add a bizarre encounter with some random stranger to the mix.

Halfway to Marta's house, I slammed on my brakes, stopping in the middle of the road. My recollection of the woman in the store finally took root.

My last encounter with her was four weeks ago when I was lying in a field, rain pelting down on me as her brother, Set, tore into my body, looking for my magick as if it had been woven into my internal organs. She had worn no clothing, looking feral as her skin blazed gold. Ezra stood next to her, looking like an Egyptian warrior. Turns out, he had been one.

She had healed me that night. And when I was six years old, she blocked my memories and my magick.

Hathor.

A car horn blared, pulling me out of my thoughts. I eased to the curb and parked. Cool air buffeted my face while I sat there, trying to wrap my mind around the strange conversation I'd had with her. Everything in me was screaming to turn around and go find her, despite the obvious lunacy of it. After all, I had no idea where she could have danced off to.

And what about the man she was talking to? I got the impression he knew her. Was he an Old One as well? Ezra's warning to me weeks ago popped into my head. Both Hathor and Ezra had marked me for protection. Even Set had. So, if the man I just ran into was an Old One, that meant I'd just had another brush with death.

I glanced over at the magazine sitting on the seat. Why the hell did I even buy it? Impulse? Or was it more of me hoping I could find an easy way to self-healing and the utterings of what I believed was a random stranger, had wiggled their way inside my head and pushed me toward the purchase? Damn. I was trying to rationalize buying a magazine advertising the secrets to a man's heart. If it hadn't cost so much, I would have chucked it out the window.

"Fuck," I said, looking at my watch. If I didn't get going now, I'd be late.

I pulled away from the curb. I wasn't going to solve this right now. I would tell the others. And maybe I'd go see Ezra. Maybe he would know who the man was. And if anything, Hathor had to be staying with him.

When I pulled onto Marta's street, I spotted five-year-old Maria standing in the porchlight's glow. She was wearing a white, flower print sundress, her hair braided into two long ponytails, and she held the doll I bought her last week. She bounced from one foot to the other with a huge smile on her adorable little face. She should not have been outside—not by herself, at least. How could she not be afraid? Especially after what she had been subjected to at the hands of pedophile blood magick users. Hell, I could barely get through an hour-long sermon without my past pain rearing its ugly little head, and here she was bouncing around with a smile on her face.

The employees at the Sinclair at-risk youth facility had sexually abused her and her siblings. And while the Sinclair family tried to pretend they were not a threat; going as far as to try and convince Marta they were on her side and troubled by the events that took place in their facility. I didn't buy their P.R. crafted bullshit for a minute. Especially since we had taken Marta's kids from the house before the authorities arrived.

Given that, there was no way they could have known the Martinez kids had been at their facility in the first place, which meant they were involved in what had gone on. Might have even taken part in its sickness.

I slowed my car down, still watching her, and pulled up to the house.

I glanced across the street and noticed Mr. Magee sitting on the porch. I knew he had a rifle by his side. He'd shown it to us this week; said he would not let anyone touch Marta and her family again. I appreciated it. While I didn't blame him for not stepping in when he noticed something nefarious going on weeks ago, I did hold a little anger inside of me that Marta and the kids could be kidnapped right under his watchful eye.

He was, however, making up for that oversight now by keeping a constant vigil on Marta's home. And that had to count for something.

I pulled into the driveway and parked next to Kara's Honda. Before I could get out of the car, Maria ran toward me, dragging her doll along with her.

"Hi, sweet girl," I said, wiping the concern from my face. She didn't need to see that.

"Hi, Aunt Cole!" I braced myself as she launched into my arms.

I pulled her in close and snuggled her neck, inhaling her strawberry scent and taking solace in the fact that she was safe. Still holding Maria, I turned and waved at Joe. He dipped his head in acknowledgement.

"What are you doing outside?" I asked her.

She leaned back and stared at me out of solemn hazel eyes.

I'd never seen her look like that before, and it concerned me. "What's wrong, sweet girl?"

"I can see you sometimes, Aunt Cole." She leaned in and whispered, "When I'm dreaming."

"What am I doing in your dreams?" I asked, rubbing her back. She was the first one I saw when we entered the basement at the Sinclair family at-risk home. Locked in a cage, she had been naked, covered in grime and blood. I seriously hoped she wasn't reliving that nightmare in her dreams.

The door banged open, and Marta came running out. "Oh, thank god!" She snatched Maria from me and squeezed her so hard, I was afraid she was going to break the little girl.

I placed my hand on Marta's arm, and she blinked at me. It was as if she'd just registered, I was standing there. "She's fine, Marta," I said, my voice soft.

Marta continued to stare at me, tears welling up in her eyes. I glanced over at the porch as Kara stepped outside, holding Juan's hand. José stood next to them with a bat clutched in his hands. His gaze roamed over the neighborhood—searching for threats. He was too young to be worrying about danger. Too young to believe he had to protect himself and everyone around him. He should have been riding through the neighborhood on his bike with his brother and sisters playing with him. But instead, they had been exposed to a kind of evil that would always impact their lives. I was living proof of that.

Kara gave me a look filled with sorrow and helplessness, mirroring my own feelings. We didn't know what we were doing. Despite our best efforts, none of them were getting any better. Marta and the kids needed professional help. But Marta kept refusing, kept telling us they would be fine. That their pastor was helping them.

They weren't fine.

Isabel came out of the house and took in the scene—eyes roaming over all of us. I lifted my hand in a wave and she blinked a few times while she chewed on her lips. She'd been doing that a lot lately; like she was swallowing the pain, ignoring her need to let it all out.

"*Mija*, you can't go off alone. Please," Marta said finally. My heart seized at the anguish in her voice. She tightened her grip on Maria, making the little girl cry out.

Isabel rushed over. "Mom, it's fine," she wailed, her voice cracking. "Maria is okay," Isabel said, trying to soothe her. She wrapped her arms around her mother. "We're all okay." Even I could hear the hollowness in her words. Isabel knew they weren't all right.

I reached for a crying Maria. "Here, Marta, I got her."

Marta nodded and let me take her. Isabel wiped the tears from her mother's face. After shifting Maria to my hip, I grabbed my purse out of the car along with the bag of cookies. Maria seized the cookies, letting her doll drop to the ground. Isabel scooped up the abandoned toy and guided her mother into the house, with us following behind.

After Marta and her kids had been taken, someone came in and cleaned out their house, trying to sell the illusion that they had moved. Even her neighbor Joe had believed it strange that Marta would pack up in the middle of the night and leave, then send a moving truck later for her things. He found it even more odd that she hadn't said goodbye. We had just rekindled our relationship after a few years of us not speaking, but even I knew that Marta wasn't like that.

Turned out, the Sinclair family—not the Stewarts—had sent the moving van. And a week after we found Marta and the kids, another moving company delivered their belongings, along with a check from Bradley Sinclair. Everything was intact. The Sinclairs even repaired the furniture that had been broken prior to their men taking it. Marta threw all of it away, only keeping their personal mementos. As for the check, she ripped it up and mailed it back to him. I didn't blame her. I would have done the same thing...most likely with some violence involved.

Despite the new furniture and the walls being painted, there was still an ugly stain simmering just below the surface. Its poison showed in the clothes strewn about and the dirt on the floor and counters. Marta had always taken pride in her home. She would never let it get to this point. Yet every time we tried to help her clean it up, she would yell at us to leave it. As if she didn't see what was going on around her. Or even worse, how the disarray was affecting her kids.

I wanted so badly to fix it. To go back in time and never step foot in Tribec Insurance. My being there, coupled with my determination to leave, were the reasons Ronald had ensnared Marta and the kids in his scheme. He needed to make sure I stayed and continued asking questions, so I could expose his family's Harvest ritual. I wanted to dedicate myself to pursuing Ronald, but I needed to be here to make sure we took down everyone involved in blood magick. Including the Sinclair family.

They couldn't hide behind their P.R. firm forever.

Besides, if Devlin was right, Ronald would save me the trouble of hunting him down and instead return to Tulare hoping to add me to his list of victims. And by that time, I will have mastered my magick.

After helping the kids get cleaned up for dinner, we all sat down at the table. Isabel set a plate of spaghetti in front of me. "Thank you," I said, smiling up at her.

She wrung her hands and looked from me to the plate. "I hope it's all right. I followed the recipe like Mom said." She looked over at Marta, who sat staring at Juan as he colored.

"Yes, you did good, *Mija*," Marta said, not looking up. Isabel's shoulders dropped and she walked away.

One of the other troubling changes we'd noticed about Marta was that she had stopped cooking for her children. Like her mother before her, she took pride in cooking for her family—always made big, elaborate meals, including dessert. Before we'd had a falling out a few years ago, she would invite us to dinner often. I think I gained five pounds at every meal she fed us.

But now, Isabel was cooking, using her mother's recipes to fix food for the family. Sad thing was, Marta never helped her; never gave her guidance—just sat in this catatonic state at the dinner table, staring at her children. And barely eating herself.

Kara started to get up. I raised my hand to stop her. "I'll go," I whispered and followed Marta's eldest into the kitchen. "Isabel?" She scooped spaghetti on another plate. "You want to talk?"

"No, Aunt Nicole. I must feed everyone and then make sure Maria and Juan bathe. And then..." Her voice caught, and she dropped the plate on the counter. "I don't know."

I pulled her to me. Her small body shook as she cried on my shoulder. "It's okay, baby," I said, rubbing her back.

"I can't fix it, Aunt Nicole. No matter how hard I try.

Mommy doesn't help me. She doesn't see how much we need her."

"She does."

She stepped away from me and swiped her hand across her cheek. "We prayed. Like Daddy taught us when we...when we were locked in that basement. We just kept praying and..."

I took her face in my hands. Let her see the strength I couldn't give myself, but I damn sure was going to give her and said, "You're safe now. Understand?" She nodded. "There is no way I'm going to allow anyone to hurt you all again." Even if it destroyed me, put me in danger, I would fight to my very last breath, making damn sure I kept that promise.

She closed her eyes. "Mommy was hurt, too. I heard her tell Ms. Lena." Mr. Magee's daughter Lena had started coming over when Kara or I could not be there. We appreciated the help and, in case something should happen, there was someone close enough to intervene.

I hugged her again. She should not have heard that. No wonder she was trying to do everything. She believed Marta couldn't.

She jerked away and walked over to the kitchen drawer. After glancing out toward the living room, she opened the drawer and took a card out. "Ms. Lena gave me this." She handed it to me.

Reid Family Counseling Services was etched across the front.

Even Lena Magee knew Marta needed help but was either shut down when she tried to offer some or too afraid to approach her in the first place. Most likely, Marta shut her down. "I will talk to her about it, okay?"

Isabel gave me a half smile. Relief shone like a bright light all over her face. "Thank you," she said, and then turned and finished dishing up spaghetti.

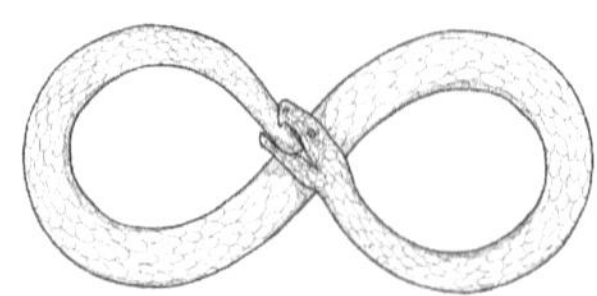

AFTER DINNER, I helped Isabel give Maria and Juan their baths. While Maria bounced around with enough energy to power a small city, Juan went about getting ready for bed as if he were being forced to do so. He didn't complain. He just remained silent and did as he was told. I didn't know which one of them worried me the most: Maria, obviously blocking the memory of what happened to her, or Juan, reliving it in everything he did—including his drawings. And José, he didn't put his bat down once. He was always checking outside, keeping a watch over his family while Marta ghosted around, seeming lost.

When Isabel went upstairs to take a bath, I did the dishes and straightened the kitchen. Kara helped José get ready, then went outside. After a short while, I went outside and joined her.

She stood on the porch, staring out at the darkened street, seemingly deep in thought. "We have to help them," she said, not turning around.

I pulled the card from my back pocket and handed it to her. "Isabel gave this to me."

She took the card and studied it. "Lena mentioned talking to Marta about counseling for the family." She handed it back to me. "But you know Marta. She believes her pastor can help them."

I snorted and took a seat on the porch swing. "Well, he's not doing a good job."

I didn't believe for a second that their pastor could help. I was willing to admit my own mistrust in religion and its practices could be coloring my views, but I was also tired of my friend and her kids suffering. Something had to give.

"Give them time, Nicole." She sat next to me and kicked off, setting the swing in motion.

My head fell back. The squeaking filled the silence between us, mixing in with the light from the firebugs dancing around the bushes in front of the wooden handrail. A comfortable warmth settled over my skin.

"I ran into Hathor today," I said, closing my eyes.

"It's a little scary how casually you said that." I could feel her eyes on me.

I lifted my head and looked over at her. "You're right; I should be freaking out." I laid my head back again. "Truth is, I haven't decided how I should feel. My encounter with her was a little... strange. She kept talking about the desert and restoring power. She implied it took heat to do so. Maybe her efforts are affecting the weather."

"How can restoring power change the weather?" Kara asked. "Elemental magick, maybe?"

"She's a god. We really don't know how their power works or what they're capable of." I chuckled. "She also told me to take a quiz in a self-help magazine to find my purpose."

Kara laughed. "Your purpose?" She turned to me. "When she..." She looked down at my chest and cleared her throat. "Healed you. She kept rambling on about the sun. And your mom had to practically dress her when she refused to put clothes on." Kara laid her hand on my arm. "I wouldn't put too much stock in what she said. Ezra said she's been a little out of touch for a while. And I got the same impression."

I nodded, mostly to reassure her because out of touch or not, I had the distinct impression she was trying to help me.

The screen door opened, and Marta stepped out onto the porch. "They are finally asleep," she said. We made room for her on the swing, and she sat down between us, a white envelope clutched in her hand. "This came yesterday." She handed it to me.

Scrawled across the front was Marta's name along with the kids. Bradley Sinclair had sent another check with a yellow post-it note attached to the front.

In case you lost the last one.

Bradley Sinclair, the twisted bastard, knew if Marta cashed the check, she would confirm her children had been at their facility. His checks were a sick form of harassment.

I stared down at the crumpled envelope in my hand. *Soon, Bradley. Real soon, I will put a bullet in your head.*

"Devlin offered me a job," Marta said after a short while. "I think I might take it."

I turned to her. "I thought you were going to work for my father."

"I think I'd feel too lost trying to work at an apothecary shop."

"Are you sure you want to go back to work so soon?" Kara asked.

Marta looked off down the street. "Yes." Even I could hear the hesitation in her voice.

"You are aware of the type of work they do," I said. "Marta? Are you sure this is something you want to get involved in?"

She leaned back. "Before we moved to Tulare, my dad had his own P.I. firm." She tapped her fingers on her thigh and bit her bottom lip. "My mom hated what he did. She said he put himself in danger too much. So, when we moved to Tulare, he sold his business and started working as a janitor at the elementary school." She glanced at me. "He told me some years ago that he would have quit sooner if she had stopped nagging him."

Kara and I laughed. That was one of the many things Marta's mom was good at: nagging. We loved to listen to her parents argue. Of course, it would always end in a big meal and them sneaking off to "talk", while we watched *Columbo.*

Marta smiled. "I miss my parents. They would have been a godsend right now." I placed my hand over hers. They had died in a car crash a year after she got married. "My mother never knew my dad would share his stories with me. I found the work fascinating and told him when I got older, I would open my own firm so he could do what he loved so much again. He liked the idea. Even believed we could work together." She shook her head and frowned. "When I told Manuel what I wanted to do for a living, he laughed and said a woman's place is raising a family." Marta chewed her lip again. This had to be where Isabel had gotten that nervous habit from.

I placed my hand on hers. After a brief pause, she continued,

"I miss him. And I hate him. He cheated on me constantly. But I stayed. Raising my family. When he died, leaving me with four kids and little money, I hated myself for not leaving a long time ago."

We often wondered why Marta stayed with Manuel. He had hit on both Kara and I and when we tried to tell Marta about it, she'd stopped talking to us for a few years. I wished we had known she was suffering.

"Working for Devlin will help me take care of my kids. I may not be the *best* investigator, but at least, in a way, I can fulfill my promise to my father." She shrugged. "Who knows? I might be good at it." Her face darkened. "It will also get me that much closer to the monsters who hurt my babies."

"Marta," I said. "When the time comes, we'll take care of the Sinclair family." I didn't want her to get her hands dirty.

"No, Nicole. When the time comes, I will take care of the Sinclair family." She looked at me, her eyes hard. "You will let me have my revenge."

How could I broach the subject of counseling after her declaration of retribution? Kara and I shared a look, both of us knowing this wasn't the time. Even so, I pulled the card from my pocket. Maybe if I gave it to her, she would think about it. Rubbing the smooth surface of the card, I leaned back and contemplated my options. Who was I to encourage someone to seek therapy when I wouldn't do it myself? Hell, I was getting advice out of magazines.

"It's getting late," I said finally. "Kara is staying with you tonight. I can come back later this week."

"You and Kara have lives. I can take care of myself and the kids." The words sounded right. Too bad her tone didn't. She still had that quiver of uncertainty in her voice.

"I like being here with them," Kara said. "I can help out still."

Marta turned to her. "You're teaching summer school, right?"

Kara turned away. "No. I told them I wasn't available."

This was news to me. I also believed she was teaching summer school.

"I've already arranged for Anne to watch them this week."

"My mom?" The swing jostled as I shifted toward her.

Marta studied me for a minute. "You should call your parents. Don't let anything keep you from a relationship with them." Tears welled up in her eyes. "I almost lost my babies." She trembled, arms going around herself. "I couldn't manage thinking I would never see my kids again." She stared me. "Your mother…"

"I don't want to talk about it." I cut her off. I couldn't make this conversation about me. Besides, I wasn't ready to deal with my own issues yet.

Marta stood up. "I should get some rest. I told Devlin I'd be there early in the morning."

She was dismissing us. Why?

"Marta," I said, reaching for her.

She narrowed her eyes, and for a minute, I saw hatred swimming in them. I let go of her arm and looked at Kara. The look of confusion on her face told me she, too, didn't understand Marta's sudden change in demeanor.

Marta sighed. "I'm sorry." She placed her hand on her stomach as if she were trying to hold in her emotions. "This is hard. I have to do the right thing. And"—she sucked in a breath. Her eyes swam with unshed tears—"I need to heal. You two love me so much. It's crippling me. I must be strong for them. But as long as you two continue to coddle me, I won't try to get better."

I extended the card to her. "Start here," I said and got up. "You want to prove to us that you can manage, prove to the kids that you can take care of them?" I pointed at the card as she stared down at it. "Isabel gave that to me. She's trying, Marta. She needs you to do this for her. For all of you." I pulled her to me and wrapped my arms around her. "Please."

Kara got up and put her arms around both of us. "Yes, Marta, please."

Marta held on to us, silently weeping.

Finally, she nodded. I'd take that as a yes for now.

A Bargain With the Devil

Alek pulled into the parking lot of *Carnavalul de Fear* and navigated around the bottleneck of cars lined up to exit. Families, towing sluggish children behind them, made their way toward their vehicles, while large groups of teens and young adults swarmed in the direction of the front entrance. They were ready to be thrilled and scared to death, or—he noted, looking at the roller coaster as it made its way around the entire carnival lot— brought to the brink of it. People craved danger; always sought to walk the fine line between life and death.

And that's what the carnival offered: a chance to come dangerously close without having to step over the line.

Despite his windows being up, the muffled sounds of cheers still penetrated his peace. He rubbed his head, trying to bury his growing need to reach out with his magick and invade the minds of the people blocking his path, giving them just a little nudge to move the hell out of the way. But as soon as he touched their minds, he knew he wouldn't be able to control himself. Not in his current agitated state.

This was the main reason he avoided crowds. His magick had always sought to do dark things, always wanted to lash out and twist other people's minds. Break them, even. Nicole, having the protection against magickal attacks embedded in her, was a welcome distraction. He would never dream of hurting her. But sometimes his magick had a mind of its own. Her protective mark forced him to keep his magick constantly in check. And her mere presence brought him a peace he so desperately craved.

He had discarded his suit jacket and tie after the funeral and currently had the air-conditioning on full blast. Nevertheless, an unwelcomed heat had settled over him, cocooning him in a stifling embrace. Maybe it wasn't so much the humidity in the air but the unrest that currently rode him like an unwanted lover. Petronela had asked him to come, and he couldn't refuse his great aunt, but he knew working for her would eventually lead to him losing control. And he was not looking forward to that.

A break in the crowd had him surging forward. A man whipped his head around and glared at Alek. *It would be so easy*, Alek thought, *to crush the man's mind.* He reigned those dark thoughts in. Not here. Not now. Didn't mean he was going to back down. So he continued to inch forward. The man, possibly seeing the threat in Alek's eyes, finally shifted to the side, allowing Alek to pass.

The lights from the Ferris Wheel, more beacon than illumination, penetrated the darkness inside his car. He glanced up at the familiar friend as it turned at a sedate pace. That's where he always found solace. His mother had brought him to Tulare when he was seven, nine years after Petronela had settled here. He'd told his mother he wanted to ride the Ferris wheel. And it was on that first ride where he learned how to control the darkness inside of him.

But that control didn't last long.

Finally able to move past the parking lot, Alek made his way around the back of the building. An unfamiliar guard sat stationed at the entrance. Mid-twenties with scruff on his face, he wore a uniform that was too big for him, with a dark stain between two of the buttons. Alek was surprised the man hadn't taken better care of his appearance. Even more surprising was that Petronela allowed it.

Alek rolled down the tinted window so the guard could see him.

"Does she know you're coming?" the man asked.

No one was crazy enough to show up here unannounced. He would have said as much, but it wasn't his place to teach the man about Petronela. If he worked here long enough, he'd learn on his own. Instead, Alek leaned back and waited. After a short while, the man lifted the bar and Alek drove forward and pulled into a space near the back door.

The sweet scent of caramel candy and buttery popcorn filled the car. He should have eaten at Vincent's house, but the knots in his stomach kept him from consuming anything but a few sips of water. He couldn't figure out why Petronela wanted to see him. She already told him she wouldn't help Nicole, reneging on the promise she'd made when Nicole lay in a coma recovering from the injuries inflicted on her by Set.

Damn. She could have died that day. He still couldn't get the image of her lying in a pool of blood, her chest torn open while rain filled her insides. But somehow Hathor, along with Nicole's father, Henri, had saved her.

The security door opened, spilling light onto the blacktop. Stefan Baciu stepped out, and his young niece, Elena, scrambled close to his side. The little girl had her thumb in her mouth. Last week, Stefan told him that the nightmares continued to wake her every night. And sometimes she would even cry out for Alek—the man she believed to be her savior. He didn't think of himself as such. Never had. But he had helped rescue her and the other children who had been caged in the basement of the Sinclair family at-risk youth house.

Alek got out of the car. "Do you know what this is about?" he asked when he joined them at the door.

Stefan pushed the back door open further. "She said she needed someone to find a man associated with the old families who has come to the island and failed to check in."

Elena reached for Alek, and he scooped her up. "How are you?" he asked her.

She didn't respond, except to rest her head on his shoulder and continue sucking her thumb.

"She's still not sleeping," Stefan said, rubbing Elena's head.

Alek squeezed her close. He wished he could take away her nightmares. Hell, even he had bad dreams about finding the kids in cages. They learned Elena's parents had applied for insurance at Tribec. The Stewarts, using Ronald Stewart's bogus blood test, had determined that the Bacius had in their blood the compound needed for their Harvest ritual. Elena had been given to Andrew Snow to deal with, and he in turn sold her to the Sinclair family. With her parents dead, Elena's uncle had taken her in.

Petronela said she would give Devlin and his team time to bring down the Sinclair family since Marta Hernandez, too, had a stake in their demise. Not a lot, mind you. But she did say she expected them to handle it soon. And Stefan demanded he be there when it happened.

Stefan went inside, signaling for Alek to follow.

"Why ask me? She has plenty of people who could handle this for her," Alek said.

Stefan turned and said, "You are family."

He should have refused, but Petronela had always been kind to him when he was a child. Back before he even knew she had a ruthless reputation, she always looked out for those who were different. She understood the darkness inside him; had even offered to help him tame it. But his family had grown distant from her because she settled on Tulare Island instead of continuing to Travel with the rest of the family. So, he never got the opportunity.

Still, she had gone back on her word and refused to help Nicole. And that bothered him.

Muted sounds from outside filled the darkened hallway as they walked. More than once, Alek had to yank his foot up to keep it from sticking to the ground. He glanced down at the brownish substance. *Blood.*

"What happened?" he asked, stopping in the middle of the hall.

Stefan stopped and turned to him. "Someone was stealing from Petronela. Gregor still needs to clean up."

Everyone knew the lengths Petronela would go through to protect herself and her family. Her brutality had garnered her a reputation that few ever tested. It had been years since she'd had to prove her strength. It surprised him anyone would dare steal from her. He was also surprised someone from one of the old families would show up without checking in first. It just wasn't done. Could someone be testing Petronela? Trying to find weaknesses?

Alek dipped his head once and signaled for Stefan to continue. Besides, it wasn't his concern what went on at the carnival.

At the end of the hall, Stefan pushed a red, velvet curtain back and stepped aside, allowing Alek to enter.

"She'll be here in a minute," Stefan said, taking his niece from Alek.

Alek dipped his head in thanks, smiled at Elena, and took up a position with his back to the wall. He didn't dare sit until Petronela invited him to.

"That service was an insult," Petronela said, stepping into the room. Alek turned toward the hidden door and watched her walk in, face covered in wrinkles that spoke of age and wisdom and sights seen. Her sharp brown eyes studied him as she stood in the entryway.

Two young girls stood closely behind her. The taller of the two had hair so dark it looked bluish. She wore it straight down her back with a single braid woven into it. She wore a peasant blouse with embroidered flowers stitched into the collar and a long red skirt that came to her ankles. Her face held a scornful smile. And her blue eyes seemed to look out on the world with hatred.

The shorter girl had her dark brown hair braided down her back. She wore the same outfit, only her skirt was green. Her small mouth trembled as her green gaze roamed over the room, finally landing on Alek.

Petronela made her way to the deep red lounge chair by the back wall, covered with plush gold pillows. It reminded Alek of a throne—not surprising since Petronela fancied herself as a sort of monarch to her people. She sat down and stared at him. "You should have advised Vincent on the proper customs."

"Vincent's mother wasn't Romanian. She was Christian," Alek said.

Petronela waved the comment away as if it were insignificant. She picked up a long ivory pipe. "I might have to remind him of our ways when he comes to work Monday."

This was news to Alek. He thought the big guy was going to continue working with them.

Petronela turned to the girls and raised a single sculpted eyebrow.

The short girl rushed over to a small white dais in the corner of the room. An onyx jewel-covered box sat on top. She picked it up and gave it to Petronela.

Petronela took the box and opened it. She hummed as she stuffed the pipe with sweet-smelling herbs and lit it. Pulling in a deep lung full of smoke, she stared at the two girls—blowing smoke in their direction.

"Daniella and Ileana believe my rule can be questioned. What punishment should I give them?" she asked finally, her gaze turning to Alek.

Alek shifted under the weight of Petronela's question. It didn't matter what he said; she had already decided what to do with them. But for some reason, she wanted his opinion. He wondered why but didn't dare ask.

Another man stepped into the room, holding a file under his arm and a bucket in his hands. He thrust the bucket at the girls.

"We are not cleaning!" the taller of the two screamed.

Petronela got up, quicker than her old frame would suggest she could, and slapped the girl across the face. "You will not raise your voice to me, Daniella." She stared at the girl.

Daniella placed her hand over her cheek and stared down at Petronela out of those hate-filled eyes. It was always the young ones, Alek noted, who liked to challenge authority. They must have shielded Daniella from Petronela's reputation. Otherwise, she wouldn't dare try to test his great aunt.

The other girl, Ileana, grabbed Daniella's hand and took the bucket from the man.

"Go clean the blood from the floor. Or yours will soon join it," Petronela said, her voice laced with venom.

"Yes, Auntie," Ileana said, and pulled Daniella out of the room.

Alek opened his mouth to protest the treatment of the girls but stopped. It wasn't his place. However, he wondered what the girls had done to deserve her wrath.

Petronela sat on the couch and picked up her pipe. "Gregor," she prompted.

The man handed Alek the file. "One of the cousins spotted Unrie Nevsky at the gas station two nights ago," Gregor said. "He can be linked to the Lazarescu family." He paused and looked at Petronela. She signaled for him to continue. "He hasn't checked in with Petronela, which could mean... Tribe has come back."

Thirty years ago, fifteen families of Roma, calling themselves Tribe, had come to Tulare intent on taking down Petronela. A minor war cnsucd, resulting in many fatalities. And when it was all over, only four families of Tribe remained. Petronela, after eliciting an oath, welcomed two of the families still standing while the other two left the island, promising never to return.

Alek glanced at his aunt. If Tribe were back, it would explain why someone would believe they could steal from Petronela.

He opened the file and read through its contents. Someone had compiled a dossier on Unrie Nevsky, which read more like a police rap sheet. They had linked him to seventeen murders and twelve kidnappings across the globe. Yet he had never committed a crime on Tulare. So why now? Alek kept reading and stopped when he came to an address on Tulare Island.

"Unrie lived on Tulare?" he asked, looking at his aunt.

She nodded. He stared at her, trying to see past the rigid visage she showed everyone. But she only gazed back at him—unafraid, it would seem.

Gregor pointed to the information on the address. "The house belonged to Lazarescu."

Given his age, Unrie would have been ten at the time. Yet, his surname was Nevsky. Alek searched his memory for some of the old family names. None of them had any Russian ties. And he wasn't Roma. But the link was there and unnerving.

"Do you think his family was part of Tribe?" Alek asked, looking up at Petronela.

"That is what I need you to find out," she said, her face an unreadable mask.

"You have people who could do this for you," Alek said, shutting the file. Even if he didn't work for her, it would be a good idea if he found out. Petronela had defeated them once, but there was no telling how many people they could have amassed in the time they'd been gone. This would affect all of them.

"Yes, but I figure it will be an acceptable trade." She pulled smoke in and leaned back. "While I can't help your girl directly, I do know someone who can. I am willing to bring him to the island in exchange for your help with this."

"I need an oath from you that if I do this, you will help Nicole, Auntie."

Petronela's head jerked up and her eyes narrowed. "Do you doubt my sincerity?"

"No," Alek ground out. "Just your word."

Gregor stepped into his space. Alek ignored him. If he had to fight his way out of here, he'd break every mind that he could before Petronela shut him down. More blood for Daniella and Ileana to clean up.

Petronela raised her hand, stopping the man. "I will allow that because of our previous bargain. But I will remind you, questioning me will get you killed, Alexandros. You remember that." The words sounded right, but the heat behind them wasn't there. And Alek realized the threat was for Gregor to hear. Again, she felt the need to show her strength. Was she concerned about the people around her?

"I'm not afraid of death, Auntie. You remember that."

She smiled, the gesture pulling her wrinkles into a macabre mask. "No, I don't suppose you are. Now, go. You have until the end of this week to find him and bring him here."

"If he fights me?"

She waved her hand. "Then kill him and bring his head." She laid back on the couch, dismissing him.

"And what about the other info?" Alek asked, inquiring about the Ark.

"Some things only the Historian can answer. You remember the ways?"

Alek nodded. The Historian, calling herself Luisah now, was on the island. According to his aunt, she had been here for seventeen years. She always came years before a disaster that had the potential to drastically impact humanity's existence.

The only problem: humanity had ceased seeking out knowledge. They had instead turned to conspiracy theories and half-truths when making decisions, often leading to disaster. For knowledge, the Historian required a price: a pact to ensure the person would remember what they had learned. Before gold and gems and silver, blood was used to seal the bargain.

After a brief hesitation, Alek walked out.

He passed the girls on the way out. They stopped talking

when he got close. He paused, thinking of what he could say to bring them comfort. Then he looked into their eyes and saw he didn't need to. The evil brewing in those blue and brown depths didn't need any words of wisdom from him. So, he moved on.

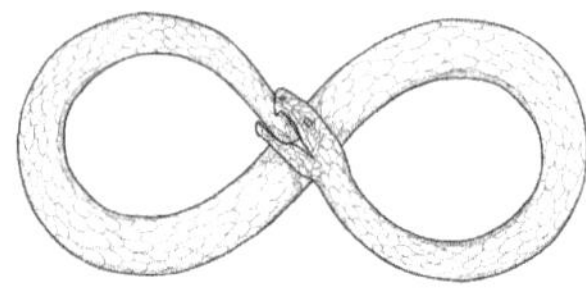

Alek pulled up to Devlin's and noted the absence of Nicole's car. He pulled his phone from his pocket and debated calling her. Or, at least, sending her a text. He needed her but didn't want to appear needy. He craved her but didn't want to push. And yet, not seeing her car here made his heart hurt.

He put his phone away, got out of the car, and made his way up the walkway to the front door. He remembered she was having dinner with Marta and the kids tonight and maybe she decided to stay over again. And since Marta would start working with them tomorrow, she and Marta could have decided they would ride to work together.

Enticing scents greeted him when he stepped inside the cool house. Jonah must have cooked. If it were left up to him or the others, they would always eat takeout. Jonah preferred home-cooked meals. Alek followed the sound of their voices down the hallway and entered the kitchen. Devlin glanced up mid-sentence and raised an eyebrow in question. Alek pulled out a chair and sat down heavily. He ran a hand down his face and pulled the tie from his hair.

"Petronela wants me to hunt down a man named Unrie Nevsky," he said in way of greeting. He gave Devlin the file. While the man read through it, Alek filled his plate with steak, potatoes, and roasted tomatoes. "Looks good, Jonah."

Jonah grunted.

Alek took a bite of the steak and closed his eyes in bliss. Jonah could cook. After sampling the potatoes, he looked at Rachel. She beamed at him. "You doing okay?" he asked her.

She nodded. "You look tired. You need coffee?"

Rachel made a coffee especially for them that not only helped give them the much-needed caffeine jolt, it also helped with the drain on their magick. Both he and Rachel constantly used their power to the point of exhaustion.

He gave her a half smile. "It's not my magick. Just..." He leaned back. "Might be leading to something bigger." He shook his head and sighed. After devouring a few more bites, he told them about Tribe.

Jonah took the file from Devlin. After reading through it, he said, "I can check out the house at this address in the morning."

"I can research the families that left Tulare and the ones that stayed," Rachel said, getting up. She squeezed his shoulder and headed to the family room they had converted into their main meeting area.

He wanted to stop her; tell Jonah he could handle it on his own. It was obvious Petronela had wanted him to deal with this by himself anyway, but he knew they wouldn't listen. They would insert themselves into the situation and help him deal with the problem. A team. A family. That's what they were.

"How do you want to handle locating Unrie?" Devlin asked.

Alek picked up the file. "He has a pattern of behavior I should be able to follow. I'll check out the more affluent hotels in the morning. If I get a lead, I'll let you know." Even though Petronela had given him the job, his loyalty lay with Devlin and the team. He would keep them updated as well. Besides, if Tribe really was back, their presence would impact the team as well.

Devlin studied him for a minute, seemingly deep in thought. "Things didn't go as planned at the church today. Gerald Stewart made an appearance, demanding we return the Ark. Might have to deal with him sooner rather than later." He blew out a frustrated breath. "I'm not sure Jonah or Nicole will receive an invitation to join the cult. So, we might have to come at this a different way. We could deal with Unrie first, and then…"

Alek shook his head. "No, I can handle it. If I need any backup, I'll let you know." He looked at Jonah. "What happened at church?"

Jonah leaned back, swinging his arm over the back of the chair. He nodded, as if trying to figure out a way to explain. "Nicole seemed…" He trailed off. "I don't know. Spooked?" He looked up. "Something disturbed her. Even before…" He studied Alek, his eyes seeming to convey something before he said it. "Even before Gavina tried to infiltrate her mind."

Alek narrowed his eyes. "I thought she was a faith mage. How the hell would she be able to infiltrate Nicole's mind?" He fought the wave of fury riding through him.

"She's fine," Devlin said, reading Alek's body language. "Her mark protected her."

Alek expelled a breath filled with anger and frustration and made a signal for Jonah to continue.

Jonah dipped his head once and continued. "When I dropped her off earlier, I got the impression she wanted to talk. But when she did finally spit out what was on her mind, she asked why I wanted to go undercover." Jonah took a sip of sweet tea. "So, I told her about my past, hoping she would open up."

"But she closed up," Alek said.

Jonah nodded. "I could tell something had bothered her. And she said Gavina's magick looked gray. I checked with my uncle, and he said gray represents Divine Evil. It happens when someone's magick becomes corrupted."

"Could it be blood magick?" Alek asked.

"No. He said it would have to do with a repeated ritual of some kind. One that alters the magick. He's going to investigate it further for us." Jonah spread his hands out. "It might take time."

"What we don't have," Devlin said. "We're just getting started, and we're already stretched thin." He glanced over at

Rachel, who now lay sprawled across the floor, staring at her laptop. "Rach, call it a night. We can research later."

She spared him a brief glance before shutting the laptop. "I'll do dishes after I watch Spongebob," she said, turning on the television.

"Do you know who she is going to bring in to work with Nicole?" Devlin asked.

"She didn't say. She also said we have to talk with the Historian, Luisah, about the Ark."

Devlin pushed up from the table. Alek glanced at his phone. "Any word from Nicole?"

Devlin looked down at him. "Give her some time."

Alek knew he was talking about more than just her coming over this evening. He stood up. "Is this going to be a problem?" Alek asked.

Devlin studied him. "You tell me."

Jonah cleared his throat. "Nicole knows the mission comes first," he said.

Both Alek and Devlin looked at Jonah. He shrugged. Even he understood what they were talking about. Alek wondered briefly if his obvious attraction to Nicole *would* become a problem.

"She's unique. And has a head full of steam," Jonah said, and stood up. "But I know we can count on her."

Devlin laughed. "She does push all my damn buttons, but..." He glanced over at Rachel. "We needed her."

They all looked at Rachel, who was now mesmerized by her favorite cartoon. Out of all of them, Rachel needed Nicole the most. Her desire to have female friends had become an obsession, and the last thing they needed was Rachel going off the deep end. She was already close to the edge to begin with. Her father's damage ran deep. The man had kept Rachel, her siblings, and her mother sequestered away from everyone. They were his secret family—the one's he went to when he needed to act out his aggressive behavior. All the while parading his other family around, spoiling them. And when he wanted to advance his career in politics, they became expendable.

After saying goodnight, Alek headed to his room to take a shower. A pang of longing rolled over him. Without second-guessing himself again, he pulled his phone from his pocket and sent Nicole a text.

Hey...

I have never had a job consume me. Never had a job where the life and wellbeing of others rested on my shoulders. Then again, all the jobs I've had have been meaningless. Just one paycheck after the next to keep me from having to ask my parents for money. Once I left for the day, I no longer worried about it. I was free to go out and let my hair down. *Literally.* Dance until my feet hurt. Drink until I got a nice enough buzz to help me forget about the day. But now, my life seemed consumed with fear and concern and a glaring sign of my own inadequacies.

And all my decisions affected someone else.

'*What if*' had been playing on repeat in my head since I left Marta's house—all the different chances and opportunities whirling through a movie-like montage with me at the center. No matter how I looked at the situation, no matter how many ways people tried to convince me otherwise, I knew I was at fault. And with this new mission, if I didn't get my shit together, I could be responsible for someone else suffering again.

I stopped at a crossroads, looking at my two possibilities. Going to Devlin's seemed like a wise decision. After all, all I had to do was get dressed in the morning and I'd be at work. But then there was Alek. If I could just shake this overwhelming need to be around him, could somehow not be attracted to him, then every-thing would be fine. Yeah, that wasn't going to happen. My feelings for him ran deep, burrowing their way into my heart and soul.

So, I drove home.

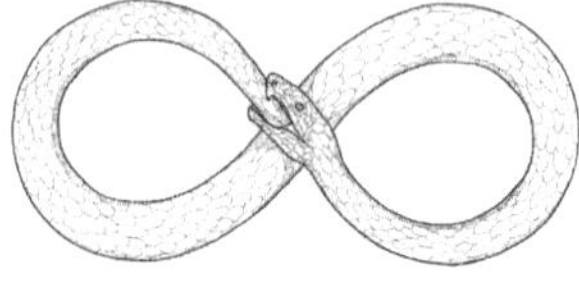

I PARKED in my lot and climbed out into the heat. Glancing up at the sky, I noticed a red haze had settled over one of the clouds. The sudden desert-like dryness in the air reminded me of the conversation I'd had with Hathor earlier. She said she'd missed the desert, but she also said it took a great deal of heat to restore power. Had she lost some saving me? And if so, was she trying to restore it? And now I had no way of finding out unless I hunted her down.

Music filled the neighborhood. The bar down the street was still open, giving the last few patrons the illusion that they didn't have anywhere to be tomorrow morning. I used to be among the partygoers. Now, it was one long day after another. Don't get me wrong—I really did like working with Devlin and the team—but sometimes, on nights like this, I missed my old carefree life. Living in a constant state of oblivion is comforting, especially after you learn the monsters are real and walk among us.

The streetlights blazed, cutting a swath of light into the darkness. As I walked toward my building, a strange, uncomfortable feeling settled over me. I peered into the night, remembering the last time I'd trekked to my building, and spotted Set's silhouette standing in the rain, watching me. While there was no rain now, the same sort of uneasiness crept up on me. I should've run inside and hidden. But I knew there was no hiding from a being who could appear anywhere.

I stared out at the empty street, expecting to see him. As I stood there, peering into the night, two cars raced by. My heart slammed into my chest, and I sucked in a frightened breath.

Dammit. I was standing here, working myself up into a fright.

I shook my head and turned away. Something pulled my gaze to the sky again. I'd never seen a fat red cloud before. The longer I stared, the more it seemed to expand. Before I could avert my gaze, it shot across the sky, quicker than I'd believed possible. I stilled, my mouth agape, and stared at the phenomenon. A meteor? No, that couldn't be right. Meteors existed in space. Not in the night sky over Tulare.

I took a step toward my building and a blast of heat rushed down and blew across my body. I gasped as the waves of warmth rolled across my skin in a torrent. It felt as if I were being cooked alive. My knees buckled and slammed to the ground. I tried to pull air into my lungs but couldn't.

The phoenix wings unfurled slowly inside my head. My protective mark was coming to life. Power surged through my veins and adrenaline rushed inside my head, cutting off all the surrounding sounds. With one mighty beat of the phoenix's wings, the current of heat stopped—leaving me on my knees, covered in sweat.

I shifted from my knees and sat down on the asphalt. My lungs still burned, and while I wanted to go inside to get some water to ease the sting, I also needed a moment to catch my breath. I chanced a look at the sky. The cloud no longer hung over me. Just the usual fat rain clouds still holding onto their water.

The need to act weighed on me, but I needed time to think. My mark wouldn't have reacted if someone or something hadn't tried to attack me. Yet, the nature of the assault made no sense and took little effort to stop. Which meant, while magick in nature, the heat wave could have been a simple inquest or probe. My skin wasn't cooked. My hair hadn't been singed.

And I was not going to solve this sitting on the dirty ground.

I slowly climbed to my feet, dusted myself off, retrieved my purse, and continued making my way inside.

Maybe Devlin would know since he was an elemental mage.

I stopped at the wall of mailboxes near Mr. Wan's apartment and stared at my box, drumming up the courage to open it.

Packages weren't the only things Ronald sent. He also sent long, flowing letters recounting in explicit detail our intimate encounters—giving me a glimpse inside his mind of the few times we had sex. They read like journal entries and, recently, had gotten more and more macabre to the point he had started recreating our time together in a fantastical, fictional way that always ended with me lying in a pool of blood.

I swallowed the fear and opened my mailbox. The mailman had stuffed it to bursting. I no longer got mail for the previous tenant, but I got enough junk mail to wallpaper my apartment. Mr. Wan set a trash can near the boxes when everyone had complained, loudly, near his door about the unwanted ads.

After shoving the junk mail inside the trash, I studied the three letters Doc had sent. His handwriting had an elegant, almost old-fashioned, look and feel to it. I could picture him sitting at a desk, quill in hand and bottle of ink by his side, as he wrote out the madness inside his head—thinking his ramblings perfectly sane. How had I not seen this?

Sitting in his office at Tribec, reciting the many oddities I'd noticed during my interview, he'd tried to convince me not to leave. While doing so, I'd seen a glimpse of mania in his eyes as he pounded back glass after glass of Asbach Uralt brandy like it was water. I'd dismissed that look because of his obvious hatred for his family and believed his drinking was an act of rebellion toward them. He'd told me in one of his earlier letters that the reason he drank so much that day was the urge to kill me had been too great, and the only way to suppress it was with alcohol.

He'd drunk even more on our first and only date. And the sex had been intense and brutal. This revelation had drilled home that I'd barely escaped death.

One of the bulbs in the hallway leading to my apartment had blown out, creating a pool of darkness near my front door. I stopped, letting my eyes adjust as I scanned the small space. I'd left the gun Devlin gave me at his house. I didn't want to take it to Marta's and have one of the kids find it. When no immediate threats presented themselves, I continued to my apartment, hurriedly opened the door, and rushed inside, only to be deposited into more darkness.

I scraped the walls with my keys as I fumbled around the plate trying to turn on the light—heart ramming inside my chest. The click of the light being switched on echoed around the room, and my apartment flooded with illumination. I blinked a few times to stop the sudden sting in my eyes and just stood there, waiting for the fear to stop its march through my body.

Why the hell was I so damn scared?

"Okay, Nicole, you've never believed in the boogeyman, so don't start believing in him now!" I yelled at myself.

Except I had a real-life boogeyman: Set.

We still needed to find out who had freed him from the Ark and what ritual they used to do it.

During the confrontation with the Stewart family, he'd pulled me out into the rain and tried to convince me to give him my magick. When I refused, he'd dug into my chest to take it. Ezra and Hathor had stopped him in time. I'd spent days healing from what should have been fatal wounds. I hadn't seen or felt him in weeks. But I had caught his acrid desert scent a few times when I'd been home alone.

I sniffed the air to make sure Set hadn't been here, then pushed off the wall and went into the kitchen. After drinking two bottles of water to ease the dryness coating my throat, I went into my bedroom and retrieved the shoe box under my bed. Fifty letters lined the inside, all but five of them unopened.

I stuffed the latest three inside and shoved the box back under my bed. I was doing that a lot lately. Hell, all my life—shoving the things I didn't want to deal with out of sight, so I could avoid the reminders.

I needed so much damn help.

My copy of *The Land Guarded by People of Colour* sat on the dresser along with the letter from Steve it came with. Louis Badet had learned enough about the Old Ones and the creation of Tulare that he'd written a record of it.

They found him dead soon after the missive, once believed to be a poem, had been written. Steve had given me a copy that Luisah had entrusted him with a week before his death. I had refused to open his letter to me until five weeks ago. If I had, I would have known all of this sooner. And would have definitely figured out that Jordin Cisco was an Old One.

It would seem I had a pattern of not reading letters.

It felt strange being home alone. I'd grown used to the sounds of others moving around in the background. Their daily routines became a soothing sort of white noise that put me at ease. I used to crave my solitude—believed that it was the only way to keep myself grounded. I still hated crowds. But I'd learned recently, I hated being alone even more.

I stared down at my unmade bed, wishing Alek was there to help warm my sheets. To hum his melody while he held me in his arms. And the only thing keeping that wish from coming true was me.

My gaze travelled around my small room, taking in the half-hearted attempts on my part to decorate. I'd painted the walls a cream color, only to change my mind and add a green accent wall later. It didn't look right with my dark burgundy sheets nor my dark wood furniture. It was as if I couldn't make up my mind what I wanted the room to look like.

The clothes on the floor of my closet caught my eye. I went over and started picking things up. I really needed to get rid of most of these things, especially the clothes I bought for Tribec. I wasn't a business dress suit sort of woman. And my current profession would call for me to dress in leathers and boots. But Tulare was too damn hot for that shit, so I'd stick with jeans and tank tops. I would, however, get one of those superhero belts Devlin, Rachel, and Kara wore.

When my clothes were all hung up, I looked around the room and noticed a thin layer of dust coating my dresser. Might as well get that out of the way, too.

An hour later, I'd cleaned my entire apartment and was still no closer to sleep. Fuck I was stubborn. I knew I wanted to go back to Devlin's, and all I had to do was walk out the damn door, climb in my car, and drive over there.

No. I could do this! After a quick shower, I got in bed and turned off the lights, only to end up turning them on again. I lay there, unable to sleep, debating my options. My sole reason for staying away was fear of me and Alek getting any closer than we already were. Fear that I would just give in. And then, when I was happy, he would leave. Because I knew I would end up fucking it up, eventually.

"I can't keep doing this to myself," I said aloud.

My phone dinged, and I picked it up and read the text.

ALEK

Hey…

Alek.

I jumped up and put my clothes back on.

After grabbing a few items from my drawer, along with my basket of laundry, I turned off my bedroom light and headed out, reasoning with myself it would be easier for me to get up in the morning if I was already there. And it had absolutely nothing to do with him sending me a text. Yeah, it was bullshit. But it sounded nice in my head.

On my way to the front door, the acrid scent of sand filled my nose.

I froze.

A shimmering silhouette filled the space in front of me. Adrenaline flooded my body, and my heart pounded in my chest as my mind went through a series of ideas on what I should do. When it finally settled on, 'Get the fuck out of here,' the smell dissipated, and the silhouette vanished as if it had been pulled back out of existence.

I got the fuck out of there.

I pulled up to Devlin's house and parked behind Alek's car. Seeing the Buick sitting there made my heart skip a beat. If I were smart, I'd have made a U-turn and driven myself to a motel since going home was so not an option. But sometimes, being smart was overrated. Besides, after that close call with Set, I needed to feel Alek's arms around me right now.

I got the key Devlin gave me out of my purse and slid it into the lock. Pushing open the door, I spotted Devlin, stretched out on the sofa bed; his eyes focused on the ceiling. He grunted when I came in. His relaxed posture was an illusion. He kept a gun under his pillow and his vials of elements on the bed beside him. I doubted Devlin ever relaxed.

"Are we okay?" I asked, remembering our heated discussion earlier.

He turned and looked at me. "We're always okay, Nicole." He got up and moved to the edge of the bed. After running his hand through his hair, he continued, "You're part of my team. Part of my responsibility." His gaze met mine. "I have to keep you safe. If that means drilling you until your reflexes become second nature, then that's what I'll do."

"You can't keep us all safe, Dev," I said, trying out Rachel's nickname. I liked mine better. Dev felt too personal.

His eyes rounded. He shook his head and let out a bark of laughter. "Get some sleep. We have a lot to do tomorrow."

"Yes, Boss Man."

"Better," he said, his mouth stretching into a rare smile. Maybe he didn't mind me calling him Boss Man.

I continued to stare at him. He lifted an eyebrow in question.

"I got hit with this strange red mist filled with heat outside my apartment," I said finally.

He nodded. "Heat wave. Most people can't see the elements in the air." He gave me a questioning look. "Maybe you have some elemental magick inside of you as well."

I shrugged. "I don't know. I'd have to ask." As far as I knew, there were no elemental practitioners in my family. I shifted, uncomfortable because I wanted to keep pressing.

"Spit it out, Nicole," he said.

"Why would a heat wave funnel down and target me?"

He smiled and let out a chuckle. "You assume it targeted you because you could see the actual heat. Had you not been able to see it, you would have believed you had walked into a heat patch. The elements can't target someone. They have to be wielded." He stood. "Did you see someone in the area?"

"No. No, I just saw the red mist. I didn't mean to worry you." If the heat was generated by elemental magick or an accumulation of magick, then my mark would view it as an attack. And there wasn't anyone around to direct an attack at me. Maybe he was right.

"Set tried to visit," I said after a while.

"You said that too casually," Devlin said, eyes locked with mine. "What happened?"

I went through the brief encounter. "Should I be worried?"

Devlin rubbed a hand down his face. "Since he hasn't made an appearance here, I want you to stay here for now until we figure it out."

"Yes, Boss!" I said, trying to avoid the sudden rush of joy coursing through me. I didn't know how to handle the worry in his voice. It left me in a confused state. One I knew was caused by my inability to accept anyone showing concern for me.

He chuckled.

"Thank you for helping Marta," I said, changing the subject.

"She's a strong woman." He sat and stretched back out, resting his head on his hands. "I admire that. Besides, we could use some help."

"You hired Kara, too?" I asked, curious.

"Kara changed her mind about working with us." He sounded disappointed. I didn't blame him. Kara was a damn good fighter. "She only went with you today because she thought you might need her." Kara had said as much.

"Well, thank you again."

He nodded and turned to resume his study of the ceiling.

"Devlin?"

"Yes," he said, not looking at me.

"Were you waiting up for me?"

He turned, his eyes going a little soft. "We all were."

Before he could see the smile on my face, I continued down the hall, following the glare of the television.

Rachel lay on the floor with mud mask on her face, watching Spongebob SquarePants, her favorite tv show. She glanced over when I entered the room. "This is my favorite episode," she said, her eyes dancing with joy. They were all her favorite episode.

"Where's Jonah?" I asked, sitting down on the chair.

It took a minute for her to respond. Finally, she waved her hand toward the backyard. "He's swimming." Rachel laughed and turned on her side.

After a brief pause, I got up and went to the back door. Pushing it open, a warm breeze rushed in along with the smell of chlorine. Jonah emerged from the water and gripped the side of the pool. After running his hands over his face, clearing the water, he opened his eyes and stared at me. "You okay?"

"Yeah. Just..." *Stalling*. I didn't want to rush into Alek's room. It felt too needy, and I couldn't afford to have those feelings. Not now. "You should have asked Kara to come over and swim with you," I said, taunting.

He winked at me. "Maybe I will."

I lifted an eyebrow and gave him a teasing grin. He studied me for a minute, and I realized he probably suspected why I was hanging around with him outside. Hell, everyone on the team knew Alek and I were attracted to each other. We were constantly dancing around our feelings like a couple of clueless teenagers. "Well, I will let you get back to your swim." Jonah nodded and pushed off from the edge, his body flexing as he swam across the water. Kara would have lost her mind at the sight. I was having a hard time myself pulling my gaze away from those powerful muscles working as he sliced through the water.

Once I'd seen my fill, I shut the door and went over to the kitchen cabinet and pulled out the jar of chunky peanut butter. I'd always loved eating the peanut buttery goodness directly out of the jar as a kid. My mother hated it. Said I should put the peanut butter on bread or crackers. But I preferred to dig in with my fingers or a spoon.

I used my finger to dig out some and shoved it in my mouth. I wasn't hungry. Not for food, anyway. But still I stood there, scooping peanut butter into my mouth, trying to fill in the need growing inside of me as I thought about Alek.

Seriously, Nicole stop stalling.

Rachel's laughter carried into the kitchen. I was acting like a child. After putting the peanut butter away, I swallowed the panic down and made my way toward Alek's room.

I pushed open the door and the sandalwood scent of Alek's body wash rushed out. My hormones stood up and brushed the cookie crumbs off their chest. Dammit. I should have waited. Maybe finished the entire jar of peanut butter.

The bathroom door was ajar, letting out puffs of steam. I stood in the middle of the room, debating. I'd seen Alek naked before. By accident, of course. At least, that was the lie I continued to tell myself. Now, if I walked into that bathroom, it would be deliberate on my part. So far, we had managed to keep it somewhat professional. Yes, I slept in the bed with him. Yes, I fantasized about him doing more than just holding me through the night. Yes, I was teasing him and would most likely end up in hell for it. Okay, maybe not hell since I didn't believe in it. But something was bound to happen if I kept climbing into bed with him. I just hoped it didn't change our relationship for the worse.

Three weeks ago, I'd made the rare decision to seek help for myself. The revelation that my reckless lifestyle could be a result of the abuse I suffered had me worried. So worried, I went to a bookstore and bought the book, *The Silent Voice of Molestation* by Dr. Amanda Poole. The first three chapters outlined how abuse victims dealt with the shame and hurt in many different ways. Some became overly sexual, while others retreated into themselves—gaining weight to avoid being looked at as a sexual object again.

I became overly sexual.

It also talked about the suppression of the assault and how, even though those memories were all but forgotten, the person could still act out on the deeper hurt that never truly went away.

My memories had been blocked.

The first three chapters had effectively set the stage and gave me the reasons why I behaved the way I did. Why my relationships and my views on sex were so distorted. In chapter four, Dr. Woods wanted me to dig deeper into my feelings. She wanted to break me down to my core and have me face all the pain and poor decisions I'd made in my life. She wanted me to be emotionally raw so that she could build me up again. So, I returned the book and bought my first self-help magazine. Today's purchase would add to the three I already had. At this rate, I'd have a bunch of useless magazines cluttering up my coffee table in no time.

Looking at the bed I shared with Alek, smelling his scent, feeling the warmth of the shower's mist buffeting me and knowing with just one step into that room, I could return to my old self and allow this attraction to go to the next level, was almost too hard to resist.

Two things stopped me from doing that. One: I'd promised

myself I wouldn't go there with another person I worked with. And two: I have never slept with someone I cared about. And I cared about Alek. Maybe chapter five of Dr. Poole's book would have told me why I did this. Sadly, I would never know.

So why did I keep sleeping in his bed? I could use my fear of Set as an excuse. I did have some residual fears, but I knew that was bullshit. I could stay with Kara. Hell, I could even sleep in the unoccupied room. The one that was supposed to be Devlin's, and he had offered it to me. But no, every time I came here, I crawled into bed with Alek, and peace washed over me when he pulled me toward him. Holding me for the night. I needed that connection. That feeling of someone wanting me. It consumed me so much that I believed without it, I would break.

Alek wanted me. And that made me feel safe. Which was unhealthy too, but I wasn't strong enough yet to change.

The door opened further and Alek, wrapped in a towel, stepped out into the bedroom. Every cell in my body screamed at me to move forward. Just take the next step. But instead, eyes locked on him, I just stood there. Wanting. Needing.

His long, wet hair lay plastered to his bronze skin. I watched a single line of water as it made its way down his chest. Damn his chest. *Stop it, Nicole.* I licked my lips and, fighting what felt like a powerful wind pushing against my face, I turned away.

"How was the funeral?" I managed to ask.

"Long."

I heard the towel hit the floor and swallowed against the dryness in my throat.

The dresser drawer banged open, and I peeked. Alek pulled a pair of black boxer shorts out of the drawer and slowly slid them over his powerful legs. I believe my tongue might have been hanging out of my mouth, but I was not going to acknowledge it.

"Thirsty?" Alek asked.

"Are you?" I asked, kicking my shoes off.

He smiled at me. "Come here."

I moved without thinking and went into his arms. "Okay, that was odd," I said.

"What?" he asked, stroking my hair.

"You, commanding me and my feet moving without my consent. I would say you are using your magick, but I know you can't use it on me."

He laughed and extended his arms out, looking down at me. "I wish it was that easy." My cheeks heated, and I stepped away. He snatched his towel off the floor and carried it back into the bathroom.

I followed him in. "What's going on?"

Alek picked up his brush and started brushing his hair back. "Palace intrigue," he said.

I chuckled. "What?"

He stared at me in the mirror. "Petronela gave me a job."

Crossing my arms, I leaned against the door jamb and watched him. "Why are you working for her? And what does she want you to do?"

Alek secured his hair with a band and stepped toward me. "Not important." He reached out and ran a finger down the side of my face. "Devlin told me what happened today at church. You want to talk about it?"

I looked at his mouth, just a few inches away from mine. "Not really." I bit my top lip and Alek moved in closer. I placed a hand on his warm chest. "We can't."

My hormones rebelled.

Alek kissed my cheek. "We will," he said, and then stepped around me and got into bed.

I watched him for a minute, wondering if I should go home. In the end, I climbed into the bed with him. When he pulled me to him, holding me in his warm, safe embrace, I forgot, for just a little while, that what I was doing was unhealthy. I couldn't keep sleeping next to Alek, teasing him. If I wasn't going to take the next step, then I should stop before I ended up hurting both of us.

Alek's arm tightened around me. I pushed back, letting myself relax into him. Maybe it was me who was confused. Because at this moment, in his arms, I knew it was where I belonged. He'd said before he would wait for me to make up my mind.

Looks like I already had.

My phone trilled, jolting me out of my sleep. I slapped my hand on it. When that didn't stop it from ringing, I cracked open one eye and glared. Everyone I knew understood I was not a morning person, especially before I've had my fill of caffeine and food—mostly caffeine. So whoever was calling didn't know me, and I saw no reason to answer their call this early in the morning.

When it finally stopped ringing, I turned on my side and tried to go back to sleep. Yeah, that didn't work.

Flopping on my back, I stared up at the ceiling fan, whirling, pushing the 78-degree cool air around the room. Devlin had ordered me to keep the thermostat at that exact temperature. He even put a helpful note above it when I failed to follow orders. Of course, I had written over said note with my own suggestion, which led to a simple request devolving into childish antics.

His comments about protecting me floated around inside my head. Why the hell did I continue to give him such a hard time? And why the hell hadn't he fired me yet? Maybe he was a glutton for punishment.

Rachel laughed, her voice penetrating the walls and raking over my bare skin like claws. Morning people should burn in hell. Seriously. I mean, who wakes up with a smile on their face and sunshine in their heart?

I shifted away from the sound, as if somehow my back could block the noise, and stared at the empty spot where Alek slept.

Like always, he had smoothed down his side of the bed, making it easy for me to make the rest of the bed when I got up. The first time I'd left my side unmade; he'd given me a raised eyebrow. The second time, he made a point of demonstrating how I should do it. I would have been offended had he not been wearing those lovely, form-fitting boxer shorts. Maybe I should get him to show me his technique again. I smiled at the thought and pushed myself up. I might as well join the rest of the team before Devlin came in here barking orders.

After brushing my teeth and pulling on a wrinkled t-shirt and a pair of shorts, I snatched my phone up and went to join the rest of the household. They'd have to forgive the wildness of my hair and the wrinkles in my shirt. It was too damn early to gussy myself up.

"Good morning," Rachel chirped, and I do mean chirped, as I walked into the kitchen.

"Morning," I mumbled, walked over to the counter, and lifted the coffeepot. The tantalizing black liquid sloshed around inside. But before I poured myself a cup, I turned and asked, "Is this the special coffee?" She mixed herbs in with the coffee that could keep us up for hours. It was also used to help those who expelled a lot of magick. She warned me to not drink more than four cups a day.

She smiled. "Yes."

I studied the pot for a minute, weighing my options. The first time I found out about the coffee, I spit it all over the place and crushed Rachel's heart. Now, I had the advantage of deciding not to fill my cup with the mystery brew. She never told me what she put in it.

"I can make regular coffee," Rachel said hesitantly.

I must have been standing here longer than I thought, staring. "Will you tell me what's in it?"

"Sure!" More chirping. "Apple blossom because it feeds into

the immortality of our magick. Pennyroyal for strength. Rosemary to restore memory. Yarrow for injuries, both physical and mental. And caffeine in its purest form. Not diluted with chemicals and additives. This is dangerous, but I infuse it with green tea and my intent to keep it safe." The damn mad chemist had the nerve to smile. Like casually throwing in one of the ingredients she used was dangerous should be okay.

Devlin walked in the kitchen and took the pot from me. "We have a lot of work to do this morning. Eat your breakfast fast and meet us in the living room."

I saluted him with my middle finger and poured myself some of the concoction. It sounded like I would need the extra stimulant after all.

Breakfast usually consisted of whatever food was left over from the night before. Most times Jonah would make a feast to last us days. But on occasion we ordered takeout. Since nothing was stacked on the counter, I opened the refrigerator and gave a happy sigh. Steak and potatoes: the staple of any good diet. After polishing off the food of the gods, I finally meandered into the living room. Jonah sat at the fold-out table near the sliding glass door. I smiled and rubbed my belly in appreciation for the food. He smiled and dipped his head in acknowledgement.

Rachel sat on the floor with two laptops in front of her, chewing on the end of a pencil—the light from the screen illuminating her face. She looked up at me and beamed. I tipped my coffee cup in her direction. She'd let her hair grow out some. The once-bob was now past her shoulders. She wore it pinned up in a girlish ponytail with bangs framing her face.

Marta sat next to Jonah at a newly constructed desk looking through papers that, judging from the holes, were once tacked up on the whiteboard. I glanced at the board to confirm this. Devlin must have ordered her to review all the files we had on everyone and everything. Probably said it with that bossy-like tone of his.

She, too, had her long hair tied up. She even had on a pair of slacks and a short-sleeved blouse. Why did I suddenly feel like a damn hobo?

Marta looked up and took me in. "I see you're still cheery in the morning," she said, smiling.

I smiled. Not because of what she said—she was making fun of me—but because she was smiling. And that made me feel good. "You know me so well."

"You could have ironed your clothes," she said.

I would have given her the bird, but Devlin, standing in the center of the room, cleared his throat and pointedly glanced at his watch.

"Sorry about that," I said.

Devlin scrubbed his hand down his face and sighed. I was starting to believe his sighs were curse words reserved just for me.

"I'll stop being petty," I said, offering an olive branch.

Devlin shook his head and turned away. But not fast enough for me to have missed the smile on his face. Maybe I was wearing him down. Or thin. Probably thin, judging from the tightness around his eyes.

While the notes had been removed, the pictures Jonah had taken of the different families were still tacked up to the board. I moved closer and examined Gerald Stewart. Damn. I really wanted to have another go at him. I had so many nice comebacks now that I'd had time to think of them. His wife, Louella, along with his sister, Helena, were taped next to him. They had moved down the pictures of Lisa and Thomas. I smiled at the red X I had added to their faces weeks ago.

Ronald's picture was underneath that. I took a sip of my coffee, smiling over the brim. *You're next, Doc.* I really needed to stop calling him that. It was too intimate a nickname for the sadistic asshole.

The Young family had their own board. I glanced at it as I sipped my coffee.

"Alek is working on locating someone for Petronela. I will

jump in and help if he needs me. But until then, we are following four lines of investigation."

I like how he framed what we were doing. Made it sound legitimate. Because who really says, "We have two groups to hunt down and kill?" So, making it sound official might help the group digest it.

"Killing them both would be ideal," Rachel said.

Okay, maybe not the entire group. I took another swig of coffee to hide my wince. I was working for hired killers. Which made me one. Oh, I would love to see my guidance counselor's face now. Tell her just what I ended up becoming. That acting career had seriously gone up in smoke. Who was I kidding? I never wanted to be an actress. I just wanted to piss off my guidance counselor and make her shut up.

It took a minute, but my brain finally registered what he said. "Four, Boss?"

He nodded. "Since you and Jonah will likely not obtain an invitation to the inner circle at The Better Day Church, I'm thinking we need to figure out another way to get the information we need. Possibly approaching one of the parishioners."

"But we only attended one service," I said, wondering why I was protesting. If his other avenue of finding out if they practiced blood magick meant I didn't have to go back to the church, that was a win-win. Right?

He sat on the edge of the table. "Attending their mass service might not be the answer. And..." He trailed off, his gaze steady on me.

"I'm fine. Promise."

"Okay. Then another service it is." He took a sip of his coffee and sighed. "Next up." He looked at Jonah.

Jonah leaned back in his chair. "My uncle got back to me last night and told me a gray aura represents Divine Evil. He didn't have any more information than that, but"—he dipped his head in Rachel's direction—"Rachel found a few things online."

"I don't trust most of the sources," Rachel began. "But one

item stood out. In 1340, a Buddhist monk named Khuchar was said to have achieved Divine Evil. The story goes on to say he slaughtered his entire monastery and became immortal." She stared at the screen. "I think the story is fabricated, but the reference to Divine Evil is there." She looked up at Devlin. "I need more time and maybe access to actual religious texts."

"Jonah," Devlin prompted.

"I can see if my uncle can get ahold of some." He shook his head. "But Buddhism wasn't something he studied. Might need to find a scholar on the subject."

"Agreed," Devlin said. "For now, we focus on getting as much information as possible." He looked at Marta. "Print out everything you find online about it. Most stories about the past have some kernels of truth in them. We just need to weed through them. Rachel, keep working on tracking down all the people associated with Tribe."

"Tribe?" I asked, interrupting.

"I will have to catch you up on that later," Devlin said. "Petronela said we have to go to Luisah for information on the Ark." He studied me for a minute. "You up for that?"

I wanted to say no, but then I wouldn't be doing the job he was paying me for. Besides, Luisah and I were long overdue for a talk.

"Yes. I can handle that."

"Then you and Jonah—"

My phone rang and a knock sounded at the door, cutting him off.

I glanced down at the display. Mr. Wan. A moment of panic wormed its way inside of me. I answered the phone just as Devlin left the room to answer the door.

"Mr. Wan, please tell me everything is all right," I said in way of greeting.

"Yes. Of course," he said, his tone hesitant. "Just wanted to let you know you have a visitor outside your door. She's been here for an hour."

"Umm...did she tell you what she wanted?" Who in the hell would show up at my apartment this damn early in the morning?

"Here, you can speak with her."

A rustling sounded and a female said, "Hello."

The voice sounded familiar. "Who is this?"

"Juliette. I met you at church yesterday," she said, helping me recall the dark-haired girl who had stared at us with open curiosity. The one Jonah had also been consumed with for a short while.

How the hell did she get my address? And as soon as I thought about it, I remembered the guestbook I signed before we entered the church.

"Who is it?" Jonah asked, getting up and walking over to me.

"Juliette," I said.

"Put it on speaker," he whispered.

"What are you doing at my apartment?" I placed the phone on the table while Rachel, Marta, and Jonah gathered around.

She didn't respond right away. When she spoke again, there was a slight hesitation in her voice. "I came to invite you to our women's gathering tonight."

"Why?" I asked then cursed myself. This was the opportunity we were hoping for.

"Gavina was..." she trailed off. "She was concerned and wanted to make sure you were okay. Can we meet and talk about it?"

Devlin walked back into the room and stood in the doorway. He signaled for me to respond.

"Where?" I asked.

"I saw a coffee shop around the corner from your apartment. I can meet you there."

"*Libations by R?*" I asked.

"Yes. Can you make it?"

I looked around at the team. They all nodded. "Sure. Give me an hour."

"Okay," she said and hung up.

"Well," I started. "I guess that solves one of our problems. Although, I don't buy Gavina's concern for one damn minute."

Devlin pushed off the wall. "I don't either. So be careful. I have to go have a *discussion* with Detective Barnes about our reason for being on Tulare. He asked me to meet him at the station in Perry."

Rachel stared at Devlin as if she expected him to elaborate. "I can go with you, Dev," she said, closing her laptops. There was a slight hesitation in her voice. She knew something was off, but obviously, like me, couldn't figure out what.

He shook his head and glanced at Jonah. "I can take care of this alone," he said definitively.

Devlin turned away. I looked at Jonah, and he cut his eyes in Rachel's direction. I raised an eyebrow. *What did he expect me to do?*

Jonah placed a hand on Rachel's shoulder. "I think you should go with Nicole. Juliette might try to hurt her."

Rachel whipped around, eyes narrowed. "No one hurts my friend."

I honestly believed that the phrase 'Cut a Bitch' was invented for Rachel. Her loyalty to her friends was so unshakeable that it might border on madness. Jonah knew exactly which button to push with her. And how to redirect her attention.

While the distraction might have worked on her, I was curious why a detective from Perry would show up in Pleasanton to inquire about Devlin and his team being on the island. Like Tulare was some sort of secret, members-only place. The timing of the man's presence felt too coincidental. Like someone had purposely sent him to check in on us.

"Jonah, help Marta with her search on Divine Evil." Devlin pulled his keys out of his pocket and removed a key. After giving it to Marta, he turned to me and Rachel. "You two check in when you get there and when you leave."

"Yes, Boss."

He smiled and walked out.

Marta got up and walked over to me. She grabbed my shoulders and gave me a hard look. "Be safe."

"Are you kidding? Rachel's coming. She's like an entire security detail rolled into one."

Rachel beamed at me. Yep, definitely towing the line between sanity and madness.

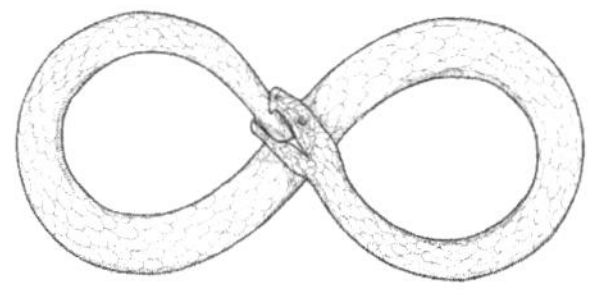

Rosalind Moore, an acquaintance from high school, owned *Libations by R*: the upscale coffee/tea/sweet shoppe that used to be an upscale bar. Brunswood, being the only settlement on the island with a vast majority of nightlife activity, had all kinds of bars. Unfortunately, upscale didn't fit the area as much as the owners had wanted. So, it closed two months after its grand opening.

A soft chime announced our arrival inside as we stepped into the moderately crowded space. I inhaled the seductive smell of banana nut muffins. Or, shall I say, ripened Chiquita gold bananas with a hint of vanilla and gluten-free walnuts baked in a mix of flour and butter. Ten dollars. Seriously, she charged ten dollars for one.

Rosalind looked up from the notebook she was writing in and studied us. Her eyes seemed to glow, making the already soft brown look like amber. She closed the notebook and made her way to the counter—her coffee connoisseur standing by to fulfill the order she predicted each customer wanted. Funny thing was, she was always right.

I had been a regular here for a short while despite the prices but stopped coming when my bank account decided I needed to change my spending habits.

"Long time, Nicole. Black coffee. Sugar-free Banana nut

muffin." She looked at Rachel. "Green tea with a splash of peach. Cinnamon cookie."

"Impressive," Rachel said.

"Thank you. Thirty-two dollars even."

I cried a little as I handed her the money. She must have raised the prices.

"Yes, ritual is always the key. Right? Like without it"—she gave me my change—"people would lose their way. Descend into chaos, even."

"What happens if they do?" I asked. I'd learned to expect her little tidbits of wisdom.

Her eyes went amber-like again. "I suppose you'll find out soon enough." She smiled and pushed our order toward us. "It really is nice seeing you again, Nicole."

"You too, Rosalind." I looked over at her notebook. "New novel?"

She wiggled her eyebrows. "Yes. And I've just gotten to the good part." She glanced out the window. "She'll be here soon."

"You're a mage," Rachel said.

Rosalind cocked her head to the side. "No. I'm a connoisseur of people." She leaned forward. "You broadcast so loudly."

I urged Rachel away from the counter. "Forgot to mention Rosalind can read minds. Of course, now I know it's because she's a mage. I knew magick had to be involved." Her magick must have never been viewed as a threat. Otherwise, my mark would have reacted to her reading my thoughts in the past.

"Should we wait outside on the patio?" Rachel asked.

The haphazard patio sat on the busy intersection where cars, trying to defy the speed of gravity, took the corner at more than forty miles per hour. Only the brave or stupid sat outside.

"No, it's safer in here."

We took a seat at a table near the back, facing the door. We were twenty minutes early and so was Juliette, who came strolling in, her gaze immediately landing on us. She wore a plain white t-shirt and a pair of tight blue jeans. At least it wasn't the frock she had to wear yesterday. She smiled at Rosalind as she stood at the counter waiting. Rosalind paused several times before snapping her fingers.

"I got it! Chai," she said, her voice carrying across the room.

Juliette shook her head. "Just herbal tea, please."

Rosalind turned to the server, a frown on her face. She never got a customer's order wrong.

After collecting her tea and an oatmeal cookie, Juliette made her way over to us, her steps hesitant, keeping her eyes focused on me.

We watched her set her cup down and pull a chair over to our table. Before she sat down, she looked at Rachel.

"Sorry. This is my friend Rachel."

She hesitated before extending her hand. "It's nice to meet you."

Rachel gave her a small smile.

"Sit," I said.

She nodded and sat. "I like your neighborhood." She blew on her tea, watching me over the rim of her mug. "I live in a house with the rest of the girls. I'd rather have my own place. But Gavina says we must not stray from her. And being on our own—" She shook her head and took a sip of tea. Her face scrunched up and she set the mug down.

Why was she telling us this?"

Juliette looked at us. "Sorry," she said, tearing into her napkin. "I ramble when I get nervous." She pushed up in her chair—her back going straight. "I apologize for just showing up at your apartment. I would have called first, but you didn't put your number in the guestbook." She gave me a questioning look. I had to give her credit. She did a nice job of asking for my number without really asking.

"Of course," I said, pulling a pen from my purse. After scribbling down my number on a napkin, I gave it to her.

She stared at it for a minute, as if she needed to memorize it. Finally, she folded it up and shoved it in her pocket. "Gavina wanted me to invite you to a gathering of The Daughters of the Vine," she said in a rush. "She sensed your power at the church and thought you might consider joining our community."

"Is this part of the main church?" I asked.

She shook her head. "No. Boyd..." She let out a small chuckle. "No. He fancies himself as some divine guide. Gavina lets him run the church how he wants. Her focus is on the women. She believes we need a safe space to worship as we please. Away from the tyranny of man."

The Daughters of the Vine. Sounded like a cult. Even the way she described it screamed secret religious faction. And the wording itself was a bit odd. Why the tyranny of man? Did they hate men?

"What goes on at the gatherings?" Rachel asked.

Juliette turned to her. "Spiritual enlightenment and worship. Mostly, we allow ourselves to be free."

She was being vague. I wanted to press her more, but feared if I did, she would rescind her offer. But before I did commit, I had to know why Gavina had invaded my mind. We'd find out how later.

"Why would she probe my mind?" I asked.

Juliette smiled. "She does that to everyone. Her whispers have become so familiar that their absence can sometimes be disturbing." She stared down at her shredded napkin. "She stopped whispering to us a few weeks ago. We don't know why." She swiveled her head toward the window, looking out at the parking lot. "I have to go. The meeting is at seven tonight. I truly hope you are able to attend." She reached in her purse and pulled out a piece of paper. After setting it on the table, she got up. "Thank you for meeting with me." She smiled then turned and walked out the door—leaving her food and beverage behind.

"Well. That was odd. She sure seemed in a hurry to get out of here," I noted.

"Yeah, she did," Rachel said.

I picked up the scrap of paper she left and studied it. She'd written down an address located in the East Gate Estates community.

"It might be a trap," Rachel said, glancing at the note. "And you're not going alone."

"If it is a trap, I shouldn't go at all." I shoved the paper in my purse and polished off the rest of my lukewarm coffee. "And I'm getting some strange vibes about this." I wrapped my muffin in a napkin to eat on the way back to Devlin's.

A crazed smile stretched across Rachel's face. "You think it's a game?"

If it was a game, Rachel seemed a little too eager to play. Since I'd seen her in a fight, I wasn't concerned.

Before we stepped outside, I turned. "Rosalind?" She looked up. "How come you couldn't guess her order?"

"Your friend?"

I didn't correct her assumption. Instead, I made a non-committal noise, encouraging her to continue.

She put her pen tip in her mouth and stared out the window. "Her thoughts." She shook her head as if she were casting off something she was thinking about.

"What about them?"

She looked back at me. "They're not her own."

A Dangerous Game of Hide and Seek

Alek walked into The Brentworth hotel at a little after nine in the morning. The swanky hotel was located on the border of Tulare and Dulean just off the Tulare River. They'd left the glass doors open, letting in the warm air. Wicker fans circled overhead, pushing the heavy citrus scent through the spacious lobby. Polished wood floors stretched toward a bay of heavily polished elevators. Plush couches lay scattered throughout. Swanky, but not overly so. The view of the Tulare River the primary draw.

He'd set out at seven to avoid the rush of guests checking out of the hotels he had on his list. Thankfully, there were only so many posh hotels on Tulare Island. He had eliminated all of them in a few short hours.

He should have remained in bed with Nicole, he thought. At least for a few more hours. Her body pressed up against his felt right, and it was getting harder and harder not to make a move. The hungry look she gave him last night had almost broken his resolve. But he didn't want to scare her. So, he'd continue to let her set the pace.

Alek looked around. The five-hundred-room upscale hotel was the last place he would have ever considered searching for

Unrie Nevsky. After all, *Carnavalul de Fear* was only a ten-minute walk from the hotel.

If Unrie was in fact staying at the hotel, he was either brazen or unaware of Petronela's reputation. He thought about the man his great aunt caught stealing from her and the hallway caked in blood. Maybe people didn't fear her like they did in the past.

A tall, redheaded woman looked up from behind the concierge desk and took him in, her face scrunching up into a distasteful sneer. A man stood next to her, staring with a touch of hostility in his eyes. Wearing jeans and a black t-shirt, with his long hair pulled back with cord, Alek knew he didn't fit in. The old couple swerving around him like he was a dangerous obstacle they must avoid on their quest to get outside, cemented the fact.

"Afternoon," he said, rattling the old woman. He didn't relish making her uncomfortable, but he did enjoy the spark of indignation in the man's eyes as he ushered his wife more quickly through the glass doors.

A short woman wearing a blue blazer and matching skirt walked up to him with a smile stretching across her entire face. "Can I help you?" Her eyes roamed over him as she played with the collar of her white blouse, exposing a black bra underneath. She wore a single gold bracelet with a tiny charm of a record player.

Alek glanced at her name tag: *Candace Rebel, Hotel Manager.* He smiled. "Yes, Ms. Rebel."

"Candace, please," she said, sidling closer.

It seemed she didn't have an issue with him being there. Good. Alek pulled a picture of Unrie from his pocket and unfolded it. "Is this man a guest at your hotel?" He didn't do finesse. He preferred the direct approach.

"Ms. Rebel," the man behind the reception desk called. "Can I speak with you for a moment?"

Candace glanced behind her at the man staring daggers at them. She chuckled under her breath and leaned toward Alek. "Timothy likes to believe he runs this hotel." She played with her necklace, drawing his attention back to her. "Put it in writing, Timmy," she called out and steered Alek out of the lobby. "He's also a spy. We better talk in my office."

He left glamorous behind and entered an era long forgotten. Posters of '80s bands covered the office walls. A hand-written sign that said, 'I'm the damn manager' hung on the wall directly across from the office door.

"Nice," Alek said, looking around. "What do the owners think?"

Candace perched on the edge of the desk and crossed her arms under her breast. "You mean dear, old *Daddy*?" She laughed. "He's still trying to get me to use the Brentworth name." She winked. "I legally changed it to Rebel when I was eighteen. He cut off my allowance and made me work here."

"Rebellion at its finest."

Candace nodded. "Absolutely!" She got up and took the chair next to him, leaning in close. "So, who's this guy you're looking for and what did he do?"

Alek leaned back and smiled at her. "Are you flirting with me, Candace?"

"Why, yes, I am," she paused. "I didn't catch your name."

"Alek Vaduva."

"Alek. Is it working?"

He shook his head. "Nice necklace. Now"—he leaned forward—"can you give me the information I need? Or should I put it in writing?"

She laughed and stood up. "Finally! Someone who doesn't annoy the hell out of me. Daddy prefers Timothy to check in the guests. I figured since he's also Daddy's spy, he should write down everything he needs to say." She winked. "Makes it easier for him to report."

"You could always quit," Alek said. He liked the woman. She had a way about her that demanded people shut up and take notice. She must drive her parents crazy.

She gasped with mock indignation. "And tarnish the family

name? Never!" She shrugged and moved to sit behind the desk. "The pay is good. And I get to stay here for free rather than the stuffy family estate in Dulean. I like to give my dad a hard time. He likes to pretend I'm not related to him." She tapped some keys on her computer. "My mother has found solace in lounging in the living room with her pearls on."

"Sounds horrific." He couldn't decide if she was a spoiled rich kid or a woman who was just trying to find her own way.

Someone knocked at the door.

Candace looked up from the computer. "Yes."

"Ms. Rebel, the guests are complaining about the doors being open."

She returned her attention to the computer. "Put it in writing, Timmy."

Alek chuckled. "Seems you like to get under everyone's skin."

"The joys of life." The printer came to life, spitting out several sheets of paper. Candace stood and retrieved them. Next, she put a disk in the computer drive. "I should probably give you a copy of the surveillance video with him in it, too." She copied the video on a disk and smiled at him. "Now, detective," she said, putting the disk in a case. "Is there anything else I can get for you?" She handed him the papers and the disk.

Alek smiled and took them. "Never said I was a detective."

"You didn't?" She gasped, feigning a mock surprise. "My mistake. Is there anything else you need?"

Alek stood, folded the papers, and stuffed them in his pocket along with the disk. "This should help. Thanks."

He turned to leave. Candace reached out and grabbed his arm. "Should I be concerned about the safety of my guests?" All the sarcasm and teasing was gone from her voice. It had been replaced with worry.

"Keep this between us, and you should be fine."

Candace walked him to the lobby where Timothy stood in the middle of the room, trying to console a young couple wearing tennis outfits. He glared at both Candace and Alek.

"Looks like I have a fire to put out. Nice meeting you, Mr. Vaduva," she said and walked over to them.

Alek stepped outside into the humid air and made his way to his car. Once inside, he reviewed the paperwork Candace had given him. According to the information, Unrie had been staying at The Brentworth for a month and had checked out two hours prior to him arriving.

How had Unrie escaped Petronela's radar for an entire month? Had someone warned him that Alek was looking for him? Why else would he have suddenly checked out after staying at the hotel all this time.

As he stared down at the name of the man that had been staying with Unrie, he pulled out his phone and called Devlin. He answered on the second ring. "I have information on Logan," Alek said. "I'll pick you up in twenty."

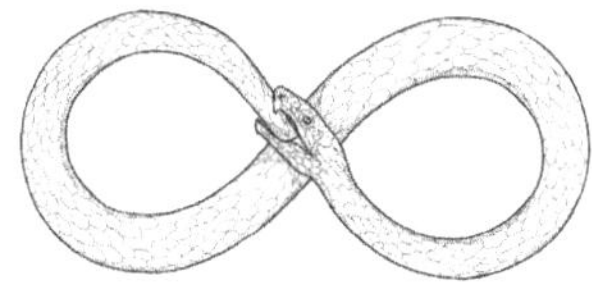

Devlin climbed into Alek's car and sighed. Alek noted the dark circles around his eyes, and that his boss had lost some weight as well. The Markum family had placed a tremendous burden on him. Forcing him to act in a way he wasn't comfortable with. Yes, they had often ended up in similar situations in the past. Like Devlin had told Nicole, the team had decided they would be the checks and balances for magick. Yet, investigating someone and purposely setting out to kill were two different things. Their job on Tulare would get bloody. And for Devlin, it was a line he didn't cross lightly. But I knew he had to. They all did.

Alek handed him the paperwork he got from Candace and pulled away from the curb. "According to what the manager gave me, Unrie Nevsky checked in a month ago and checked out two hours before I arrived."

"Convenient." Devlin scanned the pages. "Logan Magellan.

Name sounds Portuguese." Devlin looked up from the file and stared out the window. "Jonah thought he might be Spanish or Italian." He paused. "What I'm wondering is why would he stay at the hotel with Unrie? Better question. Why is his ID on file? Last I checked, you only need one ID to check into a room."

"I think we can thank Timothy for that." Devlin looked at him. "Don't ask." Explaining Candace Rebel and her relationship with her employees might take a while and besides, it wasn't important. "I'm curious why he stayed with him for ten days. Especially since he has a place on Tulare."

Devlin flipped through the papers again. "Looks like both our cases have merged. But what does it all mean?"

Alek didn't know.

Devlin set the papers on the seat and leaned back. "So, we have a man the Stewarts use as a fixer, and a hitman working with a man Petronela believes is here to settle some old scores. Gerald Stewart believes we have the Ark. And I got a visit from a Detective Barnes from the Perry Police Department this morning, inviting me to the precinct. He asked me a few questions about my time at Tribec and said we need a license to practice on Tulare." Devlin shook his head. "I put a call in to the Markums."

"Why would a detective from Perry be concerned about what was going on in Pleasanton?"

"He wouldn't say. And I asked him several times." Devlin shook his head.

"You think the Young family is working with Gerald?"

"They have to be. Gerald was at their church." Devlin told Alek about the phone call Nicole received. "We have our way in. But I'm concerned it might be a trap. Especially since Gavina tried to work magick on her. She has to know Nicole has some power."

Alek's grip tightened on the steering wheel. "Is Nicole okay with this?"

Devlin laughed. "I don't think Nicole will be okay until this is over." Devlin glanced at him. "Can't understand why she doesn't just ask her father to help her with her magick."

Alek thought about Candace and her petty rebellion. Which, given her concern for her guests, said that it wasn't just life she was angry at—it was her father. Maybe some wounds never healed.

"If I help Petronela, she won't have to."

Devlin turned to Alek. "But she should."

"Can't argue with that."

"Rachel found a brief mention on Divine Evil. She wants to check a few more sources before she's sure the information online is correct." Devlin scrubbed his hand down his face. "This case is already a major headache with more avenues than answers."

"Yeah," Alek said. "We might need to hire a few more people."

Devlin sighed. "I'm hoping Kara will agree to work with us. I know she's a teacher, but I get the impression she might give that up." He looked down at his hands. "She wanted to be there for Nicole yesterday, but said she wasn't able to do more than that. I'm hoping I can change her mind." He smiled. "She's a damn good fighter."

Alek nodded, remembering the way the fiery redhead had taken down the blood magick users in the barn weeks ago. Her command of her magick was pure poetry. And Jonah could barely keep his eyes off her. He smiled. It was good to see the big man smiling more. They all needed a break in the constant deluge of danger they stayed in. Or, thinking of Nicole and Kara, some strong women to take their mind off things.

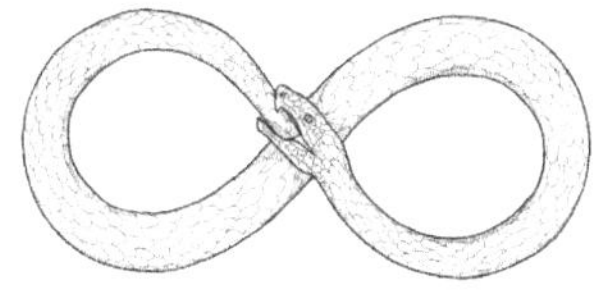

The address for Logan took them to the Greenwood Apartments in Perry, what the locals referred to as 'The War Zone.' Alek pulled to the curb in front of the dilapidated building and looked out over the bleak landscape. Despite the sun riding high in the sky, the area still seemed to swallow the light, as if the sun couldn't penetrate the darkness the area exuded.

Children skipped in the streets—their faces devoid of any joy. Two cars drove by slowly, the passengers watching him and Devlin.

All eyes landed on them when they climbed out of the car. One kid broke free from the pack and cycled over to them, the bike weaving around the street in a menacing dance. The child's eyes remained fixed on them.

Alek stood there, staring, seeing the resemblance to the albino who had tried to attack him and Nicole when they drove through this area over a month ago on their way to question a guard from Tribec Insurance. The albino had wanted to kill him, take his car, and force Nicole into prostitution. Alek, in a fit of rage, unleashed his magick on all the people who had gathered on the street to help. His attack on the albino, Alek learned later, had caused the man's brain to bleed.

He had told Devlin about the run-in but left off his use of magick to put everyone to sleep. Devlin knew the slippery slope Alek traversed on and worried that his dark urges would emerge again if he stepped over the line. And using magick on so many people at once was stepping over the line. At least for him it was.

The girl had the same pale skin and wore her light-brown hair in braids. A pale orange light pulsed around her.

"You the one put my brother in a coma?" she asked.

Alek nodded. "We gonna have a problem?"

She got off her bike and let it fall to the ground. The *clank* echoed down the street as if they were inside a soundless void.

She stared up at him out of pale eyes. "Nah. He was getting soft. Someone was bound to kill him one day." The way she said it made Alek believe she might have been that someone. She jerked her chin toward his car. "Give me a twenty, and I'll make sure no one touches your car."

"No one *will* touch it," Alek said. "But..." He pulled Logan's picture from his back pocket and handed it to her. "If you tell me which apartment this man lives in, I'll give you fifty."

She took the photo and studied it. "Yeah. We know him." She

looked up at the apartments. "You think your magick will keep you safe inside there? Most people learn real quick that ain't true."

"How do you know we have magick?" Alek asked.

She stared at him out of those translucent eyes. "I can see it," she said finally. She dipped her head at the picture in Alek's hand. "He was crazy powerful, too."

Devlin pulled a hundred from his pocket. "Fifty for any information you have on him and fifty for the escort."

She nodded. "That I can do." She slid the money into her pocket. "Just remember, it's your funeral." She looked over her shoulder at the kids watching them. "No one touches the car." One of the taller kids nodded. She started for the front entrance. "Come on."

Alek leaned toward Devlin. "You sure you want to get her involved?"

"This is her territory. By showing respect, we get what we need and don't have to engage with the locals." He glanced back at the kids. "I don't want to end up hurting a child. " He slipped a belt around his waist that contained small vials filled with the four elements. As an elemental mage, he could wield them in battle.

Alek hoped their time here wouldn't end in tragedy and death.

They stepped past the foggy glass doors and into the apartment lobby. Dark gray concrete covered the floor with stains saturating the surface. An overloaded metal garbage can rested at the foot of the stairs with flies swarming around it. A coppery scent mixed with urine and old trash hung in the air as though it had weight. Alek's eyes stung as he pushed forward, swallowing down the bile that rose in his throat.

The walls were stripped to the stained boards underneath. Five thick plastic bags bulged out of a section in the wall. A short, round man wearing dirty overalls stood in front of one of the openings, holding a spackle knife in one hand. Alek watched as he moved a board in front of one of the bags. It was then he noticed the body inside.

"Elevator don't work. We gotta take the stairs," the girl said, but Alek didn't move.

Seeming to understand why he stopped, the girl said, "Your man brought them here yesterday and paid Mr. White to board them up."

Why had Logan buried someone in the walls?

"Did he say who they were?" Devlin asked, his voice strained.

The girl shrugged. "No. And nobody here is going to ask, either." She glanced around at the walls. "My mom told me when the mayor pushed all the crime out of the other settlements and forced us into this small area, factions rose and fell. The only way to keep that chaos from continuing, someone got the idea that burying the people they killed in the walls would be the best way to instill fear and keep people in check." She ran her hand over her head, looking around. "I don't know. Maybe they saw it in some movie." She chuckled. But there wasn't any joy in the sound, only sadness. "My uncle put the first person in the wall. My brother even put a few in there."

The fact that Logan had done the same suggested he had a familiarity with the area and their brutal practices. Alek pulled his phone from his pocket and took pictures of the people's faces. He'd have Rachel do an image search to see if they could identify them.

She looked around. "Looks bad, I know. But it's all an illusion. And at least I can see past all this to something better."

"You live here?" Devlin asked, surprised.

"For now. Later, when I make enough money, I'll live in Dulean. Mix with rich folks." She smiled. "Date their daughters." She turned and continued up the stairs. "Come on. And stick close. People will try and kill you in here just because they're bored." She glanced at one of the plastic bags sticking out the wall. "Then keep you close as a warning to others."

"What's your name?" Alek asked.

On the first step, she turned. "They call me Rae." She cocked her head to the side in question.

"Alek."

She looked at Devlin.

"Devlin." He studied her for a minute, eyes narrowed. "Will you take up the mantle?" he asked finally.

"No. I'll be in Dulean, remember?"

Devlin nodded.

"Okay, lead the way," Alek said.

They walked up four flights of stairs. Rae took them down a long hallway covered in trash to the last apartment on the left. "This is it. You want me to come in with you?" She seemed eager.

"Can you stand guard?" Alek asked, handing her another fifty.

She pocketed the money and smiled. "That I can do."

Alek tried the door. It opened without resistance, and they stepped into the room. The stench from the hallway washed away, depositing them into a room with bare white walls and a stale, almost void-like smell saturating the air. It was as if no one had ever lived in the apartment. A clean spot in a sea of decay. Given the condition of the rest of the building, it was definitely odd.

Alek studied the rest of the room.

A black leather couch sat on the left side of the small living room with a dark, wooden coffee table in front. Beige carpet covered the entire floor, flowing into a small kitchen covered with yellow linoleum.

Neat and orderly. Without much in the way of personality. If not for the couch and coffee table, Alek would have sworn nobody lived there.

It took only a few minutes for them to go through each room, noting the absence of furniture or personal effects. In the kitchen, Alek picked up a stack of mail addressed to Logan Magellan for an address in Alice.

Devlin walked into the kitchen. "Why would he rent this place and not furnish it?" he asked, taking the mail from Alek.

Alek pondered Devlin's question. Going back to his earlier

confusion about why Logan would be staying at a hotel if he had a place on Tulare to begin with.

"It feels like some elaborate ruse," Alek said eventually, letting his mind work through the clues. "Why else would he go through all this trouble?"

Devlin shoved a piece of mail in his pocket and glanced around the apartment. "I agree. This apartment isn't set up for someone to live in." He tossed the rest of the mail on the counter. "My question is why?"

Alek shook his head.

"To stash the people he killed in the walls?" Devlin offered.

Alek thought about that for a moment. "Since he was obviously aware of their practices, he must be from the area. Maybe even lived here at some point in the past."

Devlin drummed his fingers on the counter, thinking, then turned and called Rae. She popped her head in the door. "Has Logan lived here before?" he asked her.

She nodded slowly. "I got the feeling he did. When he came here. He knew who Mr. White was. And Mr. White has been here forever."

A sound came from the hallway. Rae snapped her head around. "Hey, we have company," she said a note of warning in her tone.

"How many?" Devlin asked.

"Four," Rae said, stepping into the apartment.

Alek turned to Devlin. "You want me to shut them down?"

Devlin shook his head. "Too risky. We use only what's necessary."

Alek dipped his head in acknowledgement and rushed into the living room. Rae stood off to the side, with a blade in her hand. He wanted to push her behind him but knew she wouldn't stay put. He'd just have to keep the men focused on him and Devlin.

A few seconds later, four young men entered the apartment, guns drawn.

Devlin stepped into the room, holding a small tornado in his hand.

"You must be the welcome wagon," Alek said, and rushed the first man.

Tall, lanky, with more attitude than common sense. The man raised his gun and fired, the shot going wide. The bullet got caught in the wind and ended up embedded in the wall.

Alek surged forward and shoved the man up against the wall, slamming his head back against the plywood. A *crack* resounded as the wall split open from the force. Blood ran down its surface and Alek released the man. He grabbed his gun, ejected the bullet into the chamber, and took the magazine out, then tossed it away.

The other three tried to step in to help but found themselves fighting against a strong wind as Devlin released the tornado in his hand. Several shots rang out. The bullets circled the room before finally embedding in the thin walls. Their guns were ripped from their hands, flying into the kitchen out of reach.

The couch rattled, lifting up off the ground. Devlin was bathed in a dark blue light, his magick working fiercely. Alek knew the men couldn't see the crackle of the luminescence as it bathed the room, but he could, and the sheer magnitude of it momentarily gave him pause, solidifying his earlier assessment of Devlin's anger. Too bad he couldn't use his own magick. The fight would have been over before it started.

The couch flew across the room. One of the men didn't move in time and was caught in front of it as it slammed into the opposite wall.

Rae yelled, and Alek turned in time to see a man pick her up to use as a shield. With her arm arcing down, blade at the ready, she drove the polished steel into the man's side. He bellowed and dropped her to the ground.

That left one man. Devlin shoved him to the ground and put a boot on his chest as the wind finally died down and his magick settled.

Alek walked over and crouched down, studying him. He

looked no older than twenty, yet he already had the lines on his face and the hatred in his eyes of someone who'd lived a lifetime filled with brutality, death, and chaos.

Rae dropped to her knees and wiped the blood from her blade on the floor. "This is Zane," she said identifying the man under Devlin's boot. She glanced around the room. "Those are his crew. They've been trying to take over since my brother went to sleep."

Alek wanted to tell her to wait outside or in the kitchen, any place but right here. But then he remembered she saw this type of brutality daily. And judging from the hardened look in her eyes, it had stopped phasing her a long time ago.

"You workin' with them now?" the man asked, glaring at Rae.

"Money's good." She leaned down. "You tried to kill me."

He turned away and looked at Alek. "Man paid us to keep an eye out for anyone coming to his apartment."

Alek pulled the picture of Logan from his back pocket. "This man?" he asked, showing the picture.

He nodded and looked over at one of his friends lying on the floor. "That was some freaky shit you did," he said, stealing a glance at Devlin's belt. "Is that fire in one of them glass things?"

"You don't know about magick?" Devlin asked, removing his foot from the man's chest. He offered him a hand, and the man grabbed it and stood.

"Nobody uses magick in Perry." He looked down at his gun. It was on the floor near the entrance to the kitchen. "Maybe we need to find us someone who can. Guns don't seem to be workin' no more."

"Tell me about the man who paid you," Alek said.

Zane ran his hands down his pants as if he were dusting them off. Alek figured it was an effort to look tough and suppressed his smile.

"He moved in two weeks ago. Paid Brittany." He looked at Rae. "She went missing yesterday." Rae nodded. "Anyway. He paid Brittany to clean the apartment and a few of us to put the couch and coffee table in here. Yesterday, he asked us..." He looked at the man Alek had put down, easing up off the floor. Alek breathed a sigh of relief that he hadn't killed him. "He told us to watch the place. Paid us a grand each."

"What were you supposed to do if someone came in?" Devlin asked.

Zane looked down at the floor; his feet twitched like he wanted to run. "Supposed to kill whoever came knocking." He looked at Devlin. "You think he'll know we didn't get the job done?"

"Why?" Alek gritted out.

"Man scared the hell out of us. Don't need him coming back." He looked around at his friends. Only one remained down, hidden behind the couch.

Alek didn't give a damn if Logan came back. These boys chose to get involved and they had come in here intent on killing them. He glanced at Devlin. The man shook his head and stepped over to the couch. Alek walked over and helped him push it from the wall.

Even though the man lay motionless, he had a pulse. Weak, but it was there. And that was all they could do about it.

After pocketing the mail, Alek and Devlin left, bringing Rae with them.

"You going to be okay?" Alek opened his car door. The kids had done what they were told. No one had touched his car.

She lifted her bike off the sidewalk. "This is my domain. I'm always going to be all right." She looked out over the street. "Maybe I can work for you again," she said. The hope in her voice sent a pang of sadness through him. She didn't want to be in this place.

Alek wished he could take her with them. But that would be wrong. She was a minor, and her world was already filled with ugliness. And the work they did would expose her to even more violence. He couldn't do that. Or even worse, get her killed "Maybe. If we need some backup," he said, despite him knowing they might never see her again.

She smiled and pedaled away. Alek climbed in the car and started the engine. "You want to check out the next place?" he asked and pulled away from the curb.

Devlin stared down at his phone. "Looks like Nicole has been invited to a gathering of The Daughters of the Vine." He glanced at Alek. "That ring any bells with you?"

Alek shook his head, his hands tightening on the steering wheel. He didn't want Nicole to go to that meeting. Not alone, at least. "You sending Rachel with her?"

"Yeah. And I just texted Kara to see if she would go, too. Nicole might get pissed, but too bad. Until she learns battle magick, I don't want her working alone."

"Agreed," Alek said. Although, he would never tell Nicole that, because Devlin was right: She would be pissed. "Am I dropping you off?"

Devlin leaned back. "Yeah. Gotta check on the team."

"And let Nicole yell at you?"

Devlin smiled. "That too."

We pulled up to Devlin's at a little after two in the afternoon. Rosalind's revelation about Juliette's thoughts not being her own still bothered me, and I couldn't shake the feeling we had missed something. But no matter how many times I reviewed our meeting with her, I just couldn't find anything. Rachel did, however, confirm Juliette had a pale blue aura, which meant she could have elemental magick. I should have checked, too, but I'd been too distracted, trying to determine what her end game was. Maybe one day soon it would become second nature for me to check if a person had magick. Like it was for Rachel and Alek.

Rachel opened the door, and we made our way toward the back—only to stop dead in our tracks. Gone was the single desk set up for Marta as well as the plastic fold-out table for everyone else. They had been replaced with two wooden tables. Each table held two laptops, lamps, and chairs. Our whiteboards remained. However, a collapsible projector screen and projector sat on a table next to it.

"I see you decided to redecorate," I said to Marta.

She looked up from her laptop and glanced around the room. "I think this works better." She got up and stretched. "It felt awkward being the only one with a desk."

"We've only been gone for a couple of hours," I said, moving further into the room. It was just like Marta. She always had to make a space her own. I would say she had OCD, but it wasn't like that. It was more of a need to have a space for everything and everyone. She needed order in her life, which made the disarray at her house even more jarring. It wasn't in Marta's nature to let her immediate area become so disorderly.

"I made a list when I got here at seven this morning. Devlin said it was okay for me to make changes. So, I ordered the items we needed, and Jonah went and picked them up."

I nodded, fighting the urge to laugh. She had come in here like a *boss* and reordered everything to her liking. Devlin and she had to be twin souls. "I don't see any nameplates. Can you direct me to my desk, ma'am?" I asked, smiling.

"You are such a smartass, Nicole," she said and extended her hand out to the table on the left. "You and Alek can work there."

"Okay," I said, ignoring the obvious matchmaking she had set up. "There are only four spots and six of us."

"Rachel said she preferred to work from the floor. I got her a bean bag chair and floor desk. Jonah and Devlin both rotate standing and sitting."

"So does Alek," I said, visualizing him sitting on the edge of the desk. He rarely worked at a computer.

Marta gave me a half smile. "I know."

I shook my head at her and sat at my newly assigned seat. At least the chair was comfortable. And I had my own brand-new laptop. Maybe Devlin would let me make improvements as well. We could start by adjusting the temperature on the thermostat.

Rachel grinned from ear to ear as she plopped down on her bean bag chair. The *whoosh* of the leather giving almost made me laugh. I could so picture her playing on that thing. "Thank you, Marta. I love it!" she said and leaned back with a smile on her face.

Rachel really was a kid at heart. A dangerous one, mind you. But still, she could manifest enough joy to light up a city block. It was confusing at first, seeing how deadly she could be. But then I remembered what Devlin had told me about her past. I still needed to work up enough nerve to ask her about it. He didn't give me all the details, just enough to help lay things out. Of course, I could always wait for her to open up. Otherwise, she might expect the same from me. Yeah, not going to happen.

Jonah came into the room with a pan of French bread pizza covered in pepperoni.

"Oh, bless you," I said, taking a piece. I had polished off the muffin on the way home, and I was still hungry. Or needing to eat my feelings. Since I wasn't above lying to myself, I'd go for saying I was hungry.

After handing out pizza to everyone, he sat on the edge of the table and said, "Update."

I gave him a rundown of our meeting with Juliette while Marta took notes. Once done, Rachel told him about the texted image she received from Alek and the circumstances behind it.

Jonah looked at me. "When you..." He trailed off.

I knew what he wanted to ask: If I'd seen them putting bodies in the walls when I was at Greenwood Apartments. "No," I said. "But I did spend most of my time high." Jonah gave me a look. Not pitying or judgmental—one that said, *'I appreciate you opening up.'* I could have hugged him. Instead, I settled on getting myself another slice of pizza.

"Seems morbid," Marta said. "And...showy. Like he wanted to prove he was the biggest, baddest person around."

She was right on both fronts. Why stick bodies in the wall? It screamed, *'Look at what I can do!'* Only people who needed to prove themselves did things like that.

Rachel plugged her phone into her laptop. "I can run an image search. It might take a while." She took a large bite of her pizza and smiled. "You put extra cheese on it!"

Jonah laughed and turned to Marta. "What have you found so far on Divine Evil?"

Marta got up and retrieved some papers from the printer. "I printed out all the stories that came up. I figured I'd highlight all the similar information in each article and post. I can compile a list from there." She set the papers on her desk. "One thing stands out, though: the name of the monk and hints of him being both Divine Evil and immortal." She looked at Rachel. "So, I'm thinking that part is true at least."

Rachel nodded as she chewed the last of her pizza. "If we can get some religious texts, there might be more."

"Yeah," Marta said. "Like what ritual helped him become Divine Evil and immortal in the first place."

Jonah looked at me. "When you're done eating all the pizza, search for any references on The Daughters of the Vine."

I covered my mouth. "Oh, should I have saved some for Alek and Boss Man?" I asked, my voice filled with sarcasm. It was on the tip of my tongue to call him Boss Man Junior, then I remembered him telling me he didn't like leading; hated being in charge. So, I swallowed the joke along with my pizza. Even I wasn't that crass.

Rachel laughed and grabbed another slice. "They can make their own." We shared an air toast with our pizza and chuckled.

Jonah shook his head and pulled out the chair next to Marta and straddled it. "I guess they'll have to," he said finally, a smirk on his face. He opened *The Wisdom of Boyd* and started reading.

"Oh, please tell me you are not reading that book," I said.

"Never know where the clues are unless you look." He shrugged. "But so far, I've found nothing; only Boyd taking scripture from the Bible and writing his own interpretation of it."

I knew there wasn't going to be any wisdom in that damn book—just double-talk and pretty words. Boyd was an idiot. A charlatan. A snake oil salesman in a nice suit. Hell, even his wife thought so. But sadly, Jonah was right. If we wanted to find answers, we'd have to examine everything. Including text written by a hack.

What we weren't talking about was what came next. After we found the connection to blood magick, did we storm the church guns blazing magick at the ready? Or did we execute a sneak attack and take them out while they were sleeping? What if they had more followers involved? Did we take them out as well? The Markums did say, 'Kill them all.' Should we assume that meant every single blood magick user, or just the main families that practiced? So many questions that I wasn't going to ask because I doubted Devlin, or the rest of the team, knew either.

So, after polishing off my third slice of pizza, I turned on my laptop and searched for The Daughters of the Vine. A host of items popped up. Damn. I might need another snack. Or drink. Maybe even a cigar to weed through all of it.

A few hours later, we all sat back and went over what we'd found.

Jonah confirmed Boyd had no wisdom, and no command of English vocabulary, either. He did, however, have a load of charisma and self-love. All those qualities were necessary if you wanted to con a bunch of people into believing your bullshit. And to think, people—including us—paid for that damn book.

The Daughters of the Vine presented themselves as a woman empowerment movement. Gavina held seminars teaching women about taking charge in their lives and not bowing to the demands of male partners. Her rhetoric walked a fine line between outright hatred of men and simply helping women deal with the few males who believed they set the sun. So why was she still married to Boyd if she didn't like men?

They also bottled and sold wine they called, 'Nectar of the Gods,' which was a blend of organic grapes and a secret ingredient they didn't want to disclose. They also gave all their profits to charity. It looked nice on the surface, but I wasn't buying it for a second. And neither was the rest of the team.

I rubbed my eyes and leaned back. "It's not like I expected them to announce they were a cult. But I did expect to get some salacious tidbit or a damn complaint at least." My brain hurt from reading an overload of pretty, well-cultivated words, aimed to sell me on the idea I should join their 'movement.' I hated salespeople. And I hated bullshit as well.

"We might need to dig deeper," Rachel said. "The Young

family is powerful. If anyone did complain, they would have buried it." '*Or killed them*', she left unsaid.

"Still." I looked at Jonah. "Can you make us something else to eat?"

He gave me a look that, to the casual onlooker, would appear to be scornful. But I knew it was loaded with sarcasm and a touch of irritation. Damn. I was such a bad influence on everyone.

"So, that's a no, then," I said, fighting my smile.

"Are you hungry, Nicole?"

I shook my head. "No. Just frustrated."

"We all are," he said, his tone placating. He was trying to help. I appreciated that.

I smiled and he winked at me, then turned to Marta. "Any luck?"

She nodded, staring at the pile of highlighted papers in front of her. "So, all the stories had the same three elements we learned before." She stood up and taped notecards to the whiteboard. "The events took place in a monastery in Tibet in 1340 A.D. The monk involved was named Khuchar and he had managed to achieve Divine Evil and immortality." She added two more cards to the board. "Five sources claim he killed all the members in his brotherhood. And one source claimed he had made a blood sacrifice." She turned to us. "Despite it only being mentioned once, I'm thinking the blood sacrifice is significant."

"Magick is in the blood," Jonah said. He got up and went into the kitchen. When he returned, he had a bag of chips and four sodas. After handing them out, he continued, "I'm sure Devlin would want us to follow that lead." He checked his watch. "Your meeting is at seven, right?"

I groaned. I really didn't want to go, but knew I had to. I also had to work on not being sarcastic and asking questions laced with sarcasm. Looks like I was going to need a new mantra. Or I could just recycle the other one.

My phone buzzed, and I looked down at the display. "Well, looks like Kara is coming with me tonight." I gave the team an accusing glare. "Who told Kara about the meeting?" As soon as I said it, I knew: Devlin. Damn him. He probably thought I needed some emotional support. Or that I couldn't handle it myself.

"Probably Dev," Rachel said, grabbing a handful of chips. "He might want you to have backup."

Well, there was that, too. Why did my mind always latch onto people thinking the worst of me? Like everyone believed I wasn't good enough.

Rachel stared at me. "That's okay, right?"

I laughed. It sounded forced. "Of course," I said and downed my soda.

Marta gave me a questioning look. I shook my head and turned to Rachel. "Did you find out who Logan had buried in the walls at Greenwood Apartments?"

She nodded and looked at her computer. "Leonard Beltran. He was a business associate of the Stewarts."

"Why would they have Logan kill their business associate?" I asked, not expecting an answer. There was no way any of us could figure this out. We'd have to ask Gerald himself. It might give me the opportunity for a rematch. It still needled me I hadn't been able to come up with a better comeback. And yes, I sounded like a juvenile.

Jonah rubbed his head. "We'll put that to the side for now."
We all agreed.

The front door opened, and I turned toward the sound. Devlin walked in the room, and his gaze landed on me.

"Nicole," he said, and ticked his head toward the front room. "Alek wants to talk with you." He glanced around the room with a look of admiration, then walked over to the new table and tossed a wrinkled file folder on top.

I glanced at my shorts and the now-stained tank top and groaned. Too late to change now. I got up and ran outside.

Alek's Buick sat idling in front of the house with the passenger window down. He stared transfixed at me as I walked to the car. I flushed under the weight of his gaze and had to fight the urge to run back inside and clean myself up. Fuck. He was turning me into a girly, girl.

"Hi," I said, leaning in the open window. "You're not coming in?"

He smiled. "No. Have work to do. I wanted to see you before you left."

I licked my lips. Damn. Even rumpled, this man looked good enough to eat. "What did you and Devlin do all day?"

"Play hide and seek."

"What?"

"Get in, Nicole." His smooth voice rolled over me and I had to suppress a shiver.

I opened the car and climbed inside. He reached over and pulled me onto his lap—my legs resting on the seat. "You okay?" he asked as he slipped a strand of hair behind my ear.

"Why am I sitting in your lap?" I asked, avoiding the question.

"Because I want you here." He glanced down at my lips. "I'm worried about you."

"I can take care of myself."

He laughed softly; his eyes fixed on mine. "I met someone today who reminded me of you."

"Oh, really?" I gave him a teasing smile. "Are you cheating on me already?"

Our lips were inches apart. Did I move or did he? My eyes fluttered and my stomach dipped. I pulled in a breath and inhaled his familiar scent.

His hand gently pressed into my side, moving me closer. That answered my question. At first I moved, but now, he was moving me. I really needed to stop this before we went too far.

"Are we doing things my way now?" he asked, his voice soft. Just one last millimeter and our lips would touch. He'd told me weeks ago, after I told him we shouldn't be in a relationship since we were going to be working together, that we would do it my way first and his way forever.

"We can't," I whispered. My hormones cried foul.

He leaned forward and kissed me on the side of my face, his lips dangerously close to mine. I sighed. Why couldn't I just take the next step?

"Let me know when we can," he said, easing away.

I leaned back, trying to put even more distance between us. My body felt tight, and need was making my head a little foggy. "I will."

"I would tell you to take your gun, but..." He trailed off, a smile playing on his mouth. His sexy damn mouth.

I narrowed my eyes. "But I don't know how to use it, so it's better I leave it. Is that what you were going to say?" I tried to put some heat in my tone, but it came out breathy instead. This man really did fuck with my head.

He laughed, his body shaking, and I fought the sudden urge to rip my tank top off and straddle him at the feel of him pressing into me. Boy, that vision got hot really quick.

"Kara's coming so she can act as my gun."

"You forget I witnessed just what you could do when you're cornered." He glanced down between us. I remembered our attack and how I almost ripped a man's dick off.

"We're meeting with a group of women."

"Well, I'm sure you can improvise."

"I will not stoop to titty-twisting!" That was a lie. I would definitely twist the hell out of a bitch's titty if she tried to come for me.

His laughter filled the car. He cupped the back of my head. "We need to work on your magick again soon. I'm not happy Petronela didn't train you."

"Did she say why?" I asked, shifting.

Alek grinned. "Stop that. And no. But when I bring her Unrie, she promised to have someone else help you."

He studied me for a minute, his eyes roaming all over my face. He did that sometimes, and it made me think, despite my protective mark preventing magick attacks against me, he was trying to find a way inside my head. Especially since I refused to open up to him, no matter how many times he tried.

"What are you thinking?" he asked, his voice barely a whisper. I looked away, and he gently turned my head back to him. "Haven't we moved past this?"

"I don't know. I want to." We weren't talking about Petronela anymore. The intensity of his gaze was scaring the hell out of me. "Is Devlin going with you?" I moved off his lap and tried to ignore the impressive evidence of his desire.

He was silent for a minute. I could feel his gaze on my back. But I refused to turn around. "No," he said. "I won't be long." He reached over and squeezed my hand. "I'll see you tonight?"

I nodded. "Be safe," I said and got out of the car.

He winked as I shut the car door. After a brief hesitation, he drove away. It was getting really damn hard to resist Alek. Really damn hard.

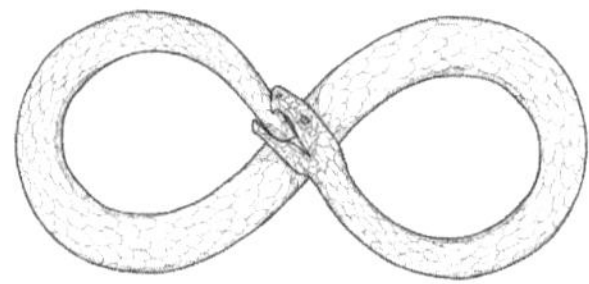

After a quick shower, I stood in Alek's room and surveyed my now—washed and folded—clothes. Rachel had done laundry. While I appreciated the gesture, it felt a little strange to let someone else wash my underwear. She even ironed my tank tops and shorts. I picked up my short, pale blue sundress. It was the closest garment I had to white. And it also said I didn't care about modesty. So, just a subtle middle finger. Should work just fine.

My hair was a problem. No amount of gel was going to tame the wild curls sticking out all over my head. Well, the amount I had, anyway. A ponytail was out of the question. I didn't have a headband, and I wasn't wearing a hat. Wild and free, it was.

A knock on the front door sounded, and I stepped into the hall and rushed to answer it. Kara stood on the porch, her copy of *The Wisdom of Boyd* tucked under her arm, wearing a white dress.

"Seriously, Kara?"

She stepped inside and looked at my outfit. "I should be asking you the same thing."

I shrugged. "It's all I have."

"I wish I could go," Rachel said, coming into the room. "Better for me to watch your back."

"I don't think they will attack us," I said, not completely sure. We all knew it could be a trap, and if it were, they would outnumber us. But sadly, it was a risk we had to take.

Devlin came in the room and handed me a switch blade. "Here. Leave the gun and keep this with you."

"And where am I supposed to stick it?" I looked down at myself. When I glanced up, Devlin gave me a look so loaded, I thought he might have had a stroke. His eye twitched. Dammit. I managed to push his buttons again. But how?

"I saw a fourteen-year-old girl take down a guy today with a knife just like that. You mean to tell me you don't know what to do with a knife?" he asked, his eye now jumping. That wasn't what I asked but apparently it was what he heard.

I got in his face. "We need to talk," I said, and left the room, trusting he would follow. I stepped into the empty bedroom and waited. A few minutes later, the door slammed, and I tried not to flinch, then wheeled around and faced Devlin. "Why are you so angry with me?"

Devlin stared at me for a while, his gaze going slightly distant. Finally, he leaned back against the wall and closed his eyes. "I didn't want you working with us."

"Well, fuck. I can just—"

He lifted his hand. "Hear me out." His eyes searched mine. "Please."

It was the 'please' that did it. Otherwise, I would have run out of there.

"I didn't start that off right. So, I apologize." I crossed my arms over my chest and waited. He blew out a frustrated breath and continued, "I'm sure you know by now I have trust issues.

You were…" He trailed off and gave me a half smile. "Wild." His eyes danced with laughter. I fought against the pull of that merriment. I knew what he was saying. But his revelation still stung a little. "But also, damn observant. Rachel convinced me you would be a great addition to the team." He shook his head and closed his eyes. "I'm rambling. I know." He opened his eyes and stared at me. "Rachel was right. You are a good addition to the team. In more ways than one. But…"

My heart felt heavy in my chest. He was putting his cards on the table, and he didn't know just how much I needed that right now.

"I'm afraid I can't keep you safe," he said finally. "No matter how much I want to. Seeing you out on that field." He shook his head. "The entire team was distraught. Alek stopped talking and eating until you woke up. Hell, we had to force him to take a damn shower." He stepped away, his movements jerky. "The one time we've fought together, and you ended up with your insides practically spread out all over the place."

"Shit." I moved toward him. "I'm sorry. I thought you were just…I don't know." I looked away. "Why don't you stay in here instead of the living room?"

"Stop trying to change the subject."

I nodded and turned back to him. "I don't know what to say, Devlin. I'm trying." I sat down heavily on the floor. My eyes brimmed with unshed tears. "This is not what I expected to be doing with my life. But at the same time, it's what I should be doing." I looked up at him. "If that makes sense."

He stared down at me. "It does." His gaze went distant. "I always wanted to work in law enforcement. Turns out, that's not where I belonged either." He crouched in front of me. "The thing is, we learn to adapt and improve. Your power… It worries me. And your stubbornness grates on my nerves. I will never give you another gun to use because you might shoot one of us. And so, that leaves the knife."

I opened my hand and stared at the knife—encased in black

metal. "I'll need to learn how to use it." It felt pretty good in my hand—almost like it belonged.

"I'll train you."

I shoved it down between my breasts.

"Looks like you found a place to stick it."

I laughed. Devlin making jokes was such a rarity. "I don't want to flash you, so you'll have to help me up."

He extended his hand, and I grabbed it. "It's too late for that."

"Oh, well." I gave him a teasing grin. "Lady-like was never in my vocabulary."

I started for the door, then stopped. He had put his cards on the table. I needed to give him something. "I'm scared, too, Devlin." I turned and looked at him. "When Gerald accused us of having the Ark, it was the first time someone had ever rendered me speechless. Like I couldn't form a single thought or question if my life depended on it."

"Wish I could have seen it."

"Ah, two jokes in a row. What will the others think, Boss Man?"

He smiled and moved forward. "I know the burden I have placed on you. That, too, keeps me up at night." He glanced around the room. "I can't sleep in here because the minute I relax —the minute I let my guard down—that's when I know they'll come for us." He dipped his head toward the wall that connected to the living room. "Out there, I can see it coming. Stop it before it reaches any of my people."

I placed my hand on his arm. "I give you my word. I will fight like crazy to make sure no harm comes to any of you. Ever. I will not be a burden to you."

He nodded. I took a minute to collect myself, then followed him out of the room.

Everyone had moved to the war room. When we walked in, Kara and Jonah jerked their attention away from each other and looked at us. How cute. They were giving each other heated glances.

"What did we miss?" I asked, smiling at Kara. She refused to look at me.

"Jonah and Kara want to sleep together. The room has filled up with their lustful pheromones," Rachel said, staring at us. She shrugged. "We all went over what we could find. It's not much, Dev. And I still think it's a trap."

Humor danced in Jonah's eyes while Kara turned red.

And I didn't know which part of what she just said to react to first. Okay, I did. But that wouldn't be productive. Instead, I focused on the mission. Mission. Like we were going to battle. Damn. Now that I'd put it out there, things were bound to devolve into madness. And of course, the first thought that popped into my head just had to be, 'Would I end up having to twist someone's titties?' Maybe I should have focused on Jonah and Kara's desire to sleep with each other.

Jonah cleared his throat. "Gavina will try to break you down," he said. "Try to get in your head and use any emotional weakness you have." He looked at me. "You're in a fragile state right now; she will be able to sense it." He lifted a hand when I opened my mouth. "You can also use it to your advantage. Tell her some things but leave out the most important information."

"So, feed them a line of bullshit," I said. "And I'm not fragile." All eyes focused on me. I flipped them off and continued, "What do you suggest I say?" I left off the sarcastic remark hovering on the tip of my tongue.

Jonah stared at me. "What part of *fragile state* bothered you the most?"

Okay, maybe I had let my tone slip. I pulled in a calming breath. Perhaps I was in a fragile, hostile state. "So, tell them a mean bastard left me, but don't tell them he was a serial killer, and I want to kill him."

Devlin nodded. "Exactly. You okay to do this?"

I stared at him. "Not really. But we all have to do our part. My part is to walk into a women's empowerment group and hope they don't convince me to join the movement." I patted my chest. "I have a secret weapon, though. So, we should be good."

"You're planning on flashing them?" Kara struggled to keep from laughing. "You think that might work?"

"Oh, fuck you. Devlin gave me a knife, and it was the only place I could stick it." I turned away from them. "Shit. I'll just shut up now." I started for the front room and ignored the laughter that followed me.

I stepped into the warm air and waited. A few seconds later, Kara came out, smile still plastered on her face, and put her arm around me. "Have I told you lately just how much I love and appreciate you?"

I swiveled my head toward her. "I will cut you with my new knife."

"Dev said I should go and wait outside for you," Rachel said, walking out onto the porch. "I don't trust them. Might need to go in and fight." The light in her eyes, and the superhero belt clutched in her hands, screamed she hoped she would get to go inside and start a fight.

"I need one of those," I said, dipping my head toward her belt.

She smiled. "I'll make you one."

She stepped off the porch, and we followed. Damn. Well, I guess she was coming with us. Now, all I had to worry about was keeping her from coming inside. 'Cause if she did, the night would dissolve into madness, and everyone would end up dead.

Maybe that wasn't such a bad idea.

The 'oh shit' handle shook in my hand, and I was seriously questioning my decision to let Kara drive us to the gathering. Her quest to get us there on time had her pushing her little Honda Civic to the point where I feared the compact car might rattle apart, leaving us stranded in the dark in the middle of the highway.

"Hold on," she announced as she took the next turn, tires smoking.

"Are your trying to break the speed of sound?" I asked, hand throbbing as I gripped the handle.

She shook her head, tsking at me. "And here I thought you didn't like being late."

"This is fun!" Rachel announced from the back seat.

"Okay," I said, eyes glued to the windshield. It was probably wise not to distract her.

While the majority of Tulare's wealthy elite lived in Dulean, some had separated themselves completely and carved out space in the crevices of the small hills in the island's center, creating a sort of commune-type environment. The only access to the community was off the highway that circled the entire island.

Kara slowed down when we reached the *East Gate Estates* brick and wooden sign, illuminated by five ground floodlights. She navigated her car around the steep curve; her headlights barely pushing back the darkness.

"These rich assholes couldn't afford lights for the road?" Rachel asked. She sat in the backseat, most likely feeling very proud of herself for convincing us we should let her come inside with us.

I believe Devlin had something to do with her dogged determination. However, I couldn't prove it. And I wasn't about to accuse her of plotting with him either. The talk Devlin and I had earlier had me rethinking my behavior. Wondering if I should work on how I responded to his wanting to keep me safe.

"They don't want to give people the impression they're welcome," Kara said.

Hard to argue with that. After all, the residents could have easily created an entrance on the other side of the hills, giving them access from Legare Street, which ran alongside the man-made lake in Dulean.

And the lack of light along the road screamed, '*fuck off*'. Like, '*We hope you crash your car in the steep ditch you won't see coming.*'

I rested my head against the seat and stared out at the darkness —trying to order my thoughts. I really hated having to go to this gathering in the first place. But if it meant not having to attend their church services next Sunday and listen to Boyd wax on about being a chosen vessel full of wisdom, then I'd gladly go to a few of their meetings.

My stomach dropped when Kara took the next turn too fast.

"Ha!" Rachel barked. "We almost drove off the road!"

I was glad she found humor in it. I was still trying to unclench my hand from the 'oh shit' handle.

"Sorry about that," Kara said, slowing down.

"Maybe we should walk the rest of the way," I suggested.

"Shut up, Nicole," Kara said.

"Okay."

A mile in, we came to a sign that read, *Hollingsworth Manor*. Kara made the sharp turn onto the gravel path and, thankfully, drove slowly up the incline. Large cypress trees stood on either side of the pathway. Their dark silhouettes seemed to close in on us. Kara finally switched on her high-beams and slowed the car down even more.

"I can barely see out here," she said, her voice a mere whisper.

"Should we turn around?" I asked hesitantly.

Kara shook her head. "No, we've come this far." There was a note of curiosity in her voice that matched my own feelings. Why would they build their home so far off the beaten path?

A short while later, a blaze of brightness filled the car. We all gasped as we took in the large mansion bathed in a beacon of light. I thought their church was a dedication to the gods. But looking at their home, the church paled in comparison.

The architect had obviously used some of the church's design. Roman columns encased a large porch covered with clay pots that were filled with every flower and plant one could imagine. Windows you could walk through sat on either side of two Mahogany doors that currently stood open with torch stands erected on both sides. Two men wearing loin clothes and elaborate gold and white masks stood on either side, holding flutes filled with red liquid.

An apple tree rested in the yard, surrounded by a group of women wearing white sleeveless garments that hung off their shoulders. They wore their hair down, with bands of decorative metal covering their heads. It would seem the Young family had a fascination with Greek customs. It made me wonder about the next family we investigated. Would they be obsessed with Roman culture? Would we have to infiltrate a bath house filled with naked men? I smiled. That would be a sight to see.

Kara parked near the other cars lining the large driveway.

"I'm going to stand out." I climbed out the car. I glanced at Rachel, just now noticing she was wearing a white skirt and cream blouse. "Well played, Rachel. Well played." It had been her plan all along to come with us. Or should I say Devlin's plan. I couldn't be mad, though; I knew he was worried about me.

She smiled and lifted her skirt, showing me her favorite pair of brass knuckles strapped to her thigh in a special leather holder.

"Just in case." I contemplated the many ways they could end up forcing Rachel to use her brass knuckles. And the many ways I might be goaded into yanking the knife from between my breasts, pulling the blade out, and stabbing someone. But if they had a gun, by the time I completed those steps, I'd be shot.

If any of them had a gun, I'd just brought a knife to a gun fight. Damn, I couldn't get any stupider if I tried.

Kara joined us at the passenger side door. "They have an apple tree in the yard," she said.

"Yes. Their very own Garden of Eden." It looked like one. All that was missing was a massive snake wrapped around the tree trunk.

As we took in the gardens, warmth settled over me.

I glanced over at Kara. While her face held a hint of skepticism, her eyes were alight with interest. Rachel had crossed her arms and stood staring with a smirk on her face and admiration in her eyes.

"Is there magick on the grounds?" I asked them.

Rachel pointed at the shrubbery. "They covered the bushes in the spell. A mage must be feeding magick into them. It's the only way the spell would remain active."

I followed her line of sight and found a mix of catnip and lemon balm. Combined, the two plants gave off a powerful fragrance that would induce calm. But with magick, the effect would be amplified. No wonder I felt like my legs would give way at any moment.

"How can you see a spell?" I asked, curious.

"You look at it the same way you would a person's aura," Rachel said.

I focused on the plants and let my vision go distant.

A shimmery, gauze-like mist blinked into existence, and I could just make out the faint pattern of color that coated everything. It looked like a hazy film had been draped across the lawn. Not a rainbow of colors, more a concentration of gold and red and a bronze-like color.

"Most of the women lounging on the grass are mages," Kara said.

"They also look on the verge of stripping down," I said, staring at them. A few of the women had leaned back, letting the legs fall open—their dresses sliding down their thighs.

"Maybe there is too much magick."

I tipped my head toward the men standing at the double doors. "Or they've been sampling the contents in those glasses."

We all chuckled.

"Hello," a familiar voice called. I turned and found Juliette striding toward us. She, too, had on one of the long dresses the other women were wearing.

Kara looked at me. "They're wearing Peplos. And the metal crowns on their head are called Stephane."

"Oh," I said.

Juliette stopped in front of us and smiled. When I saw her earlier in the day, she had worn no makeup. Now, she wore dark eyeliner around her eyes and dark red lipstick. Gold shadow covered her eyelids, and a dusting of it was on her cheeks as well.

"I'm so glad you're here." She sucked in a deep breath. "I was worried I hadn't convinced you to come." She looked at Rachel and Kara. "I'm glad you could join us as well."

Kara and Rachel smiled at her.

Convinced me to come? I turned away to hide my suspicion.

"I was just telling my friends this place looks like your own little Garden of Eden." I forced a smile. I needed to show interest.

Juliette nodded and looked over at the garden again. "Gavina wanted the place to be one of peace. We even make our own wine. Nectar of the Gods," she said, turning back to us. "You will sample it tonight, and if you like it, you can purchase a bottle or two."

We already paid for that useless book at their church—there was no way in hell we were buying the wine, too.

"Is there a spell on the plants?" Kara asked, cutting off my reply.

"It's a calming spell," she said, rubbing her bare arms. "Most of the girls who come to us are scared and confused. Some are even a little lost. Gavina's daughter, Salome, laid the spell over the plants to help calm them."

Juliette looked at her watch. "We should head in. The gathering will begin shortly." She linked her arm in mine as if she was afraid, I would suddenly decide to run away.

I'll admit, I was entertained by the idea. Especially if they expected me to purchase some of their wine. Please tell me we weren't walking into a Greek themed multi-level marketing scheme where we all got our own case of wine, dressed in Peplos and Stephane, and sent out to sell enough to reach the top of the pyramid.

I would cut the first woman who even suggested it.

We passed the two sculpted males and stepped into the foyer. Between two twin staircases sat an enormous fountain with a marble statue of a naked woman in the middle, holding a golden apple in one hand and a scroll in the other. Water cascaded down between her breasts, curving around her leg to fall into a pool of water. I circled the statue and found gold glyphs lining the spine of her back. Before I could take my phone out and snap a picture, Juliette came over, carrying a flute of wine.

"No, thank you," I said.

"It's just wine." Juliette signaled behind her. "Your friends are drinking it."

She said that as if I should follow their lead, but even as a teenager, I always did my own thing—which, honestly, was worse.

"Dammit." I grabbed the glass from her and threw back the contents in one large gulp. "What the hell?" I asked as the world shifted. "You said it was..." My words faded as I tried to maintain my balance. My skin flushed and a warmth settled over me again. Only, this one felt...heated. Sexual. My clothes felt as if they were on fire, and I needed to take them off.

"Oh, that was too sweet for even me." Kara joined us. "I'm

surprised you drank it, Nicole," she slurred. She moaned, dropped forward, and put her head between her knees.

My vision blurred. Bursts of light popped off around her. The phoenix wings unfurled inside my head. I stared at the glass on the floor.

She said there was no magick in it. So why was my mark suddenly waking up?

I glanced over at Rachel, who was studying the glass intently. She looked at me and Kara with alarm. Then, she rounded on Juliette. "What did you do to my friends?" she yelled; her voice raked across my skin.

Juliette's eyes rounded and her arms went up as if she were warding off an attack. "Nothing. I swear. Maybe the wine is too potent for them," she said in a rush.

Rachel helped Kara stand. "We should leave," she said to us. I shook my head, clearing the last dregs of the wine's effect. The phoenix wings settled. My protective mark was beginning to confuse me. Just like with the heat wave, it had only reacted once. Like it was responding to, not an attack, but my thoughts of being attacked. Could I control it?

"Nicole," Kara said, her tone even. "Are you sure you're okay?"

I closed my eyes and nodded. "Yeah. Maybe it was just a sugar rush." I glanced at Rachel. "How come you didn't react?"

"Hello," someone said behind us before she could respond. I turned to find Gavina standing behind me. She placed a hand on my back and leaned in. "Are you all right?"

"Yeah." I fought the urge to knock her hand off me. "The wine is just too sugary for my taste."

"I'm sorry about that. It is a dessert wine, after all. But it does take some getting used to." She looked behind me. "And who are these lovely ladies?"

Kara stepped forward. "I'm Kara." She extended her hand, and Gavina reached out and shook it. "I attended your church service this past Sunday."

"Yes, I remember. You're welcome, of course." She smiled at Rachel. "And you? I don't recall seeing you at our service."

"I'm here to learn," Rachel said, her voice flat.

Gavina gave us a loaded look. The smile she wore suggested she wanted us to feel welcome, but the look in her eyes screamed *predator*. She turned and motioned to her daughter. "This is my daughter, Salome. She's here to make sure our guests are comfortable."

Salome smiled at us. "It's nice to meet all of you." She glanced down at our clothes. "If you like, I can provide you with some garments to change into." It wasn't a question. Nor was it meant as an innocent suggestion.

"We would be more comfortable in our own clothes, if you don't mind," I said, adding just a tad of saccharine to my voice.

She gazed at me out of scorn-filled eyes. "Of course. Whatever works for you." She stepped into my space and let her eyes travel down my body slowly. "If you change your mind"—she met my eyes—"please let me know."

Gavina touched her lightly on the back. "If you will excuse us, we must change for the gathering. While it's okay if you decide to stay in your current attire, I will ask if you at least let us provide you with masks." Again, it wasn't a question.

I would have said no, but I didn't want to make waves.

"That will be fine," Kara said for us.

"I'll get them." Juliette rushed toward a room on the left. She returned moments later and handed each of us one. Made of a strong thick plastic like material, the entire half-mask was painted an ivory color with gray tones underneath. Gold glitter covered the black-lined eyes and cheeks. Almost identical to the way Juliette had painted her face.

We slid them on and followed Juliette into the next room.

Soft music played in the background. Gold glyphs and depictions of nude Greek women in robes holding jugs, walking, lounging, and bathing covered the white walls. Overly large gold, red, and bronze pillows lay on Persian rugs with gold trays filled with fruit and various cheeses. The patio glass doors opened to the night sky, letting in a warm breeze filled with a sickly-sweet scent.

Women lay across the pillows, their shoulders now bare. They had removed their clothes. All of them were chatting, eating, and drinking more wine. Gazes turned our way—a few of them filled with heat and longing. One woman watched me out of hooded eyes as she slid her Peplos up her thigh. It was the same woman I saw outside under the apple tree.

Given the description of The Daughters of the Vine being a women's empowerment movement, I expected a more homey, comforting environment with helpful quotes written on the walls. Bookshelves lined with self-help books. Women in both casual wear and business suits all congregating to uplift one another. Or, given the fact they made and sold wine, at least displays of their vintage.

But not this. This reminded me of the orgies depicted in old Greek mythology paintings where men and women gathered to celebrate in excess. Yet, there were only two men here, and they appeared to be more decoration than anything.

I glanced at Kara and Rachel. "My alarm bells are going off," I whispered.

Kara scanned the room, taking everything in. "As long as they don't expect us to join them, we should be fine." She looked at me. "Besides, you do have a knife shoved down between your breasts. You can pull it out if things get out of hand."

"Sarcasm is my thing, not yours," I said, eyes narrowing as I gave her a half smile. I appreciated the distraction because my flight or fight response had kicked in. "And I don't think these women would mind me pulling the blade from between my breasts."

"It's a good tactic," Rachel said. "They will be too focused on your breasts to see the knife." She patted her leg. "And my legs."

We all shared a chuckle before sitting down on the pillows closest to the exit.

The enchantment on the grounds, the sweet wine I drank, and now the extremely comfortable pillows. And I could smell a rich herbal scent in the air. Everything had been engineered to coax us into letting our guard down.

Rachel picked up a piece of cheese from one of the fruit trays in front of us and studied it.

"I wouldn't if I were you," I said, laying back. So many fairy-tales warned against eating the food. Sadly, I'd already drunk the liquid.

"You think it's poisoned?" Kara asked.

I glanced at Rachel. She had checked the alcohol Ronald kept sending. "Can you test it?" I asked Rachel. I should have asked her to test the wine, too.

She continued to study the cheese, finally popping a piece into her mouth. "There's no magick coming off it."

"Did the wine have any?" I asked.

She started to shake her head no, then stopped. "Didn't seem like it. But you and Kara both reacted to it. I would have to test it."

Which meant we were going to have to buy some damn wine.

Gavina walked into the room, wearing a white robe with gold embroidery on the front. A large hood hung down the back. When she passed by, filling the air with a heavy floral scent, I noticed her robe was opened down the front, allowing us to glimpse her nakedness underneath.

Oh, hell no. I started to get up. Kara placed a hand on my arm, drawing my attention to her. She shook her head and whispered, "Wait."

Wait for what? Everyone to be given a robe and told to strip down? No, not going to happen. She jerked her head toward the door. Gavina's girls stood in front of the door wearing the same robe their mother wore. Each of them had on a mask.

"Daughters of the Vine," Gavina started. The women moaned. I risked a look and saw the woman who had been flirting with me earlier was now completely naked. This gathering had gone from zero to a hundred in mere minutes.

We had to get out of here.

"You do not have to hide who you are here." She let her robe fall to the ground.

The two men who were at the door when we came in started circulating, handing out gold goblets filled with wine. When I refused to take one, he set it down beside me and moved on. I was not drinking any more of that shit. Gavina took a glass, slowly brought the goblet to her mouth, and leaned back, letting the liquid drain into her mouth and down her breast, following the same path as the water flowing down the statue in the foyer.

A gray light pulsed around her. She lifted her head and her gaze locked with mine. "Drink," she said, her whisper carrying to me. "Become whole with us."

My eyes grew heavy, and my heart fluttered in my chest. But my protective mark remained silent. How was she affecting me? Before I knew it, I had put my hand on the goblet, letting the warmth sink into my skin.

Kara placed her hand on my arm, pulling my gaze away from Gavina. She stared at me, willing me to snap out of it. "Fight her," she said. I nodded and turned away. I didn't want her to see how close I had come to raising that goblet to my mouth.

The woman eyeing me earlier knelt in front of me. On full display. Her aura, a bright green. Earth mage. "You have so much power," she whispered. "It's beautiful to see."

Rachel moved toward me. I stopped her with my hand. If I was honest, there was no real threat here. And if we were going to find out if Gavina was using blood magick, we needed to hold out as long as possible. Show interest in their activities to a point. But I did draw the line at participating in what was turning out to look like one big orgy.

Jonah's words flitted through my head.

"Sex has always been used in cults... It's the best way to control someone's mind, body, and soul."

The woman lifted the goblet and moved it slowly toward my face. "The grapes we use are grown with magick, which gives them the added sugar. But I assure you, it is harmless." Her voice was a mere whisper. Again, the urge to drink overwhelmed me. She placed a soft finger on my chin, and I froze.

I've had women flirt with me before. I never minded. If I had been attracted to them, I might have even slept with a few. I was never a prude when it came to sex. Yes, I had sworn it off recently but that was because I learned I had an unhealthy view of relationships. The need was there. Always. Especially when I was around Alek. My keeping him at a distance had more to do with the mounting feelings I had for him than anything else, because believe me...I wanted to rip that man's damn clothes off.

But as I sat there, motionless, staring at this gorgeous, naked woman, a strange longing overcame me. A bone-deep ache consumed every fiber of my being. And I had to fight the desire to touch her.

She gave me a questioning look as she held the glass near my lips. I gave her the smallest nod of consent. She tipped the goblet, and I opened my mouth, allowing the too-sweet nectar to coat my tongue.

"Nicole," Kara said, her voice seeming to come from far away.

The woman urged my chin up and poured the rest of the liquid down my throat.

Once again, my vision wavered. I fought the surge of convulsions making their way down my body. A moan escaped my lips. The woman lay me back against the pillows, and it was then I noticed that two women stood in front of Kara and Rachel, doing the same thing. Kara lay back against the pillow, her body shaking as she ran her hand down herself. Rachel lay motionless, staring up at the woman in front of her.

I assumed when Kara had called my name, it was to pull me out of the haze. But it wasn't. She was trying to get my attention. That thought circled in my head as I rode the sensual high of the wine and writhed on the pillow, trying to ease the ache inside of me.

Gavina knelt in front of me, her perfumed body sending chills along my arms. The woman stepped away, having completed her task. "Monique is right," Gavina said, her voice soothing. "You have so much power in you." Her hand cupped the back of my neck. She pulled me toward her, until we were mere millimeters away from each other, our lips almost touching.

"What I wouldn't do to get a glimpse of that power," she said, her sickly, sweet breath blowing over my face. She pressed her warm lips to my cheek. I shuddered at the contact.

After setting me back down, she moved away. I turned my head and watched her as she stopped at each of the now-naked women and ran her hands over them. Petting them. They writhed under her touch.

Rachel came into view. She stared down at me, her eyes imploring. "Do you want to get out of here?" she asked in a whisper.

I nodded as tears streamed down my face. Sad thing was the tears weren't because of what Monique or Gavina did. It was because I wanted so badly to give in to them.

I reached out and grabbed Kara's hand. She squeezed mine in return. She, too, must have been riding a high. So, why wasn't Rachel?

"We were once called Maenads. Followers of Dionysus. The only god who we will give ourselves to freely," Gavina said, returning to her chair. "Our bodies are temples. And when we give to another, they receive a blessing. That is what I give all of you tonight and forever. My eternal blessing. There will be no shame in this room. No need to hide our desires." Juliette walked out of a room behind Gavina's chair and joined Gavina on the dais. "Drink. Eat. And make love," she said, and pulled Juliette into her arms.

I turned away.

Kara leaned over. "Maenads are created by sending women into a wine and sex-induced frenzy," she said.

I nodded, letting the knowledge slide over me. I knew the stories about Maenads. Even worried that the women at Jordin's had become the famed women of excess. But the way the girls responded to Gavina, made me wonder if she too could create them. "Are you okay?"

She blew out a breath laced with wine. "I need to get out of here. Or..." She trailed off as she stared across the room at the woman who had given her wine. The heated look in her eyes told me what she was going to say. Because when I made eye contact with Monique, I felt the same way. She stared back at me with a questioning look in her eye. All I had to do was signal that I was willing, and I knew she would be across the room in seconds.

Thankfully, a small part of my brain was functioning enough for me to realize it wasn't a good idea. I stood up on shaky legs and smoothed down my dress. Kara stood as well. No one rushed to stop us, which made me wonder why they had plied us with wine in the first place. If the idea was to put us in the mood, they had succeeded. Now, except for the lustful looks from Monique, no one paid us any attention. They carried on as if we weren't even there. I was missing something. Something important. I just couldn't figure out what.

What I did know was there was no blood magick here—only sex and wine. And women, who wanted the freedom to engage in sexual activity that some would consider taboo. And yes, also pass judgment. But why did they need the calming spell and the wine that, I was positive, was laced with something other than excessive sugar? Monique said the grapes were magick-infused. Could that have been it? Was that the reason my mark stirred?

Gavina had mentioned Dionysus. The god of wine, insanity, and ritual madness. That yes, led to the creation of Maenads. Maybe that was what we were looking at: Maenads, acting out what they had been driven to do.

I rubbed my head, trying to ward off the brewing headache. I wasn't going to figure this out tonight. Not in this state. So, I followed Rachel and Kara out of the room.

As we stepped out into the warm evening air, I thought about the god Dionysus. All myths derived from a kernel of truth. Each civilization borrows the religious beliefs from the ones that came before them. Before they worshiped Dionysus in Greece, another god had been revered as the god of wine, insanity, and ritual madness.

The Egyptian god Shezmu.

Which meant, The Daughters of the Vine were worshiping Jordin Cisco.

We rode home in silence, each of us too consumed with our own thoughts. Rachel, surprisingly, had managed to get a bottle of the wine to test while we sat on the grass trying to fight off the residual effects of the wine. As it turned out, the herbs in the air had played a part in our reaction as well.

A short time later, Kara pulled up to Devlin's and parked behind my car and turned off the engine. She sat there for a moment, staring out at the street. "I have never been so confused in my life," she said. "I'm trying to drum up some outrage or anger. But all I keep feeling is deep-down longing." She turned to me her green eyes filled with tears. "What should I be feeling?"

I shook my head. I didn't have the answer.

"I can give you something," Rachel said. "It should help."

"No. I'll be fine. Just need to take a cold shower and hold my cat." I took her hand in mine. She squeezed it. "I'm fine. Seriously. Just need to get my bearings."

"Well, at least we learned they weren't practicing blood magick," I offered.

Kara harrumphed. "Yeah. They're just plying themselves with wine and having sex. Oh!" She snapped her finger. "And worshipping Jordin Cisco." She turned to me. "How do you feel about that?"

"I want to say I don't blame them. But like you, I'm having a hard time wrapping my mind around how I should be feeling right now." I ran my fingers through my hair, yanking at the ends. "I need air." I shoved open the door and got out of the car. After a beat, they joined me. "You know, Gavina is no different than her husband," I said after a while. "Both of them are full of shit."

"Yeah," Rachel started. "That definitely wasn't a women's empowerment group." She shook her head. "She hurt you both, and I should have done something about it," she said, her voice filled with regret.

"Not your fault, Rachel. I had the option to get up and leave. Hell, Monique even asked if she could pour wine down my throat. It was just..." I trailed off.

"Too enticing to leave," Kara offered. "Like the calming spell on the grounds. You just felt at ease and..." She pushed off the car. "I should go. Maybe I'll have some clarity in the morning. And if I feel as if they violated us, I'll pick you both up and we will go over there and beat the ever-loving S out of Gavina and her daughters."

"Yes!" Rachel pulled out her brass knuckles. "I get to use these."

I yanked out my knife. "And I get to use this."

We all shared a humorless laugh and said goodnight to Kara. When she drove away, Rachel turned to me. "Tell me. Truthfully. Are you okay?"

I smiled at her. "Yes, Rachel. Just need a few minutes to myself." I pointed at the front door. "Go on in. I'm sure Devlin is up pacing the floor, waiting for us to report on what happened. I will be in in a minute." I lied. I had no intention of going inside. I knew that if I did, I wouldn't be able to hide the confusion and turmoil storming inside of me.

Alek had started asking me about my past recently, always looking for ways to make me talk about how I felt. To distract him, I'd flirt. But he never took the bait. Finally, I'd try to make him laugh. He'd smile, but his steady, dark blue, watchful gaze would never leave my face, and I knew he was waiting for me to stop being silly and just open up. But after a while, he would laugh, then he'd take my face in his hands and whisper, "One day."

After our song and dance, once we were laying in the bed in his room, he'd pull me close and just hold me. Tonight, I didn't have the strength to go through that now familiar routine. My fear and pain were too close to the surface, and if he asked, I would tell him.

I wasn't ready for that.

Rachel stood there. Studying me. Looking for the truth in my words. I kept my face blank. Even offered her a brief smile. Finally, she gave me a quick hug and went inside. I stood there for a while, studying the front door. I knew I should go inside. But I wasn't in a good place and in no mood to face them right now. So, I climbed in my car and went to see the one person who I knew wouldn't look beyond the surface. The person who I needed in that moment to help me understand just what the hell was going on.

Shezmu—Jordin Cisco.

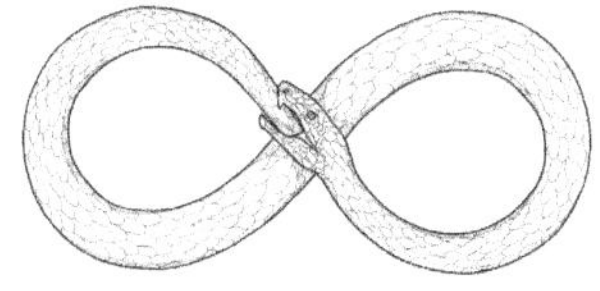

THE SIGN at Jordin Cisco's still hadn't been fixed. Dino's flashed red, while the remaining letters were blacked out. I don't know why I expected the sign to be repaired. After all, in the years I had frequented the place, it had never worked correctly, so why did I suddenly expect it to now? Maybe the knowledge of Jordin being an Old One had something to do with it. Or the fact that I'd just left a cult gathering dedicated to worshipping him. It was as if I had this secret knowledge that should somehow cast the establishment in a new light.

But what did that have to do with his sign? I stared at it, trying to find the ominous undertones. I came up with nothing.

"Fuck it," I said and made my way to the building.

Smoke billowed out when I pulled open the door. The familiar scents of cooked meat and cigarette smoke rushed at me, and I sighed. I stood in the doorway, letting the nostalgia wash over me. So many of mine and Kara's Friday nights were spent here being our silly selves. And damn I missed the juicy burgers, pile of crispy fries, and Samuel Adams.

The song on the jukebox skipped, but no one rushed to change it. I wondered how long it had been doing that.

I took in the harem of women that sat camped out at the bar. Had he driven them to madness? I thought about my obsession with him in the past. Had he driven me to the same frenzied state?

My gaze landed on Jordin. He stood behind the bar with his hair tied and tapered at the back of his neck. A neck I used to bite when we had sex. His white sleeveless shirt stood out against his bronze skin. I could still smell the scent of his skin and the feel of him inside of me.

He looked up as if sensing someone was watching him. A slow smile spread across his face. My stomach twisted in knots, thinking of all the ways he used to make love to me.

The dangers of sinking into the familiar and wanting to latch on to my old life reared its head when Jordin smiled. I could easily forget that he was an Old One—a powerful being who'd made a pact to kill or protect me. I could easily allow him to lead me to his apartment around back and forget that my life was now filled with magick and blood.

I shouldn't have come here.

So many things about my past I wasn't ready to face. But I had to. And confronting Jordin was the easiest right now. Besides, he wouldn't ask questions. He didn't care about me enough to be concerned about my wellbeing. If he had been, he would have called.

I swallowed the fear and worry and returned his smile.

He came around the bar, his stride pushing a memory of us in bed together to the forefront of my mind. I tried to shove the image down, but it stayed there, playing in real color. My skin flushed and need filled me to the point of discomfort.

Again, I shouldn't have come here.

He leaned down and kissed me on the lips. "Where have you been?" A groan escaped me as he nuzzled my neck.

My hand came up slowly, fighting through the weight of emotions and confusion consuming me. "Don't," I barely whispered. The music seemed to grow louder; that constant skipping was like daggers against my ears. I closed my eyes to the onslaught of too much sensory overload. "Just don't. I know you're an Old One. I know you were sworn to either protect or kill me." I pushed him back, finally gaining the strength I needed. "So, which are you going to do?"

He stared down at me. His eyes roamed over me as if he were searching for something. A light gold sheen pulsed around him. I'd seen it before—the last time we were in bed together. I should have guessed at it then, connected the dots flashing in front of me, but I'd been too focused on forgetting what was going on in my life to really understand. If I'm honest, I'd always seen this gold sheen around him, especially when we were having sex.

"Let's talk outside." He took my elbow and ushered me out the back door.

When we stepped out into the warm night, it reminded me of us being in this very spot not so long ago. With me against the wall, and him between my legs, while rain pelted down on us. I pulled away from him. "I'm not going upstairs with you."

He moved closer, backing me against the wall. "Why?"

Was he serious? I just told him I knew he was an Old One and he wanted to fuck me? "Answer my question, dammit! Are you going to kill me?" Did I really just yell that as if I wanted him to slaughter me on the spot?

He leaned in close, his breath mixing with mine. "I think I've shown you what I want from you." He ran his finger down between my breasts. Need flowed through me like a tidal wave. "Do you want me to show you again?"

"No," I whispered. Thoughts of Alek holding me filled my head. His laughter at my silliness echoed inside of me. Guilt wormed its way through my heart. He'd asked me once if I trusted him. I told him yes. Now, here I stood, barely able to keep myself from letting Jordin take me. Alek and I had a bond that went beyond the physical. Of course, I would never admit that to him. I craved him in a way that scared the living hell out of me. I had from the start. From the moment I saw him leaning up against the table in Devlin's house watching me out of those dark blue eyes.

A puzzled look crossed Jordin's face. He wasn't used to women saying no. He moved in, his scent filled me, and a small tremor ran through my body. "Why?" he asked, his lips near my ear. "We are good together. You know that."

His breath was warm on my skin. I tried to step away but couldn't.

He ran his tongue over the ridge of my ear. "Tell me you want me, Nicole."

I didn't respond.

"Tell me!" he demanded.

"I want you," I breathed out.

My mind went blank as Jordin attacked my mouth. My arms came around him and I pulled him in even closer. His hand went to the hem of my dress, yanking it up between us. He wrapped my leg around him as he fumbled with his zipper.

When I heard the metal slide down, an image of Alek popped in my head. He was sitting next to my bed when I'd woken up from my coma a week after Set had attacked and almost killed me. He had looked worn, bruises marring his skin. The concern in his eyes when he looked at me was the moment I realized I needed to pull away from him. The moment I knew, given the chance, I'd fall in love with him.

Jordin's finger slid under the hem of my panties, pushing them to the side. "Stop," I said, guilt gnawing at me. "Just stop." His erection pushed at my core. Just one thrust, and he would be inside of me. I shoved him away. "I said stop!"

"Nicole." He stepped forward. I raised my hand to stop him. "I'm sorry. I thought you wanted this," he said, confusion etched across his face.

This was the second time tonight I'd been in this situation. I bit back the tears and asked, "Do you know there is a cult on Tulare that worships you?"

He smiled, and I wanted to scream. "There are cults all over the world that worship me."

"Including The Daughters of the Vine."

He harrumphed and looked away. "They don't want to worship me. They want my power."

"Can they take it?" I asked, curious. Nothing in what I'd learned about the Old Ones suggested someone could take their power. And the only power Gavina had been interested in was mine.

He turned back to me. "No. And I should have taken care of them a while ago. But..." He shook his head. The anger rolling off him made me take a step back. His eyes had gone completely black. All this time, I believed Jordin was just a man who loved sex. Now, after learning his true identity, it dawned on me just how close I'd come to death.

"You mean kill them?" I asked finally.

He stared at me. His eyes grew heated and sadly, yes, my body responded again. "Come inside with me." He stepped closer, leaning in. "You, I will give some of my power to freely."

"Have you done that before?" I asked, my voice a mere whisper.

He ran a finger down the side of my face. "Every time I slid inside of you; I gave you a piece of me. Some of my essence. Yes, my brothers and sister marked you. Mine was different."

A group of men cheered, pulling our attention to them. One of them fumbled with his pants as if to take a piss, and Jordin made a noise I didn't think was humanly possible. It sounded like thunder being shoved through a funnel made of wind. The men looked up, their faces filled with terror, before running away. I would have run too, but I needed answers.

"Despite not wanting to fight in their wars, I was good at it," Jordin said. "I knew what you were when you first walked in my bar. First time I bent you across my table, I had decided I would have to kill you. I am incapable of love. It's weakness. And I refuse to be weak."

He moved toward me. I pulled the knife from between my breasts and clicked open the blade. Jordin took my bladed hand and pressed the knife to his throat. "I can't die. For a while, that was a blessing. Now, it's a hinderance." He pushed until the blade bit into his skin. Gold liquid slid down his throat.

"Your blood is gold," I whispered.

"It's not blood. The next time we had sex, I climbed on top of you, inhaling your jasmine scent and put my hands around your neck. It would have been so easy to snap your neck. But my sister, Hathor, had laid a protection on you. I had missed it before." He paused, his eyes going distant. "It pulsed so brightly. I became curious. Why would she protect you when we were sworn to kill you? So, I woke you up and made love to you again and again. Until you lay limp in my arms." He pushed in further, his lips ran along my neck. "I can smell the need on you. Come upstairs. Let me fill you. Let me satisfy that need."

"You just told me you were going to kill me. Why would I come upstairs with you?" There was no conviction in my voice. Just longing. It would have been so easy to follow him. So easy to strip down right now and let him satisfy the need making me weak. I remembered that time he woke me up and we made love. So many times, I could barely walk. Another brush with death, only this time I wasn't high on drugs.

He placed his hand on my stomach. "I buried my mark deep inside of you."

"You tried to get me pregnant!" I yelled.

He shook his head. "I can't bear to watch any more children

grow old and die. No. The mark I gave you is power. One day, you might learn to tap into it. He kissed me lightly on the lips. "When you thirst for more, come back." He kissed me again, this time, his lips lingering. "And I will mark you again," he said against my lips.

Before I could respond, or gain some balance, he walked away.

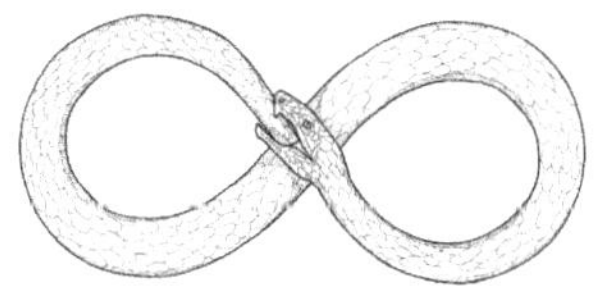

IF SOMEONE HAD TAKEN my life and reduced it down to bullet points, the list would consist of: sex, sabotage, alcohol, and denial. I lived with those things on repeat for most of my adult life. I'd convinced myself it didn't matter how many partners I'd been with and that I shouldn't worry about what others thought. I was having fun. Escaping into an activity that required no emotional input on my part. I had, as I've recently learned, been wrong.

There was an emotional impact. But I'd buried it along with the other shit I didn't want to deal with and instead used sex as a tool. It gave me, in those vigorous moments, a reprieve from the repeating admonishments going on inside my head, telling me I wasn't worthy of love. I never knew where that thought came from until the block on my memories was gone. The floodgates were open. And the knowledge of being violated when I was a child became a permanent fixture in my thoughts.

Tonight, I had struggled to understand why I couldn't feel rage at what happened at Gavina's. But now I knew, it was all part of my pattern. They had violated me. And I would have to acknowledge and deal with that soon.

But for now, staying true to my list, after leaving Jordin's and almost sabotaging the few steps I'd taken in the right direction with Alek, not to mention the possibility of destroying a relationship still in the making, I stopped at the liquor store around the corner from my house and bought a bottle of Captain Morgan.

Then I went back to my apartment, hoping I could drown my sorrow in enough liquor to avoid dealing with the next item.

Denial.

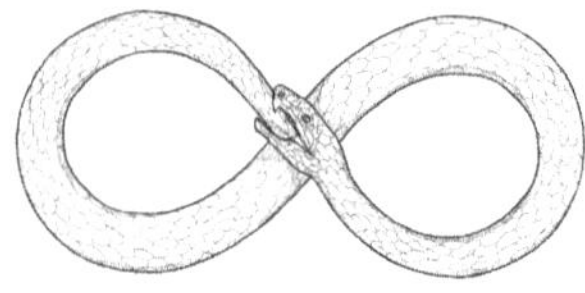

THE *THUNK* of the empty bottle hitting the floor pulled me from the depths of my self-reflection. I stared at it as it rolled across the floor, and when it hit the wall leading to the hallway, I winced as if I'd been struck.

I laid my head back against the couch cushion. Riding the euphoria of my high, as tears rolled down the side of my face, I let the sweet oblivion take me. The first glass had gone down smoothly, waking my body as it welcomed my familiar friend. After the fifth glass, I could no longer taste the rum and its many intricate flavors. But still I drank, never letting my glass get completely empty. And with each swallow, I pushed the pain down further.

An alcohol-laced sigh escaped my mouth and scented the air.

My pity party was getting boring. Even the usual guests—self-doubt, angst, and self-destruction—were staring at an empty salsa bowl, waiting for the party to end. The pattern I'd established—always turning away from the difficulties and trauma in my life to bury myself under mounds of judgment, and when that didn't work, just burying it—was getting old.

Well, at least I'd moved past denial.

I pushed up from the couch and stood, swaying a little as I surveyed my apartment. Why in the hell was I fighting so hard to keep this cursed place? And I do mean cursed. The previous tenant? In jail. The tenants before him, stretching back to when this place belonged to a cult? One I just learned Gavina was part of. Killed. Was this really the best I could do? Sure, it had pretty paint on the walls and some decent furniture thanks to my recent purchases, but that was it. It wasn't a home. It was a reflection of my poor choices and refusal to acknowledge them.

I couldn't accept the fact I didn't belong here anymore. Not in this apartment. Hell, not even in this neighborhood, filled with adult activities geared toward, not just fun, but escape.

"That might make better sense when I'm sober," I said.

I walked over to the bottle resting against the wall and picked it up. "This is the last time I drink like this." Yes, I was tempted to throw the bottle at the wall to emphasize my slurred declaration, but at least I had enough sense to see the stupidity in the action. Also, knowing me, I'd end up with a shard of glass embedded in my heel.

After depositing the bottle in the trash, I picked up my cell phone and saw the five texts from Alek. I didn't read them. There was no way in hell I could give a coherent response in my current situation. I could, however, tell him in person. Because right now, more than anything, I wanted to feel Alek's arms around me and his light touch on my thigh. I still wasn't going to go there with him, but I did want, *need,* his comforting embrace for a while. Maybe he could also make the room stop spinning.

I searched online for the number to the local cab company. The numbers blurred as I tried to press them. I had to go back online a few times to recheck the number. On my third try, I realized I could just click on the little phone icon and have the website connect me.

A woman's bored voice boomed in my ear. Before I could respond to her request, the smell of sand funneled its way into my nose and open mouth. I coughed, my eyes going out of focus as I fought past the acrid scent.

Only for it to be replaced by the smell of blood.

My skin itched. A clicking sound started echoing in my head. I dropped the phone. The woman's voice filled my living room.

The mark on my wrist that Set gave me heated, followed by the one Ezra gave me on my lips.

Dark brown eyes shimmered into existence in front of me.

The woman from the cab company cursed and hung up.
Set knocked me to the floor.
Pain.
Then darkness.

A Quiet Place

Alek stared at the bottle of Achel Brown in front of him. The alcohol flowed through him, easing the tension currently riding him. Its caramel taste lingered on his tongue.

He'd finished giving Devlin his update on the search for Logan and now sat, contemplating his next move. Logan had occupied all of his time today playing a game of cat and mouse. Putting him off his primary target—Unrie Nevsky. Gregor had contacted him earlier looking for an update. He told the man he needed more time. But Alek got the impression that time was something he had precious little of. He just needed another lead. Something to point him in the right direction.

Devlin had pulled Rachel off locating the remaining families involved with Tribe. The team's case had become complicated, and he needed her help untangling all the avenues they were being sent down.

He took a swig of his beer. Jonah had already checked out the address for Unrie that was in the file Petronela gave him. The house had been abandoned for several years. Alek drove by there after checking out the address Logan had left for them to find at Greenwood Apartments.

Both had been dead ends.

This was not what Alek did. He didn't work on puzzles or complicated mysteries. He tore down impenetrable walls and broke the minds of those standing in the way. Devlin understood this. Petronela should have too.

Devlin walked into the kitchen, carrying a pizza. "Hungry?" he asked, setting the pie down.

Alek stared at the greasy box, inhaling the cheese and pepperoni scent, and shook his head. "No."

Devlin clapped him on the back. "We'll get there."

Jonah came in the room and sat down heavily in the chair across from them. "They haven't checked in yet," he said and grabbed a slice of pizza. "I think they should have been back by now."

Alek glanced at him. "Did they say how long the gathering lasted?" Jonah shook his head.

The front door opened, and they all turned to the sound.

"Better grab what you want now," Jonah said, dipping his head toward the pizza box. "Before Nicole comes in here and polishes off the whole pie." He smiled and took another large bite of his slice.

Alek laughed, picturing his girl doing just that.

Rachel came in the room and sat down, setting a bottle of wine on the table. She leaned forward, resting her head in her hands. "That was horrible," she mumbled. "Nicole is outside. She needs a minute to herself."

"What happened?" Devlin asked, picking up the wine.

Rachel turned to him, her hands still caressing her head. "That was no women's empowerment group. It was a wine and sex club. They served us some really sweet wine made from magick grapes and then everyone got nude and started having sex."

Devlin narrowed his eyes. "Were any of you hurt?"

Rachel's face darkened. "Nicole and Kara said they were okay. But I don't know." She took a slice of pizza out of the box and set it in front of her. "They had a reaction to the wine and the herbs being pumped in the air."

Alek took the bottle from Devlin and read the label. *Nectar of the Gods.* Jonah had told him The Daughters of the Vine made and sold the stuff. "What else happened?" Alek asked, anger rising. If they hurt Nicole, he would go over there and break every last one of their minds. Damn the consequences.

Rachel shrugged. "Nothing. After Gavina talked to Nicole about her magick, they left us alone. Well, except for the girl who gave Nicole wine. She kept making eye contact with her." She chewed on her pizza. "They didn't say anything when we left." She tapped the bottle of wine. "And one of the men there let me have this."

"There were men there?" Alek gritted out.

Rachel shook her head. "Only for pretty decoration. The whole place was set up like some Greek orgy scene in a painting. Gavina talked about being Maenads and said they all worshiped Dionysus."

"Did they use blood magick?" Devlin asked.

Rachel shook her head. "No. Just earth."

"Dionysus, huh? I guess it fits with him being the god of wine and sex," Jonah said. "Are you sure Nicole is all right?"

Rachel looked down the hall. "I don't know. I'm worried about her. She seemed distraught. But she kept telling me she was okay."

Alek knew Nicole was not okay. He pushed up from the chair and walked down the hall to the front room. Pulling the shade on the front window to the side, he peered out.

Nicole stood on the sidewalk, staring at the house. He wanted to go out and check on her. But he also understood that when a woman wanted time alone, he should give it to her. He would wait.

Ten minutes later, Alek paced his bedroom. Impatience chewed at him, making him restless. He had asked Rachel to check on Nicole a few minutes ago, and she told him to let Nicole have the time she needed and just to wait.

He did not enjoy having to wait.

He looked out the window. Her car was gone. Dammit. Why did she leave? He snatched up his phone and stared at it. If he called, she would clam up, maybe even feel as if he was pushing her too hard. So, he sent her a text.

Thinking of you

No reply.

He walked out of his room and stopped in the hallway. His magick snapped out, seeking a place to land, seeking a mind to break. Sweat dotted his forehead as he worked through his rage. His fear of being abandoned. Of not being enough. He was enough. He had to remind himself of that. Letting his gaze go distant, he focused on the orange tendrils of his magick as they slid across the floor and walls.

Rachel came rushing down the hall, her footfalls heavy. She could always feel his magick when it was unleashed. When he first joined the team, she was the one who was able to calm him down enough to think. She was also the one to give him the much-needed energy when he drained himself to the point of exhaustion. They both needed the extra boost in their energy because of the constant use of their magick.

"Alek?" she asked.

He didn't respond, just stood there, staring down at the look of concern on her face.

She placed a hand on his chest and started humming. Her magick pulsed out in warm, soothing bursts of green. Healing magick. It was an ability, along with immunity to poison, that her grandmother Mei-Lien had passed down to Rachel's mother, Hai. She'd told them it was rooted in their family's past. And so few people knew how to use it today.

She stared up at him while she hummed. He pulled air into

his lungs, letting it out slowly as his body relaxed and the turmoil inside his head eased.

"Better?" she asked.

He placed his hand over hers. "Thanks, Rach."

She smiled up at him. "Our girl will be okay."

Devlin walked around the corner and stopped in the doorway, hands on his hips. Watchful.

Rachel looked over at Devlin. Devlin's gaze remained fixed on Alek. "Alek," he said in warning. "You're on the edge. I need you to take it down a notch," Devlin said.

"She left," Alek said. He hated how frantic he sounded.

"She'll be back," Devlin countered.

Alek stepped around them. He couldn't stay inside any longer. The walls were closing in on him, and his emotions were all over the place. He had a feeling in his gut that Nicole would go see Jordin Cisco. It was the next logical step. At least in her mind it would be. He knew she could be reckless, and he tried not to let his worry show too much, but right now, all he could think about was her getting hurt. Emotionally and physically.

He found Jonah outside in the pool. Arms splayed out on the edge, with his head resting on the concrete, seeming deep in thought. Normally, he would have let his demon out to thrash around in the pool, looking for a way out of the water. It never found one. Alek remembered the first time he'd seen the mangled thing. It had stopped its relentless circle around the water to study Alek, jaws with too many teeth gashed, gnawing at the air as if it could suck Alek inside its deformed mouth.

Jonah had to reassure him more than once the demon couldn't get out of the water. It was pure evil, and as such, couldn't cross the space between water and land unless it was inside a host. This information didn't stop any of them from being wary of its presence and those calculating eyes that watched them.

Alek pulled a lawn chair over and sat facing Jonah. "You talk to Kara?" he asked.

Jonah opened his eyes and looked across the water at him. "Yeah. She said she was doing okay. Went into a little more detail about what went on at the gathering." Jonah ran a hand down his face. "Sounds just like what Rachel said. A sex cult. Only, once they had given the girls enough wine to make them amenable, they left them alone. Didn't even protest when the three of them walked out." Jonah looked at the water. "It doesn't feel right."

Alek nodded, thinking. If they had no plans to harm them, or god forbid, take advantage of them, then why would they put them in a vulnerable state in the first place? Jonah was right. Something didn't feel right. "Rachel said Gavina talked about Nicole's magick. You think that's why they did it?"

"Yeah. It also explains the reason they invited Nicole to the gathering in the first place. She must have sensed how powerful Nicole was when she tried to infiltrate her mind on Sunday. Maybe she was curious?" Jonah swam across the pool and pushed himself out of the water. Alek handed him the towel from the lawn chair next to him. "Have you heard from her?

Alek leaned forward, resting his arms on his legs. "No."

The backdoor opened, spilling a muted light onto the concrete. Rachel stepped outside, carrying a cup of coffee. She handed Alek the cup and pulled a chair over and sat next to him.

He took a large sip of the warm liquid and closed his eyes as the jolt of energy pulsed through him.

"Devlin worried about me?" he asked.

"No. He's seen you at your worst," Rachel said.

Jonah stared at Alek. "Don't worry, man. She'll be back. Devlin wants her staying here after her encounter with Set Sunday night, anyway." Jonah rubbed the water off his head and chest, pausing when he caught a glimpse of the look of horror on Alek's face. "You knew about that, right?" he asked, cocking his head to the side.

Alek shot up and ran for his car.

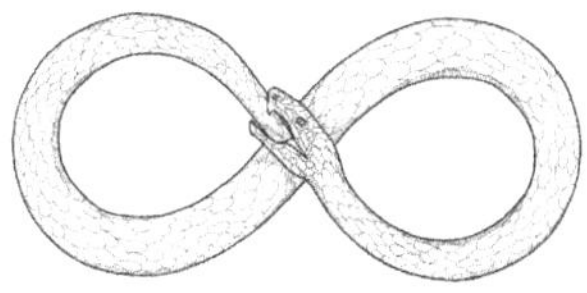

Alek couldn't get the key Nicole gave him in the lock quick enough, but when he finally managed to get the door open, his heart almost leaped from his chest. Nicole lay in a pool of blood in the middle of the floor. He rushed over, his knees hitting the ground, and pulled her into his arms. Her chest rose and fell slowly. Not dead.

After laying her down, he pulled his phone from his pocket and called Devlin. "Nicole's been attacked," he said in way of greeting. "I'll take care of it," he said and hung up.

Her shirt, seeped in blood, had one long slash across it. Alcohol wafted off her. He thought she'd given up drinking. He was right to think she had been hurting. He kicked himself for not going outside to comfort her. Careful not to stir her, he lifted her shirt and examined the wound.

Rachel had discovered the last time Nicole had been wounded that she healed quickly. It was another one of those odd things about her magick that they didn't understand. And until Nicole talked with her parents, they would remain in the dark. The cut along her abdomen was shallow, but the amount of blood surrounding her suggested it had been a deep cut. He was just thankful it hadn't been too deep. The Old One, Hathor, had to heal her from what should have been a death wound when Set attacked her before. If the laceration had been the same as that one, he doubted she would have been alive now.

His phone rang, and he glanced down at the display. Rachel.

"She's fine," he said, answering.

"Devlin said we're coming over."

"No!" Alek yelled before he could catch himself. "I got this. The wound is shallow." Why didn't he want them here? Rachel could patch her wounds and they could take her back to the safe house. Dammit, he was having a hard time focusing. "Let me do this, Rach, please?"

She didn't answer right away. "Tell me about the wound," she said carefully.

Alek laid out his theory about the wound healing on its own. Rachel remained quiet for a short while.

He could hear Devlin arguing in the background. If anyone could get Devlin to change his mind, it was Rachel. "Okay," she said finally. "I understand. Call me if you need me." It was softness in her tone that made him understand as well. It wasn't that he didn't want them to come, he just wanted to help Nicole on his own. Selfish, yes. But necessary. It would calm the turmoil going on inside of him. Assuage his constant feeling of not being enough.

"Thanks," he said finally and hung up.

After getting Nicole situated on the bed, Alek went into the bathroom and found the first aid kit, along with a towel. He returned to the bedroom. She hadn't even stirred. How much had she drunk? He pushed the thought down and focused on cleaning up her wound. He went to his knees on the side of the bed and stared at the washcloth in his hands. Dammit, he'd need water. After a fruitless search for a bucket, he filled a saucepan with warm water and returned to Nicole.

"Nicole," he said, moving the hair out of her face.

She mumbled but didn't open her eyes. He set the pan on the side of the bed and submerged the towel. Once the wound was clean, he applied antibiotic ointment and clear-strip band aids. That would hold until Rachel could patch the wound if it needed it. Was he being unreasonable keeping them away? He stared down at his hands, now smeared in blood. He was a mind mage, for fuck's sake. He didn't know a damn thing about healing.

Still, stubbornness rode him. He could do this. He was enough. And no one was going to hurt his girl again.

Once Nicole was settled and he'd put on a fresh shirt for her to sleep in, he went out and scrubbed the blood out of the carpet.

He would need industrial strength cleaner to get the stain up completely, and there was no way he was leaving her side to go buy some.

So, he did what he could for it, took a quick shower, and went back to lay next to Nicole.

And his heart and mind settled as he hummed her a song.

A door closed. The sound drove spikes into my brain. A familiar softness cradled my back. I cracked open one eye and slammed it shut immediately. Someone had captured the sun and crammed it into my small bedroom. I let out a groan as I tried to ease up. My stomach rolled with the movement. When a cold sweat broke out on my bare skin, I laid back down and tried to stop the world from spinning.

Memories from last night marched through my mind in a twisted procession, each remembrance more painful than the last. The first rush of pain and euphoria I received when I drank the wine at The Daughters of the Vine gathering. The phoenix wings on my protective mark beat once. Now, in this semi-lucid state, I could look at the strange way my mark had reacted in both instances with some clarity. It *had* been a warning. Just like the heat wave, I thought there wasn't any danger, but there had been.

Then came Monique and my drug-induced attraction to her. The wine coupled with the herbs they had been pumping through the air acted like ecstasy, waking my body up to need and desire. I had given her permission before she poured wine down my throat. I drank it, believing it would lead to something more. But she had stepped away, allowing Gavina to touch me and invade my space. An innocent kiss on my cheek wasn't innocent. She had ulterior motives. They just didn't involve sex. No, she was more interested in my magick. And she didn't need to kiss or touch me to see it.

The reel of memories continued.

Why had I gone to Jordin Cisco's? I knew in my gut that he didn't have the answers I needed. And even if he had, he wouldn't share them with me. The only thing he wanted to share with me was his power. But that would involve letting him inside of me again. And that wasn't going to happen. Sadly, the only way I would be able to locate the mark he claimed to have given me was if I found a gynecologist who specialized in magick.

Again, not going to happen.

That left Set. He had materialized in my apartment again. And judging from the pain radiating across my stomach, he had also attacked me.

Someone placed a cool rag on my forehead, and I sighed. Turning my head slightly, I opened my eyes again, blinking a few times, clearing not only the grit, but the unforgiving light filling my bedroom. The room slowly came into focus. Alek, shirtless, his hair hanging around him making him resemble a god, stood over me with worry in his dark blue eyes.

"How are you feeling?" he asked, his voice soft and soothing.

"Bucket," I mumbled, as a rush of bile rose in my throat. I surged up, biting back the pain and the wave of dizziness that rushed through me.

"Right in...oh. Here," Alek said.

No sooner had he stuck the trash can in my lap, vomit spewed from my mouth in a torrent. Alek held my hair back as more and more foul-smelling liquid flew from my mouth. My stomach churned as I continued to spew up all the alcohol and wine, I had drunk last night. My chest heaved as I tried to suck in air between episodes. Black spots dotted my vision. And my head grew light from oxygen deprivation. If I didn't stop throwing up, I would pass out from lack of air.

"Try to breathe," Alek said.

I sucked in a ragged breath. Not good.

"Damn. Please step back. This is...disgusting." I kept my head over the trash can. Inhaling the contents was not helping but I didn't want to face Alek right now. Or blow my rancid breath in his face.

He didn't move. Just stood there, watchful.

When I was sure I wasn't going to vomit anymore, I lifted my head.

Alek set the trash can on the floor. When he started to move toward me, I put my hand up to stop him. Covering my mouth, I said, "Please. It's bad."

He gave me a half smile.

I glanced down at myself. "Did you dress me?" I was wearing a snug, green tank top and green silk panties. I wanted to smile, but it would have hurt. Seems Alek liked green.

Alek sat next to me. "Yes. I found you on the floor last night with a shallow wound across your stomach." I winced at the pain in his tone. "Why didn't you come back home last night?"

Home. He called Devlin's rental house *home*. And said it like I belonged there, too.

I couldn't take this tenderness right now. Couldn't face the undeserved love and concern in his eyes. Especially not after what I did last night. I pushed up from the bed, not only to get out of having to answer his question but also avoid blowing vomit breath in his face. "Give me a minute," I said, and walked out of the room.

I went into the bathroom and flipped on the light. A deep throbbing pain pressed at the back of my head like someone was trying to drive a spike into my skull.

That would be the absolute last time I drank like that again. And yes, I vowed the same thing last night, but I really meant it now. I never wanted to feel this way again.

After splashing my face with cold water and brushing my teeth twice, I lifted my top to survey my stomach. There wasn't any blood on the bandage. That was good. I peeled back the tape and winced at the sting. Exposed, I examined the thin, jagged scar running halfway across my stomach. Small, clear strips of tape lay across it and an angry patch of red skin surrounded it. Except for the redness, the wound looked days old.

Alek knocked on the door, pushing it open before I could tell him to come in. I wanted to be mad, but the anxiety in his eyes rendered me speechless.

"Was there a lot of blood?" I asked.

"The right question is, why didn't you come back to the house last night? Even better," he said, his eye jumping, "who did this to you?"

I turned away and carefully pressed the tape back onto my skin. "Set." I gripped the bathroom sink, fighting the urge to scream. "I blacked out when he appeared."

"Did your magick stop him?"

I shook my head, and a wave of nausea came over me. I had to remind myself not to do that again. "I don't know why he stopped."

Alek nodded. "Rachel told us what happened at the gathering." He stepped forward and placed a warm hand on my back. "You want to talk about it?"

I looked at him in the mirror. "If she gave you the details, there's not much more I can add." He frowned and I pulled my gaze away from him. I knew he wasn't asking about what happened. He wanted to know about me. And how I was feeling. "I'm still trying to sort through my..." He gripped my waist, turned me around, and pulled me into his arms. Crying, although cathartic, would have hurt, so I settled on allowing Alek to hold me while the emotional turmoil tore my body in half.

As he held me, my heart filled with guilt when I remembered the way Jordin had backed me into the wall. How I had wanted him to. I hurt Alek without him even knowing. Yes, we weren't a couple. At least, not in any way that had been spoken aloud and confirmed. But we were something. More than friends.

He rubbed my back, giving me his strength until finally I was able to tell him. "Gavina violated me."

"And she is not long for this world," he whispered.

I pulled away and stared up at him. "My revenge," I said, remembering a similar statement from Marta. She wanted to be the one to take down the Sinclair family for what they had done to her children. And now, I understood just how she felt. Gavina would die by my hands. Because I doubted I was the only one she had been inappropriate with.

The front door opened, spilling noise into the apartment. I looked at Alek in alarm.

"Probably Kara," he said. "She's been coming over every twenty minutes, checking on you."

"You called her?" I asked, wiping the wetness off my cheek.

"Jonah did."

I nodded and went out to greet my friend.

"Nicole!" She rushed toward me, only to stop short before throwing her arms around me. "I was freaking out over there." She stepped back and gave me a once-over. "Alek told me what happened. How are you feeling?"

"Like a marching band is practicing inside my head and my guts might spill out at any moment."

She closed her eyes. "Attacked, and you're still being sarcastic."

"It might be a character flaw," I offered. More like my go-to when things got too heavy.

"Jonah asked me about the gathering," Kara said hesitantly. "Do you want—"

"I'm going to need coffee before we get into that."

She glanced at Alek. "Okay. We can talk about it later," she said slowly. "But coffee might not be a good idea. Do you have any ginger ale?"

"I might kill someone if I don't get any coffee."

"You might kill someone if you do. Trust me. Your stomach will thank me for it."

"Wait." I moved over to the couch and sat down. The room had started tilting. Seriously, I was not going to drink like that again. "Were you waiting in your car all this time?" I asked, just now registering what Alek had said earlier.

She crouched in front of me. "No. I was helping Paul move in."

Paul? Damn, I had completely forgotten she was going to tell Paul about the apartment.

"He signed the papers yesterday."

"Wow. That was quick." I rubbed my head. "I would help, but I'm not in the best shape." I glanced at the floor and noticed the large dark spot. It looked as if Alek had tried to wash the blood out of the carpet.

"While she gets you some ginger ale, pack some clothes. I don't want you coming back here."

"Are you channeling Devlin?" I asked, trying really hard not to smile. Yes, he was being bossy, but a part of me loved it. He was worried and wanted to protect me.

I pushed up from the couch, pressing my hand to my stomach when the pain flared. "Damn. I need pain meds and sleep and water."

"All at once," Kara said, reaching forward to steady me. Alek beat her to it.

"Probably a shower, too. So, I can drink the water while I'm in the shower."

Kara looked at Alek. "She should probably go lay back down."

I shook my head. I really needed to stop doing that. "I can manage." I glanced up at Alek. "Seriously, I need coffee." Screw ginger ale. I needed something strong to help kill this damn headache.

"And a shower," Alek said.

"I want to laugh at your implying I stink. Or get upset. But —" The floor rushed up and the world went black.

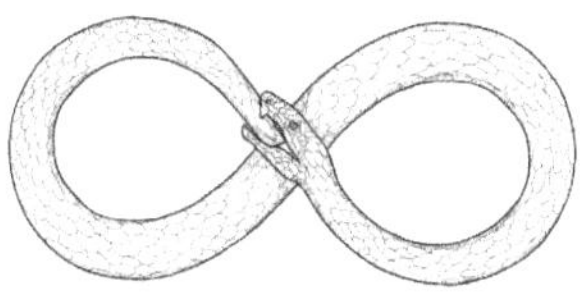

WARM WATER CASCADED down my body, waking me. I was sitting in the shower. Naked. While Alek and Kara and Paul stared down at me.

"You look like crap, Nicole," Paul said, a smile playing on his mouth.

I scowled at him and shifted so I could get up. They all moved back in unison. Seriously. "I know I've never had a problem with modesty in the past, but this is a bit much."

"Okay. She's fine. You guys can leave," Kara said, helping me stand. "Alek carried you in here for me," she said as the two men walked out of the room. "And Paul didn't know what was going on and came in the bathroom just as you woke up." Humor danced in her eyes.

"You're laughing at me in your head, aren't you?"

She put her thumb and finger together. "A little bit." Then she sobered. "Do you want to talk about last night?"

"While the shower pelts down on me?" I turned off the water, then stood there, staring at the chrome water nozzle. "You first," I said, realizing her persistence meant she was the one who needed to discuss what happened to us last night.

She gave me a towel then leaned against the sink and crossed her arms. "When Jonah called me last night to check on me…" She hesitated. "No. It's better if I start with the wine." She moved from the sink and sat down heavily on the toilet lid. "The first glass gave me an unexpected sugar rush. Of course, you know all this, but I need to talk this out."

I wrapped a towel around me and sat on the edge of the tub. "I understand."

"I had decided not to drink anymore. Even when the women came over to offer goblets to Rachel and me, I was adamant about not drinking any more. But then you let that woman give you some, so I figured it couldn't hurt. We were there to blend in, right?"

"Yeah, but we also didn't know what we were walking into. Hell, I thought we were going to be recruited for a marketing scheme."

Kara's eyes narrowed. "Oh, I would have hurt someone if they busted out a sample case and uniform for us."

We shared a humorless chuckle.

"I need to back up again," she said, continuing. "By the time the women had come over, I was already feeling the effects of the herbs in the air. Every pleasure point on my body had started to…" She clasped her hands in front of her. "Thrum?" She shook her head. "I don't know if that's the right word. But I was definitely in a sexual mood. Add in the wine, and the slightest touch would send me over the edge." She looked over at me. "After the woman poured the wine down my throat, I kissed her." Kara stood up. "It just happened. The barest touch of our lips. And the next thing I know, I'm writhing on the ground riding an orgasm." Kara bit her lip. "Last night, when Jonah called, he asked if I was okay. If they had hurt me."

Tears welled up in her eyes. I got up and pulled her into a hug. "They didn't, Nicole. If we hadn't left when we did, I'm sure I would have slept with that woman. I was so turned on, and it was the knowledge…no, the understanding of that fact that has me…"

I moved back and looked at her. "Did you feel violated?"

She shook her head. "I enjoyed it." She said it like it should be a question. "I'm not attracted to women." She swiped at the tears on her cheeks. "But hell, she was beautiful. And I wanted to feel her touch. I was more confused than anything." She smiled. "I was tempted to ask Jonah to come over and help me work off some of my pent-up need."

I gave her a half smile. "And I'm sure he would have come."

We both laughed.

She slid her hair behind her ear. "No. When Jonah and I make that leap, I want to make sure it's him I'm thinking about. Not some strange woman who didn't even give me her name."

She stared at me for a while, then said, "Your turn."

I rubbed my eyes and sat back down. "To save time, I will say ditto to everything you said. Only I know the woman's name was Monique and I didn't kiss her." I shook my head and blew out a frustrated breath. "Monique asked. Gavina stepped over the line. But I think that was the point."

"What do you mean?" Kara asked, sitting down beside me.

I told her about my theory and how the whole situation had been engineered for Gavina to study my magick. I gave her all the details we had on Divine Evil. We still needed to learn the exact circumstances that ended in Gavina's magick being changed. At first, I believed it had to do with blood magick, now I was wondering if sex had something to do with it.

"There are cults who use sex to gain power," Kara said, once I finished explaining. "But yeah. It's probably a good idea to find some religious texts on the subject." She got up. "Now. About Set?"

"I'll be careful," I said. A fruitless utterance. How could I be cautious against something that could pop in and out of existence without warning?

"How?" she asked.

"I need time to think on that. But I also need to finish taking a shower." Kara leaned against the sink. "Alone."

She smiled. "I've seen you naked before. Why are you suddenly acting like you're shy?"

I tossed the towel on the sink then pulled the shower curtain closed and restarted the water. "It's a little...strange." It did feel a little weird having Kara in here with me. When had I become so sensitive? Lately, I'd been swinging from one emotion to the next like I was on some freaky pendulum ride. One minute, consumed with anger. The next, ready to burst into tears. I wasn't about to start my period and definitely wasn't pregnant. So, what was my issue? Well, besides the past.

"If you're going to stay in here with me, please talk." I pulled the wet bandage from my skin and set it on the side of the tub, then used my loofah to scrub the stench from my skin.

"About what?"

"How is Paul's move going?"

"He's got most of his stuff moved in. He was living with some people before, but all the furniture was theirs, so he has to go shopping."

"Have you been to his old house?" I asked, letting the water cascade over me easing the knots in my back.

"Yeah. His roommates were a little strange. Kept making excuses so they could be in the same room with us."

I turned off the water and opened the curtain. "Hand me my towel."

Kara extended the towel to me and stepped away from the sink.

My hair lay plastered to my shoulders. I picked up my brush to work out the kinks before it dried, only to stop when what Kara said finally penetrated my crowded brain. I stared at her through the mirror. "In the bedroom?"

"That's just wrong, Nicole."

I resumed my efforts to detangle my hair. Sadly, it wasn't going well. "You two did have a sort of awkward attraction to each other. He liked you, but boys too. You liked him, but only for a short while." I shook my head and set my comb on the counter. "I had hoped you would figure it out. But you didn't."

"Did you hit your head?" Kara asked, picking up the comb. "Turn around so I can comb the back."

I sat down on the toilet seat and let her comb my hair. Except for the occasional fight to get the comb through, causing her to yank a little too hard on my head, it was pretty soothing. "Why do you ask?" I asked eventually.

"You've been talking in riddles. You know Paul and I settled that a while ago."

Had I? I sighed heavily, trying to figure out if she was right. I did feel...off. Like something big was just simmering underneath. And at any moment, I would break. I'd hate to think that all my vices were the things that kept me balanced. After last night, I had no plans to drink again. And the more I said it, the more it would be the truth. But a cigar might help.

I reached up and caught Kara's hand, stilling it. "I think it should be fine now." I twisted around and looked up at her. "Thank you. And maybe you're right. I might have hit my head. But I'll be all right. Just need to get my bearings."

"What are you going to do about Jordin?"

"You mean Shezmu." I was not calling him Jordin anymore. I stood up. "Nothing yet. We need more information. But honestly, I wouldn't blame anyone for worshipping him. I'm just not going to." I laughed. But the humor wasn't there.

Once I finished getting dressed, and yes, packing more clothes and supplies, Alek and I headed out to Devlin's.

Or as Alek said, home.

aria's sweet voice greeted us when we entered Devlin's house. I dropped my bag and rushed down the hall to see her. She stood in the middle of the room, wearing a pale-yellow tank top with flowers and a pair of jean shorts. Her dark, curly hair surrounded her little cherub face. She held a new teddy bear in her hands while more stuffed animals lay at her feet. Devlin was crouched in front of her, his face filled with so much adoration, she could have asked him to hang the moon and he would have found a way to do it.

I understood how he felt.

When I stopped in the doorway, he gave me a quick glance before he returned his attention to Maria. I smiled at seeing the most uptight man I have ever met let a little girl wrap his heart around her finger.

"Did you want to keep one?" she asked.

He smiled. "I think you should take care of them."

She nodded, her chin striking her chest. "Yeah. They will get sad if I don't keep them."

"Hi, sweet girl," I said, making my way toward her.

She whipped around. Her eyes rounded as she stared at me. Her face looked puffy, and her eyes were red as if she'd been crying. I eased down, bringing myself to her level, trying to keep the wince off my face, and braced myself. Maria had a tendency to launch herself at me. And I just knew the pain would be unbearable if she managed to ram her knee into my abdomen.

"I see you, Aunt Cole," she said finally.

Marta walked over and took her hand. "See, *Mija?* She's fine." She tried to urge Maria over, but the little girl wouldn't budge. Marta gave me a sad look, her mouth turning down in a frown. "She wouldn't stop crying when I tried dropping her off this morning. She kept insisting you needed her."

I cocked my head to the side. "What do you see?" I asked her, remembering her telling me she could see me sometimes when she's dreaming. Most children her age would have had little experience with the outside world to influence their dreams. Maria had more than most. Given her abduction and abuse she could have suffered countless nightmares recalling those memories. But Marta said she hadn't. So, when she said she dreamed of me, I didn't know what to think.

"He hurt you?"

"Who, sweet girl?" I asked, opening my arms. Damn the pain.

She pulled away from Marta and launched herself at me. And yes, her knee struck my abdomen hard. I swallowed the discomfort as I rubbed her back.

"The bright one," she said between sobs.

I looked up at Marta in question. She turned away. "Marta," I said, trying to draw her attention back to me. "Does Maria have active magick?"

Marta refused to look at me. I wanted to press the issue, because it was obvious to everyone in this room that she did, but Marta had shut down. And no matter how many times I asked, she wouldn't answer until she was ready.

She called Set the Bright One. That had to mean something. And despite my not confirming who she was referring to, somehow, I just knew. He did, when manifesting, look bright.

I glanced over at Rachel. She nodded, tapping her head as she studied Maria, who still hadn't stopped crying. Mind magick.

Easing her away from me, I stared into her tear-filled eyes. "I'm fine, sweet girl." I let my gaze go a little distant. A pale orange light surrounded her. Marta and I had to talk.

She looked down at my stomach. Reaching out, she placed a single finger on the spot Set had cut. "Hurt?"

"No, not at all," I lied.

"Your mother is coming to pick her up," Marta said. I had completely forgotten my mother was watching the kids.

My first instinct was to get up and run out the room like a child. I didn't want to face my mother. I damn sure didn't want to be *forced* into facing her, which was exactly what was going to happen. My mother wasn't the pouting type to take offense at my reluctance. She, like myself, would see it as a challenge. We were alike in so many ways.

I eased up, keeping hold of Maria. If I let go, it would hurt her, and I wasn't about to do that.

"Maybe I should wait in the other room," I said, looking at no one. They all remained silent. I started for Alek's room and stopped. I was being a coward. Why? Because my parents had kept something painful from me? If I could take away the pain Marta's kids experienced—wipe the memory completely, I would. So why did I have such a hard time understanding why my parents did it for me?

A knock at the door drew all our attention. I stood frozen in place with tears building in my eyes. My heart grew so heavy with sadness, it felt as if it were being shoved down inside of me. I squeezed Maria's hand, and she squeezed mine in return. It was all the courage I needed.

"I'll get it," I said.

Marta came and took Maria's hand. I smiled my thanks, turned, and walked with hesitant footsteps to the front room.

I stood in front of the door, my hands clammy with trepidation, and as I reached for the door, suddenly I was a teenager again, coming home late and knowing my parents were waiting on the other side of the door. Back then, it wasn't fear that kept me from going inside. It was the knowledge of having disappointed them yet again. They never yelled. If they had, I could have lashed out despite knowing I was in the wrong. No, they always met me with a quiet disappointment in their eyes and a lecture filled with love.

And I could only feel shame and resentment for them making me feel that way.

The doorbell sounded; its chime jarred me out of the past. Finally, with my hand firmly around the knob, I yanked it open.

My mother's vanilla scent rushed out and wrapped around me in a familiar embrace. I gasped at the onslaught of pain that suddenly rode through me. She wore a pale green sundress that clung to her damp skin. My father loved her in those dresses. Another memory of them surfaced. This time, it was their endless puppy-love that always embarrassed me.

"Nicole," she said, her voice hesitant while her eyes danced with joy and sadness.

"Maria's in there," I said, my voice thick with melancholy. "Come in."

I turned away from her love and motioned down the hall. She reached for me, and I hurried away like a coward.

I sank to the floor just inside the room and tried to avoid making eye contact with her. Maria rushed over and sat down on my lap. I was behaving like a damn child.

Marta's words floated through my mind. *Don't let anything keep you from a relationship with them.*

"Bonjour, everyone," my mother said, walking into the room.

Devlin walked over and took her hand. "Anne, how are you?"

She smiled at him. "Fine, just enjoying my time with the kids."

"Four kids." He shook his head. "They must be a handful."

My mother laughed. Oh, how much I missed her laugh. "Only Maria. She is such an energetic little one. But Fi' keeps her entertained." Her accent thickened. It always did when her emotions were high. Rachel was the same way. Almost as if they found more comfort in their native tongue.

I turned and stared at her. Alek glanced at me. I could feel the weight of his eyes—not judging, just encouraging me to take the first step.

I'm trying. Fuck knows I want to. It's just too damn hard.

No matter how much I wanted to call her mommy again, feel the joy I felt when I was four and she would chase me around the house because I didn't like wearing clothes. I'd hide them, not even realizing all she had to do was go in my room and get more. Or the times she would come in my room and lay down beside me and tell me tales of ancient times. Stories she made up to amuse me. She always told me the stories in French to help me learn the language.

I turned away, despite the anguish inside of me. Stubborn to the core. I gave Maria another hug. She patted my back as if she knew I needed comfort.

"Are you ready to go, Maria?" my mother asked.

Maria smiled and ran over to her. "Yes, Aunt Cole fine now. Can we get ice cream?"

"Yes." My mother bent down and kissed her forehead. "We can get ice cream."

Marta scooped Maria up, along with her stuffed animals, and headed toward the door.

Her familiar vanilla scent washed over me. The smell that screamed home and safety. She kissed my forehead, and a single tear slid down my cheek. Fingers under my chin, she turned me toward her. "I miss you, my sweet girl."

"I miss you, too, Mommy," I said, trying to put on a brave face. The look in her eyes said it wasn't working.

"Your father wants to see you," she said.

I turned away. "I'm not ready." Which was too bad because I missed my father so much, I couldn't breathe.

"My stubborn girl." She kissed me again, said goodbye to everyone, and left.

When I heard the door shut, I pushed up from the floor and ran into Alek's room.

Stopping short of flinging myself across the bed, I eased down the wall and laid my head back. My mind felt too full. My heart too broken. And I just needed a minute to collect myself.

The door opened and Alek came in. "You okay?"

I laughed as tears streamed down my face. "Not at all." I looked up at him. "But what else is new?"

He came over and crouched in front of me. "Forgiveness is hard," he said, placing his hand on my knee. "But you have to try and forgive your parents. Despite the pain. Holding all of it inside of you will eat you up." He ran a finger down the side of my face, drying my tears. "I don't want to see that happen to you." The rawness in his voice made me wonder if he was speaking from experience. He never talked about his family. Or why they disowned him. But I knew it bothered him.

I swiped my hand across my face. "I just need time."

He extended his hand, and I took it. The warmth of his palms against mine helped steady me. He pulled me into a hug, and I wrapped my arms around him, hearing his heartbeat in my ear. His hands slid up my back, cupping the back of my head. I leaned back so I could look at him. His dark blue eyes penetrated mine. Slowly, his head came down. His breath tickled my face, and I knew if I didn't stop him now, he was going to kiss me.

"Alek," I breathed out, trying to convince myself we should stop. But I didn't move.

The way he looked at me wasn't out of lust or sexual need. It was the way Steve used to look at me. With pure love and adoration in his eyes. Like I hung the moon and the stars, and I knew that wasn't right. I couldn't handle this amount of caring. I didn't deserve this type of love.

But I craved it.

My stomach quivered with anticipation. Alek slowly moved closer. Our breaths mingled. I shoved down the doubt and moved with him. Our lips were so close now, I could practically feel them on mine. My eyes grew heavy. I leaned in, wanting to close the last millimeter between us.

Then someone knocked at the door.

We pushed away from each other. I was going to kill the person on the other side of the door. And from the murderous look in Alek's eyes, he was going to kill them, too.

"Is Nicole okay?" Marta asked.

I sighed. I'd completely forgotten why I had run in the room. "Yes," I cleared my throat. "I'm fine." I was not fine. My body thrummed with need, and I couldn't do anything about it.

"Okay," she said hesitantly.

"We better go fill everyone in," Alek said, resting his forehead on mine.

"Maybe they can wait a little longer." I put my arms around him.

He smiled, bent down, and placed a soft kiss on my cheek. "Later."

He walked out the room before I could respond.

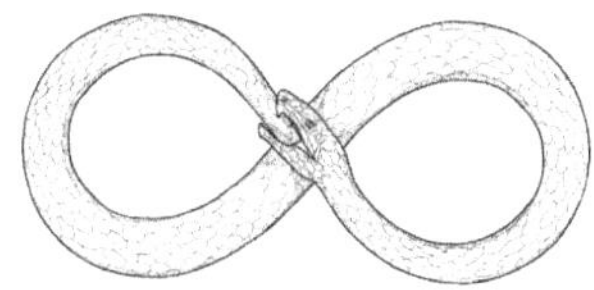

EVERYONE BUT ALEK was seated when I entered the room. Waiting. I took a seat next to Marta, choosing to forgo my assigned seat. I needed the comfort of my friend at the moment. Alek set a mug of coffee in front of me, and I smiled up at him in thanks. After a few sips, I placed the mug on my desk and told them what happened last night with Jordin and then Set. I figured we would cover the gathering at some point, but I had to prepare myself for it.

Devlin leaned back and laced his fingers together behind his head. "Why did Set stop?"

"I don't know. But..." I looked at Marta. "When did Maria tell you something was wrong with me?"

Marta wrung her hands together, her lips thinning. I knew this was hard, but we needed to know. "She woke up around one and started screaming. She just kept saying your name. Then a minute later, she just fell back against the pillow and went to sleep."

The room grew silent. Finally, Devlin said, "Alek? What time did you get to Nicole's house?"

"It was a little after one," Alek said with anger and frustration in his voice. "So, I just missed the bastard."

I got up and walked over to him. "You can't defeat him," I said, taking his hand. "Hell, I don't know how I did, either." I lifted my shirt. "He didn't use magick to do this."

"I would have tried," Alek said, his eyes locked with mine.

"Nicole's right," Devlin said. "He seems to, thus far, only be able to interact with her. We need to figure out how. I'm also curious as to why he waited so long."

"Oh, well thanks, Boss Man. I guess my safety isn't a concern," I said and immediately regretted it. "Sorry," I said before he could respond.

"Your emotions are high, Nicole. Trust me. We understand."

We? I swallowed the lump in my throat. Devlin was right, of course—my emotions were all over the place. Otherwise, I would have understood what he was saying instead of snapping at him.

"Thanks," I mumbled. "I think...well, the few times I've felt his presence in my apartment. I got the distinct feeling that he was trying to manifest but couldn't."

"So, we need to find out what's changed," Devlin said.

I nodded. I did not want the focus to be on me. But it was also important I find out how, after all this time, Set was finally able to fully manifest in my apartment again. And what kept him from doing so before. Otherwise, no place was safe.

He stared at me. His eyes searching. "Rachel told us what happened at the gathering," he said hesitantly. "Are you up to giving us your impression of the evening?"

I bit my upper lip. It was either now or never. After taking a deep breath, I went over what happened and my assumptions about why. Devlin asked me to repeat the order of events a few times, and Rachel was curious when the herbs started affecting me. She had already got the information from Kara. Marta went from shaking her head to cursing in Spanish. Jonah kept asking about the specifics of what the room looked like and if there were any ritual items being used. He even asked the specifics, aside from sex, of what the women were doing. Neither Rachel nor I could recount any of those details.

When I was done, Jonah said, "I don't think The Daughters of the Vine are a cult." We all stared bug-eyed at him. "Most of faith magick deals with creation. But it's also used as a way to channel power. Prayer circles are designed for this. But in some cultures, sex magick is also used. As far as I know, the practice died out in the early fifties. However, some believe it merely went underground."

"Do they use blood magick as well?" I asked.

Jonah shook his head no. "But..." He paused. "I'm wondering if it could account for her aura. Divine Evil, from our understanding thus far, needs to be achieved."

Devlin looked at Rachel. "Did you test the wine?"

She nodded. "Yeah. I can't determine the spell she used on the grapes. But there isn't anything else in them. It had to be the herbs."

"Or the combination of the two," I said. "Together, they acted like ecstasy."

Rachel agreed.

I hesitated. I wanted to ask her about her immunity to poison. But I also didn't want to put her on the spot. "Umm..."

"You want to know why I didn't react?" she asked.

I sighed in relief. "Yes."

"It works like your protective mark. Most of the women in my family have an immunity to substances used in magick. It's what makes me expel magick all the time."

I thought about what she said. She and Alek drank coffee she created to help replenish their magick. I'd been drinking the coffee as well. She'd also told me recently that my magick looked over-charged. Could I be expelling magick, too? I made a mental note to revisit that thought. It wasn't important. Besides, we had too much on our plate already.

Devlin got up. "I'm still curious about the wine, and if Jonah is right, we need to understand Gavina's ritual more." He looked at me. "She was interested in your magick for a reason. We need to know why." He scrubbed his hands down his face. "Alek and I will visit Petronela to get more leads on Logan and Unrie. When we get back"—he glanced at me—"the three of us can check with Luisah about the Ark and also see if she has any information on how one would become Divine Evil."

He looked at Marta. "Marta, see what you can dig up on the wine. I've never heard of the brand before. See if they are selling it exclusively, and if so, compile a list of people buying it. Maybe Gavina isn't the only one using it in a ritual." She nodded and opened her laptop.

"Rachel, finish locating the properties of the families associated with Tribe. Start compiling as much as you can on them. Including family trees. I don't want us to be caught off-guard if they do decide to return to Tulare."

"Jonah, talk to your contacts. See if you can find more information on sex magick. If anything, we need to confirm blood magick is not involved."

He looked at me. "Let Rachel check your wound and then get some rest. We'll come get you before we go to Luisah's."

"Do I look that bad?" I asked. I was not looking forward to confronting Luisah.

"Do you want me to answer that?" The look on his face suggested he really wanted to.

"No, Boss Man!"

He fought a smile and turned away.

Alek kissed me on the cheek. "See you."

"Um...okay." Why did I suddenly feel like a teenager?

Alek and Devlin left, and Jonah stepped out of the room.

Rachel got up. "Take your shirt off. I'll go get my supplies," she said, walking into the other room.

"I seem to be exposing myself a lot lately." I pulled off my shirt. Pain raced across my stomach.

"What else is new," Marta said, her tone teasing while she stared at my stomach.

I grinned at her. Slowly, I removed the new gauze. I didn't want Rachel to rip it off.

"It doesn't look so bad," she said, moving closer. She placed a cool hand on the barely visible scar.

In the short time it took Alek and me to drive to Devlin's house, it had healed even more. Just one more strange thing about me I needed to get answers for. But as long as it wasn't something life-threatening, I wouldn't worry about it.

Rachel came back in the room. While she examined my wound, I asked, "Hey. Jonah said you used healing magick on Devlin to make him calm down yesterday."

She leaned back and studied me. "You want me to help you, too?"

I lifted my hand. "No. I was just curious about it."

She resumed her study of my wound. "It's something the women in my family can do. We push our magick out, creating a sense of peace. Dev can usually maintain his control. But..." She sighed, leaning back again. "I'm worried about everyone."

I touched her hand. "We'll be okay.

She smiled and stood. "Might have to kill a few people before we are. You want something for pain?"

I pulled my shirt down. "No. No, I'm good." I didn't dare chance taking something she created for pain. There was no telling what she would put in it.

Rachel walked out of the room.

"She's a little intense," Marta said.

I nodded. "Yeah. You'll get used to her."

While Rachel and Marta worked, I did think about getting

rest. But I couldn't just lay there and do nothing. Besides, I knew sleep would not come easy. Not until I confronted Gavina.

So, when Jonah came back in the room, I asked him to give me a ride to my apartment so I could retrieve my car. When we got there, I'd have to come up with a reason why I couldn't follow him back. One that didn't involve the truth.

W hen it came down to it, giving Jonah a load of bullshit so he would overlook me driving off alone after what happened last night wasn't going to work. So, I opted for the truth. I might have rambled on a bit, but at least I was honest. And when I was done, he told me he would follow me and park out of the way so as to not draw any attention to himself. I would have kissed him, but Kara might have hurt me. So, I settled on a quick hug, hopped in my car, and made the long journey to Hollingsworth Manor.

My reason for going was personal. Gavina had pushed me off-balance, and until I confronted her about the violation, my mind could not rest. Our investigation required my full attention. I'd already spent a great deal of time on an emotional rollercoaster. It was time I did something about it. Besides, there was no way I was going to let this slide.

But I had to do this on my own. Jonah, god bless him, understood that. I doubted Devlin or Alek would have. No, they would have wanted to protect me. I didn't need that right now.

And who knows, maybe I could confirm if she was in fact practicing blood magick once and for all. If she said no, I would walk away and deal with her another day. If she said yes, well, I had packed my gun. And of course, the knife Devlin gave me was wedged between my breasts. If she didn't drug me, I might be able to pull it out and stab her.

Now I just needed to find the right words to say that wasn't a string of expletives.

The apple tree was the first thing that caught my eye when I parked in front of Gavina's house. According to the Bible, it was the fruit that gave mankind all its knowledge. Given to Adam by Eve because a snake had tempted her into eating it. I never did like that story. It implied women were weak and easily manipulated.

And if time and history have taught us anything, that bullshit belief was simply not true.

Women could be manipulative, yes. But we were hardly responsible for all of mankind's sins.

I parked closer to the end of the driveway and walked up the slight incline to the house, steering clear of the gardens. I didn't want calm right now. Only rage.

A thick, gold rope with a tassel at the end hung to the side of the mahogany double doors. I pulled it, and a loud melody rang out. A few minutes later, a familiar woman opened the door.

Monique.

A red ribbon held her long black hair away from her makeup-free face. She wore a pair of red shorts and a tank top with no bra. As she stared at me, her mouth stretched into a beautiful smile, making her green eyes light up.

"I hoped I would be able to see you again," she said, stepping forward. Her eyes roamed down me briefly. This close, I could smell a sweet, floral scent wafting off her.

"Yeah. Hi," I said, feeling a little off-center. I hadn't counted on running into anyone from the gathering last night, especially not her.

Her face fell. "You're not here for me, are you?"

I shook my head no, unable to voice my feelings. Last night, I had been ready to sleep with this woman. Looking at her now, all I could feel was...confusion. Yes, the wine and the herbs had something to do with my attraction to her. But some of that residual appeal was still there—just not enough that I would ever act on it.

She gave me a sad smile. "Well, it was a nice thought, anyway. Are you looking for Gavina?"

"Yes," I said, still a little tongue-tied.

"She's not here. She took some of the girls with her to drop off wine to our clients."

"You don't sell it in stores? I thought…" I trailed off. This was information I shouldn't have known.

"It's okay. I would have checked us out online, too. No, we advertise it online. We only sell to exclusive clientele." She stepped back. "Did you want to come inside and wait? I'm sure she would be happy to see you."

I was sure she would, too.

"If anything, you can come in out of that heat," she offered.

After a brief hesitation (I did not want to seem too eager), I stepped inside. Monique closed the door, and I broke out in a cold sweat. Fuck. Maybe this was not such a good idea. A phantom scent of Gavina's sickly sweet breath seemed to hang in the air. The image of her hovering over me naked coalesced inside my head. There had been a hunger in her eyes. An animal-like craving for the magick I held inside of me.

Monique placed her hand on my back, and I jumped. "Sorry," she said. "You just seemed a little lost for a minute, there."

I shook my head. "No. I'm fine. Just had a rough night."

"Yeah," she laughed. "The wine can be a little potent. It takes some getting used to."

I didn't correct her assumption. "What's in it? I mean besides grapes."

She signaled toward the door. "You saw the apple tree, right?"

"It was hard to miss."

She gave me a warm smile. "Yeah. I like to sit under it during the night. Well, on nights we aren't gathered in the Divine space." She hugged herself, her eyes lit with joy. "Anyway, a single apple is used in each batch of wine. Gavina said it gives the wine its sweetness." She leaned in. "It also helps lower inhibitions."

"I've never heard of apples being able to do that."

"Oh." She laughed. "Not on their own, no." She extended her arm toward the hallway leading toward the Divine space. "There are other plants used." She hesitated. "I could show you."

She seemed way too eager to help me. I studied her for a minute, trying to find deception in her eyes or body language. She watched me, her face growing more and more unsure.

"Are you sure you're allowed to show me?" I asked.

She sighed. "Honestly, I was hoping I could entice you to stay. Maybe even..." She stepped back. "Sorry. I sound a little desperate." She pulled her ponytail over her shoulder. "Did you maybe want something to drink?"

I shook my head. "Two glasses of that wine was more than enough."

She laughed. "No. I was thinking maybe tea or coffee or water."

"I could use a cup of coffee." I paused. "It's just coffee, right? Nothing else has been added to it?"

She raised an eyebrow in confusion. "I would call you paranoid, but I guess I understand after last night. I know Juliette invited you. I assume she didn't tell you what the gathering was about."

"No. She didn't," I said, not keeping the anger out of my voice.

"We are encouraged to bring new members in. Juliette finds hers at church. I don't go to Boyd's services. I know they're a sham. I usually go with Gavina to deliver the wine. Some of the clients bring friends that we can invite."

Damn. It *was* a pyramid scheme. Only, there was no selling involved. Just sex. "She told me Gavina invited me."

She gave me a strange, confused look. "Well," she started, nodding. "I guess that explains why she asked me to study your magick. She told me it was special and wanted me to see how powerful you were." She shook her head. "Let's get that coffee."

I hesitated. If Gavina had asked her to study my magick, she had to know something was up. And sadly, the only way I was going to find out was if I followed her into the kitchen.

We took the left hallway and entered an enormous kitchen done in chrome, white, and stainless steel. Splashes of color could be found in the appliances. Monique indicated I could take a seat at the large island bar and went over to an elaborate red coffeemaker sitting on its own cabinet.

"It took me a while to get used to all the gray in this room," she said as she worked the machine. "A few months after I got here, I asked Gavina if I could add some color." She pointed out a few items in the room. "The coffee machine was my idea, along with the red tea kettle and red popcorn machine."

"How long have you been here?" I asked. The rich coffee scent filled the air, making my mouth water. I had planned on only taking a few sips, but the smell was just too tantalizing. *Please don't let it be poisoned.*

"I've been here two years." She stood at the counter, staring down at the floor. "I first met Gavina at the church. My husband —" She shook her head. "Correction: My ex-husband and I had come to Tulare to visit his grandparents. They took us to the service." She looked up, locking eyes with me. "My marriage was crap. My husband, abusive. I'd been trying to find a way out." She smiled, her eyes going distant. "Then Gavina spoke to me. Told me she could heal me and all I had to do was let her inside."

I suppressed a shiver. It was the same phrase Gavina had said to me.

"I will heal you. Just let me inside."

"Is it too cold in here?" Monique asked.

I shook my head.

She watched me for a while, concern etched across her face, until finally she said, "After that, it was easy to leave him. I moved here a week later." She swallowed and turned back to the coffeemaker. "Do you take cream or sugar?"

"Oh, no. Just plain, please."

She set a mug down in front of me. I inhaled the tantalizing aroma. "What kind of coffee is this?" I asked, taking a sip. The jolt of caffeine had me blinking my eyes rapidly. "Strong," I said.

She smiled. "It's Kenyan Peaberry." She sat in the stool next to me, picked up her mug, and blew on her coffee. "I'm a bit of a coffee snob. Picked up the habit from my ex. Gavina was nice enough to give me the money to continue it." She took a sip. "I hate cream and sugar, too."

"What did your husband say when you told him you were leaving?"

"He slapped me and said he was going to see some friends and I should have dinner ready when he got home." She laughed. "That was the last time that bastard put his hands on me. I left after he did. And haven't heard from him since."

I started to tell her about my own ill-fated nuptials, but it would send the conversation down a personal path that might give her the wrong impression. It was too bad, though. I did enjoy her company.

"So, how often do you have to bring in new members? And where do they all stay?" I asked.

"Oh, we only recruit when others leave."

I raised an eyebrow in question.

"Gavina believes some of the women become too afraid of the freedom she offers. It can be scary letting go of all those societal rules and just...being."

"How many have left?"

"I've been here two years. Twelve women have left since then."

I made a mental note to have Rachel see if she could find some names. I doubted asking Monique would be wise. But there was one thing that was bothering me: Jonah believed sex magick might be the answer. And for us to know if it was, I needed to ask about their ritual. Damn, this was going to be embarrassing.

"Does everyone sleep with each other?" I asked in a rush.

She smiled. "Yes. But not outside of the Divine space." She leaned in. "Well, that's not true. Some have developed relationships and end up together. Gavina doesn't mind, as long as they are able to participate in the gatherings."

"What is the purpose of the gatherings? Besides the sex?"

"It's not just sex. It's Enlightment and freedom and the best damn magickal orgasm you will ever have." She closed her eyes as if she were savoring the memory. "It goes on for hours. Pulsing through you in this wave of energy."

"And where does all that energy go?"

She opened her eyes. "We simply release it."

I could guess exactly where the energy went. Into Gavina.

"So, you all live here? With Gavina and Boyd?"

She laughed. "Oh, gosh no. Boyd and Xavier live down the road. Gavina doesn't pretend to be married outside of church. She married him to appease her parents and to have children." She laughed. "I thought you knew that."

I shook my head. "Why stay married, then?"

Monique shrugged. "Convenience. Who knows? She doesn't talk about it much. I do think some of the girls sneak Xavier in when Gavina is away."

Interesting. We had to find out exactly where Boyd and Xavier were living. It could be they were the ones practicing blood magick.

Monique eased off the stool. "Did you want me to show you?"

My eyes rounded.

"No," she said in protest. "Not that." She paused. "At least, not unless you want me to." She waited, and when I didn't respond, she continued, "No. I can show you the room and the outside garden." There was a note of hurt in her voice.

I stood up and reached out to her. After a brief hesitation, she took my hand. "I'm sorry. I'm not attracted to women." I smiled. "But if I were…" I trailed off, unable to go much further than that.

She ran her thumb over my fingers. "I understand. I hope I didn't upset you."

"Not at all. It's kind of flattering. And I've been hit on by women before."

She gave me a knowing smile. "Okay. Well, did you want to see the room?"

Yes. I did want to see it. But not for the reasons she was thinking. Despite what I'd said, I knew she was still actively trying to recruit me. If I hadn't liked her, I would have charged forward without a second thought. But I couldn't do that. She was a kind woman who, I was guessing, was being used by Gavina. I did not want to use her, too.

She tugged my hand. "At least let me show you the garden." She gave me a hopeful look.

Fuck.

After a short while, I nodded. "That would be nice."

She didn't let go of my hand as she led me back through the front foyer and into the familiar room. The plush pillows still covered the floor. I wondered how often they had to have them cleaned.

"This place reminds me of those paintings you see of Greek and Roman orgies," I said.

She laughed and let go of my hand. "It does, doesn't it," she said, gaze circling the room. "I guess I never really thought about it."

I glanced at her. She turned to me and smiled. "You are truly a beautiful woman," she said. "And that is the last time I will flirt with you." She raised her hand. "Promise."

I smiled. "I told you it was fine."

She nodded and made her way toward the glass doors leading to the outside. I took a moment to examine the room, looking for any ritual items or symbols. Aside from the depictions of women on the walls, there was nothing.

"Coming?" Monique called, standing in front of the open doors.

I started for her and then stopped. "What about Gavina's

daughters?" I asked, remembering them standing in front of the archway leading into the room. "Do they participate?"

"No, they just watch and make sure everyone is okay." She glanced outside and then turned back to me. "Between you and me, I think they like standing over us, casting judgement. They always have these arrogant looks on their faces."

They gave me the same impression.

Monique showed me the outside garden. Like the front, it was covered in a plethora of bushes and flowers, some of which weren't native to Tulare. She told me the earth mages helped keep them alive. What I was most interested in was the small, encased pond that sat right outside the doors with lilies floating on the surface. Nymphaea Lotus, known as Egyptian water lily, and blue lotus flower, both of which could account for the euphoria we felt. And the opium poppy and passion flowers surrounding the pond would only intensify the effects, especially if they were infused with magick.

It was like I had guessed: a magickal form of Ecstasy.

After thanking Monique and telling her I would try and reach Gavina another time, I texted Jonah and told him I was heading out and needed to stop at the drug store. While I had no plans to drink myself into oblivion like I did last night, I did need something to settle the anxiety running through me.

And the pain of knowing I couldn't help Monique.

A Spider's Web

As soon as they had got in the car, Devlin had leaned back and shut his eyes. Alek knew the man was tired. Hell, even he could use a nap. But rest was not something he could concentrate on right now. His great aunt would not be happy with his failure. In his defense, he had tried to warn her she should use someone else. But she had insisted he track down Unrie and bring the man to her. Or at least his head. What she hadn't told him was that Unrie had been on the island for a month. Yes, he had only been spotted two nights ago, but surely someone would have been able to confirm how long he'd been here. They had managed to compile a dossier on the man, for fuck's sake.

Then there was Logan's involvement. Had she known Unrie was working with him? If so, why not warn him in advance? Something wasn't quite right with the whole situation. And while Devlin wanted to get more leads, Alek wanted to find out what game his great aunt was playing. And why.

Carnavalul de Fear wasn't open until just after dusk. The rides were built to elicit fear, and most people had a misguided belief that nothing bad could ever happen to them during the day. The carnival preyed on this assumption nightly. They arrived just after two in the afternoon. The ground crew moved about, readying the park for the night's visitors.

"It doesn't look as appealing during the day," Devlin said, staring out the window.

Alek grunted. "You sure you want to talk with her?"

Devlin turned to him. "I understand she's family, but she must understand you are part of my team. If she needs something from you, she should have come to me."

Alek smiled. "Just make sure you don't tell her that."

Devlin chuckled. "I don't have a death wish."

They continued toward the back in silence.

Alek stopped at the guard station and rolled down his window. It was the same man from Sunday, wearing a uniform too big for him with the same stain on the front. He was surprised the man was still there.

Recognition dawned in the guard's eyes. His gaze swiveled between Alek and Devlin, and the surprise was replaced with a questioning look. He narrowed his eyes. "Is she expecting you?"

Usually, Alek would have been upset by the question, but this time, he understood. Petronela had no idea he was coming—let alone that he was bringing someone with him. It didn't mean he was going to answer. Alek stared at the man, avoiding the question, until the guard waved them forward.

Alek parked in the same spot he did the other night. Before they could get out of the car, his phone dinged. He looked down at the display. Jonah had sent a text. It would seem Nicole couldn't rest, either.

"Nicole is on her way to Hollingsworth Manor to confront Gavina. Jonah is following her." He was surprised Jonah hadn't sent the text to Devlin.

Devlin nodded. "Figured she would. Tell him to stick close."

Alek sent a quick text then they climbed out of the car.

They made their way over to the back entrance. Unlike before, the door was closed, and Alek had to pound on it several times before another unfamiliar man opened it. The man looked no older than his early twenties, with cool blue eyes and long, dark hair. His skin was fairer than most Roma. He must have had mixed blood.

"Can I help you?" the man asked.

"We're here to see her," Alek said, shifting his weight. He noticed the man had placed his hand behind his back, possibly going to for a gun.

The man dipped his head and stepped to the side, sparing Devlin a brief glance as he did so. Alek didn't want the stranger at their backs, so once inside, he paused just in the doorway and waited. He could see the calculations going on behind the man's eyes as he took in both Alek and Devlin, waiting. Finally, with an audible sigh, he led the way to Petronela's room.

The dark hallway pressed in on them. The muffled sounds of people talking were their only company. When they arrived at the curtained room, the man shifted the curtain to the side and signaled for Alek and Devlin to enter.

When they stepped inside, Alek was surprised to see Petronela sitting on her lounge chair while two couples stood in front of her. The women looked close to tears, while the men stood firm, as if waiting for orders. Petronela glanced over at them. Her dark gaze took in Devlin as if he were a rare specimen she needed to understand. There was calculation in her eyes. She smiled at them both and then waved her hand at the people in front of her.

"We will find them. Now, leave. I have business to attend to," she said, her eyes still focused on Devlin. The couples glanced back, anger playing across their faces. But they didn't say anything, only nodded and left the room.

"Devlin Grey," Petronela started. "Tell me, do you know the power you have? Do you know the man who sired you?"

Devlin shifted and clasped his hands behind his back. "I never met my father. And I'm aware of my power."

Petronela nodded, her eyes scanning the room, taking in the books lining the shelfs. "So much knowledge. You are welcome to it when you need it." She turned her gaze to Alek. "Have you found him?"

"Who?" Alek asked, testing her. She didn't say Unrie, and he had the feeling she really meant Logan.

She shifted in her seat, stretching out a bit. Pain had her face drawing taut. "The one I sent you to find."

"Logan or Unrie?"

She sighed, locking her gaze with his. "Both. You needed to find both." She tilted her head. A smile played across her face. "But of course, you already figured that out."

"What game are you playing?" Alek studied her. She looked on the verge of collapse. Like she had too much on her shoulders and couldn't handle any of it. He had never seen his aunt look like this before. "What is wrong with you, Auntie?" he asked, his tone softening.

"Tell me, Devlin, how do you like Tulare?" Petronela asked, ignoring Alek.

"It's an interesting place," Devlin said.

Petronela nodded. "Yes. That is a good description." She pushed forward, grabbing the long cigarette resting on the small table by her side. "It will be even more interesting soon." After taking a drag on the cigarette, she looked at Alek. "I'm getting old. If not for my usefulness, I would be dust by now. Able to finally rest."

"You've always been old," Alek said. "Even when I was a boy and first met you, you were old." He went over and knelt in front of her. "Now, tell me, Auntie, why would you send me after a man who has been here for weeks? Why the game?"

She touched his face—a rare act of open kindness that made Alek flinch. "I always have my reasons. You know this, Alexandros. Even when I tried to get you to come to me, to let me help you...I had my reasons. And those reasons were a promise given in blood. I became bound long ago when our people first Traveled with the Historian." She gripped Alek's face when he tried to pull away in alarm. "I have a part to play in all this. And I have set you on the right path. That is all I can say. Now, I must concern myself with Daniella and Ileana." Her mouth turned down, eyes going sad. "Some..." She sighed. "You can never save."

She shifted; again, pain raced across her face. "The players are not what they seem. Make sure you bring Unrie to me soon."

"We need more leads," Alek said. "Unrie has become a ghost."

Petronela closed her eyes. Alek could feel the magick rushing off her. A dark orange glow radiated from her as she used her rare gift of foresight. She'd told him once that she could only see parts of future events, not the full picture. And she always had to decipher what she saw. Had she seen Unrie? When she gave him the assignment, he had been too preoccupied with her request to ask.

After a short while, she opened her eyes. "I have been unable to see much lately." She grimaced. "But I do know you will succeed in this." She stared at him out of sad eyes. "That much I do know. It is the reason I asked you to do this."

"Do you need my help finding the girls?" Alek asked.

Petronela leaned back. "Not now. Now, you need to expose the players in the game we are currently playing. These ones are the key to understanding everything."

"You promised to bring someone to Tulare to help Nicole if I helped you. Will you still honor that promise?"

"I will." She waved her hand, dismissing them. "Go. You don't have much time."

"What can you tell us about this path and your part in all this?" Devlin asked.

"War is coming to this island. And we'll all be in the thick of it." She studied Devlin. "You have your role as well. More than anyone else." She looked at Alek, her eyes penetrating him. He felt her inside his head, but he didn't turn away. "Bring me the girl."

"Nicole?"

Petronela shook her head and closed her eyes. "No. The one who shines in the murky waters."

I sat at my desk, staring at the advertisement for *Nectar of the Gods* while I waited for Devlin and Alek to come pick me up. I'd filled the rest of the team in on what Monique had told me, and Rachel started looking for information on the women who used to belong to The Daughters of the Vine. We all agreed Gavina, despite any evidence, had lied to Monique. The women didn't leave. Now, we just needed to prove it.

Marta had found the same information I'd gotten from Monique about the wine. It wasn't mass produced and was only given to a select group of clients. Unfortunately, the client list wasn't available. I kicked myself for not asking Monique when I could have, but I also knew that if I had, she would have become suspicious of my motives and possibly asked me to leave. And it was imperative that I at least got an understanding of their ritual.

Jonah's contacts didn't have any further information on sex magick other than it was still practiced in secret circles. I filled him in on how it worked. Again, we had all come to the agreement that Gavina was absorbing the power unleashed when everyone climaxed. I had to admit, I was curious to see what that kind of power looked like. But not enough to go back there ever again.

Rachel had found fifteen properties associated with the families who used to be part of Tribe. According to her, all but one had been bought. And the owner of the last one had died six months ago, leaving his estate in limbo. His family was still fighting over who would take ownership of the house and land.

All this information, and absolutely none related to blood magick. We had to be missing something.

"Did you ever find out what happened to Lemuel Oren?" I asked Rachel.

She looked up from her search. It took a minute for her to respond. "Oh. Yeah. I found a death certificate for him this morning," she said, looking back down at the computer. "I have one of my friends checking it."

Rachel blinked a few times and cocked her head to the side. "I can't remember why."

"Take a break, Rach," Jonah said. Then he looked at me. "Unless you think that ad has a hidden message in it, you should do the same." I nodded and shut my computer.

Damn. We were all overworked. Stretched so thin, I was surprised we were all still functioning. I glanced at my phone to check the date. Tuesday. Given all the craziness we'd been through, I could have sworn it was Friday already. I ran my hand through my hair, thinking. We had managed to cram a week's worth of shit into two days. At this rate, I'd be spiking Rachel's special coffee with alcohol and chain smoking while shoving copious amounts of food into my mouth and begging Alek for a quickie every few hours in no time.

All my vices rolled into one long day.

Well, maybe I'd forgo the alcohol. I didn't want to revisit that horrific hangover again any time soon.

The front door opened, and I stretched. The day wasn't over with yet. I still had to go and confront Luisah. I went and poured myself a cup of coffee.

Devlin walked in the room, Alek following behind him. After greeting everyone, he turned to me. "Want to fill me in on what happened?" he asked. Jonah told me he had sent Alek a text, telling them where I was going.

"My brain hurts," I said, taking a sip of my coffee.

Devlin's face softened. He gave me a look of understanding and turned to Jonah.

While Jonah filled him in, Alek came over, took my hand, and guided me to his room. After he shut the door, I put my coffee mug on the dresser and let him pull me in for a hug. "You know," I whispered to him, "I was just entertaining the idea, that if all our investigations end up like this, I might have to corner you for some quickies throughout the day."

He laughed, then stepped back and stared at me. "Sounds like a plan." He winked. "Of course, we'd have to work out a signal."

"How about, 'My brain hurts?'"

He raised his eyebrow in question. I gave him a teasing grin and leaned back against the dresser. "Seriously. I'm worn thin."

He scrubbed his hand down his face and pulled the tie from his hair. "We all are." He studied me for a minute. "You up to seeing Luisah?"

I closed my eyes and nodded. "Yeah. Have to get it over with, and we need the information."

A rap sounded at the door.

Alek leaned down and gave me a soft kiss on the lips. "Time to go," he said.

I sighed. Yeah, time to face Luisah.

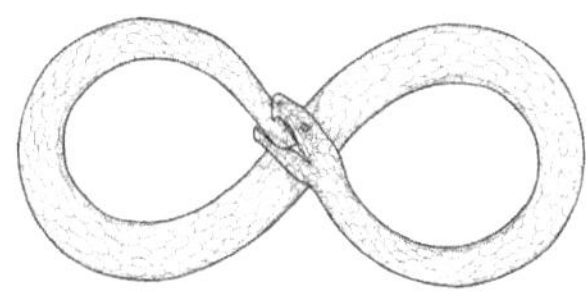

ORANGE LIGHT FILLED THE SKY, keeping the darkness at bay for just a little while longer.

No one spoke as we drove down Williams Avenue making our way to Coeur d'Alene. We rode in Devlin's SUV. While Alek rested in the back, I stared out at the changing landscape with nervous energy dancing around inside of me. I had not seen Luisah since my recovery, but like my parents, Luisah had lied to me. Well, more like omitted some of the information I needed. And I wanted to avoid talking to her about it. It was easier.

The road narrowed and Williams became Route 73.

The land bridge Coeur d'Alene rested on was populated by small settlement of Creole people. After reading *The Land Guarded by People of Colour*, we learned that the people here *were* the people of Colour the document referred to. We also learned they, along with the Gullah people in Sandpoint and the Cherokee Indians residing in the small Cherokee Nation at the bottom half of the island, were all immortal. Tasked with keeping Set from leaving the island.

Most of the locals referred to Coeur d'Alene as the town that time forgot. I used to believe it was because of the small, scrap-wood homes with tin roofs and dilapidated brick chimneys. And the fact that most of the homes didn't have electricity. But now, I knew why. The people who lived here were truly from another time.

We passed the handmade sign for Coeur d'Alene, along with a cluster of shops. A pang of guilt and sadness overcame me when we drove by my father's apothecary shop.

Devlin pulled his car to the curb in front of Luisah's. He turned it off, and we climbed out into the heat. A warm breeze blew over me, carrying the varying scents of eucalyptus, lavender, and salt. I inhaled the familiar smell. I shouldn't have stayed away so long.

Luisah came out of her shop, and her gaze locked with mine. I had to fight the urge to squirm under her scrutiny.

"The Historian," Alek said, coming to stand next to me. "She is one of the three gods that created humanity."

"What?" I said, my gaze going between him and her.

Alek studied me, his eyes shining in the darkness. "Why don't you know this?"

"Wait, wait." My head spun as I tried to absorb what he said. I'd realized four weeks ago that there was something more to her. Something ancient. But I would have never guessed she was a god.

"Most religions talk about the one true god creating the world, not three," I said.

"When organized religion was created, the three converged into one. However, the triumvirate has always remained. The Father, the Son, and the Holy Spirit for Christianity; the Mother, the Maiden, and the Crone for Wiccan..."

I held my hand up to stall him then returned my attention to Luisah. She stood directly under a streetlamp in the pool of light, the darkness surrounding her, waiting patiently for us.

A chill went down my spine as I stared at her. *Historian.* The title made sense, I thought, as I stole a glance at the bookstore, it suddenly dawning on me that I'd never seen her sell a book—only collect fees for use of the knowledge she kept packed inside her store. And Alek wasn't the only one who had referred to Luisah as the Historian. Ezra had as well. But I was so focused on finding out what he knew and what he was that I didn't connect the dots.

She watched me for a minute as the smoke from her cigarette circled around her head, floating out into the night. "You broke your word to me, girl," she said.

"And you lied to me."

"I am incapable of lying. I can only provide the information you need."

"Then why didn't you tell me about my magick?" I asked, my tone accusing. "Why keep something so important from me?" I was on the verge of tears.

The smoke from her cigarette parted. She stared at me out of those ancient eyes. "The knot that kept your magick locked inside is gone." Her gaze went to my lips. "And you've been marked again." She took in Alek and Devlin. "You have to protect her."

"Luisah," I said, my voice small.

"Come inside. War is coming. And you all have to be prepared." She gave me one last look and walked inside the store. The bell over the door rang out, filling the quiet.

I walked into the familiar store. The scent of clove hung in the air. The floorboards creaked as we made our way to the long wooden table that ran down the center aisle. I kept my gaze averted from the remembrance of Steve she kept on the wall. I didn't need to visit that pain right now. "Why did you not tell me you were a god? And I thought the Old Ones were gods? How many damn gods are there on this island?" I drew in a ragged breath. There were so many secrets being kept from me; it was hard keeping track.

"The Old Ones are not gods." She dismissed me and looked at Alek. "Pay the price, and I will give you what you need."

"You're seriously going to charge us ten dollars?" I yelled.

She stared at me, her eyes filled with sadness. "It is the only way I can answer. And you have already paid the price for information."

"What do you mean, I already paid the price?" As soon as I asked it, I remembered my promise to her. After getting hired at Tribec Insurance, curiosity about the Gerzean culture and the artwork displayed on their walls had driven me to see Luisah. I hadn't visited her in years, and when I finally did go see her, she made me promise never to stay away again. At the time, I felt as if there was something more to her request—something significant that I was not seeing. "My promise?" I asked, my voice soft.

She nodded.

"Does the price require blood?" Alek asked.

"Blood?" I said, my eyes darting between them.

Alek turned to me. "Blood used to be the required price for information," Alek said. "Later, gold was used."

She stared at him. "No. Keep your blood in your veins, mage. You will need it for the battle to come. An oath from both of you will get you the answers you seek," she said, looking at both Alek and Devlin.

"What oath do you seek?" Alek asked.

"Your promise to return with your entire team in ten days."

"Why ten?" I asked.

Luisah regarded me. "It is not your concern. For this one..." She inclined her head toward Devlin. "The need for knowledge will become overwhelming." She turned back to Devlin. "Your promise?"

Devlin looked at Alek, a silent question playing across his face. Alek regarded him for a minute, then turned back to Luisah. "You have our word."

Luisah stared at Devlin, waiting for an answer. After a brief hesitation, he agreed to return as well. Why was it so important we return? Before I could ask, Devlin took out the picture of the Ark and gave it to Luisah. "We also need any information you have on Divine Evil."

She went in search of the information and returned a short while later with two books, one of which was *Naqada* written by Professor Shukuma. She set it and a worn brown journal on the table.

I picked up the journal and opened it.

"Divine Evil can only be achieved when one absorbs the magick of another. It must be done in ritual and freely given." She tapped her finger on the journal. "The first to achieve this was a Tibetan monk named Khuchar. He grew tired of trying to achieve Enlightenment and instead turned to a darker path. He stole the magick from his brothers—leaving them as empty shells."

"Did he kill them?" Devlin asked.

She shook her head. "No. Just empty."

"I've seen this before," I said, picking up the slim gold and black book with *Naqada* stenciled on front.

"It is what you need," she said. "Take both of them with you."

Maybe there was something I missed.

Devlin took the book from me and flipped through the pages. "Professor Shukuma works at Morehouse University," he said, looking at me. "It says he went on several excavations with his wife, searching for the Ark."

And there it was. I never thought to focus on the author of the book, just the contents. I would say I felt like an idiot, but that would be an understatement. After all, she showed me the book when I first asked about the Naqada culture. Maybe she had been trying to guide me all along.

"How do I protect myself from the rest of the Old Ones?" I asked, getting up. It was obvious she wasn't going to give us any more information, and I at least needed to know that; especially after Set attacked me again Monday night. True, he stopped, but until I figured out what had made him, I needed something to reassure me that if I were attacked again, I could defend myself.

"Only another Old One can help you." She looked at Alek and Devlin. "Remember your promise."

"Ten days," Devlin said.

She nodded.

"One last question," I said and paused. I had to ask this the right way. Devlin believed the red mist that hit me was a heat pocket, but he did say something about stored power. Hathor said it took a great deal of heat to restore power. We didn't have the time to get into it. Like Devlin said, we were being pulled in too many directions. Weather would not be a priority right now. But to me, it was important. I'd suffered through that brief inferno, and I wanted to know why.

"What sort of power causes an immense amount of heat?"

"One that is being restored," she said without hesitation and with a note of finality in her tone.

Hathor said she was restoring power. Now, I just needed to find her and find out whose power she was restoring. Along with all the other shit we had to deal with. Shouldn't be a problem.

After one last glance at her, I followed Alek and Devlin out the door.

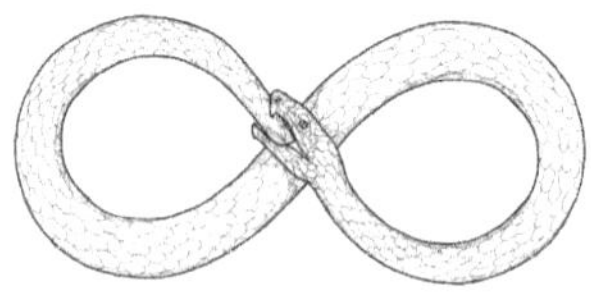

WE RODE in silence for a short while, each of us deep in our own thoughts, before Alek said, "In ancient times, before there was gold and silver and other such things to distinguish one's wealth and power, knowledge was the source of power. Over the years, those who had the most power sought to control others by limiting their knowledge. That was the start of religion. The first holy decrees outlawed libraries and prohibited the people from learning, and even convinced the masses that knowledge was evil. The Historian is there for those who seek her out."

I turned and found his eyes in the darkness.

"She is always present during tragic events in history."

"As a record keeper?" I asked.

He turned away from me, his face haunted. "No, as a source of information. She comes years before disaster strikes, hoping that humanity would remember that knowledge is power and use that to stop whatever tragedy is going to take place. A blood oath would rob us of our free will; an oath given freely would give us a choice. Our choice is far more valuable than money. Luisah needs that to help us in the days to come."

It was what I had been fearing. The scene was being set for something big. If what Alek said was true—and I had no reason to doubt him—about why Luisah had come to this island, then the final pieces would soon be put in place.

"Petronela said something about being bound in blood," Devlin said. "How old is she?"

"No one knows for sure," Alek said. "But I have to wonder if she, too, made a pact with the Historian. It would make sense." He paused. "After all, she does have part of the Alexandria library."

D evlin decided, since we knew how Gavina had achieved Divine Evil, we should switch our attention to the Ark. He did, however, ask Rachel to get the journal Luisah gave us transcribed from Tibetic to English just to be sure we weren't missing something.

Our focus on the Ark meant we were going to concentrate on the Stewart family for a while. I had to admit, I appreciated the change. I needed to cleanse my mind. Forgetting about Gavina would help me achieve that. However, I was still going to make her pay for what she did.

Sitting down heavily on the front porch, my hand shook as I tried to light my cigar, the flame dancing around the tip. When it finally caught, I pulled heavily on it, letting the apple coat my throat. The smoke curled out into the humid air. I rested my arms on my knees, letting the cigar dangle from my fingertips.

The answers we got at Luisah's worried me. How had I missed that important piece of information? True, the time she gave me the book, I wasn't looking for information about an Ark. But if I had paid attention to what I was reading, it probably could have saved us some precious time. Not much, but at least we would have known who to talk to about the Ark in the first place.

The solution to my Set problem wasn't going to be simple. Ezra had warned me about contacting him again unless he reached out first. And I refused to ask Jordin for help. So, that left doing nothing and possibly getting killed. Or going to see Ezra and possibly getting killed. Either option left me dead.

I took another pull on my cigar. Damn, I was screwed.

My gaze travelled back toward the black Nissan parked a few houses down from us. It had been there when we got back over an hour ago. I could just make out a person sitting inside. I would have dismissed it, but we had a few people currently gunning for us. I thought about going inside to get my gun, but I had my switchblade and a cigar to finish. So, fuck it. If whoever was in the car wanted to come for me, let them come. They could help me break in my knife.

Headlights flooded the street, and Kara's car came into view. I took another pull on my cigar and blew out a ring of smoke, watching as she pulled in behind Devlin's SUV. Needing to vent, I'd called her when we got back. Something in my voice must have alarmed her, because she'd told me she would be over and hung up.

Kara got out of the car and her gaze landed on me. "Why are you out here by yourself?" She walked up and sat next to me. "Smoking?"

"Yeah, Madeline can kiss my ass."

Kara reached for my cigar, and I handed it to her. She took a long pull.

"Smoking?" I asked.

"No sense in you smoking alone." She blew smoke in the direction of the car. "Who's Madeline?" She handed me back the cigar.

"The self-help guru handing out shitty advice." She gave me a confused look. I shrugged. "You don't want to know." I ticked my head toward the car down the street. "See that car?"

"Yes. Do you know who it is?"

"Not yet. He does look familiar, though."

She leaned back on her hands; her gaze trained on the car. "You think it's Logan."

"No. The man in the car has hair."

"Something about Logan seemed familiar."

"You've seen him before that day at the church?"

"Yeah. But I can't remember where." She stared down the street, but I didn't think she was trying to figure out who the driver in the car was. There was strain around her eyes and mouth. She took the cigar from me.

"Why are you really smoking?" I asked.

"I heard from my grandmother today. She's coming back to the house." After taking another pull, she handed it back.

"And?"

Kara sighed. "Give me a minute."

We sat there in silence. Eventually, she stood up and paced in front of me. "I need a distraction for a second. Tell me what happened today."

"Okay." I told her about my day. I doubt she was listening. She just kept pacing and growing more and more agitated.

Finally, she stopped and blurted out, "My grandmother took me from my mother when I was two months old." She paused, then added, "When I was ten, my grandma told me that my mother had planned on killing me."

My eyes rounded and I stood up. She put up a hand to stop me. "Let me get this out." She looked at me. "I need to tell you why I was trained to use battle magick."

"You want to tell me now?"

"I think it ties into my memories of Logan. Something's there. Maybe if I talk it out, I'll remember."

"How long have you been worrying about this?"

She frowned. "Since we saw him at church." She peered down at the ground. "I just kept thinking. Trying to remember. When my grandma called, it was like something had clicked in place."

I looked down the street. Whoever was in the car seemed to be content to just sit there. So, they'd have to wait. "Okay," I said, turning back to her. "Let's sit back down, at least."

She nodded and let me guide her back to the step.

After a short pause, she said, "My grandmother said my

mother hated that I looked so much like my father, and she didn't want the reminder of what he'd done staring at her every day. So, she decided to drown me."

"What had your father done?" I asked.

Kara wrapped her arms around her legs. "My mother always wanted to be a teacher." She smiled. "I found some of her old college textbooks when I got older." Kara wasn't kidding when she said she needed to talk it out. I leaned toward her, offering support. "F, I'm telling this wrong."

"No, you're not."

She looked at me out of tear-filled eyes. "Thanks." She reached for the cigar, and I handed it to her. After taking a pull and blowing the smoke out, she continued. "My father was my mother's college professor. Since my grandmother refused to pay for her education, she offered to stay after class and help him grade papers for twelve dollars an hour." Her eyes hardened. "One night, he decided he wanted more and raped my mother." She turned to me. "I was the result of that rape."

She got up again. "My mother wanted to abort me. But my grandmother convinced her to keep me instead. And when I was born, my mother slipped into a deep depression. When I was two months old, my grandmother had come to visit. She found my mother holding me down in the bathtub. She took me from her."

"Did your grandmother tell you this?"

She shook her head. "No. I read about it in my mother's journals. The only time my grandma talked about my mother was to put her down and call her weak."

"What happened to her?"

Kara shrugged. "Sometimes I think about trying to find her. But..." She turned to me. "Then I remember she didn't want the reminder."

I've always known Kara's grandmother was horrible. As kids, we rarely spent any time at her house. I couldn't imagine what type of mother would force her own child to keep a baby after being raped. That level of cruelty did not make sense to me. But then again, if she hadn't, Kara wouldn't be here.

I ground the cigar out. I didn't know how to feel about what she'd just told me.

"When I was ten, she started training me how to kill," Kara continued. "My father was my first lesson. That's where my memories of Logan start to surface."

Part of me was curious how she managed to kill her father. Another part of me didn't want the memory of my ten-year-old friend slaughtering someone floating around in my head.

She looked at me. "Marta wanted a family. She even stayed with a man she didn't love to keep that family. You were always obsessed with magick and tried to pretend otherwise. I think you knew deep down you had more power than you were led to believe you had. I was trained to kill and have stayed hidden in a classroom full of children so I would never have to use those skills." She said all this as if she were ticking off a list.

"I'm so sorry, Kara."

"But one day, I know I will step out of that safe space and become what I was trained to be." She took my hand. "But I promise you'll be the first to know when I do."

We sat in silence for a while. I didn't know what to say. My best friend had been trained to be an assassin. My sweet, somewhat bubbly friend, who hated curse words and loved sugar could kill at the drop of a hat. And now, she was promising to tell me when she decided to start killing. There was no follow-up to that.

"Is working with Devlin bringing it all back up?" I said finally, my voice a little rough. I couldn't help but feel as if I had let her down in some way. She had to have been struggling during that training. And I was her friend the whole time.

She sat up. "Yes. A memory of her teaching me keeps surfacing. And in it, a bald teenaged boy is talking to her." She turned to me. "I think it was Logan."

I remembered what Alek had done to the guard from Tribec. He'd altered the man's memory to remove Jonah from his mind. I told Kara about it and how Alek had explained it to me; that while the details didn't change, the understanding of what went on did.

"You think Logan did that to me?"

I nodded. "It sounds like it. And he did briefly seem concerned about your presence."

The front door opened, and we turned. Alek stood in the doorway, looking down the street. "He's still there."

"Oh, so you noticed him, too?" I asked. He gave me a look. "Of course, you did." I got up. "Should we go have a chat with him?"

He looked at Kara. "As long as you two are done talking."

"We're done," Kara said, pulling a blade from the sheath around her ankle.

"Umm...Kara? What the hell?"

"Where's your gun?" she asked.

I looked at Alek. "Don't you dare say anything."

He laughed and stepped down off the porch. As soon as he did, the car started and, rubber burning, the driver sped by, giving me a brief look at him. His familiarity finally kicked into place, along with memories of his smell.

"That's the bastard who asked me to give more at church on Sunday." Everything about what I said sounded wrong.

We rushed down the walkway. Alek tossed me his keys, a clear sign he wanted me to drive, and jumped in the passenger seat. My hand shook as I tried to shove the key into the ignition. Okay. I could do this.

Sweat dripped into my eyes.

Adrenaline coursed through my body.

I gripped the steering wheel to the point of cutting off my own circulation.

I punched the gas pedal, the car lurching forward.

I slammed on the brakes, and my chest rammed into the steering wheel.

Alek reached over me and yanked the seatbelt around me.

Once I heard the click, I peeled out, trying to make up the lost time.

My hands ached, my grip on the steering wheel too tight. Alek's magick flared, filling the car. He hummed a dark, familiar melody as I wove in and out of traffic.

The man in the Nissan swerved into traffic. Horns blared as he clipped two cars trying to get away from him. I kept my foot down on the pedal by sheer will and prayed to whoever was listening that I didn't kill us.

The scene before me was like a fast-moving train wreck.

"Nicole, watch out!" Kara yelled as we barely missed the car merging in front of us.

Alek continued humming. It was that same tune he hummed when we were ambushed in Perry. Alek's power seemed to cut off all the oxygen. I blinked rapidly, trying to clear the haze from my vision, while I jerked the steering wheel back and forth.

"Fuck," Alek yelled.

The Nissan merged onto the highway. Car horns blared as he weaved in and out of traffic. He clipped a car when he changed lanes, sending it into a spin. I yanked the wheel to the left, barely missing him.

"We need to control the situation," Alek said.

"And how exactly are we going to do that?" I said, inching the car up to ninety miles an hour.

An orange light filled the car. The Nissan cut across traffic, making its way toward the exit. "Get closer!" Alek yelled.

I would have flipped him off, but I needed to keep both hands on the wheel.

The Nissan took the exit too fast, running the red light. I slammed on the breaks just as a semi passed in front of me.

"Kara, drive. Nicole, in my lap."

Before I could protest, Alek unclicked my seatbelt and pulled me in his lap. Kara scrambled over the center console just as the light turned green. She punched the gas, going from zero to fifty in less than a second. She should have been driving in the first place.

We caught up to the Nissan just as it turned down another residential street.

"Where are we?" Alek asked.

I looked around. "Tulare," I said.

"Are there any abandoned areas up ahead? Alleys?"

I thought about it for a minute. Tulare had most of the tourist attractions with a small residential population. It also had a ton of strip malls. "A few streets down, there's a strip mall."

Alek nodded then looked at me. "I need you to reach out and touch his soul."

"What?" I asked, turning to him.

He cupped my face. "You can do it. I need him afraid so I can send him down that alley."

"If you're going to do it, I suggest you do it now," Kara said. "We're almost there."

Okay. So. No pressure. I turned toward the Nissan. Alek had started to hum again, filling the car with his magick. I tuned it out, focusing on trying to see the man's aura first. The car posed a problem. My mind kept telling me there was no way I could see past metal. And I was having a hard time pushing that thought down.

"The car's in the way," I announced.

"Concentrate," Alek said. "Look through the back windshield."

I blew out a breath and let my gaze go distant. Staring through the windshield, I was able to see a pale gold light that looked almost yellow emanating around the man in the car. Faith magick. I pushed past that to the small ball of light pulsing in the center. I reached out with my own magick, just as he passed the last street before the strip mall.

A cold, slippery feeling encased my hand. I was tempted to look down at it but kept my eyes on the back of the man's head.

He jerked, and the Nissan slowed. When I flexed my hand, squeezing, he yanked the car toward the curb.

Kara pulled up behind him.

"Are you holding it?"

I nodded. When I tried this on Alek weeks ago, I had only been able to run my finger across the energy. Now, I was able to feel pieces of it in my hand.

Alek's magick surged, and the man pulled away from the curb and turned down the alley. Kara followed.

Alek pulled his phone from his pocket and called Devlin. "We have the man who was watching the house. I put him to sleep," he said. "What do you want to do with him?" Alek put the phone on speaker.

"Where are you?" Devlin asked.

"In Tulare."

"Take him to a motel and text us the address. We'll meet you there."

Alek hung up and looked at Kara. "Any cheap motels in the area?"

"Yeah, near the border of Brunswood."

Alek cupped my head and turned me to him. "You okay?"

"Ask me that later. Are we really taking this man to a motel to question him?"

He nodded, studying me.

Was I disturbed by what we were about to do? I'd like to say yes, but I also knew this man had been watching us for a reason. And we needed to find out why.

"Since I assume we're taking his car, too, am I riding with you or Kara?"

"Your choice," he said.

In the end, I rode with Kara. And not because I didn't want to ride with Alek. I needed to pretend for just a little while that we weren't kidnapping a man to question him.

Sadly, it wasn't working.

The motel Kara directed us to looked as if someone had abandoned it long ago; a long brick building with a weak beam lighting the walkway. An office, cast in shadow, sat off to the right with an old man sitting inside—the glare from the TV illuminating his heavily lined face. He didn't even look up when we pulled in.

Who in the fuck basket would actually want to stay here?

"How the hell do you know about this place?" I asked, getting out of the car.

She climbed out and surveyed the lot. "It's seen better days."

"You didn't answer my question."

She winked. "And I'm not going to."

I nodded. "Oh, but you will."

She smirked and turned toward Alek. He got out of the Nissan and glanced around the lot. "This should work," he said, his gaze going to the office. "I'll get a key for the room at the end. There's less light down there."

I turned and looked at the last room in the row. He was right, there was less light. Correction: no light. Kara handed me Alek's keys and got in the man's Nissan. Once we parked, we got out and waited. Alek came strolling down the walkway just as Devlin's SUV pulled into the lot. Devlin switched off the lights as he made his way toward us.

"What did you say to the clerk?" I asked when Alek handed me a key.

He tapped his head and walked over to the Nissan. Well, I guess he wouldn't have had to say much if he used his magick. Jonah got out of the SUV and helped Alek heft the man out of the car.

Rachel came bounding over to us with a smile stretched across her face. "Wish I could have gone on a high-speed chase with you," she said with way too much enthusiasm in her voice.

"Maybe next time," Kara offered.

I turned away from their gleeful display and opened the motel room door. A smell that could only come from a mad scientist's lab rushed out and punched me in the face. "Oh, dear god," I said, blinking a few times to fight the sting in my eyes. "When is the last time they aired out this room?"

Devlin walked past me. He must have been made from stronger stuff because there was no way in hell I was going to wade into that stench. And I do mean wade. That funk had teeth.

Devlin opened the front window and motioned for us to come inside. I let Jonah and Alek carry the man in, then waited for Kara and Rachel to go inside before I sucked in a breath and stepped into the room.

"Maybe we should question him outside," I suggested, looking around at the large space. A single bed sat flush against a dingy white wall. Next to it was a lone nightstand that looked on the verge of collapse. The lampshade sported a Rorschach test of stains. The small table with two chairs rested near the bathroom. And at this point, the carpet was just loose beige threads.

I glanced at the rest of the team. They were moving around as if they had lost all sense of sight and smell. "You all don't smell that?"

"Breathe through your mouth," Jonah offered, as he positioned a chair in the middle of the room.

Alek tossed me the man's wallet. "Make yourself useful?" His smile saved him from me giving him the bird.

According to his driver's license, the man's name was Karl Hemmings. He was forty years old and lived in Tulare. In his panic, he must have decided to drive home. Probably thinking it was his best option. So, not too bright, then.

Devlin shut the front window and took up a position by the door. "Wake him up," he said.

Alek stepped in front of the man. Deep orange light flooded the room as magick saturated the air.

Karl stirred, and Rachel stepped over and crouched in front of him. He blinked a few times, then jerked back when he got a look at us. "Who the hell are you people?" he yelled, his eyes darting around the room.

Rachel smiled. "You don't know? You were watching our house."

Karl cut his gaze in my direction. "I was watching her!" He said this as if what he was doing was okay and didn't understand why we would have a problem with it. Yep, definitely not too bright.

"Nicole," Devlin said, dipping his head toward Karl. I guess I was up. I sucked in a deep breath. I could do this.

I moved in front of him. "Why were you watching me?" I asked, suddenly feeling as if I should have come up with some sinister lead-in to my question. Like villains who recite random bits of history before threatening their victims.

He looked away from me. "You all won't get away with this!"

"Get away with what?" Devlin asked.

I scowled at him, and he shrugged. "What he said," I said unnecessarily.

"I'm thinking of moving to the neighborhood," he said, smirking.

I stood up. "You know, the only reason I'm questioning you is to keep you alive. I can have my friend ask, but she likes to use chemicals when she interrogates people, and they"—I leaned forward—"never survive the questioning."

"You won't get away with this!" He didn't even blink at repeating the veiled threat.

"You have said that already. Now…" I rested my hands on the side of the chair, getting in real close. "What exactly will we not get away with?"

"Xavier will destroy you!"

"Xavier Young?" Why the hell did Karl believe a teenager with no magick could destroy us?

Karl blinked, then slammed his eyes closed. He must have slipped when he said Xavier's name.

"Why does Xavier want you to watch us? And how did you know where we were?"

Karl didn't respond. He just sat there with a smug, resolute look on his face. Maybe I should have let Rachel interrogate him.

Alek moved in close. "Would you like me to help you answer?" he asked, his tone even.

Karl spared him a brief glance before turning his gaze back to me. "Xavier told me about you."

"He did?" I asked, still trying to figure out why Xavier sent this man to watch me. "What did he say?"

Karl gave me a cynical smile. "He said you came sniffing around his mother's place, wanting to join her harem. Be a whore like the rest—"

I slapped him. When he laughed, I lost it. All those feelings of being violated came bubbling to the surface. Rage filled every pore on my body. My vision had gone red. I continued to pound on his face no matter how irrational my response to his taunting was. Fuck Gavina and fuck him for believing I would ever let that sick bitch touch me again. Someone called my name, but I ignored them and continued to take out all my pent-up anger and frustration on Karl. He showed up at Devlin's purposely to watch me. He had no right to do that. And Xavier, that useless piece of shit, should have never sent him. I was not Gavina's whore!

Karl buckled under the onslaught of my blows. I heard a loud *crack*, the chair toppled backward. Before I could follow Karl down, someone grabbed me around the waist, and the next thing I knew, I was being deposited outside.

My chest heaved as I stood there with angry tears streaming down my face.

Alek studied my face. "Better?"

Karl's manic laughter drifted out the door. Seriously? "Maybe I'm not as dangerous as I thought I was. The guy is still laughing after I just pummeled him to death." I rubbed my sore hand. "He got under my skin."

"That was the plan."

I stared up at him. "And I fell for it."

"We all do sometimes." He steered me toward the door. "Best get back in there. Show him you are not so easily defeated."

"Let me pull some fresh air into my lungs first," I said, and he smiled.

After a brief hesitation, I walked back inside. Alek shut the door behind us.

Karl had been secured to the other chair, the broken one in a heap by the bathroom door. He stared at me, hatred brewing in his eyes. I studied his bloody face. At least I'd done some damage.

"Do I need to repeat the question?" I asked as if I hadn't just gone into a rage and beat on him.

"Fuck you," he said, his tone even. Okay, so we were both going to pretend. Fine with me.

"Why does Xavier want you to watch us?" I asked again.

He didn't respond. I lifted my hand, and he flinched back. "He told me to follow you," he stammered out. "Said you are strong and if I can convince you to join him, I can move up in the church."

"Join him?"

"I'm done talking."

"You're not doing a very good job of convincing me not to let my friend question you," I said, infusing my voice with disappointment. Rachel handed me her brass knuckles.

"How did you defeat Gavina?" Karl asked, his eyes glued to the brass knuckles.

He was stalling, and it took a minute for me to figure out what he was talking about. "At church?"

He nodded. "He said you made his mother finally feel pain." A maniacal smile stretched across his face. "Women should never be put in a position of power. That's a man's place. Boyd is weak. He lets her control him. In the new order, Xavier will rule, and I will be by his side. I will finally get what I deserve."

I glanced at the others. None of this made any sense. "So, Xavier is trying to take over the church?"

"No. The church is bullshit. Boyd is a fraud. And Gavina just wants to have sex with the women. No." He shifted in his seat. "True power comes from the gods. Xavier has summoned one who was created long ago. Once we amass enough power, we will bring him back into existence." He chuckled darkly. "I will lead by Xavier's side, ushering in a new age," he said, repeating his assumed destiny again. "So, beat me all you want, you silly little tramp. I will one day rule you as well. Those that don't go willingly will be brought down." He looked down the length of me. "I will enjoy breaking you in."

I tried hard not to react. Sadly, it wasn't hard enough.

I barked out a laugh. Karl jerked back as if he'd been slapped. Seriously? What was next? They were going to take over the world. Build a kingdom? And it would *literally* be a cold day in hell before I let this foul-smelling idiot touch me. I ripped off one man's dick; I wasn't above ripping off another.

I glanced around at the others, belatedly noting that no one else was laughing. They were too busy staring at Jonah. He stood near the bathroom door, staring at Karl's back with horror in his eyes. After a brief pause, he stalked over to the man and got in his face. "Which god?"

Karl smiled again, and before I could stop her, Rachel slapped him. She must have gotten tired of standing on the sidelines.

"Legos. He is waiting for us." Karl said, his voice filled with delirious glee.

"Idiots!" Jonah yelled. "Do you even know how a god is created? And what kind of power they have if they're able to get loose?"

"Xavier is strong. He is the chosen one."

Jonah glared down at him as if he could impart common sense by simply staring and willing it into Karl's brain. Karl, like most zealots too far gone for reason, stared back with a defiance born from the constant reassurances that he was always right.

Devlin stepped between them, causing Jonah to take a step back. "When does he plan on doing this?" Devlin asked.

Karl sat back and made a point of smashing his lips together like a child refusing to talk. Seriously?

We were getting nowhere.

Karl turned from Devlin and glared at Alek. "Xavier will make you pay for hurting me." It took me a minute to figure out he was talking about Alek's mental attack.

"Why don't *you* make me pay?" Alek asked, his tone deadly.

Devlin glanced over at him. "Step out," he said.

Alek gave Karl one last look, pushed off the wall, and walked out. Jonah and Rachel followed. What was *that* all about?

I focused on Devlin, trying to figure out what the end game was. It was obvious Karl had no intention of answering our questions directly. True, Rachel could inject him with her concoction or pummel him to death. The look in her eyes said she was ready to do both. But I had already given him enough blows, and those seem to have had no effect whatsoever.

Devlin seemed, for the first time, lost, as if he didn't know how to handle Karl's brand of crazy and something had broken inside of him. Hell, I didn't know, either. And the longer he stayed tied to the chair, the worse it would get. We had to do something.

Devlin jerked his head toward the door, signaling for me to

step out. Good. I could use a break from Karl's noxious motor oil scent. Was he repairing cars, or sleeping with them?

It wasn't like we hadn't been in a similar situation. Only that time, our attackers had shown up at my apartment, killed Wade, and assaulted Alek and me. That questioning, and its eventual outcome, was justified. At least that's what I had convinced myself of. But now, we had run a man down, kidnapped him off the street, and tied him up in a seedy motel.

We were treading on dangerous ground.

It was that gray area Devlin had warned me about the first time. They didn't do black and white. He and his team colored outside the lines and operated in the gray. And now, I was part of the team, also playing in the ambiguous shade.

I glanced down the walkway and looked in the office. The clerk's head lay slumped forward, the light from the television dancing over his head. "What did you do to the clerk?" I asked.

"He's asleep," Alek said.

I nodded while trying to come up with a plan on how to deal with Karl. He was obviously hell bent on antagonizing us. He didn't even seem concerned about his wellbeing. "I think I should question him alone," I said before I could stop myself.

Alek moved next to me. "Not a good idea."

I ignored him because I knew he was angry, and I didn't want to argue with him about it. It was sweet he wanted to protect me, but I also needed to prove myself.

"What's your game plan?" Devlin asked, surprising me. I thought for sure he'd object to me putting myself in danger.

What was my game plan? Aside from keeping the crew from killing him.

"I can..." I trailed off.

"Get him talking. He's fixated on you." Devlin suggested as if he had been thinking the same thing.

I felt Alek move up beside me. I turned to him. "I can do this," I said, trying to sound brave and sure of myself. It wasn't working.

He moved closer and stared down at me out of dark blue eyes filled with a brewing storm. "Devlin is right. He is fixated on you. For the wrong reason."

I smiled, mostly to reassure myself, but also to calm Alek down a little. I needed his support if this was going to work. "Did you forget what I can do?"

He fought the smile gallantly, but in the end, his lips quirked up just enough to signal to me he understood what I was saying.

"Before you rip his dick off, make sure he tells you about Xavier's plans," Rachel said.

"Okay," I said, thankful for the brevity. I was afraid. But mostly, I just wanted to get this shit over with quickly.

"Do you need me to help?" Kara asked.

I stared at her for a minute. After what she just confessed to me, having her in the room was not a good idea. True, she could probably get a confession out of him. But she would also have to inflict enough pain to get him to open up. Maybe even place some strategic cuts on his body. Damn. I really needed to stop my imagination before it got out of hand. I had no idea what her training comprised of, and imagining it wasn't going to help me process it.

"Kara," I started, and she held up her hand to stop me from finishing the statement.

"No. I will wait out here," she said.

"I'll wait with you," Jonah offered. He put his hand on her waist and guided her toward Devlin's SUV.

"They're going to make kissy face," Rachel said. There wasn't any joy or teasing in her tone, which startled me until I looked at her and saw her face was filled with worry. It was a little surprising to see her in that state. She usually charged at danger like a kid in a candy store.

"I'm going to be okay, Rach," I said, trying out their nickname for her.

She smiled at that.

"As I was saying," Devlin said, his impatience showing, "get him talking. People often relish the idea of being able to tell you what they're doing."

"Like a villain's speech?" I asked.

"No. We don't have time to get into the psychology of it. But trust me, Karl wants to talk. He wants to gloat. Give him the opportunity to do it. If you get in trouble, yell, and Alek will shut him down."

That was reassuring. Because I had absolutely no idea how I was going to get that man to answer my questions. After a short hesitation, I turned and placed my hand on the doorknob.

When I pushed open the door, I strong gust of motor oil and sweat rushed out as if it had been building up inside the room. I hesitated, wondering about the stench and the magnitude of it. The smell had managed to snuff out the motel's stench. Easing the door shut to keep Karl from hearing, I turned to the team and asked, "Does his smell have anything to do with magick?" I asked in a hushed whisper.

Jonah pushed off the SUV and walked over. "It can. Demons have a distinct smell. Not fire and brimstone, but something close." He inhaled. "I'm not smelling anything other than motor oil." He grew quiet, his eyes cast down as if he were thinking. "If a demon were controlling him, we'd sense its presence."

I swallowed the sudden boulder in my throat. "I thought demons couldn't roam free."

Jonah looked at me, his hazel eyes blazing in the darkness. "Where do you think the stories of possession come from? All history has a kernel of truth. Once created, if they are not contained, they do roam free. Some choose destruction and mayhem. Others choose quiet assaults."

"Like Legos?" I asked as fear wormed its way up my spine.

"Like Legos," he said.

I stared at the door and could have sworn I heard the music from *The Exorcist*. Why the hell did I open my big mouth to volunteer? I turned to everyone. They all watched me. Rachel ringed her hands like she was agitated. Maybe it wasn't worry I glimpsed in her, but anxiousness. A need to be a part of the action. Damn. She really did get off on this shit.

I pushed open the door quickly, before I lost my nerve or peed on myself, and stepped into the room. After shutting the door, I walked around Karl and stood a few feet away.

Before I could speak, he said, "Where are your protectors?" I sat down on the floor and leaned up against the wall. "They're scared of me. Of my power," he continued when I didn't answer.

"They're throwing up. You smell like you bathe in motor oil and ten-year-old sweat."

"Fuck you."

"We've already established you won't get anywhere near me." I regarded him, taking in the surety in his body language. "Xavier doesn't have any magick."

"Legos will give him magick. He will give us all power, and I will bathe in his baptismal waters to cleanse myself of this plane of existence's stench."

"So, have you been keeping yourself pure until then?" *By not bathing*, I left unsaid. I could goad him all night, but I doubted it would get anywhere.

"As Xavier has instructed," he said, bobbing his head up and down. "I..." He stared at me. "I don't trust you."

"Why not? I want to know all about Legos. You want me to join you, right?"

"You have me bound to a chair. How can I possibly believe you have nothing but contempt for me if you leave me in this defenseless position?" I would have believed this bothered him if not for the glimmer of manipulation in his eyes.

I gave him a mocking frown. "You're going to have to work a little harder than that, Karl."

He closed his eyes. "Do you people really think you're going to get away with this?" He asked in an extremely reasonable tone. The switch from religious fanatic to rational human being was a bit jarring. But I was willing to play along.

"I don't know, Karl. I mean, you were watching us. Two

defenseless girls sitting outside talking, and some big, burly guy comes up, trying to hurt us."

He opened his eyes and smiled. "With those three men inside? You're going to have to try a little harder than that, *Nicole*." He laughed, the sound filling the room and taking all the available air.

A jolt of fear raced through me as I thought about Jonah's brief lesson on demons, then settled when Karl suddenly stopped and stared at me. He was trying to get a reaction.

"Let me guess: You heard our conversation outside the door."

His lips quirked up into a leering smile. "Of course, I did." A faraway look crossed his face, and he leaned back as far as he could. "But that would be something. To be possessed by the most powerful"—he snapped forward and stared daggers at me—"*god* that has ever existed."

"I hear the Old Ones are more powerful," I said casually. "You have heard of them, haven't you?" I asked, mocking.

He shook his head in disgust. "They are humans playing god. Insignificant." He paused, biting his lip as he turned away. "Xavier could create one if he wanted to."

"How?" I already knew how. I just needed to confirm that was Xavier's end game.

"Sacrifice is…" Karl started and then froze.

His eyes rounded, and suddenly, he pitched forward. Only the bindings were keeping him up. His mouth opened on a silent scream, and he began to convulse.

Shit!

"Something is happening," I yelled and quickly undid the ropes holding him to the chair. He fell to the ground in a thump. I went to my knees and turned him over, so his back was on the floor. I didn't want him to swallow his tongue. He continued to spasm as if someone were shaking him from inside. The sickly-sweet smell of burnt cherries rose around him. I scanned the room, looking for the Old One as I sniffed the air, searching for the acrid scent of sand.

Nothing. Only the cherry smell.

The others rushed into the room. Alek knelt beside me and stared down at Karl's spasming body. "Someone is locked on his mind."

"How close would they have to be to do that?" Devlin asked in a rush.

Alek looked up. "Close."

Devlin rushed out of the room; Jonah and Kara followed. Rachel knelt with us and bent forward, sniffing. "He smells like cherries." She looked up at me. "Is it Set?"

I shook my head. What the hell were we supposed to do?

"Can you stop them?" Rachel asked Alek.

"No," he said and rubbed his head. He must have tried.

"Are they too powerful?" I asked. I'd seen Alek use his magick on a crowd of people.

"Not too powerful. Karl is allowing this. It's like..." He stared at the convulsing man. "Back up," he said finally.

Rachel and I both moved back. Alek took the man's head in his hands. Bowing forward, he started to hum. The dark melody filled the room. The power pushed at me, and my protective mark woke up.

The phoenix wings unfurled, and the hands opened as if waiting. My body lit with a wave of what felt like electricity, starting from my head and launching its way down my body. I blinked once. And when I opened my eyes, I could see the orange tendrils crawling around the room—filling the space completely. Just how powerful was Alek?

"Nicole," Rachel said, sounding far away.

My protective mark must have sensed a threat to me. But I wasn't the one being assaulted. So, what if the proximity to someone who was being attacked was the reason it was reacting? No. That didn't make sense either. Especially since I was sitting on Alek's lap when he latched onto Karl's mind before. My mark hadn't reacted then. It had to be the person who was attacking Karl. They were the threat. And my magick knew it. Going out on a limb, I knelt next to Alek and placed my hand on Karl's chest. His heart rammed so hard; I could feel the pounding in my palm.

Alek turned to me. "What are you doing?" he asked, his voice low.

"Helping," I said, hoping it was true.

Alek's sudden roar told me it was working. My mark now perceived the threat and assumed it was for me. He jumped up and stepped away from me. I didn't look back to confirm he was okay. Instead, I focused all my attention on Karl.

The gold phoenix wings beat rapidly, pushing at the sudden onslaught of magick. My body shook, and a cold sweat ran down my back. Pain circled inside of me like a cyclone working its way from the center of my chest out. A steely voice suddenly echoed inside my head.

He is mine. He is mine. He is mine. The voice was too scratchy for me to determine if it was male or female.

Drool slid down Karl's cheek. "I am yours," Karl slurred.

I slapped him. "He is killing you!"

The fucking idiot didn't even want to fight. I had tried to avoid his death. But it looked as if that effort was in vain.

A smile stretched across Karl's face as his convulsions slowed. He was dying, and while my mark was protecting me, it was doing nothing for Karl. From the looks of it, he didn't care.

Some people just couldn't be saved. And I needed to accept that.

Alek pulled me up. The others came rushing back in the room.

"No one is outside," Devlin said, his voice flat.

Alek shook his head. "There's nothing we can do."

But wait for him to die, was left unsaid. This was our fault. We should not have brought him here. When Karl's body went still, I ran out of the room.

The hot water ran over my body, washing away the taint of what we'd done, along with my tears. I did not speak to anyone when Karl finally died, nor on the way home from the motel. We had left Karl there for someone else to find. I didn't even say goodbye to Kara when she came in Alek's room to try and console me. I heard her, of course, telling me it wasn't our fault and that we couldn't do anything about it. Funny, I didn't feel that way at all.

Instead, I let the weight of it consume me. Like with Tribec weeks earlier, the sense of being lost and confused occupied every fiber of my being. Once again, we'd been given a bunch of puzzle pieces with no clear picture of how they all fit together. And again, I was at the center of it.

I didn't believe I was some fabled chosen one or any other such bullshit. But given the strangeness of my magick, maybe I was a key to something. Set had told me that I was 'of the blood.' It implied there was something significant about my magick. And if I weren't so damn stubborn, I could ask my parents. Sadly, every single time I convinced myself just to get it over with, the pain of being lied to flooded back, making me dig my heels in even more.

The bathroom door opened, letting in a cool breeze. I didn't move.

"Nicole," Alek said, his voice soft.

"I don't want to talk," I mumbled.

The shower curtain whisked back. "Too bad," he said.

While water pelted my skin, I turned and stared at him. He flinched at the heated look I gave him. "If you want to yell, go ahead. But I'm not going to let you stand in here and blame yourself."

"Who says I'm blaming myself?" I asked, my voice cold.

"Your actions. If you blamed us"—he grabbed a towel off the rack and shut off the shower—"you would be in there yelling at us. Not standing in the shower having a pity party."

"Fuck you!"

"Whenever you're ready," he said, the corner of his mouth turned up.

"I'm pissed and you're flirting with me?" I grabbed the towel from him and wrapped it around myself. He stepped back, and I climbed out of the shower. Pissed or not, my stomach fluttered at the heat in his eyes and yes, the fact that he was flirting with me.

"I'm always going to do that," Alek said, stepping closer. "I figure it might help take your mind off things." He stared down at me.

"You are so damn sure of yourself." *As he should be*, I thought, staring at him.

We had known each other for such a short time. Yet, Alek had done something no one since Steve had, make me want to be soft. Not a damsel in distress who needs to carry smelling salts soft, but the softness that comes from allowing another person to care for you. Alek did that. He pulled that buried craving out of me and put it on display. I desired him. I cared for him. I wanted to be with him.

He bent forward and kissed me on the cheek.

Every nerve ending in my body came alive. My heart fluttered in my chest and my eyes grew heavy with need and emotion. Desire rode me like a tidal wave coursing through my body as I strained toward him.

I turned and pressed my lips against his.

A long-buried emotion rushed up out of my core and stilled me. My lips remained pressed to his as I let the feeling overtake me. Whispered thoughts of love kept cycling through me, and I fought the desire to profess it.

Because it could not be real.

I moved closer, and he wrapped his arms around me. Only the pressure from his body kept my towel in place. His mouth moved hesitantly as he tilted his head, and his tongue slid across my bottom lip. I parted my lips—letting him in. The towel slipped a little, and I groaned as my hardened nipples rubbed against his t-shirt.

Alek picked me up and sat me on the edge of the sink, wedging between my legs. I wrapped my legs around him, and he cupped my butt, pulling me in closer. All hesitation went out the window. Grabbing a handful of his hair, I ravaged his mouth.

The desire to have someone inside of my mind, body, and soul left me raw and aching. I needed Alek. Past the sex. Past the friendship. I just needed *him*.

And it was that exact feeling that had me pulling away from him, putting a painful distance between us.

"We should stop," I said, my voice ragged.

Alek's chest heaved. He placed his forehead against mine. It would have been so easy to resume—to tear off his clothes and let him take me. I wanted him to. But I also wanted more. And I could not go there. Not now. Not while I was so damaged. I was likely to destroy whatever built between us.

"You're right," he said finally, stepping away. "We have time."

"Do we?"

He kissed me lightly on the lips. "I'm not going anywhere." He grinned. "Well, except in the other room." His gaze slid down me, heating my core once again. "If I stay in here, I might lose my mind."

I smiled. "Thank you for taking my mind off everything." I

slid off the sink, belatedly realizing that my breasts were exposed. The hungry look in Alek's eyes clued me in.

He made a guttural sound—that sent a thrill through me—and walked backward toward the door. "Devlin"—he cleared his throat—"wants to go over what we know."

"Okay." I continued to watch him as he stepped over the threshold and slowly closed the door behind him.

Danger and sex. One potent combination.

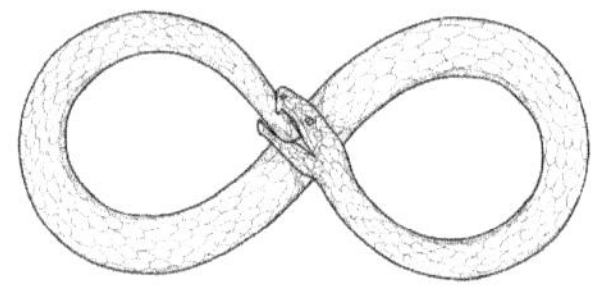

Everyone sat on chairs, looking both defeated and confused. I took a seat near Rachel and let out a heavy sigh. She pushed a mug of coffee toward me. The extra jolt of energy would help for what I was sure was going to be a long night of us circling the myriad of information we had and adding the new player to the mix. We had completely forgotten to investigate why Xavier had a void in is aura. Now, that oversight had come back to bite us in the ass.

I took a sip of my coffee. Fuck.

Devlin got up and went to the whiteboard. I studied the man as he stared at the information covering its surface. Hands on his hips, Devlin looked like he wore the weight of the universe on his shoulders. He moved Xavier's high school senior picture to the center of the board. Dressed in a white shirt, he wore a smirk on his face, as if the world were a mere joke. Given Karl's devotion to the teenager, I had to wonder just what kind of power the nineteen-year-old had that would seduce a grown man into joining him in what sounded like a quest straight out of a video game.

"How does he fit?" Devlin asked us.

I set my coffee on the table and stood. I needed to move. I wasn't kidding when I said I'd run into his type before. Both in high school and my adult life. Cocky and full of themselves, believing the world should sit up and take notice. I would put Ronald in that category, except his brand of crazy was different, and most men who walked around preening with their chests poked out weren't all that successful. However, Xavier did have one thing in common with Ronald.

They both despised their family.

"I would say he's like Ronald, wanting to break free of his family," I said eventually. "At church, he acted as if everything going on around him was beneath him. Not worth his time or energy. His smile was almost mocking. Like he viewed the parishioners as idiots or sheep. And there was tension between him and his mother." I turned and looked at everyone. "After my protective mark repelled Gavina's intrusion, The Daughters of the Vine and his siblings all rushed to her aid. Xavier took the time to find me in the crowd and smile."

Devlin nodded and took a sip of his own coffee. Noting the bags under his eyes, I checked my phone for the time. It was after two in the morning. Damn. Looked like we'd be up all night. Especially after drinking Rachel's coffee.

"Did Karl's ramblings make sense to you?" Devlin asked Jonah.

Jonah laced his fingers behind his head, leaned back, and stared at the picture of Xavier. "No. The part about Legos has some truth in it. But not completely. To sum it up, demons are the byproduct of faith magick gone wrong. When a group of faith mages decide to bring a god into existence, the understanding is that it would only be temporary. If the ritual is done correctly, they create one and then release the energy once the god's task is done. If the ritual is done wrong, or the energy is not released, then a demon is created."

"What kind of tasks?" I asked, remembering Jonah's story.

"Usually, to solidify a certain religious belief. Some people have a hard time having faith in what they can't see. Once they set eyes on the god of their religion, it restores their faith. This was a more common practice hundreds of years ago. Today, not much is needed to convince someone to believe in something." He paused. "Aside from that, gods can be created to aid in battle." He turned to me. "That is faith's battle magick. We can create a god to fight."

"Like the Naqada did when they made the Old Ones," I said.

He nodded, then glanced back at Xavier's picture. "I'm having a hard time with everything else Karl said. It was almost as if he were feeding us some made up bullshit."

"I thought the same thing," I said.

"So, who killed him?" Rachel asked. She looked at Alek. "Mind mage? I smelled cherries in the room. Nicole said Set smelled like cherries before."

"It wasn't Set," I said before Alek could answer.

"A mind mage that powerful..." He trailed off. "It could be done. But it would leave the person in a sickly state. So, if it was a mind mage, he would have to have someone else working with him. He wouldn't be functional after not only breaking Karl's mind but killing him as well."

"You said Karl wasn't fighting him," I said.

He shook his head. "No. He was definitely enthralled with the person who was killing him."

Goosebumps broke out on my arms. There was someone else working against us. Just how many damn enemies did we have? "How do you kill a demon?" I asked Jonah.

"Kill the faith mage who brought him into existence. If the demon has managed to slip the bonds of the one who created it and amassed enough people to believe in it, then only the absence of faith will destroy it. Demons need faith to keep them alive. Once people stop believing in them, they die."

I glanced at his chest. He dipped his head, acknowledging my concern. The only way to kill the demon in Jonah was for him to die. Damn.

"We table it for now," Devlin said, and picked up the slim black and gold book on the Naqada culture that Luisah had given us. "Somehow, this plays into it as well."

Jonah took the book from him and flipped through it. I had

studied that book when Luisah first showed it to me. It gave details about the battle the Old Ones were created to fight in.

Alek took the book from Jonah. "What if it's not the book itself?" he asked, studying the front. "What if it's the author? Besides Luisah, this person would know about Naqada and the Old Ones. Maybe, by giving us this book, she's telling us to contact him."

"That's what I figured as well." I sighed. "She showed me this book when I first asked questions about Tribec Insurance. I thought she was pointing out the Old Ones and the battle. After all, I did ask about the Gerzean culture. But apparently, she was giving me another clue that I completely overlooked. I never even once considered contacting the author."

"Don't beat yourself up about it," Devlin said, tone softening. "We're on the right track now."

I nodded. I should have remembered Luisah never said anything outright, only put the information in front of me so I could figure it out.

Rachel opened her laptop and typed in Professor Shukuma. "He's not at Morehouse University anymore," she said, turning the laptop toward us. "He retired last year and moved to Tulare."

Interesting—especially since he'd done so much research on the Old Ones. For him to move to a place where at least four of them resided couldn't be a coincidence.

Devlin rubbed his hand down his face. "Jonah, you and Nicole go visit him tomorrow. Rachel, when Marta shows up, have her search social media and do a deep dive on Xavier. You stay on trying to locate any women who were a part of Daughters of the Vine. Alek and I will work on the lead Rachel found today and go talk with Emilia's friend Theresa."

I must have missed something. Last I heard, we didn't have any new leads on the nurse from Tribec that Ronald had killed. The one he left for me to find on his houseboat. "How did you find one of Emilia's friends?" They must have been doing research about Ronald behind my back.

I wanted to be upset they didn't include me, but I understood their reasoning. Besides, I was keeping things from them as well. I still hadn't worked up the courage to show them the letters he sent me. Maybe I should. That way, we could work on it together. No one was going to rob me of my revenge.

"I found her online," Rachel said hesitantly. She must have sensed how this news was affecting me. "She posted about Emilia's murder and how the police aren't doing anything."

Of course, they weren't. Like the Sinclairs, the Stewart family probably had connections in high places. And her murder couldn't be tied to them, anyway. Someone had moved her dead body away from Ronald's boat and left in an alley behind a bar in Brunswood. Only a few blocks from my apartment. Definitely a message for me.

Alek stood up and stretched. "Logan?"

Devlin sighed. "Aside from the game he played, leading us around trying to find him, he hasn't attacked us. So, until he shows his hand again, we have nothing to go on. He's connected to this somehow. We just have to figure out how."

Telling everyone goodnight, Rachel grabbed her computer and left the room. Jonah followed soon after. I sat there, thinking about not just the case, but the fact that I was going to climb into bed with Alek. After our encounter in the bathroom, I didn't think that was such a good idea.

Alek hesitated for a minute as if he were waiting for me to make the first move. I kept my gaze focused on the whiteboard. When he finally left the room, I turned to Devlin. "I'm surprised you're letting Marta get involved so quickly. You made me jump through a few hoops before you trusted me." I hated sounding bitter because I really didn't feel that way. Not really. I was grateful to him for letting Marta be a part of the team. I'd told him as much.

He harrumphed. "Marta reminds me of my Aunt Daisy. They both seem forged on grit and determination. I can respect that."

"I have grit and determination!" I protested.

He laughed. "Nicole, I don't doubt it. But you also have a bad attitude and no respect for authority." He walked over and extended his hand to help me up. "I also respect the hell out of that. My hesitation with you came from not knowing just where you fit in with the Stewart family. Your involvement with Ronald was an issue."

"He was using me," I said, my voice small.

"We didn't know that at first." He pulled me into a hug.

"Oh, god," I mumbled into his chest. "Things must be terrible if you're giving me another hug, Boss Man."

His chest shook with laughter, and he pulled away, staring down at me. "Get some rest. I need you at your best tomorrow."

I stepped back and saluted him. "Yes, Boss Man!"

"Smartass," he mumbled, and made his way to the front, only to pause before leaving the room completely. "Where did you learn Tribec Insurance was hiring?"

I thought about the question for a minute. "It was right after getting fired from the shoe store," I said. "I was on my way to Jordin's and stopped at the convenience store along the way. It's the one near my apartment. They had an ad for Tribec sitting on the counter."

"Did you stop at that store often?" he asked, his face growing pensive, as if he were trying to figure something out.

"Yes," I said and hesitated. "You think someone set that ad there for me?" While I did believe someone was manipulating the situations I found myself in, I couldn't imagine how they would assume I would pick up an ad for a job they couldn't possibly know I was looking for.

Unless they were watching me.

"I'm thinking about your idea of a mastermind behind all this..." He rubbed the back of his head. "For someone to steer you toward Tribec Insurance, they would have to know you were looking for a job."

"Or just figure out my pattern," I said. Devlin had found the one small connection that led to my mastermind theory, and it terrified the hell out of me. Yes, I had thought I was at the center of it, but I never once figured out how they could have pointed me toward Tribec until now. They knew my pattern.

"The question is, why? Why focus on you specifically?"

"I guess we'll find out."

Alek's hand on my thigh woke me up to some delicious thoughts. I eased around, letting his hand travel across my body, coming to rest on my stomach, and stared at him. Damn, he was a beautiful man. His dark hair lay fanned across his pillow; his thick, long lashes rested on his lower lids, creating a small shadow underneath them. And his lips. My god, his lips. They alone could send me over the edge.

His hand slid up my abdomen. "If you keep staring at me like that, I might have to do something about it," he said, his eyes opening.

I didn't respond. He pulled me over, sliding me underneath him. He stared down at me out of those dark blue eyes filled with heat and I forgot myself. Yanking him down, I pressed my lips to his as I wrapped my legs around his waist. All that mattered in this moment was me and him—and this seductive dance we had been playing for weeks. It was time for us to do something about it.

Something akin to a growl escaped him as he devoured my mouth. I rocked forward, savoring the delicious feel of him between my legs. When I squeezed him tighter, he rose up and snatched off my shirt. He grabbed my arms and pinned them above my head. I arched up, seeking, and he brought his mouth down on my breast, sucking my sensitive nipple into his mouth. I groaned as wave after wave of pleasure rode through me.

And while his mouth continued to do some amazing things, some soon to be dead person knocked at the door.

"Can you please break their mind?" I said, my voice ragged.

He chuckled, his mouth still on my breast. "Oh, please do that again," I said.

To my complete and utter devastation, he rose up. "We will finish this," he growled.

"I vote we finish it now."

He leaned down and kissed me. "Later."

"Fine. But not here. Because I will kill the next person who interrupts us."

He laughed and slid off the bed.

He thought I was kidding.

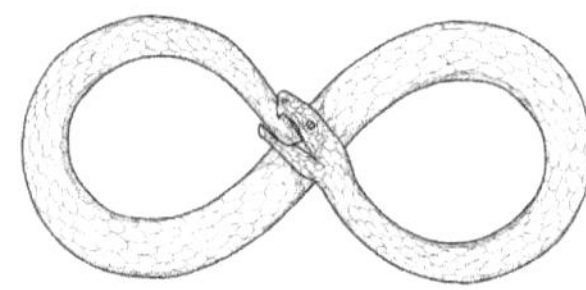

AFTER TAKING A COLD SHOWER, I joined the rest of the team in the kitchen. I might have glared at everyone as I ate my eggs and toast, but it couldn't be helped. The cold shower did not help worth a damn. And the heated looks Alek kept giving me weren't helping, either.

Once Marta arrived, Jonah and I headed out.

While he drove, I went over a bit of island history. It was a great way to take my mind off my unfulfilled need. And Jonah didn't stop me—even though he knew the information already.

There was a small settlement of Cherokee Indians already occupying the island when the first wagons travelled across the land bridge connected to Georgia in 1871. When they attempted to set up settlements, the Indians forced them back off the land and warned them never to return.

Since it had never been written down or discovered, a lot of speculation was used to explain how they were able to defend the island when they were so few in number. One of the stories told was that the land did not want the settlers there and gave the Indians power to cast them away.

Only years later, they did settle on Tulare and broke the island up into six settlements: Tulare, Dulean, Pleasanton, Brunswood, Perry, and Alice.

After reading Louis Badet's publication again, we discovered that Coeur d' Alene, Sandpoint, and the Cherokee Nation—referred to in the document as The People—at the northern part of the island, made up a triumvirate of protection that was said to help keep Set from escaping the island. It also said that The People had been tasked with guarding the Ark, keeping it out of the hands of man.

So, how had The People lost the Ark in the first place?

"What do you believe happened?" Jonah asked after I finished.

"I'm thinking that if there is a mastermind, then that person or being is the one who freed Set. And also, the one who stole the Ark from The People."

He nodded.

"But how?" he asked.

I glanced out the window. "Don't know. But we better find out soon."

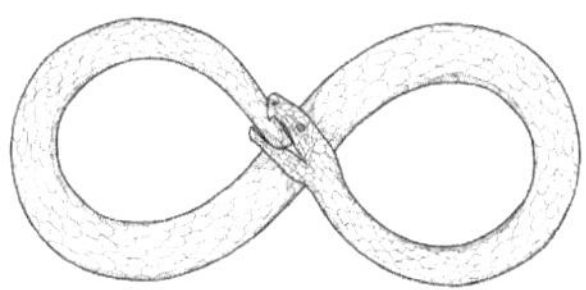

JONAH PASSED by the sign announcing we were entering the town of Sandpoint. Light traffic occupied the two-lane road. I stared out at the mom-and-pop businesses lining the road on both sides. A few outdoor restaurants were wedged in between. Smoke filled the air from the large outdoor grills. I inhaled the savory scents of meat and spices.

Unlike Coeur d'Alene, Sandpoint resembled the rest of the island, with modern family homes and schools.

"Did you ride through Sandpoint as well on your recon mission of Tulare?" I asked.

Jonah laughed. "Yes, I even stopped for some sauteed shrimp and okra." He smiled. "Reminded me of the okra my grandma used to make when we visited her in Georgia."

"You have Gullah roots?" I asked.

"No. But my grandma dated a man who did. They loved to cook together." He chuckled. "My mama said they loved to compete, always trying to outdo one another."

I smiled. "My family in New Orleans is like that. Always congregating around food." I looked out the window. "I miss them."

"When's the last time you saw them?"

"When they helped me get away from a woman who I believed was my aunt." I pulled air into my lungs, fighting the sudden tears threatening to fall. "She thought she could heal me by tying me to an altar in the bayou and having a charlatan..." I trailed off. I had no idea what Pastor Jeremiah's plans had been.

Jonah took my hand and squeezed it. "Is this what upset you at church on Sunday?"

I turned to him. "Yeah. And you are the first person I've ever talked to about it."

"You should tell Alek. And the rest of the team."

"I will." Finally, being able to tell someone about my past felt as if a weight had been lifted from me, giving me the first step toward healing. Why had I waited so long to talk about it?

A short while later, Jonah pulled up to a small white house with yellow shutters. Three small children ran around the yard, stopping when we climbed out of the car. The youngest—a little girl with dark skin and long hair—came running over to us. She smiled at me as she rubbed her head. I'd say she was maybe three years old. She reminded me of Maria with her wide-open friendliness that was often found in children her age.

"Erila, you're not supposed to talk to strangers," the older of the children said. A young boy of no more than ten who watched Jonah and me out of wary eyes.

"Hi," Erila said, still staring at me. "I'm Erila."

I knelt and smiled at her. "I'm Nicole. I love your braids."

She stepped forward and touched my hair. "Mama has hair like you."

An old man stepped onto the porch wearing jean shorts and a light green t-shirt. The wooden screen door thumped as he let it close behind him. "Hello," he called as he shielded his eyes from the sun. "Can I help you?" A note of concern laced his voice.

Jonah went up the path toward him, a smile stretched across his face. "Hi, Professor Shukuma."

Even though the professor shook Jonah's hand, his gaze remained fixed on me. I didn't blame him; a stranger was close to his grandchildren. I patted Erila's head and joined Jonah at the porch.

"I was just meeting your...grandchildren?" I said, making the statement a question as I extended my hand to him. He smiled, the skin crinkling around his dark brown eyes, as he shook my hand.

"Yes, Erila can be too friendly sometimes. But her brother, Jelani, keeps watch." He turned to the kids, eyes narrowing. "Stay in the yard. And keep your sister away from the road."

"Yes, Grandpa," Jelani said. He walked over and put a protective arm around Erila. She continued to beam at me. I hoped nothing would ever steal that joy from her heart.

"I can watch, too," the other little girl said.

Professor Shukuma smiled. "I know that Zalika." His attention returned to us. "What can I help you with?"

I pulled his book from my purse and handed it to him. "We wanted to ask you about what you wrote here."

He nodded and took the book from my hands. Rubbing a hand over the cover, he took a step backward, stopping before he got to the door. "The Old Ones," he said on a sigh. "Why don't you two come inside out the heat? I can offer you some lemonade." He opened the screen door, moved to the side, and signaled for us to enter.

I stepped inside, Jonah following directly behind me. Light filtered into the dark living-room from the large bay window. A wicker ceiling fan circled overhead, pushing a cool breeze around the room. All the furniture was dark. A large plush couch sat against the far wall with a coloring book sitting on top. Crayons lay scattered on the floor. Three small colorful plastic cups sat on a dark wood coffee table, along with paper towels covered in crumbs.

"I meant to clean this up," the professor said, picking up the paper towels and cups. "But the phone rang before I could. Please." He moved the coloring book, and I bent down and grabbed the crayons. "Thank you," he said, taking them from me. "Now, sit. I'll go get that lemonade."

"Thank you, professor."

"Please, call me Izsaka," he said.

"I'm Jonah and this is Nicole. And sir, my mama would be really disappointed if I called you by your first name."

The professor laughed. "Then your mama raised you right. But for now, in my home, I insist." He stared at us, waiting.

"Yes, sir," I said, also uncomfortable calling him by his first name.

He nodded and continued toward the back of the house. When I turned to Jonah, he was busy studying the framed photographs on the walls of desert scenes with glimpses of the pyramids. Some of the pictures had people in them—locals mixed with archeologists, all smiling into the camera. It must have been from one of the excavations he went on with his wife.

The professor returned, carrying two sweating glasses filled with ice and lemonade. "I used to make the trip to the mother-land twice a year." He handed us the glasses and napkins and sat down in the worn easy chair near the front door. "Ayanna, my late wife, and I used to take our students to Egypt for field research. Classroom learning is fine, but nothing beats seeing the places you're studying." He leaned back. "It was on one of those trips we found one of the three Arks."

"Three?" I asked. All this time, I'd thought there was only one. How had we missed this?

He nodded. "Yes. Most of man's religious history is based on the trinity. Even magick is based on the trinity. Air encompasses both mind and elemental magick. Earth has its own. And water represents the divine. Faith."

"Baptism," Jonah said.

"Correct," the professor said.

I'd seen this representation in his book and the other books Luisah had let me study when I was trying to decide if I should stay at Tribec Insurance. "Tribec," I said aloud.

"What?" the professor asked.

"Sorry. I just wondered if you'd seen the exhibits displayed at Tribec Insurance."

His face grew hard. "I've seen them. Lisa Stewart had contacted me about them some time ago." He shook his head and took a sip of his lemonade. "Didn't much care for the likes of that woman. She wanted to look through my records for information on the other Arks. Told her I couldn't help her." He laughed, but there wasn't any humor in it. "She threw a fit when I expressed the importance of having their collection behind lock and key. She wouldn't see reason and didn't take to kindly to the word no." He frowned. "I understand she and her brother were found dead some weeks ago."

Jonah and I both told him yes, but didn't elaborate.

The professor gave me a quizzical look. "How do you know about their exhibits?"

I smiled. "I had the misfortune of working there for a short while."

He nodded.

"It's not important. I'm sorry for interrupting."

He waved off my apology then sighed deeply. "The Ark we found contained two tablets with hieroglyphs on them. The students swore we had found the Ten Commandments." He laughed. "Ayanna wondered the same thing and asked one of the people from the village to send over a curator from the museum." He smiled at us. "Just in case. We were able to decipher the text. Only, later, as we reported our findings, we discovered what we'd translated was wrong." He picked up the book from the coffee table and flipped through the pages. "It wasn't the Ten Commandments. Nor was it a list of rules to live by. It was a sequence of events that led to the creation of The Old Ones. There wasn't a word for blood magick, but one of my students was familiar enough with the practice to understand the meaning behind the phrase, *Of the blood*."

A chill ran down my back as I thought of what Set had said to me in the field as he dug into my chest. *"You are of the blood..."* He believed, because of this, I would be able to free him.

"What does *of the blood* mean?" I asked.

He cut his gaze toward me. "Best guess—because that is all it would be—is it relates to a race of people or beings who were mentioned briefly in some of the writings we found later. Beings of fire. Again, the translation was off. Which, given our understanding of even the spoken languages, is possible. No one would truly know if the translations of the hieroglyphs are accurate. There is no point of reference, only guessing and assumptions."

"What was really written on the tablets?" Jonah asked.

"A list of thirteen names. Or their sounds. All The Old Ones and the families they came from."

I sat back, letting the glass cool my suddenly feverish hands. A race of people referred to as beings of fire. Mentioned in the same context with people of the blood. Could they be one and the same?

"Was magick ever mentioned?" I asked when there was a lull in the conversation.

The professor nodded. "Both before and after Christianity. In one text, the people who had magick in their blood were referred to as mages."

So, all this time, we were referring to our abilities based on Christian ideals.

"Were there any other religions referenced in what you found?" Jonah asked.

"Yes," he nodded. "Most of the well-known were mentioned. Buddhism, Christianity, Hinduism, Islam, Judaism, and even a few passages about Shintoism." He sat back. "You have to understand, in Egypt, before religion, hundreds of gods had been referenced in both myth and faith magick. These same gods had counterparts in every civilization around the world. When Christianity came on the scene, all of them were demonized, and from them, the one true god was born." He shook his head. "What they didn't realize was that the one true god had always existed, and The Old Ones were once human beings. Religions have always borrowed from one another: building, changing, corrupting. Until the truth is so deeply buried that, if ever found, it will sound like fiction."

"Maybe that was the point," I said.

"Yes, as with all men and women who seek power, corrupting the beliefs of others is the best way." He paused, staring at us. "What religion are you most curious about?"

"A sex magick cult that worships Shezmu."

"On Tulare?" He laughed. "People are more familiar with Bacchus. But yes, at one time in ancient Egypt, Shezmu was worshiped. Mostly by women who believed he bestowed power on them."

I shifted at the mention of power being given. Jordin had told me he shared some of his power with me.

"But I believe the practice has died out."

I started to tell him about Gavina but thought better of it. No need to involve anyone else in this.

"Does this help?" the professor asked.

"Yes," Jonah said. "Can you tell us anything about the other Arks?"

He grew solemn, as if something painful were weighing on

him. "Knowledge, life, and death. One to give knowledge. One to give life. And one to kill. On our last dig, after our kids were older, we found the Ark to kill. When we returned to the States, my wife...she went insane. I had to put her in the hospital to protect myself and our family." He clasped his hands in front of him. "She died three days after she was admitted."

"I am so sorry," I said, Jonah echoing my sentiment.

The professor nodded.

"What did you do with the Ark?" Jonah asked.

"Buried it. We originally found it using a map. My wife had magick in her blood. Not strong, mind you, but enough of it to recognize what we'd uncovered. She stopped me from touching that cursed thing. But not before she had laid her hands on it. She made me promise never to tell anyone where the Ark was again. I do, however, remember the inscription written on it. A single word: harbinger."

"What was written on the Ark with the tablets inside?" I asked.

"Historian. And the Ark of life, sometimes referred to as the Ark of Horus, had been removed from Egypt thousands of years ago." He leaned in. "It's rumored to have been hidden on this very island."

He had no idea those rumors were actually true.

After thanking the professor, we said goodbye to his grand-kids and left. We'd learned some things, but not nearly enough. Up until now, we'd believed there had only been one Ark. From what Professor Shukuma said, there were three. Could that be the reason Andrew Snow had been collecting information not only on his employers, the Stewart family, but the other families as well? Did he believe they had information on the other two Arks? Because if the Ark that had been hidden with The People could be found, then I had no doubt the other two had been found as well. Which made me wonder...who had the Ark of death?

A Mind in Chaos

Alek and Devlin rode in silence as they made their way to Theresa Scott's house, toward the southern part of Pleasanton near the Cherokee Nation. While Devlin read through the information on his phone that Rachel had sent, Alek kept replaying what happened between him and Nicole this morning.

He could not keep the smile off his face no matter how hard he tried. When she pulled him down into a kiss, wrapping those gorgeous legs around him, he almost lost his mind. Every imagined scenario of them together in no way compared to the actual feel of her underneath him. If they hadn't been interrupted, Alek knew it would have ended in them both satisfied and exhausted. She was right; they would have to pick up somewhere else.

"What's on your mind?" Devlin asked, interrupting his thoughts.

Alek shook his head. And thankfully, Devlin didn't press.

As painful as it was, he redirected his thoughts to Theresa.

Rachel had managed to locate a phone number for the woman despite it being unlisted. When they'd called, Theresa had been apprehensive about speaking with them. Probably believed they were acting on behalf of the Stewart family. Eventually, she relented. Rachel had asked about Emilia's family. Turns out, money had bought their silence leaving Theresa to seek justice for her friend on her own.

Before her death, Emilia had entrusted Theresa with damning information about the Stewart family. Devlin said they would help her in exchange for the information. Thankfully, she hadn't turned over her findings to the police. Chances were, it would have been buried or destroyed if she had.

Alek pulled up to a cream-colored house and parked. As they climbed out of the car, he surveyed the neighborhood. Most of the driveways were empty. Scattered toys lay on a few lawns and an ice cream truck sat at the end of the block, music off.

The sun cast a bright haze over the area, making it seem unreal; a painting had come to life. Stretching his magick out, Alek searched the homes, touching the minds of the people inside. He watched the orange tendrils of his power crawl across the pavement. Unlike the other mind mages, his magick had morphed into something dark, allowing him to expand his mind. It was almost as if his brain grew receptors—looking for a connection. The impressions he got gleaned from people temporarily became a part of him. Almost like he was being immersed inside of them. Feeling every one of their emotions.

A couple intwined with each other, making love, while guilt rode them. The feel of their connection made him flush—once again remembering Nicole. He pulled back, so the only impression he got was of their combined guilt riding them. If he wanted to, he could plant a suggestion in their mind. Telling them someone was home, and they were about to get caught. It was on their mind anyway, and a mere push from him would make it a reality for them.

He moved on, finding a young mind focused on his mother. He wanted her to pay attention to him. Alek felt a pang of familiarity with the boy. He, too, spent his childhood seeking his mother's attention while she doted on his twin brother.

Four boys hid in a basement, having skipped school. Their

minds raced with possibilities and mischief. He smiled and continued his search.

Devlin cleared his throat, and Alek turned to him. Worry briefly crossed Devlin's face. He knew the power that Alek held, and Devlin understood the cravings Alek kept at bay—the ones he had developed when he was a young boy and searching for love, only to latch onto the destruction he could cause instead.

Alek nodded, reassuring Devlin he was okay and joined his boss on the walkway leading to Theresa's house.

The house reminded Alek of a home he'd seen on a postcard in a gift shop his family had stopped at when he was seven years old. It was small and compact with a well-manicured lawn and rose bushes surrounding the porch. He couldn't remember the exact place, only that it was between the last place and the next. Traveling, to him, always felt that way. The postcard had caught his attention. He'd studied the five-by-four glossy print, running his fingers over the smooth surface. The small house pictured on the front had puzzled him. He remembered wondering what it would be like to live in a home like that. Stationary. Never having to worry about anything.

Devlin knocked on the door and pulled off his shades. Alek left his on and sent his power out, seeking the mind of the woman inside, and found chaos.

"Something's wrong," he told Devlin.

Devlin stared at him for a moment longer than Alek liked. He was probably trying to see if he needed to rein in Alek. He pulled off his shades so Devlin could see his eyes and know that he was okay.

"Dead?" Devlin asked.

"Broken."

Her mind was a chaotic symphony of memories and nightmares, all circling one another, trying to push their way to the forefront of her mind. He'd seen this before with the rental agent at Andrew Snow's apartment. Someone had used mind magick to try and create a scenario that Theresa was not familiar with, effectively breaking her mind in two. Old memories—every single worry she'd ever had was circling through her mind at once. Bills, the death of her friend, getting stood up for the prom, the promotion she didn't get at work, et cetera. All of them, on one continuous loop, warred with ones she'd never experienced. It was cruel and unnecessary. And it would take more than one mind mage to help her. In the milieu was the image of the man Alek had seen in the security tapes from the motel.

Logan Magellan.

Devlin tried the door. The knob turned easily, and after pulling his gun from his holster, he pushed his way inside. Alek glanced over his shoulder to confirm no one had come outside, then stepped inside.

The house opened to a living room that ran smoothly into the kitchen. He could see the back door from where he stood in the front room. A woman with dark hair, wearing an over-sized shirt, sat in a chair in the kitchen, her face blank. Theresa Scott. She looked a little older, but he recognized her from her driver's license photo. The lines around her mouth suggested she'd spent most of her life laughing. Sadly, her friend had chosen to work for the Stewart family, and their darkness had now touched her life, snuffing out the joy she once had.

Papers were scattered in front of her on the small table as if she had been searching for something. Or maybe Logan had been. Alek wondered if he had found what he was looking for.

Moving quickly, Devlin made his way toward her and checked her pulse. "Her pulse is a little thready," he announced. He frowned as he studied the woman. He picked up one of the scattered papers and looked over it. "Insurance bills," he said, his tone confused. He searched through the rest of them. "All of them are insurance bills. But for different people."

That was odd. Alek walked over and picked up one of the bills. "Why would Logan break Theresa's mind and leave the evidence Emilia accumulated from Tribec Insurance behind?" Alek asked, not really expecting an answer.

"Can you help her?" Devlin asked, gathering the bills together.

"I'll ask my aunt. She sent me on this chase."

Alek looked around the rest of the house. The living room had an array of clothes, handbags, and shoes strewn about, in a way that suggested Theresa had deposited them there each time she came home. No dust on the surfaces. So, she was messy but not dirty.

Alek went down the short hallway. His magick reached out ahead of him, making sure no one else was here. No one. Yet, something stirred when he searched. He stopped his advance and stretched his magick out again. A faint pulse ran through his mind. It felt as if someone were probing him. Rushing out of the hall, he snatched open the front door and stood on the porch, once again scanning the street.

The ice cream truck was gone.

He stepped back into the house and stared at the scene. The hairs on the back of his neck rose, and he rubbed at the sensation. "Something's off."

Devlin gave him a questioning look.

"Someone tried to probe my mind. When we got here, there was an ice cream truck at the end of the street. Now it's gone."

"We can call the police when we leave. Check the other rooms."

Before Alek could start toward them, they heard the sirens.

W e'd all reached the point where our exhaustion had slipped into delirium. Each of us worked on manic fumes, trying to connect the myriad of information we had accumulated. Even in our fugue state, we couldn't figure out the one thing that tied everything together.

Khuchar's translated journal clocked in at over six hundred pages. Rachel had skimmed over it, confirming what we knew already. To achieve Divine Evil, you had to absorb a massive amount of magick through ritual. It didn't specify what type of ritual, so we surmised any ritual would probably work, if the magick had been given freely.

Dead end.

When we got back from Professor Shukuma's, Jonah had gone to Karl's apartment to see if he could gain any leads on how or why a grown man would willingly allow himself to be manipulated by a teenage boy.

Another dead end.

Jonah had sent Devlin a text about the Arks and Lisa Stewart's attempt to gain information from Professor Shukuma about them. He hadn't responded yet, so we put the new information to the side and stayed focused on the Ark we did know about. We couldn't figure out who might have been able to steal it from the Stewart barn after we rescued the remaining hostages. It just didn't seem possible. While I had been in no condition to pay attention to what was going on around me, the team would have been, and they hadn't seen anyone arrive in that secluded area. It had to be someone who knew about what went on there—someone familiar with their Harvest ritual.

Could that be the reason Gerald Stewart had Logan killing off his business associates? They knew too much.

I glanced up at the whiteboard. My vision blurred as I stared at the cluttered space. What the hell were we missing? My gaze snagged on the death certificate for Lemuel Oren. According to it, he had died ten years after the building had been raided.

"Well, hell," I said aloud. Jonah and Rachel looked up. "I might have a lead," I said, hesitantly easing up. "But first, let me get my thoughts in order. The last thing I want to do is pile more information on our already overloaded pile of nowhere leads." I grabbed my purse and headed for the door.

"Do you need me to come with you?" Jonah asked.

I glanced back at him. "No. I got this."

"Khuchar said there are gods among us," Rachel called.

Jonah and I shared a look. "I'll get her to lay down for a while. Maybe watch an episode of Spongebob."

I nodded. "That might be a good idea."

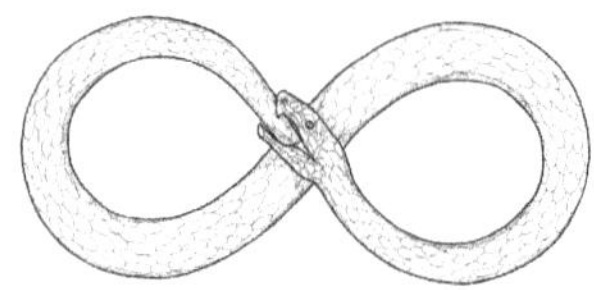

The air-conditioning in my car blew out warm air with an occasional burst of coldness. I had the money to get it fixed but didn't have the time to take it in for repair. I cracked my window to get some fresh air circulating and to alleviate the sudden feeling of the walls closing in on me. Sweat coated my back, and the discomfort had become almost unbearable, but I didn't roll up the window, or beat on my dashboard to get the air working properly. Instead, I drove the familiar streets on autopilot, focusing solely on what I needed to accomplish.

While staring at that birth certificate, I remembered Tribec wasn't the only advertisement I saw when I stopped at the store on my way to Jordin's that day. I also saw an advertisement for Rose Garden Apartments.

My apartment.

Which meant someone had steered me there as well.

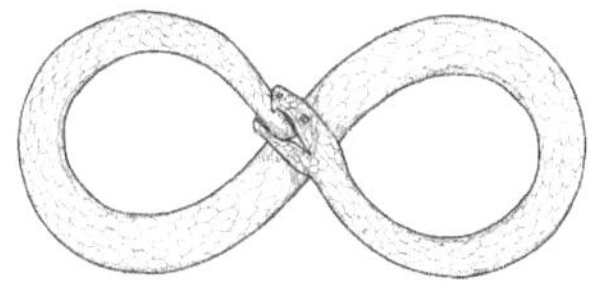

My complex was comprised of three floors and a basement. I lived on the ground floor with Mr. Wan and now Paul. The second floor had three tenants whom I had never talked to at any length, but I did know all three were occupied by singles. The third floor had a studio apartment that shared space with a storage area Mr. Wan said was off-limits to tenants. I realized how much of a stretch it was to assume any records from the asylum or cult would still be there, but we were out of options and needed just one clue to tie everything together.

I pulled into the parking lot and parked near the dumpster. I stepped out of the car into the dry heat. My tank top clung to my sweat-soaked back. All I wanted to do was stand under a cold shower, but it would have to wait. The anticipation of possibly finding the clue we needed to make everything make sense needled me, giving me the much-needed jolt of energy to keep going.

A blast of cool, refreshing air greeted me when I stepped into the lobby of my apartment complex. Mr. Wan stood in his open doorway, talking to one of my upstairs neighbors. I couldn't readily recall her name, so I hung back to avoid an awkward exchange.

She turned as if sensing me there and gave me a half smile. "Hello, Nicole."

"Umm...hello," I said, smiling.

"Barbara. My name is Barbara," she said, her tone chastising.

"I know that," I lied. I was a horrible neighbor, and it was written all over her face.

She turned away from me. "Thanks, Mr. Wan. I will let you know when they're going to deliver the furniture." She gave him a beaming smile. "You are truly a lifesaver!"

"Of course," he said, smiling, and then turned to me. "You need something?"

"Yes, I have..." Barbara was lingering. "Of course, I can wait until you and Barbara are done talking. I didn't mean to interrupt."

She made a noise I'm sure was meant to be a reprimand and walked off. Maybe I wasn't the best neighbor, but at least I wasn't purposely rude. I sighed and walked over to Mr. Wan. "I have an awkward question to ask."

"Did you want to come in?"

I hesitated for a moment, then stepped inside and was welcomed by the smokey scent of shrimp and beef. I inhaled the mouthwatering aroma, remembering I hadn't eaten since this morning. No wonder I had a headache.

Mr. Wan's apartment was a few hundred feet larger giving him a full-size kitchen instead of a half-size one like mine. His late wife had painted their walls pale green, adding Chinese lettering in the corners intertwined with roses and lilies. Mr. Wan told me the symbols spelled out a blessing meant to sanctify their new home.

Plants hung from the ceiling in ceramic pots—their lush, green vines spilling over the sides. A large brown sofa sat as the centerpiece with a marble coffee table in front. The green easy chair sat catacorner to it, facing the fifty-inch television hanging on the wall. A portrait of Mr. Wan and his late wife Lily Rose sat on the opposite wall.

After getting us both a glass of iced tea, Mr. Wan sat down in a recliner and smiled. "What awkward question you have to ask?" He took a sip of his tea.

My tongue grew heavy in my mouth, twisting at the mere

thought of having to ask Mr. Wan about the cult that used to occupy our building. I couldn't find a delicate way to broach the subject. One he had issues with given his comments on the subject before. Damn. I should have thought about this more. I drained my glass of tea and looked around.

Mr. Wan chuckled, bringing my attention back to him. "This the first time I see you with a loss for words." It was true. Usually when we talked, I had no trouble keeping up my end of the conversation.

I shook my head, smiling. "Yeah. There's a first time for everything."

"Are you hungry?" he asked, getting up.

"I'm always hungry," I said, thankful for the distraction and the food.

Mr. Wan came back in the room carrying a plate full of shrimp and beef with vegetables. My mouth watered at the sight of those large pieces of shrimp. He handed me the plate and sat back down. I shoved a shrimp in my mouth, savored the onslaught of flavors before blurting out, "Do you have any records for His Holy Need?" I asked, mouth full.

Mr. Wan's laughter filled the room. "That's the question you wanted to ask?" He tsked at me. "That's not so hard." He pushed up off the chair. "I thought you wanted to ask about your new friend moving in so quickly. You were so worried..." He walked in the other room, and I missed the end of what he was saying.

I breathed a sigh of relief that he didn't think I was crazy for asking.

"He seemed like a decent enough man," he continued, walking back in the room. "So, I let him move in early." He handed me a key ring. "This opens the attic storage space on the third floor." Before I could take the key from him, he pulled it away. "Why are you looking for this information?"

"Curious," I said. Because I really couldn't tell him the truth. He'd already had a brush with the unsavory people we were dealing with before; no need to thrust him in the middle of the current set.

He nodded and handed me the key. "Someone bought all the old records two weeks ago," Mr. Wan said. "I had kept them thinking they might be valuable one day." He sat back down. "You know people always looking for things related to true crime stories. But when I went to add some things to the attic, I found one box for the cult left behind." He sat back, eyes unfocused. "Couldn't figure out why he left that single box. I would have called him, but he didn't leave a number."

"Do you remember what the person looked like?" I asked.

Mr. Wan nodded. "Yeah. Bald man with a scar on his face. He came by a few weeks ago."

My blood ran cold. Logan had come to clean out the information and left a single box behind for me to find two weeks ago. A few weeks after our battle with the Stewart family. He had been watching me. Waiting. And it would seem, leaving little breadcrumbs for me to find. Like this was just one sick, twisted game.

I'd moved past fear and settled on rage.

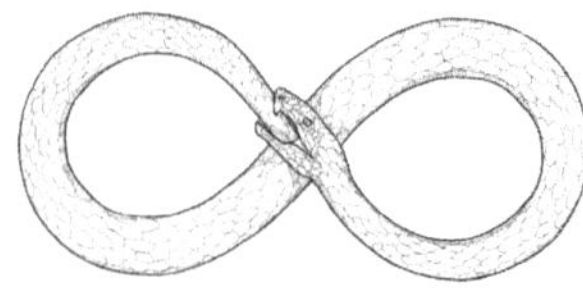

TEN MINUTES into searching all the boxes covering the dusty attic floor, and I wanted to scream. Mr. Wan could have at least told me which box to look in, or labeled them, or something. Instead, I was stuck rummaging through a bunch of creepy discarded items that smelled like abandoned hope. Well, at least what I imagined abandoned hope smelled like.

"Fuck me!" I yelled, and grabbed the next box, adding dust motes to the million already circling the weak light in the room.

The hour I'd been up here felt like a lifetime. Buried under other people's old memories. I wondered why Mr. Wan hadn't thrown away all this crap. And some of the stuff looked as if he'd gone around the neighborhood collecting junk for a yard sale he never got around to having. There was no telling what kind of diseases I might have come into contact with sifting through all this shit.

Of course, it would also help if I knew what I was looking for. I swiped at the sweaty grime covering my forehead and sighed as I stared at the broken toaster in my hand.

"Well, this looks fun," a man said.

I jumped, whirling around so fast, I heard my back crack. The toaster rattled as it hit the hardwood floor. "Dammit, Paul, you scared the hell out of me!" I rested my hand on my chest, willing my heart to stop trying to escape. "What the hell are you doing up here?"

He laughed then made his way around the maze of boxes toward me. "I saw your car out front and went to say hello. Mr. Wan said you were up here looking for information about His Holy Need. I thought I'd come help."

It would seem Paul had taken up Wade's old job, minus the creepy flirtation. But I could use the help. Otherwise, I might just go crazy in a sea of boxes and dust.

"Did he happen to tell you which box the information was in?" I asked, shoving the latest dead end out of the way. Damn, I needed a shower and a bath.

"No. He just told me you were up here." Paul rolled up his shirt sleeves. "Since I'm here, maybe I can help."

I stared at his crisp white shirt and immaculate dark brown dress pants. "Fair warning: Your clothes are going to be destroyed. But yes, please help save me from"—I waved my hands around at all the boxes I had yet to look through—"all this crap!" With him here, maybe I could find the damn box quicker. Or I could just go downstairs and ask Mr. Wan which one it was. But I got the feeling he wouldn't remember, and I wasn't in the mood to stop. Besides, if I did stop, chances were, I'd give up and just go dunk myself in the nearest large body of water.

"Okay." He grabbed a box and pulled it open. "Do you have any clue what I should keep an eye out for?"

"His Holy Need occupied this building in 1980. Maybe hair scrunches and Walkman's." I laughed, but there wasn't any humor in it. "I don't know. I was born in the nineties. What would women in a cult keep?"

"You're asking me?" Paul said, a smile playing across his mouth. "I was born in the nineties, too. But hair scrunchies seem about right. So, clothing and maybe, if we're lucky, some papers and pictures."

"Yeah. I'm holding my breath for a complete file that lays out everything," I said, shoving the latest box away.

"You sound a little delirious," Paul said. "If you want to take a break, I can search for a while."

"No. If I stop, I won't have the strength to start again." I looked over at him examining a woman's skirt. "Thank you, Paul."

He looked up and smiled. Paul really was a handsome man. "That's what neighbors are for." He said it with a little hesitation, like he was trying to figure out if being my neighbor was a problem. Maybe I had telegraphed my skepticism toward him too loudly. I could be a bitch at times, and I really wanted to stop doing that. I could start here.

"Friends," I said. "We are more than just neighbors."

His face relaxed a little. "I'm glad to hear it." He looked around the room. "Now, let's finish sifting through all this so we can order some pizza."

"Sounds like a damn good plan."

We searched in silence for a short while before I screamed. "How many boxes have we searched now?" I gritted out.

"Maybe one thousand. So, five thousand more to go," Paul said, sounding just as frustrated as I was. "Maybe if we knew what we were looking for..." He looked over at me. "Why are you looking for information on His Holy Need?" He let out a hysterical laugh. "Maybe I should have asked that first."

"I think you did," I said.

"Oh. Well, shit."

Paul was covered in dirt and grime. And his shirt had become molded to his chest. The air-conditioning up here was really going at it half-assed.

I pulled another box to me and shoved it open. "Did Kara tell you we're looking into The Better Day Church?" She told me she'd given him some details about our recent events, but she didn't tell me what she told him. I didn't want to scare the man.

"You mean The Better Day Cult," he said, opening another box. "Yes, she told me. I would have gone with you both on Sunday. Kara asked, but I haven't stepped foot in a church in years." His voice was laced with a little sadness. I wondered if his reasoning for staying away was because of his family's judgment about his lifestyle. I really hated people like that.

"Kara didn't tell me she asked you," I said. "And how does that work with you having faith magick?" I'd learned recently that Paul had latent faith magick. I thought all faith practitioners would long to go to church. Even Jonah had mentioned finding a reputable one on Tulare. Maybe he might start going with Marta.

He smiled. "I still practice my faith. But I'm not a mage. The urge to lead or preach isn't there. Just the desire to inspire."

"I read a little about faith magick. I have to admit, I would have thought inspiration came from mind mages. But I guess it makes sense that it would be part of faith." I rummaged through a few old dresses until I found a journal. Leaning back, I said, "Well, Gavina actually belonged to the cult when she was a teenager." I opened the journal and read the name inscribed on the front: Selena Peterson.

"Figures she went from one cult and started her own. I wonder what happened to the man who led it," he said.

"Lemuel Oren," I said, staring at the trinity knot on the front. Something about the symbol was familiar. Too focused on trying to figure it out, I almost missed what Paul said.

"Yeah, if I remember correctly, he disappeared after killing his disciples."

"Not everyone was killed," I said. "And supposedly, Lemuel Oren died ten years after they found the cult members in the basement."

A photograph was wedged in the back, and I pulled it out. It was an old photo of five women and one man. The man's face was obscured as if the picture had been damaged or processed wrong. The women all looked to be in their late teens or early twenties. Wearing white dresses, they crowded around the tall, long-haired man.

I sucked in a breath. My throat filled with lent and dust. Paul came over and patted my back as I coughed up the debris.

"Are you all right?" he asked, looking down at the picture in my hand.

I shook my head and continued to stare at the photograph.

Gavina looked so much like her daughter, Vidette.

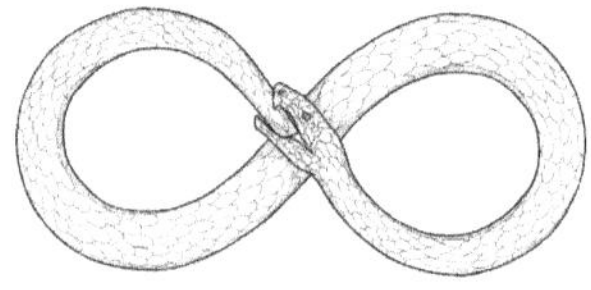

I CLIMBED out of the shower and wrapped a towel around me. Wiping away the condensation on the mirror, I stared at myself while water ran down my shoulders. After bringing the box down to my apartment, I told Paul I needed a shower. He said after he took one, he'd come back over so we could go through the rest of the box. He even offered to order the pizza. But I doubted I'd be able to eat since a large boulder currently sat in my stomach.

Being someone's puppet had sent me into a seething rage. Of course, I knew when Mr. Wan told me about Logan showing up here that I was being setup in some way. But seeing that picture of Gavina had really driven home just how elaborate the setup had been.

And not just by Logan, either.

How do you stop an individual from moving you around on a giant chessboard while you willingly step into the positions laid out for you? Should I stop following the clues? It was like I'd been left with no options. No will of my own. And that pissed me the fuck off.

I needed to let the team know what I found. But what I really needed most was to find the person manipulating me and rip their damn throat out. Oh, and burn their damn chess board, too.

"Nicole?" Paul called.

I sighed. "Be out in a minute," I told him and finished getting dressed. Maybe Paul would have some alcohol to go along with the pizza.

When I stepped out of the bathroom, I found Paul wiping down the box we found—a glass of dark liquid sitting on the coffee table beside him.

"Please say that's alcohol and you brought enough to share."

He turned and smiled. "You sure you want to drink again? You did say you were swearing off liquor."

"I was foolish and confused. Now, dammit, fix me a damn drink!"

He got up and went to the kitchen while I sat on the floor and opened the box. The sides were a little damp and gritty. "How long before the pizza gets here?"

He came back in the room carrying a glass for me. "They said an hour." He handed it to me and checked his watch. "So, another twenty minutes."

I took a sip of my drink and let the warm liquid run down my throat. It wasn't my brand, but after what I'd learned, it would do. My phone dinged, alerting me to a text message, and I snatched it up off the coffee table.

RACHEL

Dev and Alek have been arrested.

Damn. Looked like I wasn't going to get to finish my drink after all.

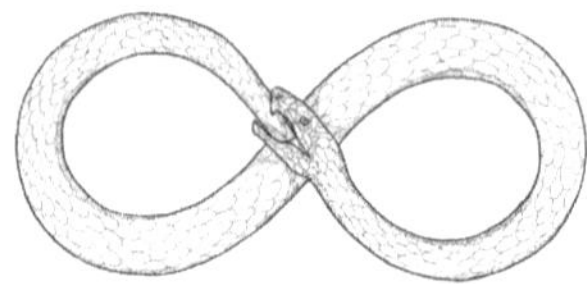

I PULLED up to Devlin's house and parked behind Kara's car. She must have come over after I left. And since she didn't call to find out where I was, I assumed she came over to see Jonah. My heart made a little happy dance at that. We weren't the type of women who encouraged each other to find boyfriends and husbands to complete us. Don't get me wrong, we talked about men, but it wasn't the only thing we focused on. Yet, knowing Kara was finally—hopefully—letting go of her obsession with unavailable men and allowing herself to enjoy the company of one who was available made me happy. And I currently needed a little brightness in this sea of darkness and subterfuge.

After wiping the sweat off my forehead, I grabbed the box from my backseat and walked up to the house, rang the bell, and waited.

Kara answered the door, wearing a green bikini top and a towel around her waist. Her red hair was braided down her back and her smattering of freckles stood out, making her look both alluring and innocent. Rachel must be giving Jonah CPR right now.

"Oh, my," I said stepping inside. "Did I miss my invitation to the pool party?"

She let out a nervous laugh. "What's in the box?" So, she wanted to change the subject. That was fine. Our focus should be on Alek and Devlin, anyway.

She followed me into the war room where Rachel sat on the floor with two laptops in front of her and her cellphone to her ear. Jonah walked into the room, wearing a pair of low-slung jeans and no shirt. Damn.

I glanced back at Kara. Her eyes were glued to him. I had never seen her this gone over a man before. Hell, even with Paul she was just entertaining the idea of a relationship.

"What's in the box?" Jonah asked.

I set the box on the floor next to Rachel. She glanced at it and then up at me with a raised eyebrow in question.

"I can wait for Rachel to get off the phone. Any news on Alek and Devlin?"

"No. Just the one call before the police arrived at Theresa's house. They found her locked inside her mind. Alek thinks it was a setup." That was happening a lot lately, and I could guess who was doing the setting up.

Rachel hung up. "They won't confirm if Dev and Alek are there. Fucking idiots!"

"Does that mean they weren't arrested?" I asked, pulling the journal out of the box.

"No. It just means the police are taking their time processing them," Jonah said. "Of course, this is all guesswork since we haven't been able to speak with them since Dev called." He rubbed his head in agitation. "We could go down there, but Dev wouldn't want us to. That Detective Barnes was already making waves about us being on the island and doing investigative work without a license. If he's involved, it could take all night." He looked at the journal in my hand. "Now, what's that?"

"It can wait. We have to do something about Alek and Devlin." I sat down heavily on the floor and stared at the box. I should have been here. Should have waited with the others for them to get back. Maybe I could have...what? What could I have done?

Tulare had a great deal of unscrupulous people in law enforcement. They seemed to go out of their way to harass people of color. Alek would be hassled. And Devlin would be too, given his dark features that hinted at his mixed heritage. Throw in the bullshit about them being on the island, investigating without a license, and we had the makings of a Molotov cocktail, ready to ignite.

Jonah crouched down in front of me. "Dev can handle this. Trust me. Did you forget he used to be a detective?"

"This is different," I said. "They will be harassed."

He shook his head. "He's dealt with his share of prejudice and cops who crossed the line. Trust me, Nicole." He laid his hand on mine. "He can handle it." The corner of his mouth quirked up. "Unless your concern is more for Alek."

"Oh, just shut up." I jerked my head toward Kara. "Took my advice, huh?"

He winked at me and stood. I appreciated his attempt to help calm me down. And he was right, of course—while I was concerned for Devlin, I was going out of my mind worrying about Alek.

Jonah dipped his head toward the box. "Are you going to keep us in suspense the rest of the night?"

"It's a present from Logan," I said, and handed him the journal. I took them through what Mr. Wan said, and they all agreed it was too much of a coincidence not to be a setup.

"So, two weeks ago, Logan goes to your apartment and buys all the information about His Holy Need, only to leave a bread crumb behind for you to find?" Kara said, her face going dark. "He would have to know you would eventually need information on the cult in the first place." Anger laced her words, and I knew Kara was struggling. I didn't want her to give in to the temptations she'd been fighting all these years because of this.

"It makes sense," Rachel said. "We started looking into the other families a few weeks ago. He must have been watching us this whole time."

I wanted to go for unfazed to keep Kara from getting any more upset than she already was, but the look on her face said I hadn't quite achieved it. Logan had been watching me this whole time. I knew it deep down in my gut. It was the only thing that made sense.

Rachel's phone rang, and she snatched it up. "Yeah," she said and then smiled. "Thank you, Benny. I owe you!" She looked up at us when she hung up. "They're at the Cross Street Precinct in Perry. Benny hacked their system."

Why hadn't they taken them to the Pleasanton precinct? "Who's Benny?" I asked.

"My hacker friend. If we're being watched, I didn't want to hack the system, so I asked Benny to hack all four stations." She beamed at us. "Dumbasses probably made it really easy."

"Barnes works out of Perry," Jonah said, his eyes narrowing. "I knew he was involved."

"So, what do we do?" Worry and fear laced my tone. Every single worst-case scenario suddenly rushed through my mind.

"We call the Markums," Rachel said, dialing.

Box and journal abandoned, I sat down with the others to wait. I had the patience of a toddler, so I spent the next two hours eating my way through the time. When the fridge was almost empty, I got up.

"I need a cigar," I said, grabbing my purse. No one stopped me as I made my way to the door. When I stepped out, the heat smacked me in the face. It was getting warmer. I really needed to find Hathor.

"Nicole," Kara said, walking out with her bag. "I'm leaving, too." She hesitated. "Unless you want me to stay."

I shook my head. "No, it's getting late, and there's no telling how long they will be at the station. No sense in all of us losing sleep." I glanced back at the house and watched Jonah make his way toward us. "I'm happy for you."

She blushed and turned toward Jonah. "Maybe we can swim another time."

I moved away, suddenly feeling like a third wheel.

"Yeah. That we will do," he said, and bent down, kissed her on the lips, and walked away.

My jaw dropped on the ground. "Well, damn," I said, watching him walk in the house. Jonah was one bold bastard. If he had looked back, I would have saluted him.

"Yeah. Definitely, damn," Kara said, her voice breathy.

My head whipped around. "You just cursed!" That must have been one hell of a pool party.

She smiled and turned away. "Text me with any news or if you need me to come back," she called over her shoulder.

I stared after her as she drove away, vowing to myself I would work on my own love life. No more uncertainty. No more hesitation. I wanted to be with Alek, and going by our morning escapade, he damn sure wanted to be with me, too. The only thing that stopped us was me and my baggage—and a house full of people.

But that could be fixed.

A Shortcut to Madness

Alek sat next to Devlin on a hard wooden bench staring at the walls inside the holding cell at the Police Precinct in Perry. Lights flickered overhead, sending the room periodically into darkness. Their constant buzz reminded him of the mosquito traps that hung on porches in the areas near water. Those bright, neon blue lights luring the pesky bugs in only to zap them to death.

He felt like one of those bugs now with the heavy weight of foreboding pressing in on him, only to be temporarily assuaged with the blaze of the weak light illuminating the room.

The smell of piss and vomit filled the warm air inside the cell. The stench seemed to be gnawing away at his skin and digging into his pores. Sweat coated his face and arms, adding fuel to the discomfort he was already feeling.

Both the bench and walls had been covered in varying degrees of madness: pleas of innocence overlapping vows of revenge; symbols of hate covering drawings of black fists and tags with names like Baby D and Lil Dawg. The walls seemed as if they were screaming in pain. There was desperation in every angry stroke of the pen.

A death mask had been drawn on the wall opposite from

them. A face outlined in white with sightless eyes surrounded by an exaggerated charcoal design. The dark paint looked as if it were bleeding onto the ivory skin. And the mouth appeared to be filled with blood.

The lights buzzed off, pitching them into complete darkness.

Seconds later, they flickered back on, and Alek's gaze landed on the scrawled message underneath the mask. *I drank her tears and swallowed her pain.*

The orange tendrils of his magick crawled along the concrete floor, seeking. In the dark, the brightness of his power looked like blood seeping up from the ground. Devlin's blue aura pulsed beside him—keeping time with his heartbeat.

They had assumed they would be going to a precinct in Pleasanton where Theresa lived. But the officers had brought them to Perry. Most likely at the request of Detective Barnes. He'd already harassed Devlin once this week. They both agreed the man had to be working for the Stewart family. Which meant the set-up Logan orchestrated had been a ploy to get them here.

The lights flickered off, leaving them in pitch dark.

Light spilled into the corridor, bringing a cool draft with it.

Alek sent his magick out further and found four eager minds moving closer to them. Three of which were intent on violence.

The light vanished.

The cell clanged open.

"Five minutes," a man whispered with anticipation in his voice.

Alek surged up, Devlin following behind him.

Adrenaline flooded his body.

A whisper of wind announced the attack.

He had only a brief second to block the blow. Pain radiated down his arm.

The next blow knocked him back. He stumbled over the bench, righting himself quickly.

Someone tried to push inside his mind with magick.

Alek lashed out with his own power.

A pained howl erupted from his attacker as Alek latched onto the man's mind. It was the elation that stopped him. Why would his attacker be happy Alek was hurting him?

In that brief second, another fist connected with the side of his head. He fell to the ground, his knees biting into the hard concrete.

Devlin bellowed and Alek heard another grunt. His boss must have landed a blow.

A foot connected with his side, and Alek reached out and grabbed it, twisting the boot covered foot. His attacker fell and Alek pounced. His eyes had finally adjusted to the dark. He planted a fist in the man's face, feeling the jaw give way under the powerful strike.

Someone jumped on his back and wrapped their arm around his neck, cutting off his air supply.

Dots flashed in his eyes as he tried to pull air into his lungs.

"Fight back," the man yelled.

Alek pushed inside the man's head and once again found elation rushing through his attacker. Why was he happy? Alek wanted to ponder it. Probably should have. But anger rode him and his magick wanted blood. Alek latched onto the man's brain, sending a message to stop his breathing. His attacker fell away, landing on the floor, sucking at the air like a dying fish. Alek pushed in further, sending another signal to the man's brain— causing him to buck on the floor.

Before Alek could shut the man down completely, Devlin grabbed him. "Stop," he yelled.

Alek blinked, releasing the man's mind and turned to Devlin. "Why," he said, his voice a deadly whisper.

"Think," Devlin said. "They went for you first."

Alek sat back on his heels and surveyed the room. All three of their attackers lay on the ground, unconscious. Just like Theresa.

Damn.

The light flickered on. A door opened down the hall. Three officers came rushing in. They spared Alek and Devlin a brief glance before opening the cell doors and pulling the unconscious men out.

A commotion carried down the hall—a woman demanding to speak with her clients.

When the door shut, all the sounds were cut off.

Alek touched the side of his head, feeling the tenderness there. It was definitely going to cause a bruise. Luckily, the kick to his side was only meant as a distraction otherwise he was sure his ribs would have been bruised.

"You all right?" Devlin asked.

"Yeah," Alek said on a sigh. He should have figured out what they were up to from the start. If he had, he wouldn't have used his magick on the man attacking him. Only his fists.

"Why would they send them in here?" Alek asked.

They both sat on the bench. Devlin turned to him. "They need a reason to justify bringing us in. If you had put that guy in the same catatonic state as Theresa, they could have blamed you for her condition."

"Fuck."

A short while later, another officer walked into the room and let Alek and Devlin out of the cell. They followed the officer down a small corridor and into a small room. An attractive woman with dark brown hair and glasses, wearing a plain white blouse, sat on the opposite side of the table, her back to the wall. She stood when they walked in. "Mr. Grey. Mr. Vaduva," she said, taking Devlin in. Her eyes narrowed. "What happened?"

Devlin rubbed his jaw and glanced at the officer still standing in the doorway. "That's something I would like to know as well."

The woman looked at the officer. "Leave us," she said, her voice hard.

The officer sneered at her and then shut the door.

When the door was closed, she looked at them. "I'm Opal Katz from Blume, Worshire, and Katz. The Markums have sent me to represent you." She moved closer to Alek and stared up at him. "Did one of the officers attack you?"

Alek shook his head and sat down.

She glanced at Devlin. "Do you know why they brought you to the precinct in Perry and not Pleasanton?"

Devlin took a seat, and after a beat, took her through it. He had to admit, it was a good plan. One that took a great deal of time. Just how long had Logan been watching them? More importantly, was he working with Barnes?

After Devlin finished, Opal sat down, leaned back, and let out a dry chuckle. "Oh, they are brazen. I will give them that."

"Too bad we can't prove it," Devlin said.

She nodded. "Well. Let's just get you out of here and worry about the rest later." She got up and rapped on the door.

An officer opened the door.

"You can send the detectives in along with a medic. Seems some of the inmates decided to attack my clients."

He gave her a hard look and shut the door.

Opal sat back down and pulled two files from her bag. "The Markum's were able to obtain a license for you," she said, sliding the folder to Devlin. "I've also got a preliminary report on Theresa Scott." She opened the second folder. "They have her at Rome General in Alice. I'm assuming mind magick has something to do with her current state?" she asked, giving Alek a pointed look. He nodded and she shook her head. "I wonder how long they've been working on this little ploy of theirs." She stared down at the file. "Doesn't matter. I will take care of it."

"Katz," Devlin said, gazing at her with an appreciative look in his eyes. "You're a partner?"

She smiled. "Yes, made partner two years ago." She straightened her glasses. Alek noticed that the lenses had no prescription in them.

"I figured they'd send a junior associate. Didn't realize any partners were on the island."

"Well, I just came down here to help with the new offices and felt this matter needed my attention." She smoothed her skirt and put her suit jacket back on.

On impulse, Alek reached inside her mind. Opal, while sure of her skills, was not particularly sure of others' acceptance of her. He studied the pale gold hue surrounding her. Faith magick. Most people with faith magick took up religious pursuits or professions that centered on helping others through persuasion and gentle guidance. He'd never seen one in the field of law.

Her plain suit and the blocky pumps she wore on her feet made him think she was trying to appear unassuming and non-threatening. A wolf in sheep's clothing.

Opal caught him staring and gave him a small smile.

The door opened and Detective Barnes entered the room followed by another man. Barnes looked like a mafia crime boss from some B rated movie. Slick black hair, shiny, olive-green suit, dark brown eyes devoid of humanity, and enough gold on his fingers to fund the police department. He wasn't even trying to hide his corruption. The other detective, short blonde hair wearing a tan suit pulled out a chair and nodded at them. He didn't look as if he wanted to be there.

Barnes set a recorder on the table in front of them and switched it on. His movements were mechanical and filled with irritation. Maybe he was upset because his little ploy didn't work.

"Detective Barnes—"

Opal lifted a finger, silencing him. "We're waiting on the medic. I want my clients' injuries treated and documented."

Barnes bristled and shut off the recorder. "What injuries?"

"Are you visually impaired?" Opal asked, her voice flat.

A knock sounded at the door and the other detective got up and answered it. A short Caucasian man wearing wrinkled scrubs, entered the room. He gave them a cursory glance before settling his gaze on Barnes.

"You can treat them," Barnes said eventually.

The man walked over and set a black bag on the table. "If you gentlemen could please stand," he said, his tone nasal. He wore a look of boredom on his face, keeping his gaze somewhat averted as if he didn't dare make eye contact with either of them.

Opal pulled a phone from her purse and stood. "We'll need photos first," she said to the man.

He didn't look at her as he pulled a camera from his case and stood waiting.

After getting pictures of his face and ribs and repeating the process with Devlin, the medic gave them a half-ass assessment and offered to call an ambulance if they needed one. Both he and Devlin declined. There was no telling where they would end up if they did agree to get treatment.

"As I was saying," Barnes continued, still bristling at the interruption. "Detective—"

Opal held up a finger again. Barnes turned red. "I would like both your badge numbers first and an explanation as to why my clients are in the Perry Precinct instead of Pleasanton."

Barnes glared at her. Opal glared right back.

"We were asked to handle the preliminary investigation," Barnes said, eventually.

Opal scribbled a note on her notepad. "Okay. I will need the name of the Detective who asked you to handle the investigation." She looked up. "I will need to confirm this with," she took her time reading through the notes on her pad, "Chief Lancaster in Pleasanton." She smiled.

"Detective Hardgrove," Barnes gritted out.

His partner cleared his throat, and Barnes shot him a hateful glance.

"And your badge numbers, please," Opal said.

Both men hesitated for a moment before pulling their badges out and sliding them to her. After she wrote down the numbers, she gave them back. "Now, Detective Barnes. Why weren't my clients given their phone call?"

"The duty sergeant had a backlog. He advised me he was getting around to it," he said through clenched teeth.

"Getting around to it?" she asked, a single eyebrow rising.

He leaned back and crossed his arms. "They hadn't been here long. We were—"

"Long enough for you to orchestrate the attack on their person," she said, gaze level.

"We will be looking into that," he turned to Devlin. "It would help if you could describe your attacker."

The man knew full well they couldn't.

"I'll get that to you," Devlin said.

"I'll be looking into it as well." Opal pulled another folder out of her bag. "I believe you were harassing my client about a license to operate on Tulare." She slid the folder to him. "Section 5-E768 of the business code only requires Private Investigators who live on Tulare to obtain a license to practice. However, to appease your concerns, we have secured one for Devlin and his team."

Barnes looked as if he were ready to explode. Alek gave Opal an appreciative glance. She reminded him so much of Nicole. Able to get under anyone's skin. Even the man's partner was looking at Opal in awe.

Opal sat back and signaled for Barnes to continue.

He ground his teeth and said, "Detective Barnes and Detective Kneadsome are present, interviewing one..." He flipped open a file. "Grey, Devlin and Vaduva, Alexandros. Present for the suspects..."

"Excuse me, correct that, please," Opal said.

"What?" Detective Barnes yelled.

"My clients aren't suspects. You will refer to them as witnesses."

"Ma'am, they were found in the woman's home!"

Opal opened the file in front of her. "It says here that the EMTs were unable to determine what was wrong with Theresa Scott. The only notation is that she didn't respond when asked a question." She looked up, her eyes narrowing. "So, what exactly are my clients suspects of?"

"Why were they in her house?"

"They can answer that for you. But please"—she dipped her head toward the recorder—"correct it for the record."

Detective Barnes glared at her. Opal didn't flinch. After a few seconds, he said, "Present for the *witnesses* is one Opal Katz, *attorney at law*." He put a sneer on his face and in his tone, then turned to Devlin. "Mr. Grey, I understand you used to work as a detective in the Los Angeles Police Department?"

"That's not essential to your investigation, Detective Barnes," Opal said. "Please stick to questions regarding Ms. Scott."

He slammed his fist on the table. "I want to know why he's on my island, acting like a detective!"

She didn't even flinch.

"If you don't have any questions," Opal said, standing, "then my clients and I will leave."

Barnes shoved up, the chair fell back clattering to the ground. "I want to know why they were in the house!"

It was the first time Alek noted the question Barnes kept asking. Not, 'What happened to Theresa?' but 'Why they were there in the first place?'

Devlin stood. "My team and I have been hired to look into the disappearance of Felicity Markum and her boyfriend Jesse Lombardi. Our investigation took us to Theresa Scott's house. That is all the information I can give you."

Alek stayed seated, not only to keep his anger at bay, but also to give him the opportunity to study the situation further. Barnes wasn't ready to accept Devlin's answer. Alek didn't need to search his mind to determine that—it was written all over his flushed face.

After an angry standoff, Detective Kneadsome stood and placed his hand on his partner's arm. "We're done here," he said. Barnes jerked his head toward his partner. "We're done," Kneadsome repeated. "Mr. Grey, Mr. Vaduva... Thank you for your time."

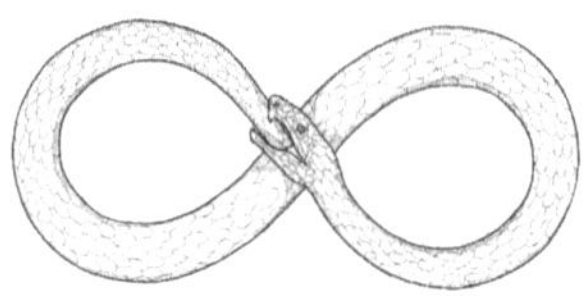

It had grown dark while they were inside. The heat still buffeted the air, but not as thick. They stood by Opal's car. She'd removed her jacket and tossed it and her briefcase inside.

Opal took a swig of her water. "That was a little strange in there."

Devlin sighed. "Not really. It was bound to happen sooner or later. The families we're investigating are obviously connected. Like I told the Markums, Barnes had stopped by before, making a fuss about my license. His assumption that I'd be on the island longer than it took to investigate Felicity's death is what worries me."

"They said they received an anonymous call that you were in the house." She shook her head. "But that didn't ring true to me."

"It was a setup," Alek said. "And we should have seen it coming."

Opal looked at him. "Were you reading my mind in there, Mr. Vaduva?"

Alek smiled. "No. Just wondering why you hide yourself behind false glasses and ill-fitting suits."

Opal laughed. "Now, that is a long story—one I'm too tired to tell right now. What do you want me to do about the attack?" Opal asked.

"Our word against theirs," Devlin said. "So, for now, we let it go until we can prove that Barnes is working for the Stewart family."

She finished the rest of her water. "I can get a junior associate started on a background check for Detective Barnes. Until then, please keep me informed on how your investigation is going." She handed Devlin her card. "The Markums want me to be the point of contact from here on out." She studied them, eyes going hard. "Anything you need, you let me know." When they nodded, she glanced over at the precinct. "I used to babysit Felicity when she was younger. I, too, want to see all the people involved in her death pay."

"In a court of law?" Devlin asked.

"I'll let you determine that," she said as she climbed in her car.

When she drove away, Alek turned to Devlin. "I have to get to Theresa before Logan does. He set out some bait to take us out of the picture. It didn't work. Now, I think he might just kill her."

A Prospect of Chance

It was just after midnight when Alek pulled up to Petal Memorial Hospital with his two cousins: Darius and Cristian. He parked in a spot near the entrance and smiled. The woman who had occupied his thoughts all day long stood leaning against her car.

Nicole.

Her bright hazel eyes caught the light from his headlights, making the irises blaze. Her light brown hair, that wild beautiful hair, had been fanned across his pillow this morning. She licked her lips, and Alek forgot himself for a minute, remembering his lips on hers.

God, he craved this woman.

She wore one of her favorite tank tops—black, cleavage spilling over the top—and black jeans so tight, they looked molded to her skin. Her arms were crossed, so she'd most likely been waiting for a while. She wore a look of frustration until her eyes locked with his. Her smile was slow, but he took pleasure in knowing it was for him. Cristian made a sound of appreciation, and Alek turned to him. "Mine," he said, then he opened the car door. A simmering heat greeted him as he stepped out into the night.

A slight breeze blew over the parking lot, bringing the smell of the ocean with it. The hospital sat in the middle of a residential area on the southern border of Pleasanton, just a few miles from Theresa's house. The EMTs had originally taken her to Rome General in Alice, but someone had called in a request to transfer her. Rachel was still trying to figure out who.

"Nicole," Alek said, making his way toward her. The wind picked up her hair, sending the fragrant scent of jasmine toward him. He closed his eyes and inhaled. When he opened them, she had moved closer and was staring up at him.

"I thought I might—"

His crushed his lips to hers, cutting her off. She moaned as he pulled her to him. When he'd satiated his need, he stepped back and stared down at her. "What were you saying?"

She blinked at him. "I forgot," she whispered, then touched his cheek. "What happened?"

He took her hand. "Just a fight. We can talk about it later."

She stared at him for a minute as if she were going to press, then turned to his car.

He followed her gaze. Darius and Cristian had gotten out. "My cousins, Darius and Cristian," he said, returning his gaze to her.

She looked up at him. "Okay."

Cristian chuckled. "You two need a minute?" he asked.

Alek smiled and took Nicole's hand. "No. Let's get this done."

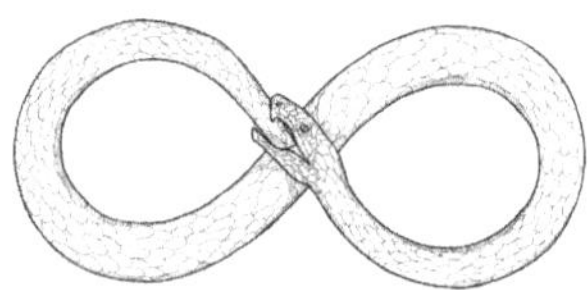

A uniformed officer stood outside Theresa's room, his head pitching forward every few minutes, only to jerk back at the slightest noise. It would be easy to push him over the edge and send him to the sleep he obviously craved, but the security cameras were a problem. And so was the man trying to blend in with the rest of the people lining the halls.

Unrie Nevsky.

If he was here, chances were, Logan Magellan was as well, only Logan chose to remain out of sight, making Unrie the bait. Which meant they knew Alek would come for Theresa. So why the ambush at the police station?

"Shouldn't we be doing something?" Nicole asked, her voice filled with irritation.

He turned and looked at her. She looked worn. He knew first-hand she hadn't been sleeping well. She should be at home, waiting in his bed for him to return. And as soon as he thought it, he pushed that image down. Nicole was no one's little woman, sitting at home and waiting for her man to return. She had fire in her. And that's what he really loved. Not some docile girl who couldn't handle herself; although, her being in his bed was a nice image.

He smiled, trying to put her at ease. "We will. But first"—he pulled her closer—"look." He jerked his chin toward Unrie. "He's a problem. We can handle him. It's his partner I'm concerned with."

He signaled to his cousins. "Subdue both Unrie and the guard. I'll send Nicole in first while I look for Logan. Give her five minutes, then I'll head in, and you two follow."

His cousins nodded and started down the hall.

Nicole tapped her head. "Why can't you find Logan?" she asked.

"He's guarding against it." He didn't tell her he already tried and came up with a void. Logan was masking his presence.

He stared down at her. He wanted to kiss her again. Before he realized it, he'd inched forward. Her breath feathered across his skin as she let out a sigh, moving forward as well.

"You are driving me crazy, Nicole," he whispered.

Leaning forward, he placed a soft kiss on her lips. Hunger for more rose inside of him. He had every intention of pulling back, but her moan sent him over the edge.

He deepened the kiss and could taste the smoke on her tongue. It sent a surge of need through him. This woman completely undid him. If he didn't know any better, he'd swear it was magick. The mere thought of her made his heart skip a beat. Her touch was like liquid fire, engulfing him in so much heat and desire.

She wrapped her arms around his neck, pulling him in even closer.

"If we don't stop," he mumbled, his tongue tracing the side of her mouth, "I might forget myself and take you in one of these empty rooms."

She pulled back and gazed up at him. "Promise?"

"Damn, woman, stop looking at me like that."

She gave him a devilish grin he knew was meant to unarm him. He leaned forward, placing his forehead on hers. "Be careful. Don't try and wake her."

Nicole didn't move, just continued to stare at him. Those eyes seemed to penetrate his soul.

Finally, she said, "I will," and walked away.

Adrenaline coursed through my body, trying to pump motion into my slow, steady steps. Nervous jitters swam around inside my stomach. The coffee I'd drunk rose in my throat, burning its way up my esophagus. Despite this, a thrill rode me with each step I took. I shouldn't be excited. After all, someone had locked Theresa Scott inside her mind, and if Alek and his cousins couldn't help her, she would forever be in that state.

But still, I was elated at the thought of getting into a confrontation, especially with the man who had been pulling our strings all this time.

I should have been afraid.

The weight of the knife between my breasts gave me some comfort. Not physically—the warm metal wasn't exactly in an ideal location—but knowing I had some protection kept my feet moving forward. The knowledge that Alek had my back also put me at ease.

Cristian had already put the guard to sleep. The man lay slumped in a chair, drool pooling at the corners of his mouth. I glanced in the direction where Alek had pointed out Unrie and couldn't see either him or Darius. And Cristian was nowhere in sight. I stopped, wondering about that. Shouldn't they be waiting?

Had Alek found Logan?

Turning back toward the way I came; I searched the now-empty hallway for Alek. He was also missing. I stood there, debating whether I should turn around.

Something didn't feel right. Where were the doctors? The nurses? Patients?

The hairs on the back of my neck rose; I rubbed the suddenly chilled spot and waited, listening, hoping either Alek or his cousins would give me a signal.

Nothing.

Had it been five minutes?

A single moan carried out into the hall from Theresa's room. I took a step forward, pushed the curtain aside, and peered in the dimly lit room.

The rhythmic beep of the monitors filled the slightly warm space. The bed sat at an angle in the corner of the room. Theresa's head lay propped up on a single pillow. She looked peaceful—an illusion masking the war going on inside her head. I started toward her bed, my feet hesitant on the polished tile floor. I'd made it a few steps in when a *click* echoed in the room.

A gun being readied.

I jerked toward the sound.

Logan stepped out of the darkness as if he'd come from a tear in space.

With the gun pointing at Theresa, he raised a single finger to his lips, signaling for me to be quiet.

"We don't have long. Step over to the window and climb out."

I crossed my arms. "No."

He took a single step toward me, putting himself halfway between Theresa and me. A smile played across his mouth. "I admire your defiance. But you have to realize, I *will* pull this trigger." His gaze roamed down my body. "Now, step over to the window and climb out."

"Why?" I asked, trying to stall.

"You're trying to stall." I really needed to work on my poker face. "I'm not going to harm you, Nicole Fontane. We just need to have a little discussion." A wicked smile stretched across his face. "Promise."

Indecision raged inside of me. He might be telling the truth. And if so, he was a threat to Theresa. The look in his eyes told me he *would* shoot her. Hell, he'd already fucked up her mind.

I started toward the window, moving slowly, hoping to delay long enough for Alek and his cousins to arrive.

"You want her to die?" he asked, his tone confused, as if he believed I was deliberately trying to get her killed. I didn't know what to make of that. It left me a little puzzled and worried about the man's state of mind. But still, he was right. Everything I did could impact her.

And he had a gun.

We were on the second floor, so jumping out the window wouldn't hurt too much. I hoped. I went over to the already cracked window; a sign that I should have registered as odd when I first walked in the room and noticed the warmth. I slid the window open further. Warm air rushed in and brushed across my skin.

"Move," he said, standing right behind me. I could elbow him. Pull the knife from between my breasts or scream. But none of those options would stop him for long.

Putting my leg over the window seat, I swung my other out so I was in a sitting position and looked down at the ground. Okay, this was going to hurt. I turned to tell him as much, and he shoved me out the window. I landed hard, barely managing to stay standing. My teeth bit into my tongue and my mouth filled with blood. I spat it out in the bushes. Pain radiated down my legs. They weren't broken, and any damage that was done would heal quickly. But it didn't stop the pain.

A *thump* alerted me to Logan's arrival. Before I could turn around fully, he brought the gun down on the back of my skull.

Everything went dark.

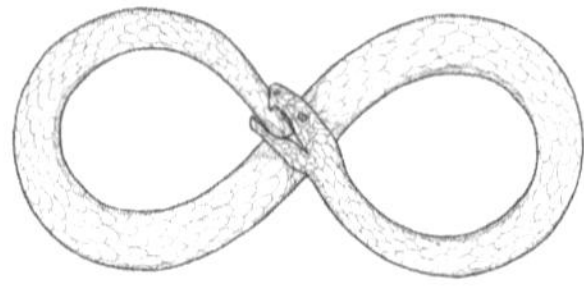

Someone laid a cool cloth on my head. I touched the person's hand, trying to figure out who it was. My mind was foggy, and I couldn't quite place where I was or what was going on. I just remembered the pain. Slowly, fighting back the stabbing sensation filling my head, I opened my eyes and stared into the eyes of my kidnapper.

"Fuck you," I muttered, and the bastard smiled.

"You were out for a while."

I shifted, trying to sit up, and he placed his hand on my back as if to help. "Seriously?" I spat. Anger helped with the pain. "You're trying to help?"

He stepped back but kept his gaze trained on me.

After a few embarrassing attempts, I finally managed to get in an upright position and regretted it immediately. The room spun. I closed my eyes. Maybe not the best idea with Logan staring at me, but if he wanted to kill me, he probably would have done it already. Besides, he said he wanted to talk. Hopefully, while he did, I could figure out how to escape.

I opened my eyes. "Where am I?" Logan pulled a knife out of his pocket. It took a minute for me to recognize the switchblade. "You actually fondled me?"

His mouth stretched into a smile. "Yes. Had to make sure you didn't have any weapons." He clicked the switch, releasing the blade. "Nice craftsmanship. Pretty sharp. It would have hurt if you stabbed me." He tossed the blade on the bed and walked over to a table in the middle of the room.

I looked around. The place reminded me of Ezra's small studio apartment in the back of his dojo. Only, unlike Ezra, Logan had furnished his space with strange knickknacks—odd figurines and decorative fans and masks.

"This place looks like a museum," I said, shifting my legs over the bed. The pain was gone. I stared at them for a moment. A strange herbal smell wafted off them. And that was not the only problem. "Where the hell are my jeans?" I yelled.

"I couldn't rub pain ointment on your jeans." Logan turned to me, holding a cup of tea. "This can help your head if you drink it."

I would ask how he knew I was in pain, but it had to be obvious. Still, his tender, loving concern was a bit creepy. "Umm... please don't tell me you kidnapped me to be your bride or some other such shit."

He barked out a laugh, the teacup shaking in his hand—spilling its contents on the floor. "Last week, I would have killed you and your friends. I would have loved to take down the great Alexandros Vaduva." His gaze went distant. "I'll confess, seeing him gave me some concern. He has a reputation, and even I had never been stupid enough to confront him." He gave me a look filled with confusion. "Was it you that neutered him? I mean, he didn't even register me in the hospital." He shook his head as if he were pained by the thought.

"Neutered?" It was my turn to look confused. And then I remembered Rachel's offhand comment about Devlin letting Alek work with them, implying that Alek was somehow dangerous. Maybe he was.

"No. It was probably Devlin Grey that reined him in. I would love to kill him, too, but, he has always been off-limits." He shrugged. "Now, do you want the tea?"

"Hard pass." *Fucking crazy bastard.* And what did he mean Devlin had always been off-limits? "Now, give me your villain speech and either kill me or let me go."

He set the cup down and pulled a chair over to the bed. "Your jeans are behind you," he said, and straddled the chair.

I turned and found them folded up near the pillow I had been laying on. I wasn't going to stand up and slide them on with him so close, so I grabbed the blanket and covered my legs. Pointless, he had already seen my legs. For all I knew, he'd seen everything. He'd touched my breasts when he took my knife from me. I should've been pissed, but no, I was more curious than anything. And my damn curiosity was still getting me in trouble. I needed to get the fuck out of here. Trouble was, I didn't know where *here* was. I mean, I could bum rush him. Take him by surprise. But I doubted that would work.

And besides, psycho had a gun.

But more worrisome was his brand of crazy. It just didn't seem real. I expected him to be all menace and brooding. But instead, he reminded me of an old, crazy grandma reincarnated into a six-foot, bald-headed, dangerously good-looking man.

Maybe I was still sleeping. Dreaming all of this. I pinched myself. Nope. Still here.

"Talk," I demanded.

He cocked his head to the side. "Gerald Stewart claimed you were extremely observant. That doesn't appear to be the case. Maybe helping you is a waste of time." He actually looked disappointed.

"What's that supposed to mean?"

He jerked his head toward the apartment. "Look again."

I glanced around the room, once again noting the strange collection of items. Were they memorabilia? "Did you inherit everything from your grandma?"

He smiled. "I'll give you a hint: I'm a mind mage." He leaned back, letting his forearms settle on the back of the chair, perfectly at ease.

I picked up the switchblade he so willingly gave me back. "I will use it." He just sat there, waiting. My eyes went to the gun resting on his thigh. "But I know the saying about bringing a knife to a gun fight, so pass. You want me to attack you, don't you?"

"Now who's talking crazy?" he asked. "I assume Devlin gave you a gun?" How the hell did this man know so much about us?

"From the look on your face, I'd say yes." He stood, gun in hand a few feet away from me. "This apartment is maybe two hundred feet. I'm standing five feet away from you. The Tueller Rule surmises that within twenty-one feet, you could successfully overtake me with that knife in your hand." He planted his feet and narrowed his eyes. "Care to try?"

Anger rose inside of me. I was sitting here, untied, allowing some deranged man who collected mystical creature figurines goad me into playing a game of Rock, Paper, Scissors. Or in this case: rock, gun, switchblade. I'd never heard of the Tueller Rule. It sounded like bullshit to me, like he'd made it up just for this scenario. His gaze bore into me. I had to choose my words carefully—not something I was used to doing. But I had to figure out what he was really up to. "You must think I'm insane," I said, changing from a question to a statement, trying to gage his reaction.

Silence.

"You have a gun."

Still nothing.

We stared at each other for a short while. I had no idea what he was thinking, but my mind was reeling from the fact that I was trapped in a tiny studio apartment with someone who obviously lost his good sense some time ago.

"So, observant. Yet"—he pushed forward—"you lack the skills to really understand what you're seeing." He smiled. "And you also have no sense of self-preservation," he said, his tone chiding.

A flash of me ripping the dick off of the last man who attacked me popped in my head, and I smiled. "Oh, I will have to argue with you on that one. I don't need a knife to do damage."

"Then why haven't you attacked me yet?"

Fuck it. I ran at him, modesty be damned, and landed a punch before he jerked me around and wrapped his arms around my waist.

"Care to try again?" He leaned closely, whispering in my ear.

"Maybe use the switchblade this time." His minty breath washed over me.

"Fuck you!" I yanked away from him and grabbed the blade off the bed. Dammit, I should have charged him with it first instead of believing I could knock him down with one damn punch. Now, he was ready for the attack.

I stood there, blade in hand, trying to run through some of Ezra's teachings when I attended his Krav Maga class. The only thing that came to mind was...no rules. I charged, blade arcing down, and was met with empty space. The bastard had moved.

My chest heaved up and down as I stood there, still trying to come up with some plan.

"When Devlin gave you a gun, did he teach you how to use it?" he asked, staring pointedly at my knife. "Might have been better if you shoved that down between your breasts."

I didn't respond.

"I could give you a few pointers." The side of his mouth ticked up in a cocky grin.

"There is something seriously wrong with you," I gritted out.

"You just have to get to know me," he winked. "But if you're done. We can move on. Unless you want another half-assed attempt at me." He looked too damn hopeful when he said that. Fucking crazy bastard.

"Why not just kill me?" Why did I keep putting that in his head?

"Do you want me to?" he asked with a smirk.

All I saw was red. Anger coursed through me, infusing my body with energy while the adrenaline pushed my heart into over-drive. He didn't see it coming. The knife sliced through his fore-arm. I aimed for more but was knocked on my ass before I could even lift the knife again. He held me down, his hand going around my throat. His eyes darkened, and I saw the caged animal behind those bottomless pits.

He was a trained killer.

One wrong move would probably break his resolve. I got the impression someone wanted me alive, and Logan was fighting his impulse to kill me.

"Touché," he said finally as he got up. He grabbed my jeans off the bed and wiped the blood off his arm. After tossing them in my face, he stepped away. "Again?"

I ignored him, partly because I knew I would never get the chance to cut him again, and mostly because I valued my life.

My heart rammed in my chest as I stood up. My ass hurt, but I swallowed the wince and sat back down on the bed. After wrapping the bedsheet around me—I was not putting those jeans on—I glanced around the room again, this time trying to figure out what he wanted me to see.

The studio apartment was one large room with pale green walls and crown-molding circling the entire space. Framed photographs of more myths and legends hung on the walls. The figurines, I noted, were of centaurs, fairies, leprechauns, and other mythical creatures. A few angels were sprinkled in as well. Four clay pots sat in each corner of the space. There was no television or radio. A large bookshelf crammed with books sat against the wall near the closet. Judging from the heavy use of myth, I could guess what the books were about. A strange, convoluted scent hung in the air. A few incense burners sat on a round table with candles and jars filled with liquid. The smell reminded me of some of the herbs my father grew.

It was the porcelain figurines that threw me, making me jump to the wrong conclusion. Logan was right; my observational skills were slipping.

Everything in the room was related to earth magick.

And Logan had made a point of telling me he was a mind mage.

"This isn't your apartment."

He dipped his head in acknowledgement and sat back down. "Now, have you all found the Ark?"

"You've lost me again. What does that have to do with this apartment?"

He glanced at his watch. "Looks like we're about out of time." He got up from the chair, went over to the table, and picked up my cell phone. Fucking bastard had taken my phone, too. "Use your skills to locate the Ark and figure out what's going on. And when you're done with that, trace the history of the phoenix."

I had two representations of the phoenix: one on my charm bracelet and another as part of the mark inside my head. "What do you know about my mark?"

He startled, pausing as he put the sim card back in my phone. "What mark?"

I didn't respond. So, he didn't know everything about me. But why would he tell me to trace the history of a mystical bird?

He made his way to the door. "Tell Kara it was nice seeing her again," he said, not turning around. "I will see you soon." He opened the door and walked out.

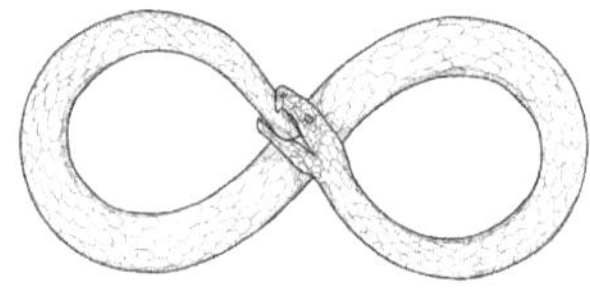

"Tell me everything he said," Alek said as I watched his cousin lay the owner of the apartment on the bed. After Logan left, I'd found her stuffed in the closet. Thankfully, he hadn't locked her inside her mind as well.

I ran through the strange conversation again. I refused to tell him about my failed attempt to fight Logan.

"Why would he want you to learn about the phoenix?" Alek asked.

I shook my head. "He kept insisting I was overlooking something."

We both looked around, taking in the various figurines and statues. It was on my second glance; I spotted the phoenix behind the angel sculpture.

I walked over and picked up the glass bird. The wings were spread out in an arc as if it were in flight. The claws were open, ready to catch prey in its grip. Jeweled eyes stared at me. I looked deeper. Inside the flames was another figure—a dark outline of what looked like a woman. She had her hands up in prayer.

The figurine was a replica of my protective mark.

I moved around the rest of the room, trying to find more objects depicting the phoenix, but the figurine I held in my hand was the only one.

I extended it to Alek when he walked up to me. "I thought Logan was crazy. But that bird resembles my protective mark. The hands, the wings. The only difference is the outline of a woman and the missing shen ring."

He studied it, running his hands over the surface. "This means something." He glanced over at the woman lying on the bed. "But what's really important is if she means something as well. He brought you here for a reason."

That much I figured out. We walked over to her, and Alek sat on the bed. Mid-sixties, her dark hair was heavily streaked with gray. Laugh lines surrounded her mouth and eyes, even at rest. No more than five feet tall, she looked small and unassuming. She seemed like someone I would immediately trust and like. But then again, she spent most of her time engrossed in fairytales, maintaining her childlike wonder. No pictures of family or lovers were anywhere in sight. And her ring finger remained unadorned and devoid of any tan line to indicate she had ever been married.

Alek stared at her. A wave of power rushed over me as he used his magick to reach inside her mind.

The woman's eyes fluttered open, and she stared at Alek. A small smile stretched across her mouth. "You are of the Roma. The Travelers. You also hold the histories bestowed to you by the Historian. I am Esmeralda. Keeper of secrets." She eased up and whispered, "Have you come to rescue me from the dark force that has set foot in my home?"

Yep, definitely maintained her childlike wonder, especially if she believed Alek was some fabled knight. I admit, he most assuredly looked like one—albeit a dark one, filled with mystery. Right up the lady's alley. And mine.

"Yes, I am of the Roma," Alek said, his voice soothing. "But I have stopped Traveling long ago." He handed her the phoenix. "Can you tell me about this, Esmeralda?"

She shrunk back, seeming to grow smaller as she tried to get away from the figurine. "The dark force gave it to me." She shook her head vehemently. "I do not like the tale of women who are birds of fire." Her face turned down in a frown; a single tear slipped down her face. "They were killed, and their power stolen."

"How?" I asked, sitting next to her.

She stared at me with her lips pressed together to keep herself from talking. Maybe it wasn't that she held onto her childhood and its fables, but that she herself remained a child. While Logan hadn't physically harmed her, he had mentally. He'd shattered her world with his presence. I should have stabbed him in the throat. I'd have to kick his ass when I saw him again.

"Will you be all right?" Alek asked.

Her face lit up again, switching so suddenly from one of fear to joy. She gazed up at him, adoration in her eyes. "Yes, I will. I have always taken care of myself." The pride in her voice made me smile. It also made me a little jealous. Even someone who society would deem feeble-minded was able to carve out a life for herself, able to live her days filled with joy and wonder. And I couldn't even manage to figure out how to stay in one place long enough to make it my home.

After ensuring Esmeralda was in fact okay, we left. When we stopped to drop off Alek's cousins, I waited in the car. My mind was too full for pleasantries, and I had no plans of seeing Petronela. The woman terrified the hell out of me.

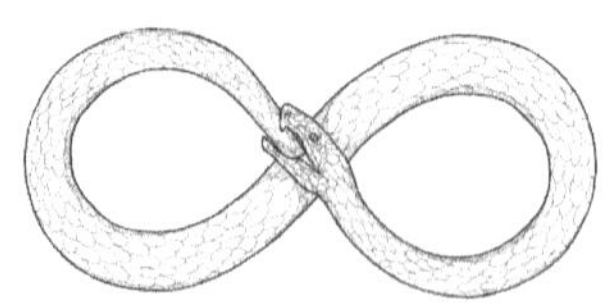

On our drive home, I studied the bruising on Alek's face. "What happened when you and Devlin were in jail?" I hated how that sounded. Like they were some common thugs always spending time behind bars.

He reached out and took my hand. "Logan..." he trailed off. "Well, I assumed Logan had set a trap so we could be attacked in the cell. But now..." he shook his head.

"You don't think it was him," I said, trying to suppress my rising anger.

"I need to give the whole thing some more thought. I know Barnes was behind it, but Logan? I get the impression he set the plan in motion, but maybe not the attack. He seems like the kind of person who would prefer to do his own dirty work. At least that's what I'm thinking."

I turned and looked out the window. "He goaded me into attacking him." Aleks hand tightened around mine. "I managed to cut him and the way he reacted made me think he was holding himself back. Like he wanted to hurt me but couldn't."

"Something about him doesn't add up," Alek said.

I turned back to him. Thinking of what Logan had alluded to about Alek's magick. It did appear to be different from when I first witnessed him using it. "Your magick," I started.

He glanced at me, raising his eyebrow in question.

"It seems...stronger. Different, even."

He nodded but didn't say anything. When we finally got to Devlin's, he turned off the engine and stared out the windshield. "My magick is different. Like Jonah, I have to keep myself in check or risk hurting everyone around me." He turned and looked at me. "You help me more than you know."

I nodded. I wanted to press, but the painful look on his face kept me from asking more. He would tell me when he was ready.

"What happened with Theresa?" I asked finally, changing the subject.

He let out a long sigh and rested his head against the seat. The sky had gone from gray to orange, and the sun crested over the horizon, filling the atmosphere with an ethereal light. I suppressed a yawn and laid my head on the seat back as well.

"It took a while, but we were able to pull her out of the chaos. She gave us information on a former employee of Tribec Insurance." He reached in his pocket, pulled out a note, and handed it to me. "Edward Clines. Devlin and I can go see him today."

"Something else is bothering you," I said, studying his face.

He stared out the windshield. "I didn't know what to think when I didn't see you in the room. Unrie led us on a wild goose chase. We lost him. Then I got a text from you, saying you went to get something to drink. I should have figured out something wasn't right. But..." He shook his head, agitation radiating off him. His hands balled into fists, and I reached out and took them in mine.

"You found me in the end."

He turned to me. "He could have hurt you."

"I'm still surprised he didn't. But what concerns me the most is that I wasn't afraid because somewhere deep inside of me, I realized I wasn't in danger. My mark didn't once react to him." I laughed. "Hell, he even gave me my knife back."

"We need to figure out what game he's playing."

I yawned. "Maybe in the morning. Or after a pot of Rachel's coffee."

He pulled me toward him. I slid over his lap, straddling him. "If you want to fool around, we will need a lot of coffee," I said.

He laughed and slid my hair away from my face. "I need sleep. And so do you." He kissed my neck, waking me up faster than any caffeine could. "But I also need to hold you."

"I need that too," I whispered. "But I hope we're not going to sleep in the car."

He pushed open the car door, and I stepped out into the chilly morning air. I pulled in the crisp scent and infused my lungs with its freshness. I hardly ever watched the magick of dawn. Alek closed the car door softly and took my hand. We walked the short distance to Devlin's house, still staring at the beauty of the suns rays spilling over the sky.

Even though my mind was wracked with so many new revelations, when Alek wrapped his warm arm around me and pulled me close, everything went silent.

The phoenix rose into the sky, beating its fiery wings against the wind, coating the horizon with an orange and red glow. A woman rode on its back, her feet planted, digging into the bird's powerful muscles. Her pitch-black eyes stared across the land. Gold hair trailed behind her as she screamed, signaling for her sisters to rise. On the ground, I stared up at her in awe. And when she passed over me, I reached for her. I wanted to ride the phoenix. I wanted to feel its heat on my skin. Her head turned toward me. I saw my reflection in her dark eyes.

'You are of my blood,' she whispered in my mind.

Fire engulfed me.

A knock on the door jolted me out of the dream. Sweat coated my skin, and my heart pounded rapidly against my chest. The bed shifted as Alek got up. I cracked open my eyes and watched him walk to the door. Mind fuzzy, I tried to concentrate on what Devlin was saying, but the blood roaring in my ears rendered me temporarily deaf.

Alek shut the door and came back to the bed. He sat down next to me and rested his hand on my hip. The weight of it on my skin—the rough texture of his fingers made my body strum with need. It seemed as if we had now settled into a natural intimacy. Each of us reaching out to the other on impulse. Like we'd been together for years. As far as I was concerned, his hand belonged on my hip. And I belonged in his bed.

"You're sweating." His fingers trailed along my thigh. "Nightmare?"

I swallowed the lump in my throat and shook my head, unable to do more than that. The emotions were still raw. I didn't believe in visions or portents or any other such things. But right now, with the dream still playing in my mind, I wondered if maybe it had been some sort of sign. Or some long-buried memory had surfaced and was trying to give me a clue.

"What time is it?" I asked, barely a whisper. My throat burned with dryness. Had I been crying out in my sleep?

"Just after eight. Devlin wants us to go over what happened yesterday."

I licked my dry lips. "Can you all do that without me?"

He smiled and dug his fingers softly into my hip, giving me a little shake. "Come on. I'll get the coffee going and coax Jonah into making breakfast."

I turned and laid on my back. "Okay. Give me fifteen minutes."

Alek kissed me on my cheek. "I'll give you ten."

I groaned and covered my face with his pillow. At the first whiff of his enticing scent, my hormones jumped up and started pacing the room.

Now that we'd taken the next step in our relationship, self-doubt had reared its ugly head. Could this work between us? I'd never been in a relationship before. Casual sex was more my speed. All this caring and concern was new to me. And I just knew I was going to fuck up eventually.

The bathroom door opened, and I removed the pillow from my face. Alek emerged, dressed, with his hair tied back. "Get up, Nicole."

"That breakfast better be good," I said, pushing up from the bed.

He laughed and walked out of the room.

The bathroom mirror didn't lie, no matter how much I wished it was really a funhouse mirror. The reflection in that unforgiving glass showed me just what no sleep really looked like: skin sallow and sunken in, eyes filmy, and hair so out of control, it looked as if it was trying to run away. Makeup might work, but I didn't own enough to make a decent-sized dent in my appearance.

I'd visited a make-up counter once in my entire life. I'd gone there after losing yet another job because I couldn't think before I spoke. The woman behind the counter had gone through what she called a skin assessment, and by the end of that torturous hour, twelve products were lined up on the counter. When she gave me the total, I gave her the finger and walked away.

Remembering that day now, I realized that I had gone there hoping to change. Only, I believed that changing my appearance would somehow change who I was inside.

I should have bought the damn products. At least I would have been able to use them to hide the obvious signs of exhaustion covering my face.

After brushing my teeth and washing my face, I stared at my wild hair, willing it to tame itself. I was completely out of gel now and would have to pick some up soon. But with the way things were going, I doubted I'd get the chance.

The dried sweat had left a sticky residue on my skin. Fuck it. They would have to wait a little longer for me to get myself together. There was no way I was going out there smelling. I climbed in the shower and let the cool water run over me. It drummed against my back, and my mind went back to the dream.

Like most of my dreams, once I was awake, I had a hard time recalling all the details. But one thing I did remember was me standing in our old yard on the bayou in New Orleans, reaching up toward the woman riding a phoenix. What did it mean? Was it something I witnessed, or something I conjured from my conversations with both Logan and Esmeralda? She'd said the women were all hunted for their power. Sadly, she wasn't able to give us more information. I knew who I could ask—the one person who might know what it all meant.

My mother.

But I had a feeling she wouldn't tell me. She'd kept her secrets this long; secrets that were now impacting my life. Could that be enough to convince her to share?

I toweled off and slipped on a pair of shorts and a tank top. My hair was manageable when it was wet, making it easy to pull back and secure at the nape of my neck. Of course, by the time it dried, it would look like a demented afro puff, but I'd have to worry about that later.

Stepping out of the room, I inhaled the delectable scents of fried onions and potatoes. The foods of the gods, as far as I was concerned. I followed the smell down the hall and stopped just before entering the kitchen.

Marta stood at the whiteboard, taping pictures of different depictions of phoenix birds to the cleared surface. All the other information had been shifted over and was now overlapping. At this rate, we'd have to start tacking things to the wall. I was somewhat in awe of her ability to fit into the team so quickly. Maybe she should have become a detective like she'd wanted to. She had the mind for it. I did too if I really thought about it. But our approaches were vastly different. While Marta organized and looked at information in a strategic way, I took to peppering people with questions and trying to find the missing pieces. Looking at the world as one great, big, confusing puzzle.

As if sensing me, she turned and made eye contact. Her mouth morphed into a sympathetic frown. "You look beat," she said.

"Exactly how I feel. How are the kids?"

She looked away, busying herself with more printouts. "They are managing." The tone in her voice wasn't convincing. It was filled with more hope than reassurance.

I went over and put my arm around her. She tensed, her shoulders rising as if she were preparing herself for an attack. I hated that. Leaning in, I whispered, "Did you call the counselor?"

She turned toward me, melancholy in her eyes. "Yes, they have an appointment next Tuesday. Will you come?"

I nodded. "Of course, I will." I squeezed her to me. I wished Marta would take more time to heal, but I wasn't going to suggest it again. Besides, everyone had their own way of coping with the shit life threw at them. Maybe she was right, and this was exactly what she needed to be doing to get past the pain.

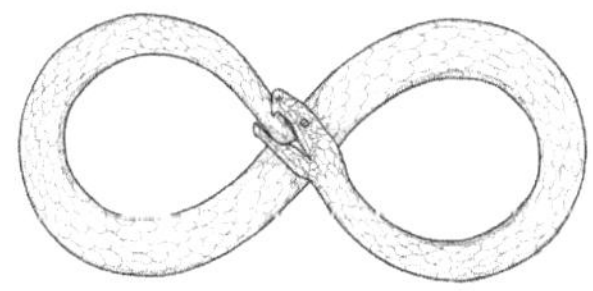

RACHEL STUDIED me as I drank my third cup of coffee. And like the first, the caffeine had yet to put a dent in my fatigue. At this point, I was just pounding the liquid back for the fun of it.

"What?" I asked Rachel and set my useless coffee down so I could finish the eggs and fried potatoes Jonah had made. If I didn't crave Alek so much, I might have asked the man to marry me. Of course, I'd have to get rid of Kara first.

"Probably shouldn't drink any more coffee. Your magick looks overcharged."

I paused, the fork halfway to my mouth. "What?" How the hell can you overcharge magick?

"You're glowing more." She said it so matter-of-factly; I was having a hard time closing my mouth.

"I didn't know magick could be overcharged." I set my fork down and stared at her, willing her to help me understand. She sipped her coffee like she had all the time in the world.

"It can't. You're just really strange, Nicole."

I'm strange. How is she so calm? Sweat broke out on my brow as I looked between her and my coffee mug. "Then how do you know it's been overcharged?"

She looked down as if ashamed. "Your magick is different. I've been keeping an eye on it since..." She trailed off, then looked up quickly. "We still best girlfriends, right?"

Creepiness aside, I understood why she was concerned. I was still trying to figure out my magick, too.

"Yes. We're still best girlfriends," I said finally. I smiled to reassure her and took a bite of my now-cold potatoes.

"Okay, team, let's get this over with," Devlin said, walking into the kitchen.

I slammed my fork down and opened my mouth to scream, only to stop when I got a good look at the grimace on Devlin's face as well as the bruise on his chin. He looked like I felt. Dark circles surrounded his eyes. His hair, normally smoothed into place, stuck out on the sides. His clothes were wrinkled like they had never been ironed before, and his face looked as if he'd lost some weight. Our conversation on Monday came rushing back. He'd been worried something like this would happen to me—that I would end up in a situation and he couldn't keep me safe. He'd been awake when Alek and I came home this morning, and while he hadn't said anything, his eyes had conveyed that worry and frustration. I'd just been too tired to really think about it.

I'd promised him I could take care of myself, and I wouldn't put the team in danger. Sadly, I'd gone back on my word, despite it not being my fault. I mouthed, "I'm sorry."

He shook his head and walked over to me. Leaning down, he whispered, "This was not your fault. We have been two steps behind Logan from the start. If anyone is to blame, it's me. I should have known you'd want to help Alek. And I should have been there to watch both your backs." He lifted my chin. "Understand?"

"Yes, Boss Man."

"Now, finish your breakfast and meet us in the other room."

"You mean the war room," I said, then shoved the rest of my food in my mouth.

He chuckled and walked out the kitchen. At least I'd made him laugh. That was something.

I followed him out of the kitchen and sat at my station next to Alek. Marta walked over and handed me a pen and notepad. It was then I realized what had been missing for a while now while we were running around, chasing our asses.

I had, for most of my life, kept journals. It was a way of dealing with all the thoughts I constantly had on loop inside my mind. It was also a way for me to keep track of events, because deep down, I knew I'd forgotten parts of my past. Of course, they came roaring back when the block on my magick and memories had been removed, but I still should have been writing stuff down. If I had been keeping notes, maybe I would have figured out what was going on a few days ago.

Devlin told everyone about their time in jail. I made a mental note to find Barnes and kick him in the nuts.

"We were able to restore Theresa's mind," Alek said. "She told us about Logan coming to her house. She remembered him clearly, but not what happened after she invited him in. He contacted her before us and said he had information about Emilia's death. I asked her about the ice cream truck, since I believe that is how Logan is getting around undetected, and she did remember seeing one outside her house." He paused. "She also said she was in contact with a female who claimed to have trained with you all. She said the woman refused to identify herself but said she would be in touch again with proof Ronald killed Emilia and the Stewarts covered it up." He dipped his head toward the note he tacked to the board. "She also gave me the name of another former employee. Edward Clines."

The female employee had to be Veronica Lockwood. She was the only other woman who had been in our training class.

"Did she have any other information? Maybe tell you about the insurance bills we found." Devlin asked. I could hear the frustration in his voice.

"Only that she had been contacted by the Stewarts' attorneys and that they had made threats of suing her for harassment and defamation. And she said Emilia gave her the bills for safe keeping."

Devlin nodded and took a sip of his coffee. "Nicole," he said, prompting me.

"Logan..." I paused, thinking of how to approach the strange encounter we had. "He was so concerned about my inability to figure things out. I think it even frustrated him a little."

"That is strange," Marta said. "But anyone who knows you would think you're not noticing something is...off?" She sat back and tapped her pen against her lips, her gaze distant. Finally, she looked up and noticed everyone was staring at her, waiting. "Sorry, just thinking aloud."

"No," Devlin said. "We need that. And I agree." He glanced over at me, and our eyes locked. "It is off. Go on, Nicole."

"Okay, so that means he knows me. Aside from his past connection with Kara, which she confirmed, I don't see how. I mean, it's not like they stayed in contact." I harrumphed. "He did have the audacity to ask me to say hello to her. Fucking crazy bastard." I stood up and started to pace as I took them through what we learned from Esmeralda, along with Logan's insistence that I learn about the phoenix myth.

"Fuck," Devlin said. "More avenues to follow."

My phone dinged, and I looked down at the display. Juliette. "Well, damn," I said. "As if we didn't have enough shit to deal with, looks like Juliette wants to meet with me at three."

"Did she say why?" Alek asked, leaning over to look at my phone.

"Maybe she wants to give us a few more clues to follow." I thrust my hand at the whiteboard. "It's not like we have enough or anything." I sounded a bit hysterical, but no one said anything.

Devlin squeezed the bridge of his nose. "Rachel," he said, his voice strained. He was barely holding it together.

Jonah pulled the projector screen down.

Rachel tapped a few keys on her laptop, and the photograph I found of the five women and one man appeared on the screen.

Rachel got up. "I spent most of the night scanning the information Nicole found in Selena Peterson's journal into the computer. Marta helped me find all of their names this morning." She smiled at Marta. "You do good work."

"Thank you," Marta said, as a grin spread across her face.

Rachel pointed at the first girl on the right. "This is Monica Sinclair at age nineteen. Yes, from that Sinclair family," she said when I gave her a questioning look. "She was the first one to join the cult. She brought her friend Rhonda Hamilton with her. Only, Rhonda ran away after staying there only a week."

"How were you able to find that out?" I asked.

She went to her desk and picked up the journal. "Selena kept detailed records."

Why would Logan want me to find this?

Rachel pointed at the next girl. "Gavina, age eighteen, and Helena Stewart, age sixteen, joined a month later. Helena is Gerald's baby sister."

Something tickled the back of my mind, like a thought was trying to form.

"Selena Peterson, age nineteen," Rachel said. "She joined four months later, and Bianca Smith, aged seventeen, was the last to join. She brought her friend Terra Long with her. Terra was one of the girls found dead when they raided the cult.

"A copy of this picture was found among Selena Peterson's things when her brother Darren found her in the bathtub, dead. She had committed suicide." Rachel clicked on the next image. "He also found this suicide note."

"What?" I asked. When had she found this out?

The note was written on pink stationary with striations of a brownish substance in the corners. As if someone had bled on the page and tried to wipe it away. The ink had been smeared, probably from water or moisture. So only a few words could be made out: 'I'm sorry,' and 'He wanted us to sacrifice ourselves.'

"Where did you find this?" I asked.

"When I scanned the photo in, I did an image search and found a forum online that still talks about the cult. Latoya Bailey, the sister of a reporter who was killed, is writing a book on the events that took place at His Holy Seed. She started the site. When I contacted her this morning, she agreed to send me this much. The rest, we have to pay for."

"Did you get any sleep?" I asked, feeling suddenly like I wasn't pulling my weight.

"No. But I don't always sleep." She turned away and clicked on another image. "This article was going to run in the paper two days after Selena Peterson was found. Only, the editor squashed the story and fired the reporter. The reporter was found dead two weeks later. Before that, he'd sent his sister this along with his notes."

"Does she know who asked the editor to squash the story?" I asked.

"Selena's parents did. And a few months later, they opened the Peterson School for Troubled Girl's in Sandpoint."

Her own damn parents didn't want the truth to come out. What the hell kind of parents did that? How much money did it take to forget your daughter's death? To let the person responsible go free? I rubbed my chest at the sudden influx of shock and sadness that overcame me. My mother buried an axe in the back of my attacker when I was six years old and buried his body in our yard. Selena's parents took money from the people who drove her daughter to take her own life. Un-fucking-believable.

We all sat in silence for a while, staring at Selena's suicide note. Why did Lemuel Oren want them to sacrifice themselves? And if Gavina had managed to escape such a nightmare, why would she start a cult and lure broken women in so she could absorb their magick? If I didn't want to kill her before, I definitely did now. She knew firsthand what kind of damage cults could cause and instead of being a force for good, she had decided to inflict the same pain on innocent girls.

Devlin finally spoke. "Alek and I will visit Edward Clines and see what he knows about Tribec. Nicole, we need to figure out what part Juliette plays in all this. Her calling you out of the blue doesn't make sense." He rubbed his head, making his hair stick out further. Glancing at the whiteboard, he said, "So many leads going nowhere. It's as if we're being led around for a reason."

"Like pieces on a chess board," I said.

His face darkened. "I don't like it. Despite Andrew's notes, we can't tie Gavina or Boyd Young to blood magick." He gave Jonah a quick glance, then looked at me. "Determine today if they are in fact practicing blood magick. Be your usual self and end this charade with them. We need to concentrate on the families that *are* using blood magick."

"My usual self?" I asked. He gave me a look that screamed, *use-your-head*. "Oh, blunt."

"Jonah, I want you to go with Nicole to meet Juliette. See if you can get anything out of her that Nicole might miss."

"I can go alone," I said without thinking. Of course, he wouldn't want me to go alone, especially not after what happened last night.

"Not going to happen," he said, his voice firm.

"Juliette is harmless. Unless she is going to puppy dog-eye me to death. I can take her."

"I'm still not letting you go alone. Logan could be the reason she's calling you now. He just kidnapped you last night. You. Are Not. Going. Alone," he gritted out.

We glared at each other, and the room fell silent around us. I knew he was worried. Hell, I was, too. But we needed a solid lead so we could stop chasing our tails. And to do that, we needed to get some straight answers out of the key players involved. Besides, Logan had kidnapped me last night. So why would he send Juliette after me now? No, she contacted me for another reason. I doubted she would be willing to share if Jonah was with me.

"Compromise?" I asked, extending an olive branch.

"I'm listening."

"Jonah comes, but he waits outside to give me a chance to talk with her alone."

"Sounds fair," Jonah said.

"Thank you," I mouthed. He dipped his head in acknowledgement.

Devlin turned to him. "First sign of trouble, handle it."

Jonah nodded, including Alek in the look. I glanced over at

him. His eyes were trained on me. I could read the storm in those blue depths; he, too, wanted to cover me in bubble wrap to keep me safe and secure.

"I'll be fine," I said. "I'm not some delicate flower, for fuck's sake. And I will have my knife with me."

His eyes went to my chest where I kept my knife. I gave him a half smile.

"That leaves Xavier," Devlin said and looked at Marta.

"His social media didn't mention anything about blood magick. Just a bunch of teenage fantasies and lewd comments about girls," she said, her chair swiveling as she looked down at her laptop.

"Jonah," Devlin said. "Check out Boyd and Xavier's place when you and Nicole finish with Juliette." He got up. "Fuck!" he yelled, making me flinch. I had never seen him like this before. Rachel got up and placed her hand on his chest. Green light filled the room as she hummed a soothing melody.

Alek leaned over and whispered, "Healing magick."

I nodded, keeping my eyes trained on Devlin and Rachel. Bit by bit, his face smoothed out, and the vein on the side of his neck ceased jumping erratically. He placed a hand over her hers. "Thanks, Rach."

She squeezed his hand and nodded. "I got you Dev."

"Sorry about that, team," he said.

"Not a problem, Dev," Jonah said. "We're all right there with you."

"I'm so damn tempted to just put a bullet in all their heads," he said, and gave a humorless chuckle. "Okay. Anyone have any questions?"

"I can work on the phoenix lead," Marta offered.

"I might have a lead on that," I said before Devlin could respond. I took them through my dream last night. "Let me ask my mother first."

Devlin nodded as he looked at the projector screen. "Marta, can you compile dossiers on the other women who escaped the cult? I need an assessment on where we should concentrate our efforts next." He paused. "We've been working off Andrew's notes. That has to end now. We need to do our own investigation into these families. I don't want any more surprises."

We all murmured in agreement.

"I'll also rearrange the boards," Marta said.

Devlin turned to her. "Thanks, Marta. I don't know what we'd do without you here."

She smiled at him. "Probably shoot everyone."

He laughed. "Yeah, probably." He glanced at his watch. "Everyone, check in at noon." He looked at me. "Nicole, keep us in the loop if you decide to follow another lead besides your mother. I want someone to be aware of your whereabouts at all times." He looked at the rest of the team. "That goes for everyone. Until we can neutralize the threats, seen and unseen, we need to keep in constant contact."

"Yes, Boss Man."

"I can add tracking apps to our phones, Dev," Rachel said. "It will help me keep an eye on everyone from my laptop."

Devlin handed her his phone and gave us all a pointed look. Well, I would have argued, but it wasn't a good idea, especially after what happened to me last night.

After Alek gave me a kiss, I fixed myself another useless cup of coffee and sat down at my computer. to review what Marta had found on Xavier's social media. It was busy work. But I needed the distraction and to kill some time before I went to see my mother.

Devlin was right. We should just put a bullet in everyone's head.

My charm bracelet glinted off the sunlight as I held it up, thinking. When my father had first given me the bracelet, he'd told me the Ankh was a symbol for his family's power and the phoenix was a symbol of my mother's. At the time, I was just excited to have a piece of jewelry and elated that my father had given it to me. I didn't put together what he had actually said: A symbol for both their magicks meant my mother had magick, too. Only later, when I'd asked her about it, she claimed she didn't.

So, what happened to her magick?

My online peek into Xavier's life had given me a headache. He spent most of his time posting about one fantasy game or another and throwing in an occasional pic of a woman's body with explicit commentary. So, pretty much a dead end. Just like Marta said.

When I hit a brick wall, I got in my car and drove to my parents' house. Now, I just needed to get the hell out of the car.

My father usually worked at his shop 'til five, but some days, he would work from home and let his clerk run the shop. I couldn't face both of them right now and had hoped he wouldn't be home. His car in the driveway meant I would have to.

I'd been sitting in my car for over thirty minutes, still not brave enough to get out and walk the short distance to the front door. True, I needed answers, but I couldn't stop thinking about the betrayal.

I picked up the phoenix figurine and stared into its blazing red eyes. Remembering my dream, I focused on the outline of the woman inside. The glass was so bright that the darkened shade of the woman stood out. How had Logan found a representation of my protective mark, yet knew nothing about it? Someone had to give him the information—tell him what to look for.

My mind drifted back to Karl and his crazed ramblings. Although Alek had confirmed a mind mage could have broken Karl's mind and killed him, I kept thinking about that voice claiming Karl as his own. And the smell of cherries. It had to be an Old One controlling him, which meant the mutterings about Xavier, demons, and power were meant to throw us off the scent. So why hadn't my marks heated, alerting me to its presence?

I touched my lips where Ezra's mark resided. Maybe the mark was only meant to warn me when Set was near.

A noise startled me, and I looked up. My mother stepped outside and started toward the street. My heart seized in my chest, and I fought the urge to hide. I reached for the door handle, only to stop when she continued across the street to Cherry's house.

Well, that made this a little easier. I pushed open my car door, grabbed the figurine, shoved it in my purse, and made my way across the street. It wasn't fair for me to use Cherry as a buffer to the argument I knew was coming, but I wasn't brave enough— no, correction—*strong* enough to do this on my own.

My mother had already gone inside by the time I got to Cherry's porch. My footfalls hesitant, I walked up the three steps and, hands shaking, knocked on the door. Cherry opened it, wearing a loose-fitting white sundress. Without saying a word, she stepped to the side, and I walked into the house, my eyes going immediately to my mother's tear-streaked face. The fireplace was ablaze as usual. The light from the flames danced over her face, making it glow. Her hair hung in limp strands down her back and her clothing was wrinkled, stains marring the fabric. I went to her, forgetting about my anger, and let her pull me into an embrace. The carpet rubbed against my exposed knees as she rocked me back and forth.

"I'll get you both some lemonade," Cherry said, and left me and my mother to our reunion.

I held on as long as I could, comforting both of us. But then, I pulled back and slid onto the couch next to her. I stared at her tear-swollen face. Steeling myself because I knew my questions would cause her more pain. "I need answers, Mom," I said, my tone soft.

She ran her hand over my hair. "Are you out of gel, *ma fille*?"

I stilled her hand and held it in my lap. "Mom, please. You owe me answers."

She swallowed hard and then got up. Pacing the room, she avoided looking at me. I'd never seen my mother so agitated. If I could choose a single word to describe her, I'd say carefree. She rarely got angry and spent a great deal of time dancing around the house—with or without music. She and my father loved each other so much, it was hard to be in the same room with them sometimes. It was as if their love was a physical thing, filling the air, making it hard to breathe. But now, seeing her in this state, my heart couldn't take it. Forgiveness crept in, trying to override the anger. The dolls on Cherry's mantle watched me with accusing eyes. I turned away from their scrutiny. I'd always hated those dolls.

Cherry returned with a glass of her special lemonade. A concoction of liquid fire. She handed it to me. I took a few sips, letting the heat course down my throat. I stared at the flames. Cherry always had one going despite the heat outside. Of course, she had her air-conditioning running the entire time, so the fire was more for comfort than anything. I used to wonder if she enjoyed watching it because of the way she had killed her husband and his mistress, but that would mean she took joy in their deaths. And I knew, while she felt it was justified, it disturbed her that she allowed herself to be pushed to those lengths.

"Anne," Cherry said, her voice soothing. "Sit down with your daughter."

My mother turned to her. I could see the anger rising, only to be suddenly snuffed out as she nodded and came and sat next to me. "Some answers, I can't give." She turned and took my hands in hers. She pulled a breath in, her chest rising, trying to expand.

Then she said, "Jean-Luke was your father's oldest friend." She gave me a bitter smile. I hadn't planned on revisiting what had happened to me, but maybe she needed to, so I prepared myself for the pain. "Your father and I used to love to go out dancing. But we rarely got the chance." She ran her hand down my cheek. "You were such an inquisitive child, and you drove your babysitters crazy." I smiled because I remembered that.

She turned away and looked at the fire again. Tears flowed freely down her face. "Jean-Luke had come to visit and offered to watch you. I should have known"—she shook her head vehemently—"when you refused to go to him that you had sensed something wrong. Children know so much. Feel so much. And all I could think about was dancing with your father."

I pulled her to me and let her cry on my shoulder, both to comfort her and to hide my own tears. I glanced over at Cherry. Her face had morphed into an angry mask. I needed that.

My mother pulled away and wiped the tear off her cheek. "When we...we got home, I heard you crying—screaming for us. And his groans." She jumped up. "Oh, dear god, his groans. I went into the room and flew into a rage. I don't know how the axe ended up in my hand, but the next thing I knew, I was burying it in his back. Over and over again." She looked down at her hands. "There was so much blood. I feared it would never come out."

"I remember," I said, my voice small. I'd been hiding behind the hutch in the kitchen while my father washed my mother's hands. "But I also remember you telling me to let go of him."

"You were keeping his soul tethered to his body. And I wanted him dead."

"I remember that. I just don't understand how. Where does my magick come from?"

She looked away. I dug in my purse and pulled out the figurine. Cherry gasped, and my mother stared at the glass phoenix, horror drying the tears on her face. "No, sweet baby, no. You cannot know about this. I will not let you come to harm."

"How will I be harmed by the truth?" I got up and went to her. "What does the history of a mythical bird have to do with us? With our lineage?"

All my fruitless searches for magick and frustration that I didn't have the same power as my father and his family. The many clues I ignored as I went about my daily life. And all the while, the answer was right in front of me. I should have known.

I'd always had this strange sort of animosity toward her when I was a teenager. I loved her, yes. We had more good times than bad. But when we fought, the anger that came out of me was always so irrational, like I was compounding a simple disagreement and turning it into an all-out war.

Was it my subconscious mind telling me something was wrong? That she was lying to me?

"Hathor took that power from me to protect both of us." She grabbed the figurine, threatening to throw it in the fire. "You will set something in motion with the knowledge of the *Nar al-nasaa*. Something terrible. When Hathor took my power, she saved us. But it is destroying her. Please, *ma fille*, leave this be."

I couldn't let it be. Despite her insistence, it was already affecting me. "A man kidnapped me and told me to learn the history of the phoenix."

"What?" My mother's eyes rounded. "Who is this man?" Her skin glowed. Fire seemed to run underneath her skin like a rapid river. It reminded me of lava. At first, I thought it was an illusion triggered by the fireplace, but the more I stared at it, the more the yellow tips stood out. I reached for her hand, only to stop short. Her hands. When I had been holding them a while ago, they were warm. Yet, ever since the night she killed my attacker when I was six, her skin had always been cold.

"You said Hathor took your power," I said, finally realizing that yes, I did need her to say it aloud. "Tell me the truth, Mom. Please."

She shook her head and turned away from me. Her hands were wrapped around the figurine. She stared down at it. "She had to give some back. Not all. It was destroying her." She jerked her head up, pinning me with her gaze. "Who. Kidnapped. You?" I flinched at the coldness in her voice.

"I took care of it," I said, purposely not elaborating. I didn't want her to shift the focus. If I kept asking, maybe she would tell me.

A knock sounded at the door, and I knew it was my father. He never liked either of us visiting Cherry. The last time I was here, she hinted at the argument she and my father had about him keeping secrets from me. Maybe he feared she would tell me the truth. The look in her eyes when she saw the figurine said she knew a lot more than I did. If we had been alone, maybe I could have gotten more details from her.

Cherry pushed up from her chair and strode to the door. My mother continued to stare at the phoenix with a look of longing and dread in her eyes.

"Come in, Henri," Cherry said, stepping back to allow my father to come inside.

As soon as he did, the room seemed to expand. His gaze traveled between my mother and me. After searching my mother's face, he finally settled on me. Those familiar hazel eyes, similar to my own, watched me now, seeking answers. He opened his arms, and as if being pulled by a string, I went into them.

All the anger flowed away from me in a wave of relief. It was always like this with him. It was part of the reason I'd stayed away. I knew if I saw him, if he opened his arms, I would forget the anger I had for them, and the lies would continue.

"You both hurt me," I mumbled into his chest.

"Shh, baby girl. It will be all right."

Those familiar words engulfed me, pushing the last of the pain away. I didn't want to hurt my parents. I missed them so damn much. My mother came forward and wrapped her arms around me. They circled me in a tight embrace. I accepted the fact that I wouldn't get what I needed from them. Well, not the answers I needed, anyway. But this—this love pouring from them, I needed, too. So, I'd take what they could give and seek my answers elsewhere.

I knew my mother wanted to protect me. My father did as well. I'd allow them that for now.

Besides, she had given me something I could use. And I had someone else I could ask. I just hoped Ezra would not make good on his promise to kill me the next time I came around, because I wasn't going to rest until I found out the truth. But first, I had to deal with Juliette.

I texted Jonah to let him know I was on my way.

I stared out the large window at Libations by R, watching the cars drive by as I waited for Juliette and her sister. Since I was early, I used the time to reflect on my past. At some point in my life, I became hyper aware of my surroundings. Constantly noting danger and strange occurrences as if I were cataloging the things in my life for a reality TV show. If I was honest with myself—hell, if I had even finished the self-help book I'd bought instead of returning it—I would know, no, more like confirm, that this hyperawareness was a result of the trauma inflicted on me when I was a child.

Pain and hurt were a constant in my life. So much so they were now like old friends, sticking around reminding me that I could never truly be happy. The need to fill the holes I had sensed inside myself led me down paths I wouldn't normally have taken —into bedrooms I should never have entered.

The book could have also explained why I craved danger. When I walked down the hospital hall last night, something kept trying to tell me to run. The adrenaline pumping through my veins, my heart pounding in my chest, and the hairs rising on my skin—all these warnings were sounding the alarm. But I pushed forward. I'd felt Logan in the corner of the room, even subconsciously made note of his presence. Yet, I stood there, wrapped up in the thrill running through my body, waiting to see what would happen.

I flipped open the magazine Hathor told me would help me find my purpose and turned to the quiz. The first question made me groan.

Circle all the traits that describe you.

None of mine were listed, so I shut the magazine and took a sip of my coffee. Was there even caffeine in it?

Rosalind walked over and sat down across from me. "You look troubled. Care to unload?" She took a sip of her tea and looked around the coffee shop.

"What would you say my purpose was?" I asked.

She glanced at the coffee cup in front of me. "Judging from the amount of coffee you've already had, I'd say you either needed to get some sleep or go pee."

"I'd say you're right. That about sums up my life right now."

"You also need to fix your hair."

I nodded. "Yes, that too. Should I sleep or pee before I fix my hair, though?"

She laughed. I'd always loved her infectious laughter. It sounded like she pulled it directly from her happy place. "On second thought," she started, "I'd say your hair looks nice. The wildness really brings out your eyes." She leaned back in the seat. "I was always jealous of you four in high school. You were all so sure of yourself. So free. I was a nerd."

"Rosalind, you still are a nerd. With a frou-frou coffee shop in the middle of a seedy neighborhood known for its eclectic nightlife."

She smiled. "Life does have a way of putting you in your place. Maybe my purpose was to open a coffee shop." A man walked in, and Rosalind focused on him. "Herbal tea with lemon and an oatmeal cookie." She shook her head and turned back to me. "Remember when you four went on that ghost hunting expedition?"

I grinned, recalling Kara, Steve, Marta, and me being fascinated with the existence of ghosts ever since the Islia Sea—a luxury yacht that was found abandoned floating off the coast of

Tulare in the Atlantic Sea—had been found. Hell, the whole island had been. We even went on a ghost hunting expedition that resulted in our getting banned from the boat for life. We never did prove the existence of ghosts.

"My friends and I had gone, too. We saw the guy throw you all out."

I turned my coffee mug around as old memories came back. The expedition had been Steve's quest. One of his many, what we called, nerdy ideas. I smiled at the memory. "That was embarrassing."

Rosalind gave me a sad smile and reached across the table to touch my hand. "I always thought you and Steve would end up together."

I leaned back in my seat, trying to get away from the discomfort suddenly overtaking me. Rosalind, as if sensing my discomfort, pulled her hand away and continued, "Anyway, it was that day my first story idea came to me."

I furrowed my brow in confusion as I tried to remember her first novel. Was it about ghosts? I could have sworn she wrote romance novels.

"Oh..." She laughed. "It wasn't about ghosts or anything. But it was about first love." She paused, staring at me, as if she were willing me to understand. After a short while, I nodded. *She was talking about Steve and me.*

"You are aware that you can read minds, right?" I asked, changing the subject.

Rosalind polished off the rest of her tea and stared at the customers. The look on her face made me think she was searching for something. Like most people who looked inside themselves, gaining perspective from their own endless life lessons and experiences. "The people who come here make the best characters," she said finally. "The man in the corner..." She dipped her head in his direction. "Last night, he entertained two women and three men in the alley. Today, he's going to work at the bank." She turned to me. "I always knew I had some magick. But your friend, the one who was sitting with you the other day, called me a mage." She shrugged. "I looked it up."

"Does it scare you?"

She smiled, shaking her head. "Not at all." She leaned in. "But please don't tell anyone. I would lose my source material."

She slapped the table, her entire face lighting up. "I sold another story."

"Oh, that's great! What's it about?" Despite her reassurances, I thought learning she was a mage did disturb her.

"You know I don't discuss that. But I will give you a signed copy."

I should have remembered Rosalind didn't discuss her stories. "Speaking of mind reading," I said carefully, "the other girl who came in. The one whose thoughts were not her own."

She nodded slowly. "Yes, the one who wanted herbal tea. I think he was confused what to order."

I lifted a brow in confusion. "You mean she?"

"No, the one controlling her. He didn't know what to order." She looked off, this time as if she were searching for a memory. Her face scrunched up in concentration. Finally, she shook her head like she was dismissing something. "That was the impression I got. A distinctive male voice inside her head."

It had to be an Old One—possibly the same one controlling Karl. But why would he be inside Juliette's head?

She frowned, staring at me the way she did when she was trying to figure out my order. "Your purpose. I got it now." She leaned in. "And so do you. Finish the quiz and check out the ads." She got up before I could respond.

Well, that wasn't cryptic at all. And now, that made two people who encouraged me to take a self-help quiz. I was so damn screwed.

My phone buzzed, and I glanced down at the display. It was a text from Jonah, telling me Juliette and her sister were walking up the sidewalk. I shoved the magazine in my purse and switched seats so Juliette wouldn't spot Jonah sitting in his car outside. Our plan was to follow her when she left. Like Devlin said, we needed answers, and I seriously doubted she would willingly give them to me.

Juliette walked in a few minutes later with her sister Bridgette in tow. They both stopped at the counter and let Rosalind decide on their drinks. This time, Rosalind guessed on the first try. Interesting.

They came to the table carrying two fancy coffees and muffins. They both wore jean shorts and tank tops. While Juliette had her hair down, Bridgette had her dark brown hair in two braids. They regarded me out of similar green eyes.

"Thank you for meeting us," Juliette said. She looked at her sister. The girl seemed to shrink back into herself. "You remember Bridgette?" She elbowed her sister. "Say hello," she whispered as if she were speaking to a toddler.

"Hello," Bridgette said, her voice soft.

They both took a seat and set their coffees in front of them.

"I almost didn't come," I said in lieu of saying hello. "You failed to give me all the details about the gathering you invited me to." I didn't keep the chastisement out of my voice.

Juliette frowned. "I apologize for that. I honestly believed you knew what went on. I mean, you came to the church and all."

I didn't know how to respond to that. We did come to the church, but even a blind man could see I hadn't wanted to be there. "I heard about some of the charitable activities and wanted to check them out for myself," I said, stumbling my way through.

She gave me a skeptical look. "The church doesn't do much charity. Only The Daughters of the Vine."

I made a noncommittal noise. I needed to move this along. "Why did you want to talk to me?"

She hesitated for a minute and then said, "I wanted to ask for your help." She held up her hand. "I know that's awkward. But... you managed to keep Gavina out of your head. Can you tell me how you did it?"

"I thought you said she'd stopped whispering to you all?" It was my turn to give her a skeptical look.

She looked down, playing with her muffin.

"Tell her," Bridgette said, nudging her.

Tears cascading down Juliette's cheeks. She swiped them away and sat up straighter. "Our parents died two years ago," she said as if in answer to a question. "We didn't have anyone to take us in on Tulare." She paused, eyes imploring mine. I nodded and she continued. "We have an uncle in California, but we didn't want to leave the island, so we lied to family services and said there was no other family. They said we'd have to go into the foster system." She looked out the window. "I went to school with Xavier. He had a crush on me." She laughed. "But I told him I wasn't interested."

"How did he take that?" I asked, thinking about his Instagram account.

She smiled. "Not well. But he got over it. Especially when he found out what happened to our parents."

Didn't seem like something Xavier would be broken up over. More likely, he saw an opportunity to try and use her grief as a way to win her over.

"He talked to his mom about our situation. He told me she was worried and offered to take us in."

I was at a loss for words. A few nights ago, I witnessed her having sex with Gavina. How did she go from being taken in by the woman to sleeping with her? "Did she take advantage of you?" I asked, anger lacing my words.

She shook her head vehemently. "No. No, nothing like that." Her eyes rounded. "Oh. You saw us having sex at the gathering?"

I nodded slowly, searching her face for any sign of discomfort. There wasn't any. She had been willing to sleep with Gavina.

She smiled. "She asked me if I wanted to join her group when I turned eighteen. I told her yes." She closed her eyes, her mouth slowly turned up in a smile. "I love all that energy we share. It's unbelievable." She opened her eyes and focused on me. "Monique said you stopped by the other day." She leaned forward. "She has a bit of a crush on you."

"Yeah, I wanted to talk to Gavina about what happened the night before."

"You didn't like it?" Juliette asked, surprised.

I shook my head and signaled for her to continue. This wasn't about me. And the only person I was going to confront about what went on the other night would be Gavina.

"Okay. Yes." She sucked in a breath. "Well, Monique also said she told you about some of the girls leaving." She glanced at her sister. "Gavina asked Bridgette if she wanted to join."

I turned to Bridgette. "How old are you?"

"Seventeen," she said. "I'll be eighteen in two weeks."

"Why did she ask Bridgette to join before she turned eighteen?" I asked, my anger once again rising. Something was seriously off here.

"Because more girls have left. The ritual only works if there are thirteen of us."

"And you don't want to join?" I asked Bridgette.

She shook her head no.

"Why can't she just say no? Why do you need to find a way to keep Gavina out of..." I trailed off. Now I got it. "She's been whispering to you," I said to Bridgette.

She glanced at her sister and then said, "Yes. For a few days now. Her pull is so strong. But I don't want to be a part of that."

"Did you tell her that?"

"She took us in," Juliette said. "We can't just say no."

"Yes the fuck you can," I said, my voice rising.

"No. I mean." Juliette blew out a noisy breath. "Not that. She won't push. It's just, we feel like we owe her. She kept us out of the foster system."

"Doesn't give her the right to take advantage of you."

"I know. We just thought if Bridgette could learn to keep her out, things would be fine. I like the gatherings. I even told her I would invite more women."

"And what did she say?"

"She was okay with it. But if we can't find enough girls..." She shook her head. "Can you please just show us how you did it? We both have magick. We can learn."

I splayed my hands on the table. "I can't tell you how I did it. I'm still learning myself." I leaned forward. "But I can help you find another place to stay."

"No. It's fine. I'm sorry we...we bothered you." She stood up; her sister did too. "Thank you for at least listening." She stared down at me. "Again, I'm sorry if you were uncomfortable at the gathering."

They walked away before I could respond. Well, that didn't go as planned.

After saying goodbye to Rosalind, I went out the back entrance and climbed into Jonah's car.

"How did it go?" he asked, pulling away from the curb. They had gotten in a car a few spaces down.

I told him what had happened.

Jonah was silent as we followed the girls across Brunswood and into Tulare. When they pulled into the mall parking lot, I screamed inside my head.

He pulled into a spot a few places down from them and turned to me. "Do you think Gavina is forcing these girls to participate?"

I shook my head, thinking. "Juliette was adamant she wasn't. But..."

"What's wrong?"

"Her story. At first, I was looking at it through my own experience with Gavina. But now, the more I think about it, the more it just doesn't make sense. If Gavina doesn't force them to join, why do they need to learn how to keep her out of Bridgette's head? And then there's what Juliette said the first time I met her outside the church. She told me Gavina had stopped whispering to them, and they didn't know why. But the way she described it sounded as if Gavina was constantly giving them encouragement.

Not forcing them to join the gathering. Why do I keep calling it that? It's a fucking cult."

"You're right, on both fronts. And it does sound strange."

I placed my head in my hands. "Devlin is going to be pissed. I wasn't my usual self in there. I forgot to ask about blood magick." Truth be told, I had not been my usual self for weeks now. "And either I'm paranoid, or everyone seems awful interested in my magick."

Jonah rubbed my back. "Don't worry about it. He'll understand. You were blindsided in there."

We climbed out into the heat. I so did not want to traverse through the damn mall.

"And Logan telling you to look into the history of the phoenix has something to do with your magick as well." We weaved around a group of teenagers who had decided to stop in the middle of the parking lot, blocking the path. "So, no. You're not paranoid."

"Do you think Logan is the one controlling them?"

Jonah shrugged. "What would be his end game?"

"I can't for the life of me figure out what he wants," I said as we made our way toward the entrance.

Juliette and Bridgette bounced along, chatting as if they hadn't just spent the last twenty minutes trying to convince me they needed my help.

"I wish I knew," Jonah said. "Are you ready to go shopping?"

"No. I'd rather gouge my eyes out. Do you see all these teenagers?" I hated coming to the mall when school let out. Way too many people milling around, getting in the way.

He laughed.

"When's the next pool party?" I asked, smiling. I needed to take my mind off things for a minute. And block out the current situation we were in. I really hated crowds.

His chest shook with laughter. "I'll let you and Alek know."

We spent the next two hours watching Juliette and her sister go from one store to the next, shoplifting. The strange thing about it, though—they were only getting items men would want. Rosalind's words came back to me. She got the impression a man was influencing Juliette's decisions. Would an Old One have her shoplift for him, too?

I was so damn confused.

I shared my theory with Jonah about an Old One possibly being involved, and he agreed it made sense.

When we got home, I told Devlin what happened, and Jonah was right—he wasn't angry. I think we all decided a few days ago that the Young family wasn't practicing blood magick. It was time to move on. I'd contact Juliette in a few days and try to encourage her to leave.

It took some doing, but I managed to convince Devlin to let me go see Ezra alone to get information on the phoenix history. Alek wasn't too keen on the idea, but he finally relented after Rachel reminded him she could track my phone. Not creepy at all. Before I walked out the door, Alek pulled me into a kiss that left us both out of breath and me wanting to rip mine and his clothes off. Sadly, it would have to wait.

Lips swollen with need coursing through me like hot lava, I got in my car and headed out to play Russian roulette with my life.

Well, if Ezra did decide to kill me, at least I got to kiss Alek first.

E zra wasn't at his dojo when I arrived. I decided to return home, then remembered him telling me he liked to play pool at the pool hall around the corner.

I arrived at the place a little after nine. It sat at a crossroads in a building that had seen better days. I'd say this was the place one would come to bargain with the devil for their soul. But then again, I doubted the devil—if he did exist—would ever show up here. Especially not at night. I made a mental note to ask the owner if he hosted parties, because this would be the perfect place for my next pity-party.

I stepped into the dimly lit hall and immediately doubled over in a coughing fit. Either they had a smoke machine going, or they were hosting a chain-smoking contest. Blinking my eyes a few times, I peered into the smoke-filled cavern, letting the outline of people and furniture come into focus. Mixed in with the smoke was the stench of stale food. I covered my nose and pushed forward.

My first step told me the D posted on the outside window should have been an F. It took force and sheer will to take additional steps and make my way across the sticky floor. No, sticky would be a step up from what I was walking on.

Music played softly in the background, some blues number to add to the already desolate feel of the place. A single woman wearing mix-match shoes and a red dress swayed in the middle of the floor. A lone biker sat in the corner, nursing a beer, casting hopeful glances at the front door as if he were expecting the rest of his gang to show up any minute now.

Once the smoke had lifted some, I took in the rest of the space. The bar ran along the right side of the room, stretching all the way to the back. A few scattered tables sat directly across from it. Five pool tables were lined up in the back, resting on a short platform.

A couple wearing tourist t-shirts for *Carnavalul de Fear* played at the table closest to the wall. At the other end, Ezra played with a man, who, at first glance, reminded me of someone. Only, I couldn't place exactly who. He had the same dark skin as Ezra, only he had light brown, sandy hair. Ezra's hair had grown since I last saw him, and he was wearing it loose, resting on his broad shoulders. I wondered if the women in class still ogled him.

Trying to avoid the worst of the sticky, unidentifiable substance on the floor, I started for them, weaving around the woman in red. She gave me a glassy-eyed once-over and continued in her drunken dance of seduction. A rat ran across my path, and I searched my memory, trying to recall if that was a bad omen or not—not that I believed in such things. But the notion I was missing something kept running through my mind. Logan's words penetrated my thoughts.

"You lack the skills to really understand what you're seeing."

The accusation really grated on my nerves. But hadn't Devlin said something similar when I didn't react to my first encounter with Logan? I pushed the thought down and continued forward.

As if sensing my presence, both Ezra and the man he was with looked up and locked gazes with me. I stopped, my feet suddenly growing heavy as I realized just how reckless I was acting. Ezra had threatened to kill me if I sought him out again. Yet, here I was, brazenly walking into the lion's den.

Ezra's eyes narrowed, and his skin lit with an amber light. I remembered that light when he threatened me. I took a step back with the full intention of running out of there, until he beckoned me forward.

My knees shaking, I climbed the three steps up to the platform and stopped in front of them.

Ezra kept his gaze on me. Cold sweat broke out on my neck as we continued to stare at one another. Ezra's eyes dipped down to my chest, and I knew he could hear my heart ramming against my rib cage.

"You're scaring her," the man said with a note of warning in his voice. Then he said something in a language I couldn't understand. Ezra slowly turned to him and responded. Their words sounded like music. It reminded me of what Luisah had said when I asked her what the Old Ones' names were. She had told me they sounded like music. This must be the language they spoke thousands of years ago.

"Why are you here?" Ezra asked finally.

"I'm looking for your sister. Do you know where she is?" My voice came out small. I had come to ask about the history of the phoenix, but I also needed to ask Hathor about my mother's magick and find a way to protect myself from his brother. Might as well kill several birds with one stone.

The man next to him laughed. "Which sister?"

Ezra remained silent, studying me out of that penetrating gaze of his. I squirmed, then caught myself. I'd shown weakness in front of too many people this week. I wouldn't do it again.

"Hathor," Ezra said, answering the man. "Nicole, this is my brother, Killion." His eyes never left mine.

"I need to talk with her. I assume she's staying with you."

He didn't respond.

I turned to his brother. I'd give Ezra another minute. "What is your original name?" It was as if I'd lost all my manners. I should have said hello first.

His eyes ran over me. "They called me Horus at one time. My name before I was changed isn't important anymore."

"Why?" I asked.

"That's a story for another day."

I thought about my theory that Karl was being controlled by another Old One. Well, I'd already been rude once. No sense in holding back now. "How long have you been on Tulare, Horus?"

"Killion. Please. We don't go by our given Egyptian names any longer. And I arrived this morning." He gave me a questioning look. "Why?"

I swallowed. Maybe interrogating an immortal being wasn't the brightest idea—especially not one sworn either to kill or protect me on sight. Well, he did chastise Ezra for scaring me. Maybe that was his way of protecting me.

"Welcome to Tulare," I said after a while, sounding like a complete idiot.

He smiled and set his pool cue on the table. "Well, brother, I see you have something to attend to. I'll go find Hathor. She probably needs clothes again." He spared me one last glance and walked away. I watched his back for a while, trying to figure out why he seemed so familiar.

"Did you forget my warning?" Ezra said, pulling my gaze to him.

I picked up the pool cue Killion abandoned and looked at the table. "I figured since you and Hathor saved me, you weren't likely to make good on that promise." It was a lie. I had believed my coming here might mean my death, but I had no plans to tell him that. I was desperate, and since my mother refused to give me answers, I figured I could try getting them from Ezra.

"Did you want to play?" he asked, staring at me.

"So, you're not going to kill me?" I tried to infuse brevity in my voice, but even I could hear the fear.

Ezra paused, his eyes roaming over me. "My brother reminded me of my mark. When I warned you before, I had never planned to see you again. Not for a long while. But yes, I did save you. So, no, Nicole, I can't kill you. By Hathor and I saving you from Set, we have made our intentions clear." He stepped closer. "Now, did you want to play pool?" He smiled and yes, my heart skipped a beat. I was gone over Alek, but it didn't mean I couldn't appreciate a good-looking man. "You know how I hate wasting my time."

"Yes, I remember." He'd drilled in those little lessons when I last went to his class. He and Devlin both were some bossy bastards.

"How about," I started and grabbed the rack, "for every ball I sink, you have to give me a straight answer." I glanced over at the couple at the far end. Ezra followed my gaze. "Can we talk in here?"

He smirked and organized the balls inside the rack. "You break."

I wouldn't call myself a pool whiz, but I could sink a few balls and figured, if I could get at least four questions answered, it would help me figure out what was going on. I leaned over the table and broke. The balls rolled across the table, each speeding toward the pockets. When the solid yellow ball landed in the left corner pocket, I turned to Ezra.

"Your brother attacked me in my home," I said. "I need to find a way to protect myself." It was obvious Ezra was concerned about me. Maybe if I started there, he would be more open and forthcoming about my other concerns.

His eyes narrowed. "I can renew the glyphs or have Killion mark you."

"What glyphs?" I asked confused. When had they put glyphs on my body? More importantly, where had they put them?

"We put some on the walls in your apartment when you were healing." He paused. "Is this the first time you saw him?"

That was an odd question. "Umm...you mean after the attack?" He nodded. I told him about the few times I smelled his scent and felt his presence.

"He must have found a way around the protection. Don't worry, I'll take care of it."

"How?"

He didn't respond.

Okay. I would let that go for now. He said he'd take care of it, and I trusted he would. I sunk another ball and turned to him. "Tell me about the *Nar al-nasaa*."

"Fuck," he said, tossing his pool cue on the table. He started down the stairs, then paused. "Outside."

I set my pool cue down and followed him out. Okay. I must have struck a nerve.

When I stepped outside, he asked, "Where's your car?"

I signaled around the corner.

"Then drive to my dojo and wait." He turned around and walked back inside the building.

Well, that didn't go as planned. Who was I kidding? I didn't have a plan.

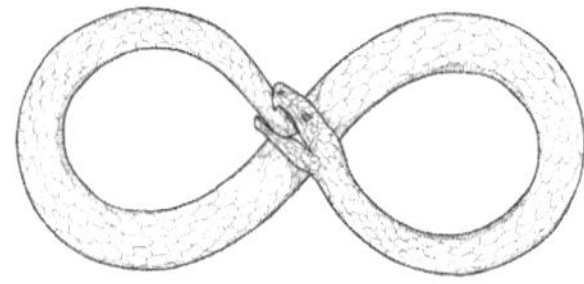

EZRA WAS STALKING around the corner by the time I had parked in the lot where his dojo was located.

Shoving open the door, I stepped out of my car, grabbed my purse, and started for him. He didn't even look up when I joined him at the door. When he opened it, the familiar lime scent rushed out and tickled my nose. I sort of missed coming to the dojo. Sure, I complained a lot, but the exercise was good. And it gave me an outlet for my anger. If I thought he would, I'd ask Ezra to start training me again. Without sex, I had too much pent-up aggression flowing through me with no outlet. Drinking myself into a drunken stupor was definitely out of the question.

Slipping off my shoes, I padded on bare feet across the cold mat toward the back room, watching Ezra the entire time. Waiting for him to pounce. Halfway to the end of the mat, Ezra turned, his eyes blazing as he stared at me. "Control your fear. Its seductive call is hard to resist."

"Stop trying to scare me," I said with absolutely no conviction. I might have even whined a little. "We keep doing this dance, and I'm tired of it."

"I might believe you if you didn't sound like you were going to fold into a ball and start crying."

Oh, that did it. I pulled the switchblade from between my breasts and charged at him. I would have succeeded in doing some damage had he not doubled over in laughter. Okay, I would have ended up on my back with him standing over me. Most likely still laughing. But at least he wasn't threatening me anymore.

"What's so funny?" I asked, putting the blade away.

"You, Nicole," he said, staring. His eyes danced with humor. "Why do you have a switchblade lodged between your breasts?"

"For protection."

"By the time you get the blade out, you'd be dead. Get a real knife, put it in a sheath, and wear it around your thigh."

"I might cut myself," I said, trying to infuse indignation in my voice. I didn't appreciate him taunting me.

"You should never fear the weapon you wield. Get a real knife, and I will train you how to use it."

"Promise?"

He turned and continued toward the back. "Promise," he called over his shoulder. "Now, come on."

We stepped into Ezra's studio apartment, and he flipped on the light. My skin heated, remembering the last time I was here. I'd been in a vulnerable place, having bared my soul to a complete stranger. I hadn't known what to do with those feelings, so I took my clothes off, hoping that it would make better. Even now, I knew that was the wrong move and definitely not healthy.

"I never did apologize for..." I made a circle with my hand, unable to voice the embarrassment. I gave him a quick glance to see if he understood and then looked away. "You didn't take advantage of me. I appreciate that."

"I've been alive for thousands of years. I know when someone is interested." He touched my arm, drawing my attention to him. "I also know when someone is hurting. You were in pain. I wasn't going to add to it." He went over to the small desk and swiveled the chair around. "Now, sit."

"I can't even imagine what you've seen in all those years," I said, taking a seat.

"War and mankind's endless obsession with power." He leaned against the wall across from me and folded his arms over his chest. "Why are you asking about the Fire Women? Did you forget about my warning of knowing too much?"

The last time I was here, Ezra told me I was safer not knowing some things. He never did elaborate on it. But at the time, I was talking about the Old Ones and assumed he was, too. "I already know about the Old Ones and that my mother is a *Nar al-nasaa*." It was a lie. I assumed she was. She never confirmed my suspicion. But he didn't need to know that.

Ezra moved a chair in front of me and straddled it. After a brief pause, he said, "The history of the *Nar al-nasaa* was destroyed in the fire that demolished part of the Alexandria library. My brother set fire to the records, and that fire spread, obliterating years of knowledge." He leaned back, his face growing pensive. Grief filled his eyes. "For Thoth—a keeper of knowledge —it was like ripping out a piece of him. But it was necessary. Not all of the *Nar al-nasaa* had been killed. Some escaped to other regions of the world. And if people learned of their abilities, they would be hunted down and sacrificed."

"How had they been killed?"

"We started off as humans with magick. But it wasn't enough. Our village wanted to conquer the entire region. And they knew the only way to do that was to launch an attack on a massive scale. So, they altered us by sacrificing most of the *Nar al-nasaa*."

"Is that why Hathor took my mother's magick?" My mother had already implied as much, but I had to be sure.

He didn't respond.

"Ezra, you have to help me."

"Did you ever stop to think that I was helping you? Despite the records being lost on how to use the *Nar al-nasaa* to create

Old Ones, someone is bound to put it together soon. This island should never have been created. My brother, trying to right a wrong, wrote about it and gave our secrets away."

"Thoth?"

He dipped his head in acknowledgement.

"Wait," I said, when what he was saying finally penetrated my brain. The only person to write about Tulare was Louis Badet. And he was dead. "I thought the Old Ones couldn't be killed." At least, I assumed that. No one said one way or the other.

"Louis Badet is my brother. And he's not dead."

"Is he here? On Tulare?"

"No. He won't come here."

"How many Old Ones are on Tulare?"

"Five."

I ticked off the ones I knew about in my head. "Does that include Set?"

He nodded.

I paused, wondering if I should tell Ezra about my concern that an Old One was controlling humans. So far, he had been willing to answer some of my questions. Here's hoping he could answer a few more. I gave him the details surrounding Karl. He silently watched me while I laid everything out.

"Sounds like something Khnum would have done. But he's not here."

Khnum was a ram god, responsible for the Nile and giving life to gods and humans.

"Could he have come to Tulare and not told you?" I asked.

Ezra thought for a minute. "Not likely," he said finally. "But I will find out."

"Thank you," I said, glancing around. "I miss class."

"You and Kara can come back anytime."

I smiled at him. "I'll let her know."

I got up to leave, satisfied I'd gotten some answers. Ezra walked me out. Before he closed the door, he told me again he would give me something to protect myself from Set. And also reminded me to buy a real knife. When I flipped him off, he laughed and closed the door.

As I walked to my car, I thought about Louis Badet. It had never occurred to me he was an Old One. But maybe it should have given him vast knowledge of Tulare's creation and the Old Ones. Ezra said it pained Thoth to destroy part of the Alexandria library. What if all that pain had morphed into rage. Forcing him to correct what he perceived as wrong. What if the mastermind behind all of this...was him?

I woke up the next morning and turned to see Alek had already gotten up. I had hoped we could at least *try* and have sex. Or is it make love when you're in a relationship? Either one would have been nice this morning. But sadly, I lay alone in the half-made bed.

Kicking the covers off, I got up and glanced at the alarm clock. It was after ten in the morning. I was surprised Devlin hadn't come in, demanding I get up and report for duty. Of course, it could be because of the worried look he had given me when I got home last night dragging my purse behind me, mumbling about subterfuge and dead ends with a cigar dangling from my lips.

My mind had decided to break in the time it took me to drive from Ezra's to Devlin's. Hence the need for sex this morning. I still had way too much tension and frustration inside of me. Of course, I could have tried to jump Alek last night, but he also seemed tired.

After a long shower, I pulled on some clothes and went to join the rest of the team, hoping Jonah had made some of his glorious fried potatoes and onions—the only *Nectar of the Gods* I wanted to partake in. Ever.

I found them in the war room, staring at a whiteboard with two pictures on it: Logan and Unrie. Everyone turned and looked at me.

"I must have slept in," I said. "Is there breakfast?" I asked Jonah.

He dipped his head toward the adjoining kitchen. "In the oven."

"There better be potatoes on that plate."

Alek came in the kitchen and leaned on the counter. "You doing okay?"

I took the plate out of the oven and smiled at the pile of potatoes and eggs. "I am now." I looked at him. "Could have used one of those quickies we discussed weeks ago."

He leaned in. "That was Tuesday."

"Oh," I said, mouth full. "Well, what day is it?"

Alek slid my hair behind my ear. "Friday."

I nodded, chewing. Five days. It had only been five days since we started the merry-go-round of a case. I sighed heavily and shoved more food in my mouth.

"Did you make the bed?" Alek asked, his eyes dancing with humor.

I stared at him while I chewed. "You might have to show me how again, even wear those black silk boxers to make sure I'm paying attention."

He smiled and cocked his head to the side. "Devlin said you looked a little off last night."

"Was it the cigar?" I asked, setting my plate on the counter.

He nodded. "Might have been. You need a break?" he asked, his tone softening.

"No," I said carefully. "What I need is for Devlin to authorize the shoot everyone option we discussed one of the days between Sunday and now so I can get some rest."

He pulled me to him. "Don't worry. We're switching gears today. And tomorrow, you and I will find a nice hotel room to spend the rest of the weekend in."

I stepped back, my eyes rounding. "Oh, please say this is true."

He smiled. "Absolutely." He took my hand. "Now, let's get this last debrief over so we can start planning our weekend."

My heart did a happy dance, and my hormones decided it was high time they threw a rave. I needed to go shopping for some sexy lingerie for Alek to take off. Maybe even a new dress in case we decide to leave the room.

"You're happy this morning," Marta said, staring at me.

"Oh, absolutely," I said with a little too much cheer in my voice. My damn, self-imposed dry spell was over, and I planned to enjoy every damn minute of it.

"I take it Alek told you I'm giving everyone the weekend off," Devlin said, studying me.

I nodded. If I opened my mouth, I feared I might blurt out our plans.

He scrutinized me for a minute before addressing the rest of the team. "Our main objective has always been to determine if the Young family is practicing blood magick. Since nothing points in that direction, we will cross them off the list. Unrie Nevsky and Logan Magellan have obviously gone underground, and according to Logan himself, they no longer pose a threat. We will continue looking for Unrie. Just not right now." He looked at Alek.

"I can update Petronela. Maybe she can have a few others help with the search."

Devlin nodded and continued. "Who is controlling who is not our concern right now. But if it ever does affect us, we will handle it—preferably with better information than we have now. Jonah?"

"Xavier and Boyd stay in a smaller house on the same road as Hollingsworth Manor. I got a look inside. Nothing to suggest they're involved with what Gavina is up to."

Devlin nodded and glanced at me. "Want to update the team on what you learned yesterday?"

"Sure," I said. I took them through what both my mother and Ezra told me about my lineage. Also told them Ezra promised to give me something to protect myself against Set.

"That explains your magick," Rachel said with a look of pure wonder on her face.

"Yeah, now I just need to learn what that means." I lifted my hand before Devlin could say anything. "But it can wait." I looked at the copy of *The Land Guarded by People of Colour*. "Louis Badet isn't dead, and he's an Old One." I walked over to the board and wrote his name next to Thoth. "And Ezra said there are five Old Ones on Tulare, including Set." I turned back to the group. "I gave him a rundown on my theory about Karl, and he said it sounded like something his brother Khnum would do. But he confirmed he wasn't on the island." I turned and wrote Killion next to Horus.

"You worried about Juliette?" Devlin asked.

I thought about it for a minute. "She...I don't know. Her story just...bothered me." I went back to my chair and sat down. "But I will call her tomorrow and check on her. She said they had an uncle in California. Maybe I can convince her to go stay with him."

"Call her Monday," Devlin said.

"Yes, Boss Man."

"I have a meeting with Opal this afternoon. I will give her an update for the Markums and brainstorm on our Barnes problem." He looked at us. "Everyone else, take the weekend. We start fresh on Monday. And before we go after another family, we will do our own research."

He walked over to Marta. "Did you pick out a gun safe?"

"What?" I asked, standing.

Devlin turned. "Marta and I are going to target practice next week. Before I give her a gun, I need to make sure she has a secure safe to lock it up in when she's home."

"No one invited me to target practice," I said.

Devlin dipped his head toward my hiding space. "Stick with the switchblade."

"It's small," I protested.

"That's the point," he said and turned away. But not before I saw the humor dancing in his eyes.

I turned and found the rest of the team smiling wide. I shook my head and walked out of the room. Alek followed behind me.

"If you really want to go to target practice, I'll take you," he said.

I shook my head. "No. He's right. I need to stick with knives. Besides, I like them better." I stepped into his space. "What's your favorite color?"

He smiled, his arms coming around me. "Why?"

"I'm going shopping and need to know what color to wear tomorrow. Green?" I smiled at the memory of him dressing me in green panties.

He leaned down and kissed my neck. "Nude."

"That I can do."

After telling everyone goodbye, I set out to go shopping. Thankfully, it was early enough in the day that I didn't have to deal with any crowds.

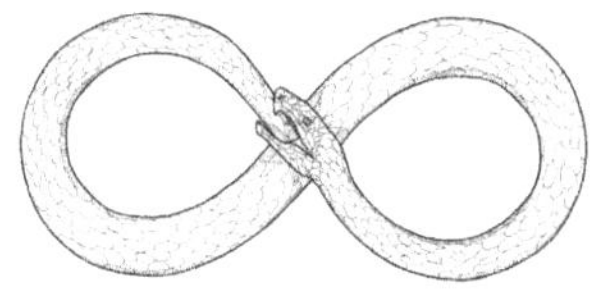

AFTER AN HOUR of trying to decide what to buy, I finally found a lingerie set that did in fact make me look like I was nude. I also got a black dress that barely covered me just in case we decided to go to dinner. Now, I just needed to figure out a place to stay. Oh, and try and squash the anxiety trying to destroy my joy. Being nervous about dating was one thing, but the constant whispers of doubt were another. I thought I had moved past this, for fuck's sake.

My phone rang, and I looked down at the display: Juliette. Alarm raced through me. I hit the answer button. "Are you okay?" I asked.

"Oh, thank god you answered. I...we need your help. Bridgette and I talked and decided we should take your advice and leave. Gavina left, and we have a chance to leave without her trying to make us stay."

"Do you have a place to go?" I asked, making a U-turn.

"I called my uncle. He agreed to let us come stay with him."

I breathed a sigh of relief but then paused. So much of this case had been one misleading thing after another. Did I trust Juliette? I pondered that for a moment as I made my way toward the main highway. While her story did seem...strange, for a lack of a better word, I couldn't just dismiss her outright. If she and her sister felt the only way to keep Gavina at bay was to learn how to shut out her whispers, then that meant there was more to it than what they had told me. And Juliette could have lied to protect her abuser.

"Meet me outside. I'm on my way," I said and hung up. After I took them where they needed to go, I could rest easier knowing I at least helped someone escape Gavina.

The traffic was light as I travelled on the main road to East Gate Estates. Once I started on the ride through the community, my shoulder blades started to itch, and an eerie feeling settled in my gut. I was being reckless again. Should I turn around?

The sign for Hollingsworth Manor loomed in front of me. *Too late now*, I thought, and turned onto the road leading to the house.

Water sprayed over the grass, creating a colorful mist. Now that I knew the spell was there, it was easy to avoid it. Juliette and her sister Bridgette stood just outside the door with bags at their feet. They came rushing over before I could make my way up the walkway.

"Thank you so much," Juliette said with urgency in her voice. Her gaze darted around, and a light sheen of sweat covered her skin. Bridgette stood rigid, her eyes focused on me, imploring.

"Where am I taking you?" I asked. I picked up one of the bags and walked to the back of my car. Opening the trunk, I shoved the bag inside and looked back at the girls. They stood closer than I liked.

"The bus station in Alice," Juliette said, her gaze steady on me.

The hairs on the back of my neck rose, and I glanced up at the house. "What about the other girls?" I asked. "Do any of them want to leave?"

Bridgette shook her head.

The phoenix wings on my protective mark beat once.

Danger.

Juliette moved behind me. "They didn't want to come." I saw it coming—a syringe she had hidden behind her. I stepped to the side, and she stumbled forward.

"Oh, you manipulative bitch!" I yelled and kicked her in the gut.

Adrenaline rushed through me as I whipped around to face her sister, who had started for me, hands curled into claws. The scream she let loose seemed to echo.

I knocked her back and kept going.

I should have listened. I should have trusted my gut instincts. Now, I was faced with two crazy bitches who wanted to sedate me. Why?

I punched Bridgette in the face, and she fell to the ground. I lifted my foot to stomp on her and felt the sting of the needle jammed into my neck.

Fuck! I should have been paying attention to Juliette, too.

A sudden warmth flooded my body. I turned in time to see Juliette sliding the needle back in her bag. "Fucking bitch!" I mumbled, my vision wavering. I stumbled, and Juliette reached out to steady me. I fruitlessly slapped her hand. Was she seriously trying to help me now?

"It's not a stick shift, so we can take her car," Bridgette called.

They were going to steal my car!

"Help me with her," Juliette said, her voice sounding far away.

Juliette shoved me, none too gently, and my body slumped

forward. I took a small amount of pleasure in their grunts as they tried to put me in the trunk. What the fuck was in that needle? My vision dimmed, going dark around the edges.

Juliette stared down at me. "He made me do it," she said, and slammed the trunk.

Well, looked like I had fucked up once again.

The world went dark.

A Road Not Taken

Alek looked at the darkened house he'd been lured to and knew right away it was a trap. He'd received a text from a blocked number an hour after he left Petronela's. She had kept him there damn near all day. He had started to dismiss the message, but he knew he couldn't. If he could deal with this tonight, then nothing would interfere with his and Nicole's weekend.

It did, however, take him a minute to figure out how the person got his number, and then he remembered Logan had access to Nicole's phone, which told him exactly who had sent him to the house: Logan.

But still, Alek showed up. Because in the end, he had to make sure he brought Unrie to Petronela. What condition the man would be in, Alek was still deciding.

A light went out in the front room, and Alek got out of the car. Closing the door silently, he sent his magick out, searching the area around him. Most people were asleep at this time of night, but a few minds remained active—including Unrie, whose agitation crawled across his mind like fire ants.

A trap. But it didn't matter. He'd take the man down.

Alek pulled the hood on his shirt over his head and made his way around the back of the house. He sent his magick out and touched Unrie's mind. All the many ways he could kill him pushed Alek into that dark place. He smiled as he tried the back door. Locked. Didn't matter. Using his lockpicks, he got the door open, and the sound of a gun racking stopped him inside the darkened doorway.

"Must have outlived my usefulness," Unrie called, his voice coming from deep inside the house. "Took you long enough to get inside."

So, the man wanted to talk. "Why wait, then?" Alek asked, stepping further into the cool house. The warmth pushed at his back. He shifted to the side to shut the door. "Open or closed?" he asked.

"Doesn't matter. One of us will be dead shortly."

Alek shut the door and seized Unrie's mind. The gun clanged to the floor, giving away Unrie's position in the house. Alek moved forward, still latched onto the man's mind, freezing his ability to breathe. Ragged sounds started. Unrie was trying to pull air into his lungs.

Stopping in front of the man, Alek reached down and picked up the gun. Moonlight filtered into the room, hitting the full glass of alcohol sitting on the little round table. Once he had the gun, Alek found the light and switched it on. He blinked against the glare, releasing Unrie's mind at the same time.

Unrie bent forward and pulled in a deep breath. He started hacking, coughing up phlegm. Alek gave him a minute to compose himself while he looked around the sparse room. It was a step down from the hotel he'd been staying at. It looked more like a hideout, a place of last resort. The walls were covered in unidentifiable stains, with similar markings on the carpet. No furniture except two chairs and the card table with an almost-empty bottle of alcohol and one glass.

"You must have realized you would eventually," Alek said, responding the man's first statement. "Why else would you be here?"

Unrie picked up his glass and drained it. He glared at Alek. "I guess that answers my question." His voice sounded strained. "Magick could win in a gun fight." He hacked again, bending over, possibly reaching for the gun taped under the table he was thinking about.

"Don't," Alek said, leaning back. "I can shut down more than just your breathing."

Unrie straightened. Licking his lips, he stared down at the bottle in front of him. "I've been killing for half my life. Never once did anyone best me. But I guess it was bound to happen." He looked up, meeting Alek's eyes. "Do the people you associate with know about your past?"

"I take it you do," Alek said, ignoring the question. Devlin and Rachel knew, and Jonah suspected. He'd have to tell the others later. Especially Nicole. That was not a conversation he was looking forward to.

"Tell me, what did it feel like to destroy your brother's mind?"

Alek lashed out and knocked Unrie to the ground. The man stayed there, blinking up at him. "If you didn't have that magick, I'd own you."

Alek smiled. "Your research on me is lacking."

Unrie got up and sat back in the chair, keeping a wary eye on Alek. "Never said I did research on you."

"Then how do know about my past?"

"It's all Logan talked about." Unrie's hand shook as he poured himself another drink. "The man has some serious hero worship." After draining the glass, he continued, "He also changed the plans on me. Told me to pull back. You all were now *off-limits*." He slammed the glass down. "Fuck! I just wanted to get paid and leave."

"Not before you see Petronela."

Unrie harrumphed. "Then you might as well kill me. I have no plans of letting that bitch torture me."

Without thinking, Alek lashed out, shutting Unrie's ability to breathe down so abruptly, the man pitched forward, banging his head on the table. He slid down and landed hard on the floor.

Alek crouched and got in his face. "Showing respect might keep you alive." He released Unrie's mind. "Tell me, what was Logan's plan?"

Unrie hacked. His eyes watered. He pushed himself up, reaching for the gun. Alek kicked him in the gut. "I already warned you. The next time I use my magick..." He got in the man's face. Rancid breath filled his nostrils. "I will break your mind." He stood, helping the man up. "What was Logan's plan?"

"The hell if I know!" Unrie slid into the chair and swiped at the tears on his face. "He told me he wanted you and Jonah dead. Along with the girl, Rachel. He was going to take care of Nicole and the rest of the people she trained with at Tribec Insurance." Rage rolled over Alek.

"What about Devlin?" Alek asked.

Unrie shook his head. "He's always been protected. Off-limits. Fuck. Do what you're going to do and get it over with!"

"Why are they killing people who worked at Tribec?" Alek asked.

"Loose ends," Unrie said, glaring at him.

Alek hummed a dark melody to put Unrie to sleep.

When Unrie pitched forward and fell to the floor again, Alek dug his phone out and called Devlin. "Logan is killing the people you trained with at Tribec. Have Rachel send me the address for Veronica, since I'm sure he's going to kill her first."

"I'll take Jesse," Devlin said.

Alek stood. "Is Nicole back yet?"

"No."

He smiled, thinking about her asking him what his favorite color was. Just what had she bought for their weekend?

He hung up, and a few seconds later, Veronica's address popped up on his screen.

On the way to the door, he sent a quick text to his cousin Cristian and told him to come pick up Unrie. He'd deal with Petronela later. Right now, he had a man to kill.

The sound of water pulled me out of my chemical sleep. My eyes opened slowly. Arms extended above my head, my wrists secured by rope, a rock bit into my back, and I shifted, trying to ease some of the discomfort. My gaze traveled around the dimly lit area. I was in a cave of some sort—white rock walls wet with condensation. The air smelled like mildew and herbs; the same herbs I smelled when I first walked into the church on Sunday. A chill traveled across my bare arms.

How long had I been here?

Muted voices carried into the room. I strained to make out what they were saying, but all I could discern was the voices belonged to women. Calling out for help would be the first logical move, but it would also be stupid. And I'd already been that, so I remained silent, listening. Testing my bonds, I stretched my arms forward, only for the ropes to dig into my wrists.

"Fuck," I whispered. "And just how the hell am I supposed to get out of this?"

Footsteps echoed off the walls, and Juliette walked into the small room. "Oh, you're awake." She came over, carrying a bottle of water and something wrapped in a napkin. "I didn't know how much to give you. At first, Bridgette worried that we might have killed you." She unscrewed the cap to the water. "It was hard trying to find your heartbeat." She looked down at the water in her hand. "He got mad. He said we should have brought you to the church and then drugged you. But I told him you were smarter than that."

"Apparently not," I said, my words slurring.

Her face brightened. "So, I did good?"

"You have got to be fucking kidding me. You drugged me and tied me to a wall in a fucking cave. No, you stupid bitch, you didn't do good."

"Did you want some water?" she asked as if I hadn't just scolded her. Why hadn't I seen her for what she was?

"Fuck you," I said, despite the dryness in my throat.

She shrugged. "Okay. Well, I'll just leave it here in case you change your mind. I even bought you one of the muffins you like. Banana nut, right?"

I didn't respond.

She hesitated, her eyes imploring mine, and then got up and walked out the room. I was so damn screwed. The muted voices started up again. I tested my bonds again for lack of anything better to do. The charms on my bracelet dug into my wrists. I bit down on the sting and yanked, trying to ease the ropes down my hands. Someone sadistic had definitely tied the knots. When blood ran down my arm, I stopped pulling.

I rested my head back against the rock. Juliette had said *he* made her do it. Since we knew it wasn't Xavier, it had to be Logan. But that didn't make sense, either. Maybe it was the same person controlling Karl. An Old One? Again, it didn't make sense. Why would an Old One control either of them? What could he possibly gain? Then again, Ezra did say the actions reminded him of his brother Khnum.

I groaned.

We had been chasing our tails, going at everything not as a team, but in pairs. Nothing made sense. And with the chemicals still riding me, I doubt it would. Closing my eyes, I started with the attack on me at church. Maybe if I looked at each thing separately, I would be able to figure it out.

Logan first appeared at the church with Gerald Stewart. He

demanded we turn over the Ark. Logan hadn't once pressed us on that. He did, however, show some concern about Kara's presence at that first encounter, only to... My mind grew fuzzy. What did he do? I swallowed, trying to coat my throat with saliva. The dryness was becoming annoying.

Think, Nicole!

Why would he be afraid of Kara? Recognition? That had to be it. So, what could Kara have told us if she had recognized him? Fuck, was this even important? I opened my eyes. The cave seemed darker for some reason, and the voices had stopped. The sound of water dripping echoed around the room. Why hadn't Rachel been able to find this place? We were under the church. Juliette had implied as much.

Concentrate!

I closed my eyes again, picturing the next encounter with Logan. Alek said the man was using an ice cream truck to get around. It was a great disguise, really. No one would think twice about it in this heat. Which meant, when Jonah took me home after church, Logan was watching the house. But I didn't see the truck after that.

Then came Alek and Devlin's visit to Greenwood Apartments. Logan had led them there. So where was he when they were at the apartment? Was he watching?

Recognition. He was worried about that. Fuck. I couldn't concentrate.

"Resting?"

My eyes flew open. Logan crouched beside me, holding the open bottle of water.

"You did this," I said slowly.

He put a finger to his lips.

The fucking bastard played this elaborate game to get me here. Had us chasing our tails for the past few days.

"Rest won't help you," he whispered, then put the bottle to my lips. Water dribbled down my cheek. "Did you want me to take a sip first?"

I opened my mouth and let water rush in. After a few mouthfuls, I turned away. Probably wasn't the brightest idea to drink the water, but my mouth was so dry, I was past caring about it.

"I should have figured you were behind everything," I said in a harsh whisper. Why were we whispering?

He put the cap back on the water bottle and sat back on his heels. "Still haven't put things together?" He shook his head. "If we had more time—if you hadn't been stupid enough to show up without some backup, maybe I could give you more time to figure it out."

"Juliette said you made her kidnap me."

"Wrong. I have nothing to do with Juliette or her sister."

"What?" I asked. "Then who is behind all this?"

"Xavier," he said.

"He has no magick!"

"And that's the point." He rested back on his heels. "Juliette has one fucked up mind. Her thirst for power borders on fanaticism. The Young family has really done a number on her and her sister, especially Xavier." He chuckled. "Her sister thinks Xavier is the handsomest. She has that shit on repeat." He shook his head and stood. Taking a deep breath, he continued, "I have to admit, when you drove to their estate, I thought you had figured it out. Then they shoved you in the trunk." He looked down at me. "You have to be in some pain. They weren't too gentle with you."

"You are one crazy fucking bastard. Did you really sit there and watch them kidnap me? And why are you here? Oh, and I learned the history of the phoenix. Any more tasks you want to send me on?" My head pounded from the strain.

He knelt in front of me. "If you had found out about the *Nar al-nasaa,* you wouldn't be here." He jumped up and dusted off his pants. "I've been here long enough." He pulled my switchblade out of his pocket and started sawing through the ropes.

"How did you get my blade?"

"They left it on the altar in the other room." He stopped cutting the ropes and shoved the knife between my breasts. "I believe this is where you keep it." He moved me none too gently to the side. "If you focus, you can see their altar room."

I tugged the ropes. "Umm…you didn't finish. I'm still tied up. And why are you helping me, anyway?"

He cast his gaze to the ground. "I might need a favor one day." He looked at my hands. "And we all have bonds we need to break." He locked eyes with me. "Free yourself. Use your magick, Nicole. Rip their souls from their bodies." He walked away, melting into the shadows before I could respond.

What the fuck?

The voices started up again. I shifted to the left and looked through the tiny doorway into a small cavern. A figure wearing a robe moved around an altar positioned in the middle. I could just make out Bridgette staring rapt at the person. That had to be Xavier.

Why was I here?

When he moved, I studied the altar. Made of marble, it had symbols etched into the side. I squinted, trying to make out the familiar drawings. Where had I seen them before?

"Have you prepared yourself for the ritual?" Xavier asked.

"Yes," Juliette and Bridgette said in unison.

"Then it's time for me to become a god."

"If you had found out about the Nar al-nasaa, you wouldn't be here."

Logan's stray comment suddenly made sense. And the drawings on the altar did as well. Ezra said the *Nar al-nasaa* were used to create the Old Ones.

Looks like I was about to be sacrificed to make Xavier an Old One.

avier strode into the room wearing a white robe with a gold sash around his waist. His dark hair lay slicked back from his head, and symbols had been drawn on his face. I wanted to laugh at my sheer stupidity. I literally walked right into this madness. My brain wanted to shut down. Or crawl in a ball and weep, but I had to get these damn ropes off my wrist. I was not going to let a teenager, and his hussy acolytes sacrifice me.

"It's time to prepare you for the sacrifice," he said, his voice modulated to sound deep and foreboding. He raised his arms up, letting the sleeves roll back to reveal intricate whorls of gold on his arms as well. "This will be..." He stopped and looked behind him. "Hurry up!"

Juliette and Bridgette rushed into the room, both wearing similar robes with red sashes. Eyes cast down, they carried clay bowls in their hands, liquid sloshing over the sides.

Oh, dear god. Why the hell did Logan leave me here? I still couldn't figure that man out. What is real angle was. But now wasn't the time to dwell on it. I had to get myself free. I eased up, tugging at the rope some more. Blood ran down my arms, to pool inside the small indentation in my armpits. By the time I did get out, my wrists would be ripped to shreds.

I should've been afraid, but for some reason, I didn't feel the threat. Yeah, they might have figured out some of the ritual to make an Old One, but they would need more than one *Nar al-*

nasaa, and Xavier didn't have any magick. All the Old Ones had magick before they were altered.

Someone screamed. The sound bounced off the walls, echoing. Xavier glanced to the right; down the opposite tunnel he had emerged from. "One of mother's acolytes must have figured out her blood was going to be used to help my mother achieve godhood." He turned and focused on me. A wicked smile of mostly teeth and lunacy crossed his mouth. "You should be happy to be a part of making me a god."

I was wrong. They didn't want to create an Old One. They wanted to become gods. How had we missed this? "Xavier," I said, infusing reason into my tone. "You have no magick. How do you expect this to work?"

"She stole it from me!" he yelled. "She told me she would make me more powerful like my sisters, and I willingly gave that bitch my magick because I believed her!"

Oh, my god. Now. Now, I understood why he had a void where is aura should have been. Gavina had stolen her son's magick. Most likely, he was her first victim—the first one she tested her ritual on. I prayed she hadn't used sex to get it.

He started taking agitated steps around the room, like he was trying to rein himself in.

I had to free myself while he was occupied. I looked at Juliette and Bridgette. They still had their eyes cast down, holding those clay bowls of water. They were no use.

"You have to listen to me," I said, hating that I was pleading with him. But if I didn't get myself free, he was going to sacrifice me in a fruitless ritual.

"Silence the sacrifice!"

Juliette and Bridgette rushed over to me. Bridgette slapped her hand over my mouth, and I bit down on the palm of her hand. Blood rushed into my mouth.

"She bit me!" she screamed.

Juliette slapped me, hard. She would pay for that.

I yanked; the last thread broke, but I kept my arms up.

"Juliette, please tell me you're smarter than this. Xavier doesn't have any magick. How could he possibly make himself a god?"

She looked at me, her face blank. But there was a slight touch of hesitation behind her eyes. Sadly, it was replaced too quickly with one of indifference.

"I have a powerful benefactor on my side. He wants me to punish my mother for her indiscretion. When I saw you hurt her on Sunday, I knew I could use you to help me."

"Is that why you sent Karl to watch me?" I asked. I knew the answer, but I still wanted to confirm he wasn't behind it.

He blinked. Staring at me in confusion. "Who is Karl?"

I shook my head. My arms were getting tired. I needed to strike soon, or I'd give myself away.

"He has given me the ritual and promised that if I get to you before my mother does, I will gain power with the spell," he continued.

His benefactor had filled this idiot's head with lies.

I tsked at him and shook my head for effect. It was now or never. "Poor Xavier. Living in the shadows of his more powerful sisters."

His robes bellowed as he lunged for me. His hands went around my neck, and I laughed. "Stop laughing at me!" His rage had consumed him so much that he failed to register my arms were no longer over my head. That I had yanked the switchblade out. Only when the click of the blade being released echoed, did he pause.

"Like I said... Absolutely no power. And no brains, either." In any other circumstance, I might have hesitated. But I knew if I gave Xavier the chance, he would have ordered Juliette and her sister to tie me to their altar so he could sacrifice me in a futile ceremony. So, I didn't hesitate. I rammed the blade in his gut and twisted. His eyes narrowed for a second, anger filling him, and then they rolled back. I twisted again, and an anguished cry escaped his mouth.

Bridgette dove for me, but Juliette kept her restrained. Her eyes were focused on Xavier while a twisted smile played across her mouth. I'd have to do something about her. I just didn't have it in me yet to kill her outright.

I shoved Xavier off me. He curled into fetal position, blood pooling around him. Juliette got up and brought a rock down on his head. I stared at her, shocked. First, trying to figure out where she got the rock, and second, trying to understand why she did it. In the end, it didn't matter. I'd wasted too much time in this cave.

"I could kill you," Juliette said, her chin going up. "I know what the ritual is."

I shook my head. "You can try. And like Xavier, I will bury my knife in your gut and your sister can watch you die."

Said sister, finally registering her handsomest man was dead, flew at me with her hands looking like claws. I didn't have time for this shit. When she was close, I reared back and socked her hard in the face. She went down. Juliette rushed to her sister's aid. "We're going to get you."

I kicked her in the head, knocking her out. "Fuck you!" I would have felt bad for kicking her, but the bitch brought me here, and if I didn't incapacitate her, she'd come after me. I'd taken Xavier by surprise. I didn't have the strength right now to fight Juliette and her sister.

With both down, I made my way toward where I'd heard the scream. Like Xavier said, the girls must have figured out they were going to be sacrificed. I wasn't leaving here without at least trying to save them.

Raised voices bounced off the rock walls, mixing with the sound of water dripping. Maybe they had an underground pool or pond they used. I followed the sounds down a tight, dark space, holding onto the smooth rock for support. The adrenaline that helped me fight Xavier had worn off, leaving me in a sluggish state.

I should have eaten the muffin.

Maybe then I would have thought about asking Xavier who his benefactor was. And I should have killed Juliette and her sister. They were bound to come after me. I just wasn't in that dark place yet. But I would be soon, especially if people kept kidnapping me.

Cries rang out. They must have started the ceremony already. How the hell was I supposed to stop Gavina and whoever else she had participating in her ritual from killing the girls? The ones who Monique had said left, because that's exactly who they were —the ones Gavina had told her followers left because they became afraid of the freedom she offered.

Bullshit.

Gavina had to be sacrificing them in a blood magick ritual to make herself a god. The only question was why. Why did she want to become a god? She showed no interest in leading her church. So, something else was driving her. Fear, maybe?

My vision blurred, and I stopped. My hand slid along the wet rock as I worked to steady myself. I should have asked Juliette what she gave me. Hell, I should have done a lot of things, like text Devlin to let him know where I was going.

If I survived this, I'd have to get that tattooed on my hand.

Another woman cried out, and I pushed forward. Doubt wiggled its way inside my head. I hadn't considered that the women might have gone into this willingly, like at the gathering when they gave their magick to her freely.

I thought back to the woman who had opened up her vein to help some blood mage's fight. She had been all too willing to serve her masters. Were the girls here similar? Would I have to fight off daggers made of blood?

A light shone ahead. I moved toward it, my hand still running along the wall. When my hand ran into an indentation in the surface, I stopped. Blinking to bring the image into focus, I stared at the glyphs on the wall. They were similar to the ones on the altar Xavier was using. The ritual depicted on the Ark. It was the same scene Set had shown me. An Ark in the middle of a clearing with bodies lined around it, their blood draining into the crevice that held the Ark. So, that meant Gavina and Boyd knew about the ritual to create an Old One. Cold sweat broke out on my skin as I took in the box like structure that had been carved out in the rock. Each wall equal in length and width to resemble a rectangular shape. Depictions covering the entire surface.

The cave had been converted into a life-size Ark.

If I walked into that room, I would be offering myself up as a sacrifice. There was no other way to look at it. A single switchblade wasn't going to protect me unless they planned to use magick to attack.

Another woman screamed, and the fear in her voice solidified my decision. Outnumbered or not, I needed to try. I could only hope the team would realize something was up and track my phone. Yeah, that wouldn't happen. Juliette was stupid, but not *that* stupid. She wouldn't have brought my car and phone to the church. Someone would have discovered it.

I had to do this alone.

I stepped out of the cave and into a hollowed-out room and was deposited at the base of a white marble dais. Makeshift altars had been erected on it. Twelve girls lay bound to them, tears streaming down their faces. One of them was Monique. Everything in me screamed. I started for her but stopped. I had to try and save them all—including myself. Fuck. I should have told her something, helped her in some way. But how?

I went further into the room. I needed to understand the ritual more; hope I could disrupt it somehow.

The altars the girls were lying on rested inside of four circles—three green, three gold, and three black, with four altars per circle.

Gavina stood in the middle of a red circle, her robe open to reveal her nudity. Gold glyphs were drawn on her skin. It was the same configuration we found on the floor at Tribec Insurance; the one used to bring a god into existence. Jonah said the red circle should not be touching the others. But here, it was.

Gavina was doing the ritual wrong.

Boyd stood to the side, arms held up in welcome, as he ran through a sermon similar to the one he gave on Sunday. Their girls went from one bound girl to the next, rubbing blood on their heads.

"Interesting ritual you have going on, here," I said, stepping up on the dais, knife held at my side. My vision wavered again, and I blinked against the sudden blurriness. "Now..." I let out a breath. "Is this the one to channel energy through combined orgasm? Or some sort of homage to Dionysus? Will there be wine? I'm so confused and might need you to enlighten me."

Everyone turned my way, including the girls on the altar. Monique locked eyes with me, and my gut wrenched. Nothing but terror inside those once-happy eyes.

"Nicole," she mouthed.

"I'll get you out," I promised. "I'll get you all out." *Including myself.* An empty promise. Because chances were, I'd die here today.

Boyd, after sparing me a brief glance, resumed his mock sermon, raising his hands to the heavens and muttering about his family's new prosperity. He showed absolutely no concern about what was going on behind him.

Gavina signaled for her children. They rushed over to her, surrounding her as if I were a threat.

I was outnumbered. The gravity of that situation was now coming into focus, along with my vision. The last dregs of the drugs started to dissipate—too bad that meant absolutely nothing in the grand scheme of things. I couldn't take five people on my own. And I didn't hold out any hope I would be found in time, either. But again, I had to try.

Monique and the other girls were counting on me.

Gavina smiled, and my heart dropped. "You have saved me some time." She stood there, robe parted, running her hungry eyes over me. "I have to say, you're not looking too good."

This was not good. I had assumed my presence would throw her, or at least make her scared. Instead, it looked as if I had offered myself up. All that was missing was a bow around my damn neck.

I was such a damn idiot. Why didn't I just leave and come back with backup? I looked down at the switchblade in my hand. Gavina couldn't attack me with magick. That meant they would come at me physically. I couldn't take them all, but I could hurt them.

Now, all I needed to do was stall them. It would give me time to figure something out. Because for some strange reason, Logan left me here. He must have believed I could win this battle with magick.

"Rip their souls from their bodies."

It should be simple. Yeah, not.

All I'd been able to do thus far was touch someone's soul, and that took both concentration and time—neither of which I had.

So, for now, I'd use the one power I knew I could wield effectively: my smart-ass mouth.

"Didn't your son tell you? He planned to make himself a god, too." I tsked. "Seems ol' junior wasn't happy with his place at the bottom of…" I glanced around. "Whatever the fuck this is."

"Mom," Vidette said. "She's by herself. We can take her." Vidette started for me, and Gavina reached out and grabbed her.

"Not yet. We don't know what type of power she has," she said, studying me along with Oralee and Salome. That's right, she didn't understand my power. Maybe I could use that to my advantage. "Let's give her the opportunity to attack. When she's done, then we'll grab her." Or maybe not.

She stared at me, her eyes hard, while a sneer slid across her face. "We're waiting. Or was your little taunt meant to goad us?" She shook her head, her face filling with disgust. "Xavier was useless. He knew that. I told him that."

"Was that before or after you took his magick?" I asked.

She didn't even have the decency to look ashamed. Oh, I was so going to relish killing this bitch. She narrowed her eyes. "His attempt to restore his power is interesting. If he had, I would have taken it, too. Men." She shook her head in disgust.

"Did you kill him?" Hedia, their youngest, asked in a soft voice. The look in her eyes told me she savored the idea of her brother's death.

I held up my knife. "Yes. I buried this in his gut."

I spared Boyd a brief glance. Still nothing.

Time to throw Gavina off her game. "He told me he had a powerful benefactor—one who wanted to punish you."

Gavina's face drained of color.

"What's wrong, Gavina? You don't look so good. Afraid?"

"If she was going to attack us, she would have done it already," Vidette said, seeming unconcerned about her mother's silence.

Gavina looked at her daughter, then at me. "You're right." She patted her daughter on the head. "Bring her to me," she said, a quiver in her voice. She knew exactly who Xavier's benefactor was.

I gripped the knife and readied myself. I might not be able to take them all, but I was not going down without cutting at least two of them. Maybe three.

Vidette started for me. I want to say I hesitated because she was just a young girl, but I was done trying to find ways to justify the actions of people who seemed innocent. Juliette and her sister had fooled me. True, I knew something was off about them—I just didn't know who the real player was. But these girls were beyond innocent.

So, when she was in range, I slashed out, running the knife across her throat. The look of surprise on her face was comical.

Did she expect me to just lay down and let her tie me to the altar?

Gavina screamed, and Boyd whipped around. His gaze went to his daughter. Vidette backed up, her hand on her throat as blood ran down her chest. He dismissed her and returned to his sermon.

I had to be in the Twilight Zone.

Gavina ran to the first girl tied up, picked up the knife that lay near her head, and slashed it across her throat. "I must complete the ritual. I need power!" Three of the kids blocked me from rushing to help. I watched in sick horror as she ran from one girl to the next.

I needed to do more than just touch her soul. I had to figure out how I could rip it out. I had to go deeper inside myself...to the magick I had yet to learn about. It was there, deep inside me—I just needed to find it.

The phoenix wings lay open, waiting. As if the mere thought of me using my magick had opened them. I looked past them for that spark of magick I'd seen inside of me when I'd been attacked before and found a pulsing red ball of energy.

Magick was in the blood. It wanted to be used. I just had to will it. I concentrated on my intent and a few tendrils separated from the mass, slithering forward. I centered my thoughts, my energy, my desire—my hatred on Gavina. She stood over the second girl; blade raised.

Letting the power flow through me, I let my gaze go distant, bringing Gavina's gray aura into focus. Divine Evil. She was so much more than that.

"She's using her power," one of the girls said; it had to be either Oralee or Salome. They were both earth mages and could see the magick in others.

"Mom said to be careful," one of them responded.

Good. Let them fear me for a little while longer.

I used that time to search deeper inside of Gavina. All the souls I'd seen before looked like bright lights in the center of a person's being. Gavina's soul looked dull and rotten. Maybe this was where Divine Evil came from. I'd have to ponder it later. With my newly tapped energy surging through me, I reached out and grabbed her soul.

Gavina suddenly stopped. Her body went rigid. A cold sensation writhed in my hand. I looked down at it. Empty. I focused inward and saw the red tendril linking from me to Gavina.

Without thinking, I yanked my hand forward. A single guttural cry rang out, and Gavina turned, eyes going completely white. She fell, sliding down to the ground in a graceful sort of way as if she were being deflated. My entire body felt encased in a frigid mass. It moved around me, twisting as pieces of it thrashed in my hand. I had Gavina's soul. Now what was I supposed to do?

Before I could decide, I was knocked to the ground, forcing me to release Gavina's soul. I heard a gasp, only to be drowned out by Salome. She loomed over me, screaming and beating at me with her fists. I blocked the worst of it. Fuck. I should have been paying attention.

A new weight was added. I moved and took in Hedia. Her eyes were wild. She snatched the switchblade from me. "Move, Salome," she yelled, raising the knife over her head.

Salome jumped up and moved away. I rolled just as she brought the knife down. It crashed into the rock floor, breaking on impact. That would have done a lot of damage. I jumped up and stepped back, keeping them all in sight. It looked like I was about to use some of that training Ezra gave me in his Krav Maga class. Since using my magick and trying to watch my own back wasn't going to work. Gavina stood, rubbing her chest as if she were in pain. I thought I'd killed her.

No time to ponder that now.

"You're outnumbered," Gavina said, leaning on Oralee. "Give up now, and it won't be painful."

"Fuck you," I gritted out. She should have died.

She laughed. "Do you think you can take us all?"

Before I could respond, someone struck me across the back of my head.

The world went black again.

A Point of No Return

Veronica Lockwood's little blue house sat on the corner of the street. It had a wraparound porch that stretched the entire length of the house. Alek climbed out of his Buick and closed the door softly behind him. Just after midnight, the street had gone to sleep. Even the streetlights cast a muted, lazy glow over the quaint neighborhood. Mindful of the traps that had most likely been laid for him, Alek cast his magick out, seeking an active mind. All he found was impressions of dreams and a few restless thoughts as someone suffered through a bout of insomnia. He'd been there before.

But inside that little blue house, he found a mind not just sleeping but completely shut down. Veronica was dead. He could have driven away, having confirmed what he suspected he would find anyway, and just report back to Devlin's house, but something kept him moving forward. He had to know; had to see for himself just what Logan had done to the woman. And if possible, locate anything that would help them find the man.

He didn't hold out much hope. But he'd try anyway.

The front door was not an option. The way the house sat, he would be too exposed. So, he moved around to the side of the house, searching for an open window or a back door. He found a side door instead. He tried the doorknob. Locked. Well, it looked like Logan was going to make this a little harder than last time.

He didn't have his lockpicks on him, so he circled the house, trying to find an unlocked window. The house had a small fence around the back and an even smaller backyard. A large tree sat between Veronica's house and the house directly behind hers. Alek only hoped it was enough to hide him. Four windows lined the back of the house, and he tried each one of them. Locked. Out of options, he found a rock, covered it with his shirt, and broke the glass on the side door. Only the sound of the shards hitting the kitchen floor could be heard.

After unlocking the door, Alek stepped into the cool darkness of Veronica's kitchen. Her dinner sat half-eaten on a small Formica table in the center of the tiny space. The drone of a floor air-conditioning filled the house. When he went into the living room, he was met with the noxious scent of flowers and metal. He knew what that metallic scent was and steeled himself for what he was about to find.

Again, he sent his magick out; the orange tendrils wove across the plush beige carpet and slithered up the walls, seeking. He followed the trail down a short hallway and stopped at a half-opened door. The scent was stronger here. Careful not to touch anything, he used his foot to push open the door and was greeted with the sight of Veronica Lockwood lying in a bathtub full of blood. A single message had been scrawled on the wall: *I'm tired.*

Not much for a suicide note, Alek thought. Most likely, Logan had used her finger to scrawl the message after she was dead.

So much life gone. For what? Anger filled him. There was nothing he could do about it. They had no way of knowing this would happen. Logan kept them too busy. Hell, the entire case had them too occupied with so many leads that if they had stopped for a single moment and really put things together, maybe—just maybe—they would have figured it out.

Yet, even as he thought this, he knew that wasn't true. They were missing the glue that tied all of these threads together; the sole purpose each of the key players had. All of them circled around, none of them fitting together.

His phone buzzed, and still staring at Veronica, he pulled it from his pocket.

"Jesse Rollins and his mother are dead," Devlin said.

"How were they killed?" Alek asked, making his way out of the house. There was nothing to find here. And if Logan did set this up, he might have called the police again.

"Going by the carbon monoxide readings on their meter, I'd say carbon monoxide. Veronica?"

"Staged suicide." Alek got in his car and started the engine. "What now?"

"We… Wait, I'm getting a call from Rachel." Devlin clicked over, and a wave of dread overcame Alek. They hadn't heard from Nicole.

"Nicole's missing," Devlin said without warning. "Rachel's texting you the address for Gavina's house."

"How does she know she's missing?" Alek asked, trying to keep calm. If he lashed out now, he'd kill everyone in the neighborhood.

"Rachel noticed she hadn't moved in over an hour and tried calling." Alek's phone dinged, and he put Devlin on speaker. "Jonah went out to find her and found her phone in the bushes. He's on his way to the church. Kara is coming to pick up Rachel so they can check out Tribec Insurance. I'll check their barn out."

Alek sped out of Veronica's neighborhood, his magick flaring as he drove.

T he cold seeping into my bare back stirred me. I cracked one eye open. Muted light danced in front of me, and I wondered if I had a concussion from the blow to my head. A searing pain running along both arms and legs registered immediately. Realization wormed its way inside of me. I had been tied naked to the empty altar in the center of the cave. Voices surrounded me, mixing with the incessant water dripping and the moans of the other women tied to the altars around me.

My trek to this room didn't reveal the water's location. Could it be part of the ritual? After all, baptism was part of the church's fabric.

But honestly, it didn't matter, anyway.

Any possible chance of escape was gone. Any hope of rescue diminished. No one knew where I was. Rachel said there wasn't any other structure under The Better Day Church. Chances were, it had been left off the building plans when they had torn down the original church and built the current one.

Moisture on my cheeks let me know that I'd started crying. The anguish inside of me had become so encompassing that any state of being before it seemed foreign and unreal. As far as I was concerned, I had always lived in this state of mind.

I tested my bindings, yanking as hard as I could, wanting to pull myself out of the melancholy—hoping they were like the bindings Pastor Jeremiah and my supposed aunt had placed on me. They weren't. Whoever had secured me to this altar made sure I wouldn't be able to escape.

My movement helped me register the sticky sensation on my skin. I lifted my head off the marble slab and stared down at the red and gold glyphs covering my entire body. A coppery metallic scent rose off me, and I cringed at the knowledge that they had drawn the elaborate spell in blood.

I had promised myself when I escaped Pastor Jeremiah that I'd never allow myself to be put in this position again. But it was a promise made by a teenager who believed her life would always venture down a dark path. Always leading to trauma like this. Unable to see the future at that age, I had no belief, no faith that I could move past all the pain and find happiness. But I had, in a way, found happiness.

At least, little snatches of it.

True, I hid behind sarcasm and foul language, but it was a hiding place I grew to love. And my friends, when pressed, would say they grew to love it, too. At least, that's what I believed.

"You're awake." Gavina stepped into my line of sight. "That's good. Everyone has just arrived." I stayed mute, studying her red-rimmed eyes and subdued demeanor. "Vidette won't be able to join us. She needs time to recover." She glared at me, eyes filled with accusation. "You almost killed my girl. If not for the urgency and my need of your power, I would have let my children slaughter you." She leaned in, and her floral scent tickled my nose. "But instead, you will die slowly while I use your blood." A single tear ran down her face. She swallowed and moved away.

From my position on the altar, I couldn't see how many people were behind me. My only view was of the rock wall in front of me. The glyphs depicted on the Ark had been etched on the surface.

"Why do you need to become a god?" I asked. If I was going to die, I needed to know why. It was the final puzzle piece that would solve this crazy mystery—not that it would really do me any good. But still, this bitch owed me the truth.

"To protect myself from Lemuel." She shook her head. "Why do I keep calling him that?" More tears streamed down her face. "His name is Khnum." She laughed without humor. "He told us that in the end. Told us he was a god created by blood magick. Some of the girls were fascinated. But not me. I knew when he told us his plans that we were powerless to protect ourselves. Can you believe he wanted us to die so he could free his brother, Set?" She glared at me as if I was supposed to answer. "He convinced us that we were special. That our sacrifice would mean something. But he lied. And when it came time for us to die, we fled. Helena, Bianca, Monica, and Selena. The four of us made a pact to amass enough power to destroy him."

"Aren't you worried about Set?" I asked.

She looked down at me. "I see you know about the Old Ones." She waved her hand around. "You hear the water? Set can't cross it unless he's inside a host. Why do you think I built my temple here?"

Seems someone had lied to her. Set could cross water.

"It's too bad you have to die," she continued. "I wish I could have drained some of your power first. It might have helped me. I have no idea if I will survive the ritual." She leaned in. "But I have to try." Without warning, she slammed a dagger into my shoulder.

The surprise registered before the pain. I hadn't even noticed she had a knife with her. I turned toward it and took in the gold and jewel-encrusted handle. Blood seeped down from the wound, coating my skin and altar beneath me. All the women around me cried out, and then came the pain. It froze me in place. All-consuming, the avalanche of agony rode me like a lover—deep and penetrating. My cries mixed in with the others', and soon, we sounded like a murder of crows screaming to the heavens.

The fucking bitch stabbed me.

Pain was replaced with fury.

I had promised myself I would never end up on the altar again, dammit. Yet, here I was, allowing some sick, twisted woman to use me in her efforts to become a god. While she had managed to use sex to twist her magick enough to make her a little more powerful, she had not achieved godhood. And the ritual she had set up wouldn't help her, either.

She was doing it wrong.

She had to know that. Because I doubted this was the first time she'd tried. Yet, she believed using my magick was the key.

"If you had found out about the Nar al-nasaa, you wouldn't be here."

Maybe it was.

I yanked at my bonds again. The knife shifted, ripping at my shoulder. I bit down and tried to ignore the agony. It was a Herculean effort, but I managed to hold onto the rage, letting that fuel me instead.

I reached inside of me and found my magick. If she had attacked me with magick, I might have had a chance, but since she didn't, I'd have to try and pull her soul out instead. With the constant pain, it wasn't going to be easy.

I twisted my head around, trying to see where she had put me. I was in the gold circle. Monique lay in the black one with a similar ceremonial dagger in her shoulder. Blood dripped down from the altar into the bowl at its base. She wasn't moving. I had no idea if she was dead, but I did know at least two of the girls were.

Maybe with enough chaos, I could disrupt their ritual and free us.

With the phoenix wings closed, it was going to be much harder to send my magick out. If I got out of this, I was so going to spend all my time practicing my damn magick.

First, I focused on the red pulse inside of me, willing it to grow. When the magick flared, I again centered my thoughts, energy, and desire on what I needed to do. This time, I had pain and fury to help fuel me. I turned slightly when the magick had slithered out of me and concentrated on the first robed figure I saw. Letting my gaze go distant, I looked past the black light surrounding her and found the bright ball of energy. Her soul.

My magick wrapped around her. When I felt her cold soul in my hand, I yanked.

She fell to the ground, and everyone stopped chanting.

Not knowing what to do next, I held onto that writhing mass and sent another tendril of magick out to the next person—repeating the process again. By the time I had three souls contained, Salome rushed up the stage and yanked the knife out of my shoulder. I tightened my grip on the souls as I fought a wave of dizziness and pain.

"Did you think we would let you stop us?" Gripping the knife in two hands, she lifted her arms above her head—her robe slid down her arms, revealing gold glyphs along each forearm—and shoved the knife into my arm.

I cried out, releasing the souls I held in my hand.

She leaned in, her eyes blazing with hatred and madness. "You can't fight us alone!" she screamed.

"She doesn't have to." Elation rushed through me at the sound of Jonah's low timbre. He stepped into the room, looking as if the cave itself had given birth to him. His eyes, usually a bright hazel, had darkened to a burnt amber color with a black-rimmed glow around them.

His demon was close to the surface.

The first time I'd seen Jonah fight, he'd ripped a man's head clean off his shoulders, making the feat look effortless. It was only recently that I'd learned he had a demon inside of him—one created by a faith magick ritual gone wrong. He'd told me back then that he had control. Seeing him now, appearing as if he'd grown two sizes, I wondered if that was true. Could he really control something so deadly?

"Nicole?" he said, making my name a question. His eyes slid toward me, taking in my predicament. "You trust me?" His voice had gone a few octaves deeper.

"With my life," I said.

He dipped his head in acknowledgement and refocused on the people who stood in complete silence. There was no warning —no, 'Brace yourself,' uttered from him at all, before he let his head fall back and his demon crawled out of his chest.

A mishappen humanoid shape with stringy white hair surveyed the room out of black-rimmed burnt amber eyes. Its skin resembled cooled lava, pock marked with craters so deep, it looked as if someone had carved out its skin. When it left Jonah, it resembled a child in shape and form. But once free, it started to grow. Someone screamed—possibly me—as it loomed up over everyone.

Jonah stepped away from it and came over to me. Salome had run back toward the safety of her family and the rest of the worshipers.

"How did you find me?" I asked while he cut me free from my bonds. The original stab wound had started knitting itself back together. Rachel had told me I healed fast. I had never been awake when this happened. Now, I could almost feel the skin as it closed in on itself. "Can you take the knife out?"

He pulled it out fast, and I bit down on a scream. Pain radiated down my arm, and I wondered if my healing would also mitigate the obvious damage done. If I went by the amount of pain I felt, my arm should have fallen off by now.

Once freed, Jonah helped me up, and I quickly scrambled off the altar. He pulled his shirt over his head and handed it to me.

The room had gone silent. I turned and got a good look at how many people were there. Damn. Along with the remaining Young family, at least fifty robed figures stood surrounding the dais. Salome was right. There would have been no way possible for me to rip all of their souls out. A pregnant pause ensued as they all stood, staring rapt at the twisted thing in front of them.

"Why isn't he attacking?" I asked.

"He's waiting for me," Jonah said.

I looked up at him. "And what are you waiting for?"

"I needed to free you first." He turned from me and focused on the demon.

It swiveled its now-massive head toward Jonah and smiled.

Slowly, the demon slithered toward the Young family and the fifty others who still stood in stunned silence. It crawled across the rock, and they all backed up until they were flush against the furthest wall.

Eyes wide, they screamed out as the demon reared up, its body expanding. In one massive rush, it dove into the first person. Blood sprayed, coating the walls, as the demon tore out of the woman's chest, sending body parts flying.

A guttural cry escaped its mouth. It mashed its mighty jaws, blood dripping from deformed teeth.

One of the girls on the dais stirred as a long strand of blood flew from her body toward a woman who, deciding she had nothing to lose, stood her ground, ready to fight.

The bowls under the altars rattled as more and more blood flew into the waiting hands of the women mages. I guess we had our confirmation: They were using blood magick.

The demon stared down at the women, who had formed a circle—backs to one another. It laughed, the sound echoing around the room.

"Help me untie the women," I said to Jonah.

I went to Monique first. After untying her, I examined her wound. While the cut shouldn't have been fatal, the blood loss could be if we didn't get her and the others out of here in time. I touched her skin. Cold. I shook her slightly. Her eyes fluttered open, and she looked up at me out of glassy eyes.

"Hold on for just a little while longer," I said.

She nodded and closed her eyes again.

After untying the rest of the girls, we turned back to the fight. They were at a standstill. Someone had thrown a blood blade at the demon. He stared at it protruding from his body. I turned away, looking for Gavina. She stood off to the side, her gray aura blazing. She locked eyes with me. Pure hatred filled her.

"Gavina is mine," I said.

"Wait," Jonah said, placing a hand in front of me.

"What is it doing?" I asked, staring at the demon. Why didn't it attack?

"It's feeding off their fear."

I glanced up at Jonah. It looked like the demon wasn't the only one feeding off their fear.

"We should attack!" I screamed.

He looked down at me. "We're outnumbered."

"Call the others."

"No cell service down here."

Fuck this. I couldn't just stand here. I centered my thoughts again, going for my magick. Turning my gaze to Gavina, I found her corrupted soul, and before I could reach in and rip it out, the demon roared, breaking my concentration.

Like some crazed ping-pong game, it dove in and out of the robed mages. They screamed, breaking their circle and dropping the blood blades. Now that the demon was attacking, they finally decided it was a good idea to try and get away.

Blood surged out with each of the demon's kills, coating the walls of the cave.

While they ran, we went around the circle and helped the women who hadn't been bled out to stand. Five remained laying on the altar. Two were dead, and three were close to it—including Monique.

Jonah helped me get her up. "I can take her out of the cave," I said.

Careful not to touch the knife, I tried to secure her arm around me, but she moved away. She opened her eyes and stared at me. "Freedom is so seductive," she slurred, then smiled. Then, faster than I believed possible, she yanked the knife out of her shoulder and lunged at me. I managed to sidestep her, but only barely. She fell to the ground and stayed there.

I didn't have time to process it; didn't have the mental space to deal with the betrayal. I snatched up the dagger and turned, waiting for the next girl to attack.

One of the other freed girls started for Jonah, dagger in hand.

"Jonah," I yelled, and he whipped around to where I was staring. The girl let out a guttural cry and ran at him. The blade made contact, slashing across his back.

I ran toward him to stop the next stab, burying the dagger in the girl's back. She screamed; the sound bounced off the walls. I turned in time to see another girl charging me. They weren't eager to save their own lives. They were going to allow themselves to be sacrificed—willing to give Gavina the blood she needed to become a god.

"Can you fight?" I asked Jonah, keeping my eye trained on the other women now closing in.

"The cut is shallow. I'll manage."

"I haven't had time to practice the moves all of you use during battle. But I will watch your back."

"Our moves?" he asked, straightening.

I gave him a quick glance. "When all of you fight, it looks choreographed. Like you all train daily for battle."

He chuckled at that. "Just try not to get hurt. Alek might break my mind in two."

I smiled at the thought and charged the first girl, slashing down as I reached her. The surprise on her face made me angry. I used that rage to fuel my movements since the pain was trying to push me down. I promised Jonah I'd have his back, and I wasn't going to break that promise.

Jonah snatched the next girl up. Her nails raked down his arm as he lifted her above his head and, in a surge of power, slammed her to the ground. I winced at the *crunch*. There was no hesitation; no allowances for her being a girl. All he saw was a threat, and he dealt with it. Some part of me wanted to scream at that—to yell, 'No fair!' like we still lived in a time when women were supposed to be put on a pedestal and treated like wilting flowers.

We no longer lived in that time. And women could be just as deadly as men.

As evidenced by the remaining girls, who despite knowing they would die, continued to charge at us. We continued to beat them off, using minimal force since they had been weakened by blood loss. As we carved our way through them, I completely lost sight of the demon. Only the cries of his victims told me he was still there, playing his bloody game of ping-pong.

When the last of the girls lay dead, I glanced out again at the destruction and found Gavina, covered in blood—chest heaving up and down, glaring at us.

I had only a moment to register this before Jonah buckled, grabbing at the side of his head. She was using her magick to hurt him.

"I will kill you," she uttered.

"Not today, bitch!" I yelled and charged. She stopped her assault on Jonah and tried to attack me. My magick flared, knocking her back. I guess she didn't learn the first couple of times.

And then, everything went silent.

The demon turned, covered in blood, and stared at me.

Shit.

I stopped in my tracks.

He continued to watch me.

"Jonah," I said in a whisper.

"He's pure magick, Nicole. If he attacks…"

"It would be a magickal attack," I finished, and ran at Gavina, knowing now I would be safe from the demon. She braced herself, her robe flying open, revealing her naked, glyph-covered body underneath.

Before I could reach her, a bloody body rammed into me, knocking me to the ground.

Salome.

Another bloody figure rushed Jonah, and when it got close enough, Jonah rammed his fist into its face. The robe fell back, revealing a man. So, there were a few men participating. I thought it would only be women. The demon rushed at the man and dove into his body, and when it flew out, blood and guts flew everywhere. It licked its fingers and once again focused on me.

I had managed to hold Salome at bay as her arms pinwheeled. She was being fueled by pure rage and frustration and possibly fear. I planted my hand on her chest and shoved her away. She scrambled back up, teeth gnashing, hands curved into claws and started for me. Why didn't she use her magick? Had she been battle trained?

The knife had skidded away when she knocked me to the ground. But given her decision to attack me with her hands rather than her magick, I figured I didn't really need it. So, when she was in range, I lifted my elbow up and slammed it into her chin. Blood flew out of her mouth as she fell back. The demon moved in close, its burnt amber eyes studying me. I stayed rooted in place. It licked its bloody lips and slowly turned away from me, setting its sights on Salome.

"Kill her," I said.

It turned back to me and smiled. My eyes widened, and a chill ran down my back.

It opened its mouth. "*Blood,*" it said and dove into Salome.

I glanced back at Jonah, who stood, his hand wrapped around a man's neck while he stared wide-eyed at me. He too seemed confused as to why his demon had followed my command.

Of course, Gavina chose that moment to attack. She drove the knife into the space between my shoulder blades. Pain radiated down my spine. I fell forward and landed hard on my stomach, smacking my face against the rock floor. The world swam, and my vision wavered in and out. Gavina's screams were like nails running along my skin. I had no idea if Jonah or his demon would save me. But it didn't really matter, anyway. If they didn't, I was going to die. Well, at least I tried.

Blackness crept around my vision.

Booted feet came into view.

The knife was yanked out of me, and I screamed.

Jonah's warm hand pressed against the wound. "Hold on, Nicole," he said, his voice sounding far way.

"Is it bad?" I mumbled.

He laughed without humor. "She managed to miss your neck by a centimeter. Can you control your healing?"

I tried to shake my head, but Jonah stilled my head. "Not a wise decision. Focus. Please."

I licked my suddenly dry lips, blinked a few times to clear the fog trying to settle over me, and looked inward at my magick. Its red mass beat against the phoenix wings as if it were trying to get free. Small tendrils licked out. A warmness settled on my skin. I reached for the magick to push my healing along, but it didn't respond. Maybe it was something I couldn't control.

"Your skin is knitting together," Jonah said with relief in his voice. "Fuck. This was my favorite shirt."

"Well, it's garbage now," I mumbled, thankful that he was trying to add some levity to the situation. "Did you kill Gavina?"

"Yes."

I shifted, trying to get up. "Let me up."

"What are you trying to do?"

"I need to kill her again." I would yank that bitch's soul back into her body and make her pay for all the pain she had caused.

He gently shifted me around and pulled me in his lap. "Why?"

He didn't need to elaborate. I thought about my need for vengeance—my need to make her pay, and realized it wasn't just her I needed to make suffer. It was Monique for making me believe she was a victim. Juliette for making me doubt my instincts. But most of all, it was the woman who claimed to be my aunt and the pastor whose twisted beliefs almost destroyed me. They were the ones I needed to hurt. So, it wouldn't just be Gavina I was killing; it'd be the pastor she represented. Along with all the others.

Jonah watched me, waiting for me to make up my mind. After a short while, I asked, "Are they all dead?"

"Yes."

"Your demon?"

"Contained."

"Then we should go," I said, and let him help me up.

I didn't need to exact revenge. I survived. That was all that mattered.

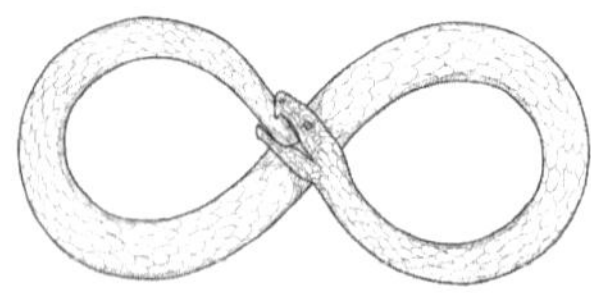

THE EARLY DAWN greeted us when we finally made our way outside. I'd been in the cave all night. Turned out, the entrance had been under Boyd's altar all along. Jonah found my clothes in the cave, drenched in blood. I had no plans on ever wearing them again. He told me on the way to the church, he had spotted my car, and when we got out of the church, he called Devlin and asked him to arrange for it to be picked up. I was in no shape to drive. Besides, I was probably going to get rid of the car, anyway. First, I needed to get my purse out of it. I only hoped those crazy bitches hadn't stolen it.

Speaking of Juliette and Bridgette, they hadn't been in the caves. I knew our paths would cross again. And this time, I was prepared to do some serious damage. I let them go free once. I was not going to do that again.

We rode in silence for a while. Before Jonah reached out and squeezed my hand. "Nicole," he said.

I shook my head. "Everything about this was…"

"Engineered," he offered when I had trailed off.

I turned to him. "By Lemuel Oren." He gave me a surprised look and then turned back to the road. "Something about my apartment building and the cult had made Rachel curious. If we had stayed focused on that, we probably would have figured it out sooner."

He nodded, his face going pensive. "We set out to stop blood magick users. Devlin—hell, all of us—believed they would be like the Stewart family. And in a way, they were. They lied to those women. The Stewarts just took what they needed. The Young family conned people into it. Different paths to reach the same point."

"I just can't wrap my head around it," I said, remembering the frenzy of the girls who tried to kill us. They were so far gone. Nothing we did could have reached them.

"Remember what I told you about how cults operate? Those women were broken before Gavina seduced them with promises of freedom and peace."

"Gavina's magick…" I trailed off. How could a faith mage attack the mind?

"She had managed to gain some mind abilities."

"I'm thinking it was Xavier's magick. He told me she stole it from him." I leaned back. "Logan told me things weren't what they seemed. I guess he knew."

"When did you see Logan?" Jonah's voice had gone cold.

I rubbed my arms. "He freed me halfway and urged me to rip their souls out. I managed to do that with Gavina. Only, when her daughter attacked, her soul returned to her body."

"We'll help you with your magick. Next time, you won't even need me to rescue you."

I nodded. Maybe next time, I could stop all of them on my own. Or maybe I would just make sure I had backup.

I turned to him. "You didn't hesitate when you came in the room," I said, thinking about the reason he had a demon in the first place. "And your demon seemed...interested in me?"

Jonah nodded and gave me a side look. "Your being tied to the altar was confirmation enough, and I have to think on the last. I don't let him out often. And when I do, it's usually in the pool."

"Is that why you're always swimming?" I asked, shocked.

"Most times, yes. I've been meaning to share that with you in case you happened to walk out when he was circling the pool but never got the opportunity."

I sat back, going through what he said. Gavina said Set couldn't enter the cave because he couldn't cross the water without a host. The Stewarts had their ritual set up in a barn on a bayou, which meant they were all aware of Set. But then again, they had to be since they knew a member of their family was meant to be sacrificed to help free him. But why had they assumed he couldn't cross water?

Lemuel Oren.

The Mastermind.

An Old One.

He had to have told them that. Or at least implied it. Which meant he knew they would betray him. What I didn't know was how I fit into his plans. But more importantly, when he became aware of me and my magick in the first place.

There were so many things we needed to figure out. But my mind was tired. So, I laid my head back and rested. My only thoughts were of the much-needed shower to wash the blood and evil taint off me.

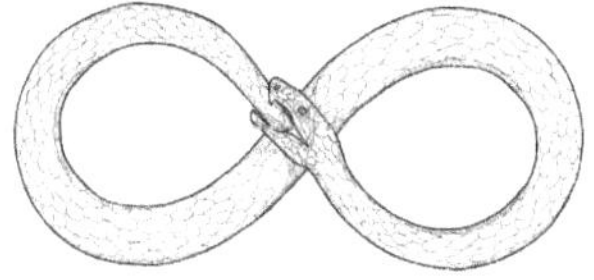

A SHORT WHILE LATER, we pulled up to the house. As soon as Jonah shut off the engine, Alek snatched open the door and pulled me out. He wrapped his arms around me; his heart pounded. I let myself relax against him.

"She's safe, man," Jonah said.

Alek nodded, then scooped me up and carried me into the house. Once inside, he strode past the front room, down the hall, kicked open the door to his room, and took me inside, not stopping until we were in the bathroom.

Without asking, he lifted Jonah's bloody shirt over my head and dropped it to the ground. His jaw clenched as he took in the many markings and deposits of blood on me. "Is this your blood?" he asked, his voice sounding strangled and so full of emotion. I was somewhat surprised I was able to make out his words.

I swallowed against my own emotions rising. "No," I whispered. "Not all of it."

He turned on the shower. He moved as if he were trying to keep himself from falling apart. I reached out and touched him. "Alek, I'm fine."

He shook his head, turned from me, and walked over to the sink. He gripped the side of it as he stared at me through the polished glass. "I should have been the one to save you," he choked out.

I stood there, naked, trying to find the words to soothe him, but came up short. No matter what I said, he was going to continue to beat himself up about it. I moved slowly toward him and wrapped my arms around him. "I know you need time to work through this. I know telling you I'm fine won't be enough." He turned in my arms and stared down at me.

"Nicole, we have been here before. You, broken and healing, and me feeling helpless. I can't..." I placed a single finger to his mouth, silencing him.

"Will you help me wash the blood off?" Maybe helping me with this would ease some of his worry. He pulled his shirt off, and I backed up. Once his jeans hit the floor, I stepped into the shower and let the warm water wash over me.

Alek climbed in behind me and pulled me to him, splaying his hands on my stomach. I relaxed against him as mist filled the room. The last time I'd taken a shower with a man, it had been Jordin Cisco. That shower had been about sex. Now, here with Alek, with his warmth pressed up against me, I could feel love building between us. The attraction and need were there, but this was about comfort, and the tenderness he showed me filled me to the point I thought I'd explode. Tears streamed down my face, and he pulled me closer, humming to comfort me.

When the water started to run cold, he washed my body down, then lifted me out of the shower and wrapped me in a towel.

Safe in his arms, I let the night's events melt away. I would deal with the emotional pain later. For now, I let Alek hold me while I held him.

"Will you sing me to sleep?" I asked, my words muffled against his chest.

"Always," he said and lifted me up and took me to his bed.

I slept most of Saturday, only to wake later in the evening to the smell of Jonah's ambrosia. AKA, fried potatoes with onions and peppers and some seasoning even after my third helping, I still couldn't identify. When I asked him to tell me what it was, he refused. I'd have to get Kara to ask him.

While we ate, we reviewed the events of our hellish week. It was somewhat of a relief that we had found out about the Young family practicing blood magick. The circumstances of our discovery weren't ideal, but at least we'd stopped them.

Now, we just had to stop the others.

Lemuel Oren had been the final piece all along. Khnum—god who gave life to gods and humans. Funny how, with just a little bit of information, Ezra was able to determine which of his siblings could possibly be behind the mayhem. If we had stayed on my building's sordid past, we would have figured it out, too.

Gavina and the rest of the girls who escaped the cult's massacre could have made a positive impact in the lives of others who found themselves in similar situations. Instead, they went from victims to predators, believing the only way to protect themselves from Khnum was to repeat his actions—to make themselves into gods. It didn't matter if the ritual wasn't working. Didn't matter if in the end, they would have died anyway. They just kept killing. Senselessly.

We had taken down two of them. That left three to deal with.

But now, we were going into this with all the knowledge we needed. But more importantly we knew the reason why they were practicing blood magick.

That left Logan. Out of all the games he played, it was his parting words to me that gave me the biggest clue. That, and his sudden change from trying to kill us to protecting us, however half-assed he went about it.

"We all have bonds we need to break..."

He was trying to free himself from someone, and I could guess who that someone was: Lemuel Oren. The man—correction, Old One, we all now knew—who oversaw The Oren Group.

The professor had led us to the three Arks: one for life, one for knowledge, and one for death—the trifecta presenting itself again. We concluded the one for life was used to create the Old Ones and could possibly be the one the families were fighting over. What we didn't know was what happened to the other two.

Louis Badet—Thoth—being the author of *The Land Guarded by People of Colour* and an Old One, was the biggest surprise of them all. It also, in hindsight, made sense that Luisah would entrust Steve with a copy of the rare document, knowing I would need it in the future. While the contents were important, it was the author in the end that was the most important, just like with the book by Professor Shukuma.

It was close to midnight when we decided to call it quits, which was a good thing since my brain had decided to call it a night an hour earlier. So, I climbed back in the bed with Alek and let him hold me. For now, that was all I wanted. My hormones, of course, rebelled.

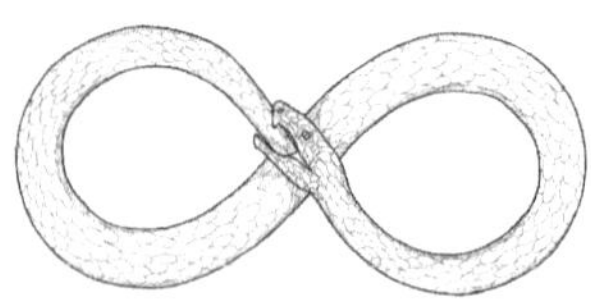

KARA and I stepped out of Devlin's house and into the heat. Sweat immediately coated my body. If the heat didn't let up soon,

I was afraid we'd all cook to death. Kara rubbed her stomach as we walked down the short path toward her car. She was taking me by my apartment to retrieve the letters Doc had been sending me. I didn't tell anyone about the purpose of my trip; just that it was important. And while I would have preferred Alek to take me, it was better if Kara did. It would give me time to talk to her about them and prepare myself for the rest of the team to read them as well.

When we got to her car, I glanced behind it and stared at my own vehicle. "I need to buy a new car," I announced as we climbed into hers. "There is no way I'm ever going to feel comfortable driving it again."

Kara started the engine, and we rolled down the windows as the air-conditioning pushed warm air out of its vents. "Give it time," she said and turned to me. "I know what those B's did was horrific, but you can't let them win."

"How would they win if I bought a new car?" I asked.

"By showing them that they got to you." She rolled up her window, and I did the same. The air-conditioning had finally started blowing cold air out. "But please, get your D air-conditioning fixed."

"So, I see you've gone back to not cursing." I leaned back in my seat. She was right, of course. Still didn't stop my determination to get rid of my car. Besides, it was time, anyway.

"For now," she said.

"What about when you and Jonah decide to move past the pool parties and into the bedroom?" I asked, smiling at her.

She winked at me. "Then I might invent a few." She licked her lips. "Seriously. That man." She made an appreciative noise that made me laugh. "One minute, we're staring at each other, and the next minute, he invites me to go swimming. I was so nervous I almost didn't show up."

"I would ask for details, but...might be a little weird. I won't be able to look at him the same way." I cringed at the thought of Kara giving me a blow-by-blow account of their time together.

"What about you and Alek? The man can't keep his eyes or hands off of you." She wiggled her eyebrows.

I groaned. "Oh, dear god. We have devolved into girly girls. What's next? Painting our nails together? Spa day? Shopping?" I was so not going to spend the entire day shopping and getting my nails done. I thought about Alek washing me down in the shower. Okay, maybe I might get my toes done, and while I was at it, a bikini wax.

"We've always been girly. We just…" She trailed off and I suddenly knew what she wanted to say. We had always talked about men, only our discussions had been about sex—not love and emotion and caring. And I also realized it had been my fault our conversations had been so shallow, because all my past relationships had been superficial.

"My fault," I said finally.

"Don't you dare," she said through clenched teeth. She pulled to the curb and turned to me.

I wanted to look away, but I knew that would be too childish, and I needed to stop doing that. I needed to take charge of my life and work through every one of the obstacles being thrown at me like I was in a sadistic game of dodgeball.

"Okay. So, not my fault?" I offered to get her to calm down.

"No. We talked about each other's lives. That's what friends do. Did I worry about you? Yes. And if I recall, I have never shied away from telling you so." I turned to her. "You hide. We all do. I have kept my secrets, and I know you have kept yours. But that ends today, got it?"

I nodded. "Got it. But…I am so not painting your nails. And you can just forget spa day."

She laughed, breaking the rising tension in the car, and pulled away from the curb. "Now, what was so important that you had to ruin my swim date?"

I didn't hesitate—a positive step in the right direction, as I told her about the letters I'd been receiving from Doc, she didn't yell—also a positive step. Maybe I could do this; allow myself to rely on others and open up about the things that bothered me. It would take time, of course, but like Kara said, we kept too many secrets from one another, and it was time we stopped doing that.

We arrived at my apartment a short time later. When we climbed out of the car, a wave of heat rushed over us. It reminded me that I hadn't told Kara about the first time I'd been caught in a massive heat wave that had drove me to my knees. As I relayed yet another kept secret, we walked into the cool hallway of my apartment complex, only to stop dead in our tracks.

Hathor stood by Mr. Wan's door, wearing a sundress with a large purse on her shoulder, chatting. And I do mean chatting, because the look on his face suggested he had not been able to get a word in edgewise. She turned when we stopped and beamed at us.

"I was hoping you would come home," she said, rushing over. She threw her arms around me. "My brother wanted me to give you something to protect you against Set," she mumbled into my hair before she stepped back and looked at me. "You look well. I'm glad." She reached into her purse and pulled out a small black box. "Here, add this to your charm bracelet. It will protect you for a while." She pulled out another, much larger box. "He also wanted me to give you one of his favorite daggers."

"Can't you just kill Set?" I asked.

She blinked at me. "We are eternal," she answered as if I should know that. "We just need to put his soul back in the Ark."

"Who let him out?"

She frowned. "Khnum. They were always so close." She smiled again. "Your mother's magick is almost restored." She stepped away and looked at Kara. "It's nice to see you again!" Before any of us could respond, she burst out the front door and into the blazing heat.

Well damn. We just spent an entire week trying to figure out who was behind all this madness and all we had to do was hunt Hathor down and ask. Un-fucking-believable!

"She your friend?" Mr. Wan asked.

"Umm…yes, I guess so." I stared down at the box in my hand. How the hell was the charm supposed to stop Set?

I looked up and found Kara and Mr. Wan studying me with confused looks on their faces. "Yeah, she's a friend," I said with more surety in my tone. "I hope she wasn't troubling you."

He shook her head. "No. She reminded me of my late wife. So chatty." He laughed and went back in his apartment.

"That was weird," Kara said, following me to my apartment. Thankfully, there were no packages leaning against the door.

"Yeah, it was." I handed her the box and fished my key out of my purse. "But then again, Hathor is a little strange. And speaking of strange, Logan wanted me to tell you hello." I gave her a brief rundown of what happened between Logan and me in the cave.

"Logan is beyond strange," she said.

I made a non-committal noise and went inside my apartment. The residual blood stain on the carpet caught my eye. There was no way to know how close to death I had come that night, but the fear of it still rested inside of me. I took the box from Kara and opened it.

A gold charm lay inside on a red cushion. I pulled it out and studied it: a Shen ring circling a trinity knot. I'd encountered so many references to the trifecta lately. Its number and symbols had to hold a significant amount of power if the history of magick and belief centered around it.

After Kara helped me put the charm on my bracelet, I opened the other box from Ezra to reveal a bone-handled dagger inside, resting on a bed of black satin. He'd written a note.

Tuesday and Thursday mornings at five.

"Well, damn," I said handing her the card so I could study the knife. "Looks like I will be resuming my training at an unholy hour in the morning." I held the six-inch dagger in the palm of my hand. Glyphs had been carved into the bone handle. "I wonder why he would give me one of his daggers."

Kara stared at the blade. "It is nice." She took it from me and admired it. "Are you going to go?"

"He invited both of us."

She regarded me, raising a single eyebrow. "So, we do this together?"

I nodded. "Maybe we can convince Marta to join us. And Rachel, too. Make it a girls' outing."

"At five in the morning?"

"If I have to suffer, everyone has to suffer."

She laughed. "Yeah, sounds like a plan. Of course, I think Rachel could kick Ezra's ass."

"This is true," I called over my shoulder as I made my way into my bedroom to retrieve the shoebox filled with letters. It was going to be hard letting the others see them. The intimate details of my time with Ronald were recounted in such lavish detail in the first few letters I read, and I had no idea what the others contained. He'd taken to re-imagining our time together by the third letter. So, I had no doubt they had gotten darker and more extravagant by now.

After grabbing the letters, I locked up my apartment and we left.

A *boom* sounded when we stepped outside.

We looked up. A streak of fire shot across the horizon.

Thick gray clouds closed in, filling the sky and completely covering the sun.

Another *boom* thundered, shaking the ground.

Then, the clouds opened up and let out a torrent of rain. It pounded down, drenching us. We ran for the car and scrambled inside.

My chest heaved as I stared out at the downpour, knowing what the sudden shower meant.

My mother had her magick back.

A Mirror for the Abyss

Alek watched Rae take command of a group of kids who had started throwing rocks at a house directly across the street from Greenwood Apartments. It had been hard leaving Nicole this morning, but he had to do this last thing for his aunt before he could spend the rest of the day in bed with her. As far as he was concerned, he could spend the rest of his life holding her. But after what was laid out last night, he knew their battle on this island had just begun.

Rae scolded one of the kids around her, bringing Alek back to the situation at hand. He saw a kindred spirit in the girl, who wanted to keep her brother in a coma. He saw a girl whose destiny walked a fine line, and with the slightest push, could go either way. She wanted to make something of herself. Of that, he was sure. But inside this darkened place, she would only rise so far. And not in the right way.

Petronela, despite her many flaws, was the ideal person to help cultivate the right qualities in Rae. She had some magick and a ruthlessness that could rival his old aunt's, but she also needed the right guidance if she was going to overcome the burdens that had been laid at her feet. He believed his aunt knew this.

"The one who shines in the murky waters."

He knew immediately who she was talking about.

Alek didn't fancy himself a savior, but he could nudge her in the right direction. It was up to her to take the first step. Not missing anything, Rae looked up and spotted him in his car. Head cocked to the side; she studied him with wide-open wonder. No, she didn't belong in this place of lost dreams. After a short while, she made her way over to him, her footsteps sure as she maneuvered around the now-curious people standing in the street. Obstacles, he thought, feeling bad for putting them in that place. But it was true. Unlike Rae, they had accepted their position in life, and from the looks on their faces, were resigned to living out a life society had shoved on them.

Petronela's words surfaced in his mind. *"You can't save them all."* She was right, of course, but he could save this one.

"You have another job for me?" Rae asked, leaning in his window. She had weed on her breath. Her eyes looked bloodshot.

"Have you been crying?" he asked.

She looked away, shame riding her. "Nah, brother died. Had to show I cared at least some. Mom draped herself across his coffin like her life had ended or some shit. She didn't give a fuck about him. And she damn sure doesn't give a fuck about me. But whatever. I'm getting out of this place. Just watch."

She cared but didn't want to show it. Maybe she believed there was shame in it.

"I wanted to talk to you about that."

She turned back to him. Her eyes had filled with hope. "So, a job then. How much you paying?"

"You want to get in the car so we can talk about it?"

"I don't do that. Never have and never will. I'll just stand here."

Alek nodded. Again, he was struck by her tenacity. Most people in areas like this, faced with the choices she must have been forced to make, usually crumbled. She stood tall, not letting anything take her down. Petronela was right—she was a bright light.

"My aunt could use some help. You heard of *Carnavalul de Fear*?"

Rae studied him. "The woman that owns that place—Petronela Vaduva. She's your aunt?"

"Yes. My great aunt."

"What she need me for?" Skepticism bloomed across her face. She wouldn't be fooled. Alek respected that. Time for a little truth, then.

"She doesn't. But I think she can help you. She's helped a lot of people." Alek looked around at the people standing around. "It's a way out, but it's your choice."

"Will I have to kill anybody?" Despite her bravado when they first met, Alek got the impression that killing bothered her—just like it bothered Nicole.

"I won't lie; I have no idea what you'd be faced with. But again, your choice." It was important that he made that clear.

Rae turned and leaned against his car. He followed her gaze to the Greenwood Apartments. "If I tell them I'm leaving..." She trailed off, looking at the people gathering around.

"Crabs in a bucket." They would try and pull her back into the fold. Keep her in the same fucked up position as them.

"Yup. Hold up. I'll let you give me a ride. I need to get a few things." She walked off. He noticed the way her back went straight; determination infused in every step.

He wished he could reassure her that being in the presence of Petronela would shield her from the ugly things life would throw at her, but he couldn't. Besides, she was used to them; had lived in them most of her life. Still, this move would help her; give her the chance she needed. Rae had been cut by cruelty and pain. She could use those skills for good or for evil. If she stayed here, it would lead to evil. With Petronela, there was a chance those skills could be used for good.

Or the gray area he and the rest of the team operated in.

She returned a few minutes later with a backpack thrown over her shoulder. "Let's get going." Alek noted the stuffed animal sticking out the side. Rae followed his line of sight. "Don't mean I'm soft."

"I didn't think you were," he said, pulling away from the curb. "Anyone you want to say bye to?"

"Nah, they'll forget I'm gone in a few."

As they drove away, a boom rocked the sky, and soon after, a torrent of rain pounded down on them.

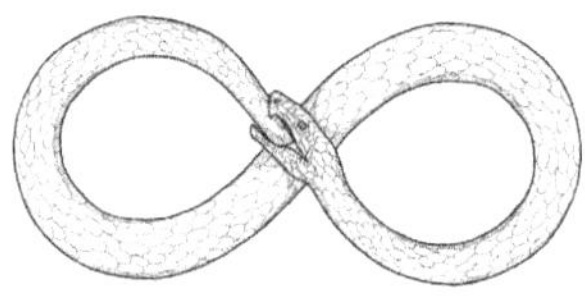

Alek pulled up to the guard station leading to the back of the carnival and noted the guard had been changed. Maybe Petronela had finally decided to get rid of the previous one. Alek knew he wouldn't last long—not with his sloppy, careless way of checking if someone was supposed to be there.

The new guard looked rattled as he directed Alek to the back. Something was going on. He pulled to the side door and found Stefan leaning against the wall smoking a cigarette, waiting for him.

"I got a bad feeling," Rae said, looking between Alek and Stefan. "You sure she wanted me to come here?"

Alek stared at the man. His head was down, eyes focused on the ground as if he'd recently been defeated. Alek surged from his car, his mind suddenly on Stefan's niece, Elena. "Stefan," he called, and motioned for Rae to wait in the car. "Is Elena okay?"

Stefan lifted his gaze and focused on Alek. "She's good. She's with..." He nodded, trailing off. "Go in. Petronela is waiting for you." His eyes moved over to the passenger seat. "Take her with you."

Alek hesitated for just a moment, debating if he should take Rae back to Devlin's until he found out what was going on. But Rae made the decision for him when she got out of the car and joined him on the driver's side. Alek glanced down at her in question. One word from her, and he'd take her away. Whatever was going on, he didn't want to involve her.

"I'm good," she said as if reading his thoughts.

His lips twitched at the reminder of Nicole. She, too, would have wanted to go in, danger be damned. When they entered the hallway, which was thankfully devoid of blood stains, Alek heard raised voices traveling down the hall. Rae looked up at him, then shoved her stuffed animal further into her bag as if showing any sign of weakness right now was a bad idea. He couldn't agree more.

On impulse, he sent his magick out, seeking the minds inside Petronela's room. He knew his family would feel his probe, but he didn't care. He had to know what he was walking into. His magick was met with a wall. They were blocking him.

"In here now, Alexandros!" Petronela roared.

"She don't sound too happy," Rae offered.

"She rarely is," Alek said and placed a hand on her shoulder, urging her forward.

Their footsteps were hesitant as they made their way down the dimly lit corridor. When they arrived at the room, all eyes turned to him—five people total, standing around Petronela, all of them crying.

"What's happened?" Alek asked, pushing Rae behind him.

"She is safe with us," Petronela said, scoffing at his gesture. She looked over at a dark-haired woman standing in the corner— his cousin Bria. "Take the girl to Dimitri's old trailer. Give her supplies and make sure she's comfortable." Petronela stood. "Everyone, leave. Alexandros and I have business."

"But we have to..." a man said before Petronela waved him off. He gave her a look filled with contempt and anger. Alek was surprised Petronela didn't respond to it. After a brief hesitation, he left with the rest of the people.

Rae hesitated. "You good?" she asked Alek, concerned.

He smiled. "Yes. And Bria's my cousin. She will take care of you."

Bria stared at him. "Come see me later, Alexandros. We have catching up to do."

Alek nodded and watched them both leave. As soon as they were gone, he turned to Petronela. "What's going on, Auntie?"

Petronela sat, falling into her chair as if the world had suddenly knocked her down. "I am tired, nephew, but there is so much work left to do." She lit one of her cigarettes, and when she had blown out a cloud of smoke, she continued, "I should have kept a closer eye on Daniella and Ileana; should have known they were up to something." She pulled a note out of her robe pocket. "But I also should have seen this was coming."

Alek took the paper and stared down at the scribbled note. His blood ran cold.

They had come for Petronela again.

"Two more girls have gone missing, and their parents killed. Bria found this note on the body of one of the mothers. Her throat had been slit." Her face grew dark.

"What do you need me to do?" Alek asked.

"The rest of us must prepare the bodies and observe our customs. We need someone on the outside to deal with everything else." Her eyes narrowed. "Find the girls. And then bring me the head of the ones who took them."

EPILOGUE

After giving Rachel the letters and promising I would talk about them later, I found Devlin in the kitchen, making himself a peanut butter and jelly sandwich. I stood there, watching him for a minute. He held himself rigid. Not even a light snack could ease the tension in his shoulders. His sandy hair had grown out. He half-turned and gave me a once-over. His profile made me pause. I'd always wondered about his heritage. His coloring suggested he was mixed, but I could never place it— not 'til now, and that realization would have to wait for another time. Right now, I needed to apologize for my actions.

"I'm sorry," I said, still standing in the doorway.

"Do you want a sandwich?"

"I prefer to eat my peanut butter with a spoon."

He harrumphed. "I used to eat it that way when I was a boy. Still do sometimes."

"We have something in common." I walked over and joined him at the counter. After pulling a spoon out, I dug in. "You know," I said, my mouth working. "I didn't mean to go off alone and not call for backup. I just wanted to keep the team safe like I promised." It was a ridiculous excuse, and I knew it. I should have called.

"And you're part of that team. So, you broke that promise. You weren't safe."

I nodded, using the mouthful of peanut butter as an excuse

not to respond. It was hard admitting I'd been wrong. Sure, I didn't really believe so at the time, but that was the benefit of hindsight. Everything became clearer when looking back, though when looking forward, the road was murky. It always would be. And now, I had people who could help me navigate it. "I've always been reckless," I said finally. "And I don't want to be that way anymore."

"Are you sure?" he asked, taking a bite of his sandwich.

I set the jar on the counter and moved in front of him. "Tell you what: I'll promise not to bicker when you're trying to teach me; promise I won't disobey an order again or put myself in danger." I placed my hand on his arm. "If you promise to take the empty bedroom, and once you furnish it, use it instead of the front room to rest. You can't stop everything. You have to let us help."

He set his sandwich down and ran his hand over his long hair. Resolve crossed his face, along with relief, like he'd been waiting for someone to give him permission to relax. "I might need help with that," he said, barely a whisper. He was still seeking permission. It was painful to see on such a strong man. This rare glimpse of vulnerability moved me.

My eyes rounded. "Devlin needs help?" I asked, trying to make light so he didn't feel so uncomfortable. Or maybe it was me not knowing how to react to this side of Devlin.

He smiled and pulled me into the third hug this week. His chest felt like solid rock, but a slight give in the hardness allowed me to relax into him. "Oh, my. Even your hugs are rigid and uptight." The rumble of his laughter soothed the last of the awkwardness. I smiled and allowed myself the reprieve, because I just knew tomorrow, we'd be back to our sparring. For now, he was relaxed—something we all knew he needed to do.

"You're like the sister I never had, Nicole."

I pulled back and stared up at him. "You mean obnoxious and annoying."

He kissed my forehead. "Exactly like that. Now..." He leaned back against the counter. "Let me finish my sandwich so I can go to the store and get a bedroom set. You're coming with me."

"Like hell, I am. I do not go shopping, especially not on a Sunday." The stores were pure hell on Sundays. All those people, fresh out of church, looking for ways to spend the money they didn't put in the collection plate.

He picked up his sandwich and smiled. "That's an order."

Well, shit. I walked right into that one. "Well played, Boss Man. Well fucking played."

He saluted me with his sandwich and closed his eyes around the next bite, enjoying the peace for just a little while. We were in the calm before the storm. Because with the new revelations, there was going to be one. Maybe even a war. And we all needed to find a little joy before the pain.

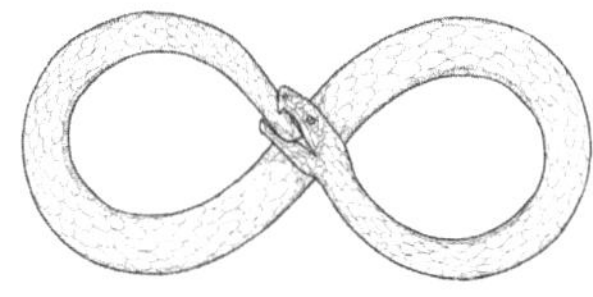

THE WATER RUSHED over me as I lay my head back, enjoying the feel of it on my skin. The sudden rain shower had mixed with the already sweaty grime covering my skin, and I felt a little unclean. I also needed time to think about the fact that my mother had magick again. The heat had been building for weeks now, keeping the rain at bay, which made me wonder just how powerful my mother was—how powerful I was as well.

I heard a commotion outside the room. On a sigh, I stepped out of my happy place, wrapped a towel around me, and made my way out of the room. Alek stood in the middle of the war room with a pained look on his face. He'd left earlier on an errand he said he'd tell me about when he got back. His eyes locked with mine.

"What's going on?"

He ran his hand down his face and looked over at Devlin. "More girls have gone missing, and Petronela needs our help."

"Does she know who took them?" Devlin asked.

"I think she believes Daniella either took them or lured them away." He pulled a piece of paper from his pocket and taped it to the board. "She found this on the body of the parents."

"They're dead?" Devlin asked.

Alek nodded.

Alek had taped a single white sheet of paper to the board underneath the Peterson family's information. The Peterson girl-school crest had been drawn on the front. Underneath the symbol were words written in another language. I turned to Alek. "What does it say?"

"Loosely translated...*We are Tribe.*"

Continue reading for an *unedited* sneak peek of Tribe
Book three
Blood & Sacrifice Chronicles

Available: October 22, 2025
Pre-order your copy now!

An hour ago, I'd made a promise to Devlin that I would not charge headfirst into danger risking my life and the lives of others. I tended to act before thinking which, as of late, put me in a great deal of trouble. I also told him I'd work more closely with the team moving forward. I'd made this pledge while eating peanut butter out of a jar. Comfort food always made things easier to deal with.

My utterance to do better and be better came with elation. I'd survived the attempt on my life despite my misguided actions.

I promise to never do this again.

In the past, this sort of proclamation came at the end of the night when the alcohol had turned sour, and I was sitting in the consequences of my actions. I'd made a similar remark earlier this week when I woke, head pounding, to learn I'd been attacked while hiding in a bottle of rum.

Now, standing in the middle of Devlin's family room—that I dubbed the war room—I made another declaration.

I was going to kill the person who dared to disrupt my peace. However, to keep my promise, I'd do so with the team. I considered that progress.

Water dripped from my wet hair and fell on my bare shoulders. A chill raced down my back, my hand flexing on the terrycloth towel secured around me. I could have tucked it in, securing it firmly to my naked body but it was probably better if I had something to hold onto. Something to grip while the anger flowed inside of me.

Not more than forty-eight hours ago, I was washing blood off my skin. Standing in the shower while Alek held me, cycling through a myriad of emotions. I'd taken a few lives in the cave underneath The Better Day Church. And had almost ended up being sacrificed in both Gavina Young and her crazed son's, fruitless effort to become gods, and now...now we had another problem to solve. But I had signed up for this. Even when Devlin gave me his bossy ultimatum about how his team worked, I stayed. No one could ever say I'd been coerced.

Even still, was it selfish of me to want just a few days to rest? To finally... *finally* spend time with Alek. The two of us had been circling each other like horny, sex-starved teenagers. The ache to do something about it was unbearable. At least, it was for me.

My mental state was also a concern. Too much had been piled on me in such a short time: memories of the abuse I'd suffered; my parents' betrayal around hiding my magick from me; dealing with the guilt of not saving Marta and her kids when I knew something at Tribec Insurance was not right; and most of all, letting a sadistic serial killer go free because I didn't listen to the warnings in my gut when I glimpsed his true nature.

I sighed, then swallowed the pain and anger and the childish need to scream *Why me?* I glared at the white slip of paper Alek had taped to the board.

We are Tribe.

It read like a battle cry screamed when the enemy charged, swords held high.

I stepped closer, examining the blood-stained paper.

Something about those words kept needling at me.

"Tribe," I whispered, hoping to dislodge the stray thought circling inside my head. It rang like a melody with no lyrics, clarity just out of reach. I shook my head in frustration. No matter how hard I concentrated, I couldn't figure out why that phrase bothered me.

Another concern pushed inside my head.

Why would the killers leave behind this note pinpointing exactly who they were? True, it would take some time to actually locate them on the island. But if they were going to announce themselves why not simply charge ahead. They'd managed to kidnap two girls and killed their parents. So obviously they had a way of getting close. Yet, they 'd left behind a note they hoped would what? Scare Petronela?

Not likely. And sadly, without further information, I had no idea what to make of it.

Jonah walked into the room carrying the scent of chlorine with him. I glanced back at him, his eyes trekked over the board while he rubbed pool water from his bald head.

He had told me recently he swam not for fun but to allow himself a moment of rest. In a faith magick ritual gone wrong, he'd created a demon—a mindless being with a thirst for blood and death. And the only way to keep that creature from harming others was to absorb its essence and keep it locked inside of him. The creature's inability to cross water gave him the respite he needed from having to keep it contained.

"What happened?" he asked, looking at me. He raised an eyebrow, gaze zeroing in on my towel.

I shook my head and turned away. I really needed to put some clothes on.

"We have another job," Devlin answered. "She does want us all working on this, right?" he asked, his question directed at Alek.

I sighed. I'd been avoiding Petronela for years. Ever since she unceremoniously fired me after my short time working at the carnival. I was not looking forward to seeing her again.

"Yes," Alek said gaze locked with mine. He knew about my misgivings.

"Maybe I should get dressed." I rushed out of the war room and just barely stopped myself from slamming my bedroom door. Well, really Alek's. I did have my own apartment and even paid the rent. Yet I never seemed to stay there longer than a single night.

I headed toward the laundry basket only to stop in my tracks. It was empty. I let the towel drop to the floor and opened the drawer Alek had cleared out for me to use.

Rachel had done my laundry again. I sighed in relief. I wouldn't have to hobble together some insane looking outfit when I went to see Alek's aunt Petronela. Muttering a curse at the dread filling my stomach, I pulled on a pair of underwear and slipped on a bra.

After slathering some lotion on, I slid into a pair of tight black jeans and a tank top. Still didn't have a superhero belt like the rest of the team, but I would get one soon. Especially if we were going to war. Well, at least that's what it felt like thus far—being in a constant state of conflict wielding magick and weapons. Always covered in so much blood.

No wonder I'd developed panic attacks.

At least, I did have a knife given to me recently that would look nice strapped to my thigh. Made me feel like a badass who knew what she was doing. A lie of course, I still had no clue how to handle myself in a fight. And I was sure blind rage wouldn't help me for long.

I dug the box out of my purse and opened it to reveal a bone-handled dagger resting on a bed of black velvet. Yep, definitely badass. My hand closed around the handle and the cool surface sent a hum of energy through me. Was there magick in it? It had belonged to an Old One. Ezra, or as he was known in ancient Egypt, Anhur, God of war and hunting. I was willing to bet this knife had been used in many battles over the years.

He'd given it to me along with dates to practice wielding it. Sadly, it didn't look as if I'd make those appointments. I took out the brown leather strap and sheath it came with and secured it around my thigh. It would take some getting used to, but I could work with it. At least it let me *pretend* I knew how to use it.

After sliding into my black boots, I looked at my hair in the mirror. An old high school acquaintance told me a few days ago while I was taking a self-help quiz in a magazine that the wildness of my hair really brought out my hazel eyes. I cocked my head to the side, trying to see what she saw. Maybe. I reached up to pull it back and stopped. Wild would definitely project the image of fierceness that I needed. So would some charcoal eyeliner around my eyes and blood red lipstick. All of it hiding the fear inside of me.

Or it could scream lunatic. Either way, it might give people pause before trying to hurt me.

"Wild it is," I said, then put on some red lipstick to complete the effect. Too bad I didn't have any eyeliner.

I pulled in a deep calming breath. Now I just needed my own battle cry. *Fuck you*, might work.

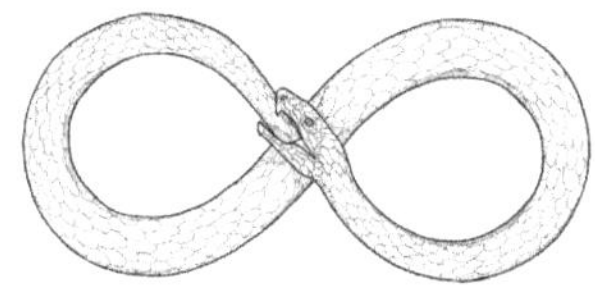

THE SMELL of coffee greeted me when I walked back into the war room. Rachel had taken down the research into the Sinclair family and added the information we had on the Peterson family. Devlin indicated he'd wanted us to do our own research into the families and not rely on what Andrew Snow, the now-deceased former employee of the Stewart family and spy for The Oren Group, had accumulated. We learned the hard way his data was incomplete. And it had cost us precious time and sent us down many wrong paths with the Young family.

I poured myself a cup of the special coffee and stood in front of the board.

The Peterson's all-girl school crest, a joining of hands circling an open book, had been sketched on the paper above the writing.

"Kara is on her way over," Devlin said, coming to stand next to me. He glanced down at the dagger secured to my thigh. "Nice." He smiled and turned back to the board. "Marta will be here tomorrow." He dipped his head toward the note. "You have any thoughts?"

I glanced at him. "The war cry." I took a sip of coffee. I was becoming obsessed with war. Was it a premonition? Or just the clues lining up to an eventual outcome? "It seems...odd," I continued. "Why announce who you are?" I tapped the crest. "And what do the Peterson's have to do with Tribe?"

"We have to find out," Devlin said.

We both gazed at the images of the Peterson family. Selena's solemn face stared at the photographer. I'd found her journal a few days ago detailing her account of what went on in the His Holy Need cult run by Lemuel Oren. Or, rather, the Old One Khnum as he was referred to in Egypt.

Like me, the Peterson family were of Creole descent. Selena's mother and father, according to Andrew's notes, no longer lived on Tulare Island. Her younger sister, Leticia ran the school. His notes also mentioned they didn't come from money. Yet, something about that didn't seem right. Yes, they had taken money from some unknown source—most likely Lemuel Oren—to *not* pursue the people responsible for their daughter, Selena, taking her own life. But they had funds before that. They had been listed as one of Tulare's prominent families.

"Yeah. I just don't want to go on a merry little chase all over the island being led from one dead end to another." I sounded bitter and on the verge of hysterics. Maybe the wild hair and dagger weren't working.

He touched my arm. "We do this together."

I turned to him. "Okay. Yeah. Together."

He narrowed his eyes. "I'm serious, Nicole. No more running off on your own."

"I promised I wouldn't." Would I break that promise? Crap, I hoped not.

The doorbell rang and I rushed out to answer it, grateful to get away from Devlin's scrutinizing gaze.

Yanking the door open, I found Kara standing on the porch, a mirror image of me except she had her long red hair pulled back in a torturous ponytail. And, of course, she wore a belt around her waist with pouches of deadly herbs inside.

"Do you think if I get the belt, I'd feel more like a badass?"

She gave me a half smile. "Is that the knife Ezra gave you?" she asked, eyeing the dagger.

"Yes," I said.

"And that doesn't make you feel savage?"

I sighed, running my finger over the dagger's hilt. "Sadly, no."

She laughed and pulled me into a tight hug.

"I'm glad you're here," I mumbled into her shoulder.

She sucked in a breath, letting it out slowly, then stepped back and stared at me. Worry creased the lines on her forehead. "Devlin and I discussed it and..." she paused, shifting her green eyes away from me. "I told him I would work with you all."

I furrowed my brow. "Permanently?"

She nodded carefully, searching my face.

"What about your teaching job?" I asked, trying to keep the worry out of my voice and off my face. Kara had told me earlier this week that her teaching job helped keep her darker urges to kill at bay. If she was willing to work full-time with a group of vigilantes, who looked at murder as a job requirement, then this would not end well.

She took my hand. "You don't have to worry about me. I got you and the rest of the team to help keep me in check." She paused, then added,. "This is what I was trained to do," she whispered, sinking heat into the words.

"Your sadistic grandmother trained you to be an assassin." Of course, Kara already knew this. But I thought maybe just saying it out loud would drum some sense into her.

She gave me a sad smile. "Doesn't matter who trained me and for what purpose. It only matters how I use that training. And I think this is a worthy cause."

Cause? She said that as if we were humanitarians out saving endangered species and the planet, not leaving a pile of bodies in an avalanche of magick and gunfire. Okay, maybe not an avalanche but close to it. And I was knee deep in it as well. But having both my best friends involved in this madness scared the hell out of me. My need to protect them reared its head, sending my thoughts into a death spiral. I gritted my teeth and pushed air out of my lungs. Red fire laced across my arms, the itch making my eyes water.

Kara pulled me into an embrace. "Relax, Nicole. Just breath normally."

Easier said than done. My vision blurred and I squeezed my eyes shut. A wall of red rolled across the back of my eyelids. Kara pushed the heel of her palm into my back, kneading the tightness. I sucked in a ragged breath, almost choking on the ball of emotion sitting in my throat.

Alek's familiar scent washed over me; his presence sent a brief wave of calm through my body. But it didn't last long.

"She's having a panic attack," Kara announced.

Warm arms circled me from behind and Kara moved back, giving us space. Alek's scent engulfed me, and I lay my head against his firm chest. His chest vibrated as he hummed a soft melody, his breath tickling my ear. He'd used this same tune before when it became difficult for me to sleep. That familiar timbre washed over me, easing the chaos inside, wrapping every disordered thought in a cocoon. "I'm okay," I said, my voice shaky. I had to get myself under control. Most important, though, was the need to figure out a way to deal with all the mess circling inside my head.

"What happened?" he asked Kara.

She frowned. "I told her I was going to work with you all permanently."

I stared at her. She looked so innocent with her red hair pulled back in a tight ponytail. Her face dusted with freckles. Yet underneath that façade was a woman who could pull elements from the earth and crush her enemies. I focused on that. On the times I'd seen her fight. She was formidable. Not some wilting flower I had to protect.

I took a deep breath and gave her a weak smile. "I'm good."

She took my hand again. "Are you sure?" The skeptical tone in her voice had me pulling myself up a little more. I didn't want her worrying about me. I, apparently, did enough of that for both of us.

I nodded. Alek still had his arms wrapped around me. I rested my head against his chest and looked up at him. "I promise. I'm okay."

He stared down at me, his dark blue gaze accessing. "We need to work on this."

I smiled. *We.* "But not now. Now we need to solve this so we can get that hotel room and not come out for a week."

"You have an apartment, Nicole," Kara said, grinning.

I reluctantly stepped away from Alek. "It's haunted." I clapped my hands together. "Now, let's go in there and get our marching orders from Boss Man!" I walked away hoping they would believe my sudden recovery. All the while, I screamed inside my head.

My assured steps faltered when I walked into the war room and found Devlin holding one of the letters Ronald Stewart had written me. Devlin's lips thinned, eyebrows drawn in a V-shape as he read what amounted to a sadistic, embellished fantasy of the time Ronald and I had spent together.

Oh, shit. I was not ready to deal with this right now.

For a few months now, Ronald Stewart, a man who hid behind ill-fitting glasses and good looks had taken to sending me packages filled with mementos of his victims who bore an uncanny resemblance to me. Along with those sick vestiges, he sent, via regular mail, long, disturbing letters of our one and only sexual encounter. He had taken that time and spun it into a dark, morbid fantasy filled with blood and pain which ended with me being carved up and eaten by him.

While I'd always given Devlin and the team the packages, I'd kept the letters and that particular madness from them, burying the missives in a shoebox under my bed and trying desperately to forget they were there.

Earlier today, in a moment of clarity or stupidity, I had decided to show them to the team. Now, I regretted the decision. Despite me not being the author of those deranged missives, I was the subject and that was more than a little embarrassing. It also telegraphed my shame and failure at not recognizing a serial killer before I let myself get swept up into his madness.

I rushed toward Devlin. "I was going to tell—"

He held up his hand, stalling my response, then gave me a look, his warm brown eyes filled with concern. "Rachel told me you brought these here earlier. She's read them." He paused, probably letting his words sink in. I nodded mutely. "We will deal with this later," he said, his tone soft. He put his hand on my shoulder. "So get that look of panic out of your eyes. We have work to do."

"Yes, Boss Man," I mumbled, and he winked, setting the letter back in the shoe box. I could have kissed him for not bringing them to everyone's attention. I turned to see Rachel standing behind me.

"We can kill him together," she said, her eyes alight with joy.

I nodded slowly and she smiled. I was a little bit scared of Rachel. Yes, on the surface she had a sweet, innocent demeanor—craving friendships and giving out nicknames whether you wanted one or not—but I saw the storm brewing underneath. Rachel was a killer. A person who took great joy in inflicting pain. Was she a threat? I'd like to say no; Devlin wouldn't keep her around if she were. But I was still getting used to the team dynamics. So all I could do was keep a watchful eye on her.

After a brief hello to everyone, Kara took a seat next to Jonah, and Devlin looked at Alek. "Did Petronela mention any connection to Tribe and the Peterson family?"

Alek shook his head.

Devlin took a sip of his coffee and sat on the side of his desk. "Kara has agreed to work with us from here on out." He dipped his head toward her. She smiled, and he continued, "We are going to need a great deal of it with our investigation into the blood magick users. We were caught off guard with the Young family." He paused and looked at the floor. The vein on the side of his neck ticked. A chill settled over the room. Power surged and Rachel stood up. Devlin shook his head, still staring at the floor.

Rachel took a step back. But waited, her eyes locked on Devlin. Something seemed to be bothering him. It wasn't like him to get so emotional. But then again, he had been on edge for a while.

Before I could say anything, he took a sip of his coffee and looked at the team—capturing everyone in his gaze. "Part of that was my unwillingness to do what was necessary. I believed we could find a way to spare some lives." He looked at me. "I told you when you first started working with us that we didn't do black and white. And yet, I went back on my own rule when we were dealing with the Young family. It almost cost you your life."

I nodded. "I'm...I'm okay with the gray," I said. The admission felt wrong. I hadn't quite reached that point in my mind. No matter the blood I spilled or the lives I took, I still wanted to look at everything as black and white. Right and wrong. But we couldn't do that. Not when so many lives were at risk.

"The Peterson school is still a priority. And with the slim connection between our current assignment, we can kill two birds with one stone. But we will need to split up to deal with the bulk of it."

I raised my hand to offer a suggestion that would save us a tremendous amount of time.

"Nicole," Devlin said, smirking.

I opened my mouth, but no words came out. My face heated and I ignored the smothered laughter behind me. "Umm...I agree," I said finally. What I really wanted to say, wanted to do, wouldn't have gone over well. We couldn't, despite what Devlin said, kick down the doors of the school and fight our way to the enemy. We weren't at war and we still had to confirm they were practicing blood magick.

He studied my face.

"What?" I asked.

"In answer to your unspoken request. No. We can't storm the school."

I really needed to work on my damn poker face.

He raised his hand. "We will need to assess the situation first before we go in." He narrowed his eyes, the lines around his mouth deepening. "But we won't be wasting a lot of time on it. Once we confirm they are practicing blood magick, we eliminate the threat. That is what we are being paid to do."

"Copy that." I emptied my cup of coffee, wincing at the burn rushing down my throat. A tremor engulfed my hand, I set the mug on my desk and leaned back in my chair. *Please don't have another panic attack.*

"We're all on edge," Devlin said, sounding a little far away. I blinked a few times and focused on him. He watched me, constantly assessing with those dark gray eyes. I gave him a miniscule smile. But he wasn't buying it.

"I'm good," I mouthed.

He nodded, and said, "I would have preferred spending a few weeks training you and Marta but..." He glanced behind him at the board. "Sometimes things just don't work out for the best. Either way,"—he stood—"we need to avoid making the same kind of mistakes we made with our last investigation." He gestured toward Alek, standing next to me. "Alek, take us through it."

Alek moved to the center of the room, hands hanging loose by his side. He seemed a little uncomfortable. I didn't blame him. "When I arrived at the carnival to drop off Rae, Petronela informed me they had found the bodies of four people."

Rachel clicked on her laptop and brought up an image of a scanned polaroid. A dark-haired man with brown eyes and creases around his mouth and forehead stared back at us. He stood next to a middle-aged woman with short brown hair and hazel eyes. "Emil Ardelean and his wife Larissa were the first to be found dead."

Rachel pulled up another image. This one was of a teen girl with a huge grin on her face. Her blue eyes danced with laughter. She wore her brown hair short, barely touching her shoulders. "Their seventeen-year-old daughter, Nadia, is missing."

Another image appeared on the screen. This one of an entire

family—none of whom were smiling. A gray-haired man with brown eyes and a woman with streaks of gray running through her disheveled brown hair. A girl stood in front of them, anger brewing in her dark brown eyes. Her long black hair had been pulled back so tight the sides of her face appeared taut.

"Petre Kotzur and his wife Florin were found next and their seventeen-year-old daughter, Sophia, is also missing." Alek sat on the edge of the desk near Rachel. "Earlier this week, two other girls had gone missing. Sisters, Daniella, and Ileana Vaduva."

"They're not all Vaduva's?" I asked.

Alek shook his head. "No. The Kotzurs and Ardeleans used to belong to Tribe."

Alek had told us before that Petronela had defeated the members of Tribe thirty years ago , yet she agreed to allow a couple of them to stay on the island. There was no way that connection was a coincidence. Someone was sending a message. "So," I paused. The stray thought returned, circling inside my head without any clarity. I was missing something. Something about Tribe's motives bothered me. But I couldn't pinpoint what it was.

"Nicole," Alek prompted.

"Sorry," I shook my head and continued. "The note could just be a way of pointing a finger at the old members," I said. "Outing them, maybe?" *Why would she let her enemies stay with her?*

"No, it wasn't a secret." Alek stared at the images on the screen. "Petronela believes some of the members that fled have returned. Unrie Nevsky, the man she had me locate and bring to her also had ties to Tribe. Thin, but they were still there." He shook his head. "Something is brewing or has been brewing; it's hard to say what until we find out more."

"Why doesn't she take care of it? She does have people for this," Jonah asked.

Alek harrumphed. "Two reasons. While she does have people to handle issues that arise, she doesn't have investigators." He looked at Devlin. "She needs us for that." He stood. "And two, when a member of the family dies, a ritual to honor the dead and send them on their journey to become ancestors must be done within three days."

"What kind of ritual?" I asked.

"*Tapiserie Soul*," Alek said. "Translated, Soul Tapestry. It's made with memories and magick, weaving them together in a kind of soul quilt."

"Don't you have to participate?" I asked. The ritual piqued my interest. Especially given my ability to touch another person's soul.

"No," he said, his voice clipped. "It's best I help the team."

I would have pressed the issue, but his body language suggested he didn't want to talk about it. I'd give him that space.

"Rachel. I want you to recheck everything that Andrew Snow accumulated on the Peterson family and cross reference it with what you've found out about the members of Tribe. See if there is a connection between the two groups."

Devlin looked at Alek. "What you've told us about their purpose thirty years ago feels incomplete. Is there anyone else besides Petronela that can give us more details?"

At least I wasn't the only one concerned about the story we'd been given.

Alek leaned against the wall, hands in his pockets. "I don't know. I'd have to ask my cousins. But anytime they've talked about it, it's always the same story. They came to usurp Petronela, and she defeated them. No one talks about how she did it. Nor why they wanted to in the first place."

"Why don't we just ask her?" I asked.

Alek gave me a half smile. "She won't answer. Not completely. She will give us clues, though." He shook his head. "Can't say I appreciate her methods. But she does have reasons for them."

"Will she at least let us examine the bodies and the scene?" Devlin asked.

Alek nodded. "They're keeping the park closed for today and

won't start the ceremony until we've had a chance to investigate. We're expected after sunset."

"Alright. You and Nicole head to the carnival and go over both crime scenes. I will examine the bodies when I get there."

"No specifics?" I asked.

Devlin studied me for a minute. "I trust your instincts."

My eyes rounded. He trusted me to take the lead. Was he out of his damn mind? I had no experience investigating a crime scene. Before I could question him about his obvious lapse in judgment, Kara spoke.

"Shouldn't we go to the school and see if the girls are there?" she asked.

Devlin nodded. "We will. But not without first confirming there is a connection." He glanced at Rachel. "What do you have on the school?"

Rachel brought up an image of a newspaper article from the late 80's. The black and white image showed a fair skinned couple and two children standing in front of a large wooden sign. "Originally named Petersons School for Troubled Girls, Brett and Gwendolyn Peterson established it in 1986 after their daughter, Selena died by suicide."

I gritted my teeth, anger bubbling to the surface. I'd found Selena's diary last week and learned she had killed herself because Lemuel Oren wanted her and the rest of his following to sacrifice themselves. When a reporter got ahold of the story, her parents had the article squashed and took money from some *unknown person* to start their school.

"They built the original school in Alice and in 2001, their daughter, Leticia took over running the school and moved it to Sandpoint." She clicked on another image. "This is the mission statement on their website."

"To help educate girls who've had a rough start in life, huh?" I read.

Both Rachel and I shared a skeptical look. Sounded like the school found troubled kids and, given what we've seen thus far with blood magick users, probably brainwashed them into being willing hosts for their rituals.

I looked at Devlin. "Are you sure we can't just storm the school?"

He shook his head.

"The students live there along with ten teachers and other faculty," Rachel said. She stood up and posted a picture of the school and a map of the area on the board. "It's located near the border of Sandpoint and South Carolina and is surrounded by trees."

I got up and studied the map. It was near the border on a patch of land that could be dubbed as its own little island. I wondered why Leticia had moved the school from Alice.

"You all notice how every place we end up, is hidden from view," I said. "A barn buried in a marsh. A ritual cave underneath the church." I turned to the team. "Maybe that is what we should focus on as well. Finding all the well-concealed crevices on this island." I shrugged. "It might save us some time."

Devlin looked at Rachel. "Keep digging into it and..." He looked at me. "The hidden places as well."

"Okay, Dev," she said.

"I need to update Opal and let her know we've added new members to the team. Our fee only covered five people; we have seven now."

"Can you ask them to get me a new car?" *Crap*. The request might have sounded reasonable in my head, out loud...not so much.

"What's wrong with your car?" Devlin asked.

"It's tainted and the air-conditioning doesn't work."

"Tainted how?"

I didn't want to answer that. I'd already put my foot in my mouth asking for a replacement. No need to ram the other one in there as well explaining why.

"She's not happy about how her kidnappers drove her car and locked her in the trunk," Kara responded.

I glared at her, and she smiled.

"We can get the air-conditioning fixed," Devlin said not even acknowledging my other concern.

"Okay," I said, feeling like a sullen teenager. I refused to drive that car again. Yes, my reasoning seemed...unreasonable. But just knowing someone else had violated me so easily using my own vehicle rubbed me the wrong way. Made me feel weak and useless. Or maybe I was just behaving like a child and should get over it.

Fuck that. I wanted a new car.

"Jonah and Kara," Devlin continued. "We have been leaving loose ends all over the place. We need to eliminate them." His gaze remained steady on Kara. "Are you okay with that?"

"Wait..." I started.

Kara shook her head at me and looked back at Devlin. "Yes. I'm ready."

Devlin looked at Jonah. "Recon first. We need to know as much as possible about each of the threats to us. When possible, we will decide as a team what to do. If not, take them down and contact Opal for cleanup."

Opal Katz was an attorney working for the family who hired Devlin to eliminate the blood magick users on Tulare Island. After Devlin and his team had discovered what happened to the Markum's daughter, they wanted him to stay on Tulare and do this. I still had questions about why, but that would also have to wait. I just hoped the reason didn't come back to haunt us.

"You will need a base of operation. Find a hotel that rents by the week."

"The Brentworth could work," Alek offered. "The manager, Candace Rebel, can be discreet. Just let her know I sent you and steer clear of her employee, Timothy. From what she told me, he spies on her for her father."

"Fancy," Kara said, smiling. "Should we use our real names?"

Devlin shook his head. "No. Check in under assumed names." He looked at Alek. "Put in a call to Candace and make the introduction."

Alek nodded and stepped away to make the call.

"Rachel, set them up with names and an ID. Have your hacker friend plant a cursory backstory. Nothing too deep. We just need something in place in case someone goes looking." She nodded and got to work.

My head spun at the speed at which things were happening.

"Why do they need fake names?" I asked. It didn't make sense to give Kara and Jonah aliases. Most of the key players we'd encountered thus far already knew everyone on the team. Well, everyone except Kara.

"We have too many people with eyes on us for my liking," Devlin said his gaze on the dagger strapped to my thigh. "For Kara and Jonah to work effectively, we need subterfuge. Not a paper trail of our activities." He continued to stare at my dagger. "Do you really need the knife?"

I lifted my chin. "Yeah. I do."

"When we need to fight, take it. Right now, I need you to use those amazing observation skills to read the crime scenes."

I stared at him, once again trying to find something to say. He was right. I didn't need it where we were going. But I also didn't like feeling vulnerable.

Alek walked back into the room. "You're all set," he told Jonah and Kara.

Rachel handed them a brown envelope. "Here is some money and IDs. I made you a married couple John and Krystal Smith." She beamed at them.

Kara stared at her, eyes watering at her fight to keep from laughing. "Thanks, Rachel."

I followed them to the door and stepped into the damp evening air.

Kara reached out and squeezed my hand. "Your mind, Nicole. That's what makes you a badass," she whispered as if she had read my mind. I turned, eyes rounding at her using a curse word. She winked at me.

"Thanks, Krystal," I said, smiling.

She smacked my arm and followed Jonah to his truck. Why did I always use sarcasm to hide my feelings?

I watched the truck lights disappear down the street, worry for my friend gnawing at my insides. Damn. I'd turned into a mother hen. Kara could handle herself. And if she got into trouble, Jonah, or was it John now, would be able to step in to help.

No. I didn't need to worry about them. I did, however, have to come up with a plausible reason to keep my dagger. 'Cause I refused to give it up.

Besides, both Devlin and Kara had said my mind made me special. And right then, my mind was telling me to never leave the dagger behind.

Thunder without Rain

Devlin pulled up to a small light-blue house in the settlement of Dulean and climbed out of his Escalade. He took in the posh neighborhood with its wide, open spaces between houses, rich, green grass, and vibrant flowers and plants. It reminded him of a golf course.

A fragrant mist covered the entire area, mixing in with a salty scent from the Atlantic Ocean carried to him on a warm breeze.

Large oak trees dotted a few of the properties, including Opal's. Acacia plants with their feathery leaves and bright yellow flowers surrounded the front area of her house and a muted porch light cast its glow along the stone walkway, highlighting a pathway toward the front door.

Devlin cracked his neck and started for her house only to stop when thunder rumbled. He looked up, searching for the streak of lightning that surely would follow. Yet, the sky remained dark, a sliver of the moon barely illuminating its vast space.

Devlin loved the feel of the storm inside of him. Power so potent and orgasmic that he had a hard time denying its pull. His magick came alive, pulsing when the white light finally cracked across the sky. He inhaled the scent of ozone, and power surged through him.

He stood there, letting the energy overtake him as he turned his face up to the sky. Warmth settled over him and he sighed. So much chaos brewed in his mind, and for that brief moment, he found order in the milieu.

A door opened, its creaking hinges piercing his peace. He let his gaze come down slowly. Opal's front door stood open, spilling more unwanted artificial light onto the walkway. He stared at the woman in front of him.

"Your body is bathed in light," she said, leaning against the doorjamb with her arms crossed under her breasts. Her white blouse molded to her body, showing a hint of red underneath. Feet bare, she wore a short red skirt with the hem set just above the knee. Something in him stirred at the sight.

"You can see magick?" Devlin asked, striding toward her.

She shook her head, dark brown hair spilling over her shoulder. "Were you projecting yours?" He climbed the few steps and stopped in front of her. Maybe a little too close. She stared up at him. "You look a little drunk," she whispered.

He pulled in a breath and stepped back. "Magick sometimes does that to me."

She glanced at the sky. "You were in your element."

He smiled at her. "Yes. You can say that." He pushed down the tension riding along with his lust and cleared his throat. "I need to update you on what's going on."

"You could have done that over the phone," she offered, still staring at him.

She was right; he could have. But he needed a moment to himself. Well, rather away from the turmoil brewing with a new assignment being thrust at them so quickly. He had wanted some time to properly train both Nicole and Marta. Get them up to speed on how the team worked. But sadly, it would have to wait. He worried their lack of understanding would lead to mistakes. Ones Nicole was likely to cause. Not because she actively sought them out, but because her penchant for charging ahead seemed to be ingrained in her DNA.

And, honestly, a small part of him had wanted to see Opal. He'd never let an attraction impede the job, but he'd been thinking about her for the past few days. The spark of interest between them when they first met had wormed its way inside of him. And despite the many internal admonishments he gave himself about the complications of a relationship between them, he couldn't get her out of his head.

She stepped back, signaling for him to come in. He moved past her, entering the room and inhaling her soft powder scent. "I figured I'd stop by instead," he said, finally responding to her remark. "Hope I didn't disturb you." Despite the casualness in her tone, Devlin still noted a tightness lining the corners of her eyes.

She shut the door and walked around him. "It's fine. Just been a long day." She glanced over her shoulder. "I'm having some wine. Did you want some?"

He shook his head. "Been handed another assignment outside of what the Markums have hired us to do."

They started down the hallway, only for Devlin to stop at the large wall. Black and white drawings of religious icons in polished silver frames covered the entire wall. There had to be at least thirty.

"Are you religious?" he asked.

She stared at the wall, a small smile resting on her face. "As a faith mage, I'm drawn to the images." She shifted closer to him as if being pulled. "This is the first one I drew." She ran her finger over the glass. "The Wheel of Dharma. It represents Siddhartha Gautama, the Buddha's path to Nirvana." Awe and longing filled her voice.

"How old were you when you drew it?" he asked, fascinated yet again by this woman.

She bit her lip. "Twelve." She paused, eyes going a little distant. "The idea of Nirvana seemed so...so much better than what my home life was like. All that preteen anger." She chuckled.

"My mother believed I got an extra dose of that hormone. We fought endlessly."

It had to be better than his home life. Hell, he'd have settled on normal teen angst any day.

"I'm surprised you didn't start with the cross," Devlin said, moving away from the topic.

She laughed. "I never did what others expected me to do. Another thing that drove my mother crazy." Her arm brushed his. The smell of her perfume stirred the air. "She's a faith mage, too. When I told her I was moving to Tulare Island, she *encouraged* me to plant acacia plants outside my home."

He turned toward her, staring into those gray eyes. The air between them charged with electricity. A magnetism that had him reaching for her with his magick. "I'm surprised you didn't go into that field of study," he said, reigning himself in.

She smiled. "In a way, I did. Faith magick allows you to exert influence." She turned away and frowned. "It helped with every case I tried. My...power...magick swayed the jury." She shook her head. "I didn't like not earning those victories because my argument was solid. It felt a little like cheating. So"—she shrugged—"I decided to work behind the scenes instead. The Markums offered me a job, and I took it."

"One could argue you traded one evil for another."

She looked up at him, eyebrows raised. "You believe what you do, what I do...is evil?"

Devlin returned his gaze to the Wheel of Dharma. Did he believe that? He let out a rough breath. "Sometimes."

"Well, then. Look at it this way." She placed a cool hand on his arm. "It's a necessary evil. I won't pretend that what we do is legal. But I also know the alternative is much worse. I can live with that." She paused, studying him. "Can you?"

He didn't answer. He *had* been living with it. This wasn't the first time he and his team had to kill. But previously, they were hunting someone whose guilt had already been confirmed. Now, they were trying to justify the kill. And that was different.

Opal waited for a beat, before continuing down the hall. He followed her into a large kitchen. Recessed lighting dotted the slate ceilings. Cream walls flowed into dark brown marble countertops and wood cabinets. He stepped onto the polished wood floor and looked down at his shoes. "Want me to take my shoes off?"

She glanced at his feet. "Do you plan on staying long?" She gave him a hopeful look that stirred low in his gut.

He grinned; the question was filled with future promise. "Not tonight." He let the comment rest and moved around her to the bench seat by the window. A laptop sat open on the small Formica table. Pages of legal briefs and law books covered a portion of the space.

"Alek's aunt," Devlin started. "She wants us to investigate two kidnappings and a quadruple murder that's taken place at the carnival."

Opal sat across from him. "I take it Petronela Vaduva doesn't want to involve the authorities." She took a sip of her wine and leaned back.

"No. They govern themselves." He studied her for a moment. "Did your research, huh?"

She smiled, nodding. "I have dossiers on all the important people on the island." She strummed her slender fingers on the tabletop. "Helps to know who's who when we need to dirty ourselves in politics."

"Politics?" Devlin asked, his eyes narrowed.

"You should know better than most that there is always a political obstacle to overcome."

"And what do the Markums really want with Tulare Island?"

She stared at him, her eyes lighting with appreciation. "You ask the right questions. Sadly,"—she took another sip of her wine—"I don't have the answers for you. For now, just concentrate on the blood magick users. And the Markums won't care if you are hired by others just as long as you complete the job they are paying you to do."

Devlin rubbed the stumble on his chin. "The Peterson family might be involved."

She raised her eyebrows in interest. "Well. That definitely helps. You can cross them off your list."

"So you believe what Andrew Snow has implied about them? That they're practicing blood magick. The man's research was sloppy."

She cocked her head to the side. "For now, just assume they are until you can confirm otherwise. It might save you some time. Your dealings with the Young family…" she trailed off.

"Was a fuck up. I know." He glanced at the bottle of wine sitting on the counter. "I think I might have a glass."

She grinned and got up. "By the way, we managed to clean up the church." She poured him a healthy glass of white wine. "The etchings on the cave walls were fascinating. I had to document them." She shook her head. "I'm afraid I fucked up in doing so. I was set to have the cleanup crew demolish it, but Gavina's siblings arrived on the island today and took over the building." She brought the glass over to him. "You really need to think about getting rid of all the key players when you do your work."

Devlin nodded, then took a sip of wine. "That seems too convenient. Why would her siblings show up today?"

Opal glanced at the papers on the table. "I'm having someone look into it."

"Well, I put Jonah and Kara on it." He set the glass on the table. "I will need another infusion of money to cover both Kara and Marta's salaries."

Opal nodded. "I can approve that." She paused, then added, "So, Kara is quitting her job?"

Devlin sighed. "Yeah. Not happy about it but now she's available full time."

"You're not worried about her spying for The Oren Group?"

He shook his head. "No. We talked about it. Her grandmother has left the island again, and she will inform me the minute she returns."

"She might be able to identify Lemuel Oren," Opal offered. "We know he's an Old One, but they don't necessarily announce who and what they are. It might be a good idea for her to use the connection and at least get a clear image of him. The one Nicole found doesn't help. I've had several people trying to compose a mockup image but...it's as if the features just won't come together."

Devlin nodded. He started to tell her about the letters from Ronald Stewart that Nicole had brought them today, but Opal would want copies and he didn't feel it was his place to share those. His jaw clenched when he remembered the few he had read. He could understand why Nicole hadn't wanted to share them with the rest of the team. But he really wished she had. He'd believed the man was only showing a passing interest in Nicole. Turned out, his obsession with her was far more intense and dangerous.

Devlin stood. "We only have a short time to examine the scene for leads."

Opal stood with him. "Let me know what other resources you might need. And did you convey our offer to cover counseling for Marta and her children?"

"I'm working up to it. Marta is complicated. She refused to just accept the money I offered to help her and her kids. She wants to work."

Opal nodded. "I can understand that. But please, tell her we can help if she needs it."

Devlin chuckled. "Nicole wants a new car. Says her old one is tainted."

Opal laughed. "I will see what I can do." She stared at him. "How is she handling everything?"

He smiled. "Better. She still's rough around the edges, but her mind...such a beautiful thing. Rachel was right. She sees so much."

"You admire her."

"Yeah. She's also a pain in the ass. Like a little sister I never had.”

They both laughed.

“Let me show you out.” She walked him back down the short hallway and opened the door. Devlin stepped outside and breathed in the smell of ozone and raspberries. “What does the acacia flower represent?” he asked, turning to look at her.

She leaned against the doorjamb. “It wards off ghosts.”

“You believe in ghosts?”

She chuckled. “As a child.” She sucked in a deep breath and let it out. “Some lessons stick.”

Devlin agreed, reluctantly turning away. “Thanks for the wine,” he said, starting down the walkway.

“Anytime,” she called out.

He didn’t turn around. His attraction to Opal had to end. He couldn’t do his job effectively and date at the same time. Both required dedication and time. And he wasn’t willing to take his focus off the threats coming at him and his team.

Thunder once again shook the sky. He sent his magick out, sensing the rain. It sat nestled in the dark clouds overhead, waiting. He looked up at the night sky, letting his magick pulse, fueling the power inside of him. In that seeking, he sensed another being. He jerked his head down, looking out over the neighborhood trying to find the one who had brushed against his consciousness.

It wasn’t the first time he’d sensed this person. They had been there all his life. But he’d never found them. And now, they had found him on Tulare Island.

Acknowledgments

I wrote this book during the year that shall not be named. It was a tough one for everyone and I am so glad it finally came to an end. But I mentioned that to say, this one was challenging. It took me on an emotional journey that, although it made me stronger, it was still difficult to traverse. Along the way, I had some truly amazing people in my corner. These are the individuals whom I truly want to thank. Without them, I wouldn't have been able to complete this book.

My husband, Bobby. He gave me so much encouragement during this time. And I will be eternally grateful for his patience, support, and love.

My mother was also there. To listen when I needed to vent and to encourage me when I felt I couldn't do it. She is my rock!

My cherished friends. The ones who stuck by me through it all:

Jessica Moore, I can't thank you enough for your insights and feedback on the icky parts. And most of all, I want to thank you for your support. You are such a positive force in my life, and I am truly glad we are friends.

Leslie Rush, you call me your Fairy Godmother, but I have to disagree. You are mine. And always will be.

Candace Robinson, thanks for being a constant cheerleader sending those positive vibes my way!

Kelley Frank for drawing such a great representation of Tulare Island. You truly brought my world to life!

Danielle K Roux for giving my girl, Nicole such a wonderful curse word. Fuck Basket is hilarious!

Leanne Treese for naming one of my characters, Karl. He really was *special*!

Loni Crittenden. Oh, sweet Loni my fabulous content editor. Girl, I am so glad you saw the diamond in the rough when I turned my book in. Without you, I would have crumbled under the weight of having to do such a BIG overhaul. I couldn't do it alone.

Erica Farner, thanks for continuing to work your magic. Finding those typos and grammar errors that tried so hard to hide.

Megan Hultberg, this is the first time I worked with you, and I seriously hope it will not be the last. Thanks for lending your keen eye to my story!

To my new publishing home. Midnight Tide Publishing!!

Oh, I can't forget my forever-home! Vicki Pettersson's Literary Haberdashery! I have found some truly wonderful people in her reading group. You all are simply THE BEST!!!

And most importantly, my constant reader. Thank you for taking another journey with my girl, Nicole. She wouldn't be here without you. Now, as I've said before, buckle up buttercup, you are in for a ride!!

About the Author

C. Vonzale Lewis is the best-selling author of the Blood & Sacrifice Chronicles and various short fiction. She resides in Hesperia, CA where she spends her days plotting the demise of her enemies. All her stories tend to be dark with a little mystery thrown in and some love to round out the mix. When not writing, she enjoys reading, spending time with her husband, and binge-watching British crime fiction.

Villainous by Lou Wilham

What makes someone a villain?

After the war, Mythikos was divided into three classes: Seelie, Unseelie, and human.

For Jericho, a werewolf a part of the Hero Alliance, the world has always been black and white. Heroes and villains. Seelie and Unseelie. Those who protect the humans and those who hurt them. Jericho has always known what side they're on.

But when the villain they've been hunting for the last six months turns out to be their childhood friend, everything Jericho knew is turned upside down. Dusk storms into Jericho's life to show them just how wrong their assumptions are, and that the world is made up of more than just good and evil.

Faced with a world that seems increasingly more grey, Jericho must decide to return to their old life, or trust their friend turned villain.

A LGBTQ+ fantasy scifi novel for fans of J. Elle's Wings of

Ebony, Marissa Meyer's Renegades, and April Daniels' Dreadnought.*Available Now*

Ragnarok Unwound by Kristin Jacques

Prophecies don't untangle themselves.

Just ask Ikepela Ives, whose estranged mother left her with the power to unravel the binding threads of fate. Stuck with immortal power in a mortal body, Ives has turned her back on the duty she never wanted.

But it turns out she can't run from her fate forever, not now that Ragnarok has been set in motion and the god at the center of that tangled mess has gone missing. With a ragtag group of companions—including a brownie, a Valkyrie, and the goddess of death herself—Ives embarks on her first official mission as Fate Cipher—to save the world from doomsday.

Nothing she can't handle. Right?

Available Now

Threads of Gold by J.C. Warren

Cinzia Clark knows two things: She inherited the same disabilities her mother has been plagued with her entire life, and no matter what her mother claims, she is not a witch.

As the voices in her head grow louder, Cin finds it difficult to cope. She's on the verge of losing the career she loves, her best friend, and her mind.

Then she meets Ian Santos, a new professor at the college where she teaches. The immediate connection between them throws her off balance, and as they grow closer, she begins to question everything she has been told over the years.

When her mom disappears, the threads begin to unravel even more, and Cin is forced to face her reality head-on.

Available Now

www.ingramcontent.com/pod-product-compliance
Lightning Source LLC
Chambersburg PA
CBHW070151310726
48976CB00001B/62